SORCERYBOUND

SORCERYBOUND

WORLD'S FIRST WIZARD™ SERIES BOOK 02

AARON D. SCHNEIDER

MICHAEL ANDERLE

DISRUPTIVE IMAGINATION

This book is a work of fiction. All of the characters, organizations, and events portrayed in this novel are either products of the author's imagination or are used fictitiously. Sometimes both.

Copyright © 2020 LMBPN Publishing
Cover copyright © LMBPN Publishing
A Michael Anderle Production

LMBPN Publishing supports the right to free expression and the value of copyright. The purpose of copyright is to encourage writers and artists to produce the creative works that enrich our culture.

The distribution of this book without permission is a theft of the author's intellectual property. If you would like permission to use material from the book (other than for review purposes), please contact support@lmbpn.com. Thank you for your support of the author's rights.

LMBPN Publishing
PMB 196, 2540 South Maryland Pkwy
Las Vegas, NV 89109

First US edition, October 2020
Version 1.01, October 2020
ebook ISBN: 978-1-64971-260-8
Paperback ISBN: 978-1-64971-261-5

THE SORCERYBOUND TEAM

Thanks to our Beta Team:

Allen Collins, Kelly O'Donnell, Jim Caplan, John Ashmore, Larry Omans, Rachel Beckford

Thanks to our JIT Team:

Dave Hicks
Diane L. Smith
Micky Cocker
Jeff Goode
Paul Westman

If I've missed anyone, please let me know!

Editor
SkyHunter Editing Team

I want to put my hands to work 'til the work's done
I want to open my heart like the ocean
— *Lit Me Up*, Brand New

It is a great evil to look upon mankind with too clear vision. You
seem to be living among wild beasts, and you become a wild
beast yourself.
— *Vathek*, William Beckford

Monsters I've Met
I met a ghost, but he didn't want my head,
He only wanted to know the way to Denver.
I met a devil, but he didn't want my soul,
He only wanted to borrow my bike awhile.
I met a vampire, but he didn't want my blood,
He only wanted two nickels for a dime.
I keep meeting all the right people—
At all the wrong times.
— *A Light in the Attic*, Shel Silverstein

I dedicate this book to my father, a man who does what is right, not what is easy. Thank you for being an example to strive for. Love you, Dad.

PROLOGUE: NE LOQUITOR

Percival Reinhart felt his fingers tingle as he tapped out the message on the telegram in the subversive little nest he'd built in the underbelly of Newcastle. Besides the thrill of victory at an operation successfully accomplished, Reinhart felt a certain degree of smugness.

The strange suit had worked, and when he was debriefed, he could tell them how all those warnings were for nothing. It had all gone swimmingly.

As a vital hub for not only the shipbuilding but also the coal trade of Great Britain, as well as a city closer to continental Europe than any port that didn't open to the much-patrolled English channel, Newcastle had become the perfect place for short-term espionage. With the help of some well-compensated and willfully ignorant locals, it had been relatively simple to set up the operational center all short-term operatives could use. Reinhart knew that no less than half a dozen other agents of the German Empire had used this location. Buried under the crumbling terraced housing area of Byker in Newcastle, the subterranean lair had everything an enterprising spy needed to prepare, carry out, and report on operations before slipping back to the continent with no one the wiser.

The operation he was tasked with was not going to be easy, and he'd expected that once he had the information, it would take some back and forth communication and supplies before things were even possible. When he'd first come, Reinhart had appreciated the setup, thankful to have a secret telegram line and a secure and concealed dead drop location nearby. The fact that a trapdoor set in the floor led to a tunnel that opened to a nearby canal let him sleep on the little cot more easily, too.

As he'd gathered information on the asset, Reinhart had become more and more comfortable in his little hidey-hole, appreciating the quiet security it offered him. After stressful days spent loafing about the shipyards pretending to work as he assessed things, it was nice to have somewhere to let his guard down. Despite multiple uses, none of those who'd come before had seen fit to furnish the place beyond the spartan facilities it had come with, but an appreciative Reinhart had begun to adorn his little abode. Bringing in small mementos from his rambles through the yard, he placed them on a small shelf here or hung them from a wall there. Nails and a hammer were easy enough to acquire for the latter purpose, and he'd also found a few rough but serviceable pieces of decorative furniture, as well as more knick-knacks and bits of local color.

Sometimes lying on the cot next to the new nightstand he'd found with a fetching print of the yards in the early 1700s, Reinhart felt almost like a local. A sense of peace suffused him even though he was a man living a lie among people who would string him up if they knew who he was or what his intentions were. He felt absorbed by the rough industrial spirit of the city, and thus, in some ways, forgiven for what he had to do.

This sense of harmony disappeared the day the suit came, which was nearly a week after he'd stated he needed supplies for a disguise.

Like a child receiving a gift from a relative, he'd torn into the parcel before even reading the missive it came with. From the feel of the package, he'd been expecting clothing, which he would have to take care of on his own, but instead, he drew out a small rectangular box and a large expanse of what seemed to be crudely stitched vellum. The box contained a bronze knife that was so sharp he nicked his finger handling it. At first, he couldn't tell what any of this could be used for by an agent like him. That, combined with the creeping sensation of dread he felt when his finger touched the hide, left Reinhart quite put out.

Confused and assuming there was some bungling involved, he'd opened the missive and read the terse lines with great bemusement.

It was a suit, somewhat akin to full body tights that also went over his face, and according to the directions, he was to slip the whole thing on to act as his disguise. The note explained that the suit was self-sealing and that once he put it on, he would need the knife to remove it. What followed was a series of rather peculiar instructions concerning the suit, describing how it was to be stored until use, the proper frame of mind to be in while wearing it, and how to remove the suit in the most careful of terms. Warnings that came with the instructions gave the sense that failure to comply would lead to catastrophic injury. It all seemed like nonsense, and as he stared at the grisly-looking thing hanging from a coat hook, Reinhart felt that the instructions implied the suit might have a will of its own.

For three days, he avoided the suit and his cozy hideaway, using the meager money they'd given him to lose himself in alcohol and partners of negotiable affection. It couldn't last, though. On the evening of the third day, looking out of the dingy window as his recent expenditure snored softly, Reinhart knew he had to go back and finish the job. If he waited much longer, the opportunity would be gone, and then Berlin would start wanting answers. Long-term plants could get away with letting operations fail, but a rapid insertion operative like him was expected to produce results. If he let this operation lapse, he might as well not return.

So he'd gone back to the nest and found to his dismay that things were not as he'd left them. The furnishings and mementos he'd procured had been…not so much rearranged as left askew. It was as if someone had picked them up or turned them about to examine them and had not had the presence of mind to put them back as they were. None of the equipment had been so handled, but everything he'd brought in to adorn his little sanctuary had. The suit of skin still hung where he'd left it, vacant eye slits in a deflated face watching him.

Reinhart had cursed and muttered to himself, turning twice to leave and face whatever Berlin's wrath was, but each time, he stopped short of the door. The suit watched him through all of this, mocking in its hollow silence. Finally, spitting invectives like a rabid tomcat, he'd yanked his clothes off, stormed over to the suit, and put it on.

The queasy feeling he'd felt handling the thing was worse by a hundredfold as he slipped into the hide, and when he felt the self-sealing action occur, he cried out in fright. The suit felt as though it were alive as it seemed to adhere to his entire body, the change occurring so rapidly and completely he wasn't sure where he ended and the suit began. As he stood naked, he shivered and felt goosebumps rise across his arms, and looking down, he saw impossibly that the suit sported goosebumps across its surface. That wasn't the only change, because instead of the stitched vellum, he was looking down at an arm that was not his own, thicker and hairier. Gaping, he'd looked down and seen his toes concealed by a paunch that was not his, and a tactile inspection told him that farther down, there were modifications to his manhood that he'd never received.

Stumbling on legs that were thicker and shorter than his own, he'd lurched to the mirror over the washbasin and found that he was not himself. Reflected in the mirror was the nude form of Douglas Murdoch, supervisory foreman for the Maritime Brush, a ship-painting company. The thickset and hirsute man was the director of several teams that painted the nautical camouflage for every British vessel that emerged from Newcastle's shipyards for military service. Reinhart's plan had been to pose as one of the man's assistants and then falsify instructions so the teams of painters would use a different shade of paint in their camouflage, a shade that German naval spotters could be trained to expect.

It seemed Reinhart would be going as the man himself, and with the deed now done, he knew it could not have gone better. The idea of posing as an assistant to Murdoch had been risky at best, dependent on proving himself in so many nuanced ways that even his considerable skills would have been put to the test. With the suit, though, all he'd needed to do was show up and growl a bit like he'd observed Murdoch do during surveillance, and the job was quickly done. He'd sent runners from the painting company to go inform the other teams of the changes, saving him time and the risk of discovery.

Practically dancing as he rushed back to his hidey-hole, the job done, Reinhart had slapped the large belly hanging from his body. Though he knew it was not his, he marveled at how he felt every wobble, as though it were his own flesh. It was amazing what the development workshops could come up with, though half the time, the stuff was less than reliable. Reinhart decided that he could appreciate something like this. A few times as he moved about the yards, he'd almost forgotten he wasn't Murdoch.

He'd forgotten he was still wearing the suit until the telegram beeped to life. He jumped, and his newly top-heavy frame made him topple to one side, catching himself on the wall with Murdoch's long arms. Reinhart felt the uncanny realization of how impossible this all was gnawing like a rodent on the back of his mind. He shoved the thoughts aside, though, as he righted himself and moved over to listen to the message coming over the secret line.

e-x-t-r-a-c-t-i-m-m-e-d-i-a-t-e   (Stop)   u-s-e-t-u-n-n-e-l (Stop) b-r-i-n-g-s-u-i-t (Stop)

Reinhart was more than a little surprised by the message: why so soon? Had he been compromised?

As he cast a glance around the room, the warm sense of belonging vanished. Reinhart remembered that he was a German spy in a city of military significance belonging to a sworn enemy of his country. If he was compromised, and every instinct told him that must be why they were in such a rush, death would be the best he could hope for if he was caught. He might have minutes before black-booted brutes came storming down the stairwell that was supposed to be a secret in the tenement building he was lurking under.

His mind racing, he snatched up what few effects he'd brought with him, shoved them into a bag, and turned a wide circle in the small room to see if he'd missed anything. As he did so, his protuberant stomach knocked over the print of the old yards, sending it clattering to the floor.

It was then that he remembered he was still wearing the suit and looked like Murdoch. If he darted down the trapdoor and squeezed his way through the tunnel to the canal, there was a good chance his boatman out of Newcastle would shoot him. They were expecting Percival Reinhart after all, short, svelte, and he flattered himself to think shockingly handsome. When a heavyset, hairy-armed man with a weak chin and a patchy mustache plopped down, they'd probably toss him into the drink on principle.

Reinhart looked about for the box containing the knife, and, spotting it on the nightstand, lunged for it. Extricating himself from this second skin might take time he didn't have, but leaving it on was not an option.

He made it four steps before his foot turned on the floor, and he fell just out of reach of the box, fingers scraping wood.

Reinhart glared at the treacherous floor, wondering what had happened. The spy knew he was a graceful man, the finest dancer he knew, and tripping on the floor like this was singularly uncharacteristic. Looking down, he saw nothing for him to trip on, but he remembered losing his balance from the telegram and assumed it had something to do with the suit. Moving as quickly as he had must have set off the bigger man's more precarious balance. That was it.

Muttering curses under his breath, he grabbed the edge of the cot to lever himself up onto his knees and reached for the box.

Coming on like a sudden muscle spasm, his left leg shot back behind him, and his right knee twisted inward. Reinhart pitched forward, one hand slapping the edge of the nightstand. He managed a cry of surprise that was cut short by his face bouncing off the stone floor. Eyes bursting with a kaleidoscope of rainbow light, the spy lay upon the floor, legs uncomfortably askew, trying to figure out what was happening.

The blow to his head didn't make that endeavor any easier, but he didn't have long to wait until further evidence appeared. Reinhart, face still pressed to the floor, felt a prickle of fear race up his back and burrow into his brain, as with agonizing slowness, he felt his body inching away from the nightstand.

He wasn't moving a muscle, but of its own volition, it seemed, his body was slithering backward across the floor.

He remembered then that the instructions had told him to keep the knife on his person at all times while wearing the suit. He remembered those odd warnings that had talked about the suit almost like a living thing. He remembered that everything seemed to have been moved around in the apartment.

As though sensing his rising panic, the skin that was not his compelled his limbs to scuttle backward faster. Feeling a scream form in his chest, Reinhart fought the movement, compelling his muscles to oppose the constricting pressure that manipulated them like a puppet.

He writhed on the floor, straining every muscle in his body to assert some control. He needed to reach the knife, needed to get this thing off him.

Spittle began to froth around his gritted teeth, and every second seemed impossible, but somehow Reinhart felt himself winning the battle against the suit. He managed to twist onto his back and then to sit up, though his arms and legs twitched and seized as the struggle continued. He convinced himself that he could feel the suit tiring, its strength slackening. His muscles were burning with exertion, but the suit was losing its hold with every frothing breath he took.

Then his right arm seemed free, and he threw himself toward the box from his seat on the floor. His hand overshot the box, and he knocked his elbow on the edge of the stand. The impact sent a tingling shock up his arm, and in that moment of weakness, the suit struck, seeming to throw its whole energy into his numbed right arm.

Unfamiliar fingers—Murdoch's fingers—wrapped around Reinhart's throat and began to squeeze.

THE ERROR

Milo heard the dogs barking and knew he'd taken too long.

The whole farmstead would be awake very soon if they weren't already, and then things would become interesting.

Gloved hands in the smoking chimney and with soot smeared across his face, Milo glared down at the dogs in the yard below. They'd been more than happy to take the scraps of meat he'd brought to distract them, but with their treats now gobbled down, the ungrateful curs had returned to their previous allegiance. If only they'd give him a few more minutes with his file.

Voices from the house beneath, angry and sharp, hollered at the baying dogs. The animals persisted and the voice sounded again, this time calling from a window. Milo realized his inability to understand the Georgian tongue meant he'd forgotten to prepare and take the elixirs that allowed him to speak and understand any language.

He swore under his breath as he extracted his hands from the chimney. He was losing track of things more and more these days. He knew why, of course. The answer was written across his black-veined body. Nightwatch was a remarkable elixir, but sustained abuse had other effects besides the unsightly discolorations.

As he shook the last of the chimney dust into a pouch, he heard a man's voice growling something, then the *clump-clump* of boots across the floor. The man of the house was headed outside to sort things out.

Milo looked skyward, cursing the bright moonlight spread over the farmstead.

If the man looked up, there was no way he wouldn't see Milo. Milo imagined the owner of the home emerging, muttering curses, and then groggily following the straining hounds to look up at the roof. What would he do upon seeing Milo perched there like a black-streaked kobold or hobgoblin alongside his chimney? Scream? Run? Start throwing rocks?

The magus had just started to sidle along the ridge of the slate roof as quietly as he could when the farmer stepped out of the house and stood at the edge of the yard. As a tube of black metal swept in front of the man, glinting in the moonlight, Milo realized that his concern about thrown rocks was grotesquely optimistic. Pennies to perogies, if the man spotted him, Milo was going to be shot.

Sliding the pouch and file into his breast pocket, careful not to jostle glass vials and collection tools, Milo began to creep back down the other side of the house. A quick glance over his shoulder spotted the outhouse a dozen yards behind the house. Another dozen or so yards from that was a vegetable garden that butted up to the family's fields. The winter wheat in the field was nearly ready for harvest and so stood over a meter tall.

If he could clear the distance to the outhouse in one leap, he could scuttle behind it, using it to block line of sight from the house until he hopped the garden wall. Then all he had to do was crawl over the other side and worm his way over the first grain hill, and he was in the clear.

Looking back, he saw the man was in the yard advancing

toward the dogs, head and gun swiveling this way and that. The man's movements were measured and suspicious. Was it just the disturbance that made him wary, or had he heard the rumors of the foreigners who'd taken up residence to the north in Shatili? Without the elixir of comprehension and tongues, Milo couldn't even have asked him if he was trespassing.

Milo turned away from the gun-toting farmer, feeling the back of his skull itch in preparation for a lead slug. He gauged the distance one more time, gathered his focus, and leaped.

His coat flapped behind him, flickering from fabric into black-feathered wings that carried him easily over the muddy stretch between buildings. So easily was it that rather than landing in front of the outhouse, he thumped down on top of it.

Milo swore as the Plutonian wings dissolved back into his coat and he fought to keep himself from tumbling headfirst to the ground. As it was, he perched atop the small roof, and the entire wooden structure gave a precarious creak as it bore his weight.

For a second after the latrine's protest faded, Milo heard only the constant yap of the dogs, and he dared to hope.

The smell of the latrine being freshly used and a soft snarl strangled that hope in its crib.

Milo barely had time to pull his leg clear when the door flew open and a sturdy young woman in a nightdress rushed out, her dark hair flying behind her. Three steps clear of the door, she whirled and saw Milo perching atop the outhouse, his silhouette clear in the silvery moonlight.

She stood gaping up at him, and Milo thought the look of horror and wonder stamped on her face might have been empowering if not for the nature of his lofty position. The smell of excrement, old and new, was potent.

"*Eshmak'i!*" she shrieked as she genuflected repeatedly. "*Ts'adi!*"

Milo stared at her for a second longer, wondering what sort

of incubus she imagined him to be, but the roar of the man at the front of the house knocked him out of his reverie.

He needed to go and quickly.

He spun and leaped into the air, applying the focus necessary to form the wings on his coat by reflex. He glided over the open ground and most of the vegetable garden. His feet nearly caught a tangle of vined stakes, but he tucked them up at the last second before slamming them down on the damp earth.

"Mamik'o! Mamik'o! Mishvelet!" the young woman screamed behind him, her voice becoming a roar. *"Mishvelet!"*

Milo didn't bother to look behind him as he vaulted the garden wall and raced across the field, stalks of wheat whipping about him. This wasn't the stealthy departure he had in mind, but he supposed it would do. A few dozen strides and he'd be over the hill, then it was only a short sprint into the forest beyond. Then it would only be a matter of tracking back west to where he'd left the bag of bones stashed along the bank of the Argun River.

He knew his elevated mood was a side effect of the night-watch, but he rode the wave of ecstatic energy, a laugh bubbling up from his throat.

"De Zauber-Schwartz strikes again!" he crowed, throwing his head back to howl wildly.

The cry was punctuated by the report of a rifle, and Milo saw the earth kick up on the slope to his right the barest heartbeat before he heard the ripping hiss of the bullet passing over his shoulder.

Absently, Milo noted that the farmer must have been a good shot to have gotten so close. His pace didn't slow but he began to weave, certain it wouldn't matter but desperate to avoid having the back of his head proven right after all. Trampling wheat in his wild escape, kernels and chaff flew up behind him in a moonlit silvery spray.

It might have been picturesque if the crack of another rifle shot hadn't shattered the stillness.

This shot came even nearer, zipping by close enough that Milo gave a cry as a sharp ripple of air slashed his ear in the bullet's wake.

"Just my luck," Milo whined with a panting snarl as he crested the hill. "I got the village deadeye!"

He plunged down the other side of the hill, glad for the dark stand of the trees looming at the edge of the field. With the hill between him and the rifle, he felt the artificial buoyancy of the alchemical drug coming back. He couldn't bring himself to cheer, but a smile spread over his face even as his breath became ragged.

"Almost in the clear," he rasped.

Then he heard the baying of the dogs and heard their sleek bodies shooting up the wheat-crowned slope. He'd be lucky to make the tree line before they were on his heels. He was going to have to decide how much of his power to display to get out of this mess, and that was assuming the marksman-farmer didn't pop over the top of the hill and blow his head off.

Milo swore as he heard canine growls coming up fast behind him.

This night was not going as he'd expected, and he imagined the drugs had given him a rosy idea of his odds.

Milo, scratched and battered, slid from the back of his unliving steed as dawn's fingers worked their magic across the gray sky.

"That could have been worse," he muttered as he straightened, feeling sinews creak as bones popped and clicked. "But then again, it could have gone much better."

The Qareen horse, nothing more than bones woven with leathery cords of sinew, stared forward without comment. The shade that animated the corpus was one of the most docile and compliant entities Milo harnessed thus far, something that had seemed essential for what basically amounted to a vehicle. To Milo's relief, despite this placidity, the animate had proven more than capable of driving its vessel at incredible speeds. Without the concerns of breath or muscle fatigue, the Qareen had torn through the countryside back to Shatili once Milo had finally managed to slip away from the dogs.

"All right." Milo sighed as he unslung the canvas bag from his shoulder and drew its mouth wide. "In you go."

The sigils inked inside the mouth of the bag flared with green light, and Milo felt a vague inhaling pressure from the bag. His soul felt it more than his skin, something like a gentle current brushing against his spirit.

The effect on the undead horse was far more dramatic.

Coming apart like a cheap children's toy, the Qareen's sinew unwound, sliding into the bag with a dry hiss. The sinew was still coiling inside when the bones danced apart from each other and tumbled into the bag, turning end over end. The bones deposited themselves in the sack, many of them vanishing inside a container that was shorter than their length. The weight of the sack barely increased as the enchanted remains slid into the ensorcelled container.

In less than half a minute, where once a skeletal animate had loomed, there was nothing but some muddy hoofprints.

"I'm sure that will get old someday." He chuckled softly, then winced at the stabbing pain in his head.

The nightwatch was wearing off.

When was the last time he'd slept?

Milo's stomach twisted and his heartbeat quickened; he couldn't remember. That wasn't good.

Nightwatch was a wonderful and potent stimulant, but extended use had its risks, not the least being a sudden loss of consciousness and even bodily trauma when it ran out. This was exactly why he'd adjusted the formula to give him a pointed reminder when it was wearing off. He'd told himself it was put in as a reminder to go get some rest, but lately, he'd been using it as a signal to take more of the stuff.

Now he wasn't sure if he hadn't slept in days or weeks, but either way, he needed to get inside and take something before the full effects of withdrawal set in.

Shatili, a small village in the Khevsureti highlands of Georgia on the northern slopes of the Caucasus, was largely untouched by time. Settled in a gorge carved by the Argun River, it would have been little more than a few simple hovels and homesteads except for the fortress complex that thrust up from the earth like a dragon spine. The Argun forked around the sheer-sided constructions of stone and mortar whose foundations predated the fall of Constantinople to the Ottoman Empire. This was the face of the defiant little hamlet, a bastion in a land familiar with war, and it had been Milo's home and laboratory for the past eight months.

When Lokkemand brought their contingent of Nicht-KAT up from Afghanistan, Milo had assumed they were heading further north, but they never made it past the Greater Caucasus Mountains. As they started to pass into Chechen territory, which was nominally held by a coalition of German and Ottoman forces, word had come for them to find a place to rest and wait. The captain had said the situation was "fluid," so they'd settle into the defensible village to wait for word from Colonel Jorge, but when winter struck the mountains and they were trapped in Shatili for months, no word came.

Now with the thaw mostly done and spring in full bloom, they still waited, though Milo had not been idle.

The magus skirted the left fork of the bridge, knowing a sentry would be keeping watch over the bridges on the approach to the fortress. The sentry wouldn't challenge him, of course, but he'd report back to Lokkemand, and that was a complication Milo wanted to avoid if at all possible.

A little farther along the bank was an outthrust of rock that stretched a few meters over the Argun, and here Milo made his crossing. Leaping into the air and trusting his coat's transmogrification to handle the rest, he swooped over the rolling gray river and came down in a series of short hops. Milo imagined he was the most ungainly of birds, but needs must, and right now, he needed to get to his study.

Typically, he would creep along and come in through a postern gate he could lock and unlock using a si'lat servant he kept in his coat pocket, but there was no time.

Impatiently checking to see that no sentry was prowling the walkway near his appointed wing of the complex, he scuttled to the rough-edged balcony that adjoined his study. It was no small distance, and even with climbing gear, it would have been difficult to scale it without at least raising a lot of ruckus.

Which was exactly why he wasn't going to climb.

In the back of his head, he knew this was a bad idea. The wings he'd fashioned into the complex fetish that was his black surcoat were meant more for gliding than flying, but another sharp stab drove the concern from his mind in a crackling wave of pain. He was confident that if he pushed them and drew deep on essence worked into the garment, he could reach the balcony. He had to.

Milo took a steadying breath and looked at the balcony, which seemed to be farther up the longer he stood there. For the first time in days, his limbs felt heavier, the fatigue beginning to seep through the insulating nightwatch like a cold, dragging tide. He had to go now or never.

"RISE," he commanded as he leaped upward with all his strength, the verbalization giving potency to his focus.

The black wings beat the air and he jerked upward, rising in fits and starts. Like an overfed vulture trying to take to the air, his progress was an uncertain thing, but by the time Milo opened eyes squeezed shut in concentration, he saw he was within arm's reach of the balcony's ledge. Drilling deeper into the latticework of essence until he felt it threatening to fray, Milo pushed the wings to propel him upward the final meter.

His arms were up over the ledge and one foot was planted against the stones below when his focus gave out and the wings collapsed into the coat. He tried not to think about how vacant the space beneath his other foot was as he hauled with his arms and pushed with the planted foot. Grunting and swearing, fresh sweat prickling across his brow, he dragged himself up and over onto the balcony. He collapsed on the stones with a groan and lay there panting and muttering incoherent promises to never do something so stupid again.

He might have stayed there for hours, except the stab in his skull told him time was running dangerously short.

Moaning half-formed curses, he dragged himself to his hands and knees to crawl into his study. The full light of the new day hadn't reached mountain-shaded Shatili yet but Milo's nightsight elixir let him spot the small bottle on his desk easily enough. Just a few drops of the nightwatch would stave off the oncoming unconsciousness long enough for him to take stock of things.

Without knowing how long he'd been awake, he couldn't let himself fall asleep since that could be fatal. However, he didn't have time to make the restorative sleepbalm he normally took to protect him from the worst of his insomniac excesses. He hoped he could take enough of the nightwatch to give him time to make the sleepbalm and not so much that his stimulated mind forgot what he was doing and went back to his research experiments. The fact that this had been his goal the last several mornings did not escape him as a point of concern, but it shrank in significance as he inched across the floor to the desk.

Arm feeling like it was laced with lead, he flopped it onto the desk and groped a clumsy hand over to the bottle. His blind fingers nearly knocked the container over, but mercifully his fatigue-softened grip was just strong enough to arrest its fall. He dragged the bottle off the desk and down to where he knelt, trembling, on the floor, his limbs threatening to abandon him altogether.

With agonizing slowness, he tugged the cork stopper out and threw the bottle's contents into his yawning mouth.

There was less in the bottle than he expected, but the taste of sweet onions in the back of his throat was soon accompanied by a rush of that pale, quivering energy he'd become fearfully accustomed to.

Milo sighed as he rose to his feet, his burdensome limbs quickening to his command. 'Well, that almost ended poorly."

Reflexively, he cast about the desk, looking for more nightwatch.

After all, the dose he'd taken had been very small, and he would need more if he was going to get the sleepbalm made. That and he had to sort his gathered materials from the night, and maybe do a little more review of *The Fluids Flow* codex, and it might not be a bad idea to get breakfast, and then check in to see if Lokkemand had anything for him, and—

"Where the hell is it?" he growled as his eyes swept over his desk and the shelves behind his desk and his thoughts raced. "I know I made more than this!"

"Which is exactly the problem." growled a gruff voice from across the room.

Milo's eyes shot up. Reclining on a couch near the door to his study was the thick, lumpy frame of Simon Ambrose.

Milo felt a rush of several feelings at once, not the least of which were confusion and anger at being so startled by his bodyguard and friend. Swearing fiercely, he threw the empty bottle at the big man, the thick glass bouncing off the couch and then rolling across the floor.

"What did you do with it?" Milo snarled, savoring the anger whose presence he didn't quite understand.

"I should have pitched it all into the river." Ambrose sniffed, casting a baleful eye at the failed missile before glaring at Milo. "But I didn't know how much you would need to get things in order after not sleeping for so long."

"It hasn't been that long," Milo lied, the anger falling out of his voice with chilling ease. "Don't be dramatic. Just tell me where it is."

Ambrose eyed his ward with a frown and then rose into a sitting position on the couch.

"Do you know how long it's been since you slept, Magus?"

The words were measured and precise, like someone talking to an ill-tempered child. This, of course, awoke Milo's anger instantly.

"I do, do you?" he asked in the most accusatory tone he could muster. "Do you, O dear nanny?"

Ambrose let the words slide off him with contemptuous ease.

"How long has it been?" he asked with infuriating steadiness.

Milo stared back, his jaw working as his lips twitched and curled.

"Five maybe six days," he said, and then, seeing Ambrose's expression, quickly added. "No, no, eight. Yes, eight days."

Ambrose stared at Milo for a few hammering heartbeats and shook his head ruefully.

"Fifteen," Ambrose said softly as he rose to his feet. "Fifteen days straight, and that's after only catching up for two days after eleven days without sleep."

"It… I mean, no, it can't… You forgot about…"

The excuses died even as he tried to force them off his shuddering tongue.

"This has got to stop," the big man declared in a voice that would brook no argument. "Bad enough you're running yourself down like this, but now your judgment is so impaired that you're running about the countryside like some witch in a fairy tale."

Milo felt part of him nodding along in acknowledgment, but he stuffed that part down deep and nursed his indignation.

"Do you even understand the pressure I'm under?" Milo asked, stalking around the desk to level a finger at Ambrose. "What they are asking me to do?"

"Only in the vaguest sense." Ambrose shrugged. "But considering Lokkemand doesn't say anything to me, whose fault is that?"

Milo snarled, throwing his hands into the air.

"One more screwup then!" he railed, pacing around the room as he began to mutter. "First, the elixirs don't activate, then fetishes don't work, and nobody takes the time to think that I'm learning this all on my own and there might be a reason no human has ever done magic before this. Now it's my fault I don't burden you with the unreasonable expectations I'm under."

Milo spun and fixed Ambrose with his most malevolent glare before speaking in an acid tone. "So terribly sorry to have inconvenienced you."

"I forgive you," Ambrose replied in placid defiance of Milo's vitriol. "We can talk about how things are going to change after you wake up, but right now, you need to take the last sleepbalm I put in your left-hand drawer."

Milo's gaze followed the big man's nod to the desk before swiveling to fix him with a furious but unsteady scowl.

"I c-can make more on my own," Milo said, his tongue suddenly feeling thick in his mouth. "Who d-do you think is in ch-char...aggh!"

A warning stab of agony in his brain rocked Milo, and he choked on his tongue as Ambrose shook his head ruefully.

"Take the elixir, Milo," the bodyguard pressed.

Milo spat out a curse between groans of pain as he staggered over to the desk and yanked out the drawer. He snatched up the balm, still spitting invectives, blind rage swirling through his tortured mind. Whirling around, he raised the bottle threateningly over his throbbing head. He wasn't sure what he was about to do in a fit of drug-addled temper, but the look in Simon Ambrose's eyes stopped him dead in his tracks.

"Take it," the Nephilim commanded, the crimson flare in his eyes pairing with a thickening pressure in the air. "Take it, or I will give it to you in a way you will not appreciate."

Hands trembling with what he told himself was withdrawal and encroaching fatigue, Milo obeyed.

2

THE ONE

Milo awoke nearly two weeks later, and for the first time since coming to Georgia, his pale skin was free of a gray tint. His veins still stood out darker than was natural, but they were not the tendrils of black that had twitched and writhed under his skin. Looking at himself in the mirror above his washbasin, he imagined he looked almost human again.

His body was recovering, but for all that, it was hard to feel truly rested.

His memory of the recovery process was a fractured series of twisted dreams where he stretched and disjointed specters circled. He recalled that they gripped his face in cold, hard hands, forced his jaws open, and poured gall down his throat. He would awaken choking and wheezing, just able to clear his raw throat before collapsing into sleep, where more wraiths crawled out of the dark to look him over before forcing more of their foul effluence upon him.

Sometimes they wore uniforms, sometimes medical lab coats, sometimes stern priestly vestments. One had even come wearing Roland's tattoos on its wrist, a skull on an orthodox cross.

Milo had wanted to run from them, but even in his dreams,

he was too tired. Limbs heavy as leaden weights, he lay and watched them come, knowing what they intended every time but always knowing he would do nothing, perhaps *could* do nothing to stop them.

The final time of this liquid violation, something sparked in him, and his limbs responded with the shuddering speed of a dream. He knocked their hands away and, grabbing one by the neck, hauled himself up to his knees. His voice roared in that dark emptiness, battering the specters into motes of unlight.

"учи учёного!"

That was when he awoke, truly awoke, and found himself naked and kneeling in his bed. The springtime sunshine filled the room, and in that fair light, he saw Ambrose staring at him, wide-eyed, from a chair at the foot of the bed.

"What was that?" the bodyguard asked, wiggling a thick finger in his ear. "Not sure I caught it."

Milo had collapsed back onto the bed, drawing the sheets across his bare form, but for the first time in a long time, he did not immediately slip back into sleep. He'd lain there for some time, wondering at how loose his skin felt on his bones before he realized that he was desperately hungry and thirsty.

Before he could finish forming a request, which was harder than he would have imagined with his neglected vocal cords, Ambrose produced a beaten copper mug full of warm, creamy broth. As Milo greedily slurped it down, the big man filled him in on the events of the last two weeks, which mostly included Ambrose keeping Lokkemand from Milo and Lokkemand keeping the locals from Shatili.

"Had a whole witch-hunting mob trudge right up the Argun," Ambrose said, a bemused smile spreading across his face. "Farmers and foresters all coming to lay their claim against the night witch, meaning you, for everything from animals miscarrying to marital disputes. I might've been tempted to see if their nerve lasted past a few warning salvos, but I'll hand it to Lokkemand; he knew exactly what to do."

Money, it turned out, was an incredible curative for all things witch-related. Lokkemand's attempt to buy off the disgruntled locals seemed to have worked a miracle.

"And after that, he stopped trying to get you up and about," the big man explained, chuckling. "I think if nothing else, he wanted to buy himself a little more time to gather funds from Command before you woke up and start making your rounds again."

More funds had come four days ago, along with an interesting announcement.

"Jorge's coming," Ambrose said simply, studying Milo. "Seems he wants to have another sit-down with you. Of course, we thought he was coming to talk to sleeping beauty, but the message he sent didn't leave room for conversation on his arrival date."

Milo stood in front of the mirror a day later, still a little unsteady on his feet, but determined to make himself presentable before the colonel arrived.

Aside from the effects of the nightwatch fading, the time off had not done much to improve his looks. His eyes were dark and contracted over his grotesquely sharp cheekbones, all riding over a collection of black facial hair made of wild wire and juvenile fuzz. As Milo reached over to start washing his face, he noted how shriveled his hands looked.

"Vulture claws," Milo muttered as his dark-veined, long-nailed hands took soap and towel in hand.

"You strike me as more of a crow," Ambrose commented from the doorway.

"No one asked," Milo croaked with more venom than he felt.

Ambrose shrugged and leaned against the doorframe, arms crossed.

Milo had tried to dismiss his bodyguard more than once, but

the indefatigable Nephilim would not be deterred. He knew the big man's supervision was more out of concern than anything else, but every time he saw Ambrose, it reminded him of how bad things had gotten. Milo hadn't only let himself go in trying to prove himself, but he'd also let Ambrose down.

The fact that this was the first time he cared about this since Roland's band only made the sting strike deeper.

"So, why is Jorge coming?" Milo asked as he plunged the towel into the warm water. "Did the message say anything about that?"

Ambrose shook his head, his eyes fixed on the dust motes dancing in a shaft of light from a hallway window.

"No, or at least Lokkemand didn't tell me," the big man said, then a lopsided grin spread across his features. "Not that he and I have chatted much."

Milo took a moment to digest the response as he washed his face. It felt like stripping off a mask, clearing away the residue of so many days of unconsciousness. When he looked up from the mirror, his flushed skin made the dark veins in his temples and forehead stand out more, but somehow, he seemed more human.

"You mentioned before that you and he exchanged words," he said as he gathered the shaving lather and brush Ambrose had brought him. "Anything I should know?"

Ambrose let out a long, lilting curse that turned into a whistle.

"He might try to tell you that I was rude to him," the body-guard explained matter-of-factly. "Which simply isn't true."

Milo paused the lather brush centimeters from his bristly face.

"And?" Milo prompted with a cocked eyebrow.

"And he might also say I told him if he came into your room again, I'd peel him like an apple," Ambrose said before muttering quickly. "Which is the truth."

Milo snorted and began to apply the lather.

"You do know that he outranks both of us," Milo said as he

turned back to the mirror. "And the one thing any army loves more than victory is the hierarchy."

"As I've said before," Ambrose declared, raising a finger to emphasize the point, "I'm not a soldier in the German Army. I am an unwilling—"

"—Conscript forced to serve under duress," Milo finished for him, rolling his eyes as he put down the lather brush and picked up the razor. "I know, you might have made mention of the fact before."

"Once or twice." Ambrose chuckled. "You sure you know how to use that thing?"

Milo, his scraggly face covered in lather, looked down at the folded straight razor and then back at the mirror to see Ambrose watching him. Without bothering to look back down, Milo flicked it open, then rolled it down his extended fingers before flipping it up to balance it on his lower two fingers. Eyes still locked on Ambrose, he walked the open razor up his hand with little flexes of his knuckles before spinning it around his index finger. The spin terminated in the razor leaping into the air and landing in his other hand.

The little display done, he began to employ the blade across his face.

"You could have just said yes." Ambrose huffed, failing to conceal how impressed he was. "What were you, apprenticed to a barber at the orphanage or something?"

Milo paused with the keen blade resting against his cheek.

"Something like that," Milo replied coolly, his eyes becoming cold and distant.

Ambrose took note of the change, and for some time, neither of them spoke.

Milo had nearly finished clearing his jawline after tending to his cheeks when Ambrose finally spoke up, his expression pensive.

"I was in a sort of gang once," he said, arms crossed over his massive chest. "Good boys, most of them, at the start. More scared than evil if you understand what I mean."

Milo flicked the blade in the water a few times before scowling incredulously through the mirror.

"How is one sort of in a gang?"

Ambrose's lips worked beneath his mustache, making it twitch and wriggle like a woolly caterpillar trying to escape from under his nose.

"July 1830. France was having another revolution, and my mother wanted none of it, so we went to Saarbrücken, where she had a cousin," Ambrose said, heaving a sigh as he settled into his tale. "First taste of a real, modern city, and didn't take long before I fell in with some other French lads whose families had also fled the turmoil in France. Told ourselves we were going to be the neighborhood protectors, keep those Prussians from mistreating us proud French."

"How noble," Milo muttered as he considered whether to apply the razor to his mustache in full or just enough to tame the growth.

"Soon enough, we found a group of hardy young men who weren't afraid of throwing their weight around and didn't have to do tedious things like work," Ambrose remarked dryly. "We set off planning to protect ourselves and our people from brutal Prussian constables, but before long, someone called those constables to protect our people from us."

It was Ambrose's turn to stare off into distant times.

"Stupid as we were, when two constables showed up to have a word with us, we attacked them," Ambrose said, a note of sad resignation in his voice. "It was a short fight and eight against two after all. Arnald Toulouse, our *capitaine*, knocked out a tooth from each man's mouth and stuck it in their pockets as a reminder. Unfortunately for us, they remembered all our faces, and with a bunch more friends, they rounded us up the next day in the street."

Ambrose shook his head.

"They beat us until we could hardly stand," Ambrose muttered, his voice softer. "And then they beat Arnald to death in front of us and made us carry him to an unmarked pauper's grave in a nearby churchyard."

Ambrose stroked his mustache pensively.

"First time I ever saw a man die, and he was my friend. I was seventeen."

Milo put the razor down, his freshly trimmed mustache and goatee shining and glossy.

"I killed my first man when I was twelve," Milo said, his tone too flat to be conversational. "Can't remember the first time I saw a man die."

Ambrose broke free from his reverie to stare at Milo.

"I can think of only a few reasons for a twelve-year-old to want to kill a man," Ambrose said, his tone level but cautious. "I'm hoping I'm wrong."

"We needed a little more money to buy a case of schnapps from a smuggler that worked the Elbe," Milo said after toweling his face off. "We were going to drink half the schnapps and sell the rest to the other children in the Krieg-Waisenhaus. We robbed a small old man in a top hat one evening. He fought back with his cane, knocked Roland to the ground. I stabbed the man under the arm seven times for that."

Ambrose's eyes narrowed, studying Milo's reflection.

"We ended up drinking all of the schnapps," Milo said, putting the towel down to inspect himself one last time in the mirror.

Ambrose frowned, nodding as he turned back toward the dust motes.

"And now here we are." He grunted. "Working for the Germans. Funny how life works out."

"That's a word for it." Milo sighed.

Jorge arrived in the late afternoon via auto caravan.

Milo and Ambrose heard the sentry call out that Jorge was inbound and moved quickly down to the courtyard, where they encountered Captain Lokkemand.

The towering officer glared down his nose at both of them but said nothing for a moment. Behind him, the platoon of soldiers they'd acquired before leaving Afghanistan, excluding those on sentry duty, of course, were arrayed behind him in immaculate parade-ground formation. To a man, the platoon stood with perfect discipline and composure, something Milo knew was the fruit of Lokkemand's efforts.

"Good to see you up and about, Volkohne," Lokkemand managed stiffly as the seconds dragged on.

"Thank you, sir," Milo said, throwing up a salute as he suddenly realized his breach of military protocol.

The captain nodded, returning the salute with a muttered "at ease" before turning back to watch the line of trucks come roll across the bridge.

Milo dropped the salute, keenly aware, not for the first time, of what a poor soldier he made. Staring at Lokkemand, with his ramrod posture, crisp movements, and towering presence, he knew the officer was in so many ways the perfect soldier that Milo never would be. The magus knew down to the bottom of his soul that he couldn't be like Lokkemand, and even if he could, he never would be. The realization of the difference between the unwilling penal conscript and the proud career officer had never been cast in sharper relief.

And yet, as they stood waiting for the colonel, Milo knew he was the one of importance. Jorge would of course give Lokkemand his due respect, especially on arrival, but no one was under any illusion as to why he'd come this far afield.

In a perverse inversion of all expectations, it was not to soldiers that the German Empire was turning for victory in this unending war.

Looking at Lokkemand standing there, most certainly aware of this fact, gave Milo a new appreciation for the man's struggle and no small amount of sympathy. No wonder Lokkemand turned to drink so often; the very foundations of his life and identity were being eroded in service to his nation. He may still have been a haughty ass with a penchant for drink, but Milo couldn't find it in himself to dislike him quite as much anymore.

The first truck rolled into the courtyard, cracking a few of the venerable stones under its weight. A squad of soldiers in matte-black uniforms scrambled out, forming a mirror formation to Lokkemand's men that waited for the second truck to deliver their ward and master. A sergeant with a face like old boot leather watched over the honor guard with a flinty stare that trailed over Lokkemand's unmoving retinue before resting on Milo.

Milo stared back until the sergeant turned to watch the second truck come to a stop.

Despite his defiant gaze, Milo found his hands starting to fiddle with the hair jutting from the back of his cap. Ambrose had promised to cut it, but Jorge had arrived before the bodyguard had gotten around to it. Milo hadn't thought anything of it before, but now, standing only a few paces from Lokkemand and the sergeant's scrutiny, he felt keenly aware of his less than immaculate appearance.

"Quit fiddling," Ambrose muttered softly under his breath.

The back ramp to the second truck opened, and Milo forced his hands to fall straight to his sides.

"Attention!" bawled the sergeant as Colonel Jorge made his unhurried way down the ramp. Everyone in the courtyard, even Ambrose, straightened and saluted as the slight, slow man came to stand on the cobbles.

His worry-worn face was browned by the sun, but other than that, he seemed very much the same man who had talked to Milo in Poland all those months before. He moved with the same senile gait, despite seeming to be a trim man in his late fifties, and his eyes still pierced through everything that fell under his gaze.

"At ease," he said with a smile as soon as he reached the end of the ramp. "No need to stand quivering as a cripple drags himself about."

It was clearly a joke, but none had the heart to laugh.

Milo never knew why Jorge moved like he did, but climbing as high as he had in the Army was evidence he hadn't always been this way. Jorge seemed determined to make light of his impairment, but no one else had the heart to.

Jorge saw this yet seemed unperturbed by it.

"So," he said as he shuffled slowly toward Lokkemand, "I hear you have had a few local entanglements since the thaw. I'm glad to hear you were able to manage them handily, Captain."

Milo noticed Lokkemand grimace for an instant as he forced his eyes to dart toward the magus.

"Yes, sir," he replied smartly. "I understand that funds are scarce, but it seemed the best way to resolve the situation without further conflict, sir."

"When I compliment you, there's no need to give explanations, Captain," Jorge said with a chuckle. "I trust your judgment; otherwise, I wouldn't have given you this assignment."

He then turned slowly toward Milo, his gray speckled brows bunching.

"And speaking of the assignment," Jorge intoned dourly, "it seems I have something important to ask him?"

"Only one, sir?" Milo asked, unable to help himself.

Jorge's eyes twinkled sharply, and a sharp smile cut across his face.

"Just the one."

3

THE QUESTION

Milo led Jorge up to his study in the western wing of the complex, suddenly eager to display his efforts to the colonel. He told himself it was because he wanted to show that the trickle of magical items he'd sent to Nicht-KAT since being stuck in Georgia was the result of great efforts, but he knew the truth.

He was doing whatever he could to avoid having to discuss the "something important."

Jorge seemed content to humor him, listening as he explained the intricacies of crafting a soul-well.

"Once the ingredients are measured to the correct proportions and you've located a point of proper resonance, resonance again being a sign that essence is pooling, which means shades, you activate the ingredients by mental effort."

Milo scooped up one of his most recently expended soul wells, a small triptych of feline bones lashed together with hair from a pregnant mare's mane.

"Once activated, the soul-well acts as negative space, a sort of low point or void," he explained, holding out the fetish to the colonel. "Just like water filling a fresh hole in the bottom of a river or lake, the essence rushes in and with it shades, which are kind of like fish caught in the current. The trick is to make sure to keep the shades there and not let them attack you in the process."

Jorge nodded as he gingerly took the used soul-well in his trembling hands.

"So, how do you accomplish that?" Jorge asked obligingly.

Milo nodded at a trio of earthen bowls on the table. The bowls were unglazed, their interiors blackened with layers of soot.

"Typical with a warding elixir that burns to form a layer of protection," Milo said, tapping each of the bowls with his finger. "At least that is the way they used to do it, but thanks to implementing my own essence, remembering the blood magic, I can construct internal wards."

The colonel inspected the triptych with a look of mild approval on his face.

"So, that is why you are letting me touch this bare-handed?" he asked with a cocked eyebrow and a smile tugging at one corner of his mouth.

"No, oh, no," Milo said quickly, shaking his head so hard he thought he might become dizzy. "That is a used soul-well. Its shades were already expended, and in fact, the last shade went into the skin-coat you had me make a month or so ago."

Milo's stomach twisted as he watched Jorge's smile vanish. It was like winter claiming a lake, a chill creeping in until there was nothing except a cold, hard expression. Milo knew the truth, but as he tried to force the words out, he found his tongue rebelling.

"The fetish, that is, the skin-coat…something went wrong?"

Jorge placed the defunct soul-well down on the desk, and without a word, shuffled over to Milo's desk chair. Milo quickly and with a few muttered apologies got out of the way and stood waiting as the colonel eased himself into the stiff wooden chair.

Milo fought back the urge to make excuses or justifications.

He'd told Lokkemand, and by extension Jorge, all the

reasons why just handing magical creations to German soldiers or operatives wouldn't work, but they'd insisted that Milo's function was to help them win the war. Saying this was the reason for his addictive binging on nightwatch would be a half-truth, but it was part of it. Yet, making excuses to Jorge now, with his eyes ready to pierce him to the marrow, seemed incredibly stupid.

The colonel had heard his protests, his complaints. Repeating them wouldn't change anything.

"The skin-coat allowed the operation to be completed flawlessly, especially in conjunction with the healing unguent you provided two months ago," Jorge said very slowly, his eyes never leaving Milo's face. "However, future use of skin-coats for infiltration is suspended indefinitely."

Milo forcibly swallowed the "Why?" before his mouth opened, deciding to nod instead.

Jorge steepled his fingers to tap his chin, clearly in no hurry. When Milo made no further response, the colonel bobbed his head in appreciation and continued.

"The agent who was using the skin-coat was very nearly killed when he tried to remove it," Jorge explained, his voice as even and steady as a man reading a routine expense report. "It appears that the shade you bound to it had different ideas."

Milo felt himself deflate but fought to keep his composure, spine straight, eyes forward, maybe a little bit like Lokkemand.

"So, the healing unguent saved him," Milo said pensively. "That's something, at least."

Jorge looked up sharply, then slowly nodded.

"No, the unguent was used to inflict a tumorous growth on the man he was imitating," Jorge corrected with a frown. "We couldn't have the man going around undoing what the agent had done. The growth put the man in the hospital, and he was unable to ascertain the changes he made."

Milo stared, feeling an off-beat rhythm in his chest at the

thought of his attempt at healing being used to critically poison a man, even if he was technically his enemy.

"They tried the unguent on a minor hand wound, and the man's hand swelled horribly," Jorge explained, pre-empting Milo's question about how they knew the unguent would do such dastardly work. "The man's wound closed, but excising the excess tissue required additional surgery. Not exactly the miracle we'd hoped."

Milo nodded, swallowing hard but still maintaining his decorum. Months of work fit for the latrine or worse.

"Well then," Milo said, not allowing his voice to tremble, "I suppose we should get to the question you wanted to ask me, sir."

Jorge nodded, the measured rise and fall of his chin signaling he'd been waiting for Milo to make the invitation.

"What am I going to do with you, Milo?"

The words hung in the air, and in the stillness, Jorge produced his cigarette tin.

Without a word, Jorge offered Milo one, then took one himself. The colonel began to probe his pockets for matches, but Milo waved off the search. His hand dipped inside his coat and emerged one thumb smeared in red. With a snap, the resin sprouted a blue flame Milo used to light the colonel's tobacco and then his own.

Another snap and Milo's thumb was free of flame, with only a small patina of ash left in testimony.

"Quite the trick." Jorge sniffed before drawing deeply and letting a slow stream of smoke slide between his lips. "That was blood on your thumb, wasn't it?"

Milo nodded as he held the first lungful of smoke for one second of searing savor.

"Razor stitched into the lining of your coat?" Jorge asked, rolling the cigarette between his fingers.

Milo nodded again.

"Old habits die hard." Milo sighed into a blue-gray cloud.

A short chuckle and a crooked smile on Jorge's face, and the two lapsed into soft, burning exhalations.

The silence deepened, and Milo let his chin drift toward his chest as he leaned against a table across from his desk. Curls of smoke wound out of his nostrils as he contemplated the floor and the yawning future.

"I told Lokkemand it wasn't going to work," Milo said at last without looking up. "I can keep trying, but there is a reason I'm the first wizard. No other human can do what I do."

Jorge's eyes penetrated the streams of tobacco smoke as he studied Milo's bowed head.

"No, they can't," the colonel agreed.

"You either need something to activate the essence, or you need activated essence in the form of a shade," Milo continued. "If a person could activate the essence, they'd be a wizard, and a shade can only be controlled by a wizard."

Jorge took an empty glass and tapped his ash. "So, it either doesn't work, or it has a mind of its own," he said, a hint of weariness in his voice. "Neither of which are acceptable for military purposes."

"Or any other purpose." Milo chuckled wryly as he raised his head and stared at the cigarette in his hand. "I could give you matches that don't work, or ones that might cook the man carrying them. As I told Lokkemand, it won't work."

Jorge stroked his chin, eyes narrowing as he watched the insistent magus.

"I think you are far too hard on the dear captain," Jorge observed, his head sliding to one side as he continued to scrutinize Milo. "But that doesn't answer my question."

"What to do with a useless wizard?" Milo asked with a cocked eyebrow.

"Don't be dramatic," Jorge chided as he dropped the butt into the glass. "And don't pretend you don't have something in mind.

Chafe under Lokkemand all you want, but the man's reports to me are always thorough."

Milo's mind raced back to all those heated conversations with Lokkemand. The shouting and cursing as he demanded to launch an operation against the Guardians, while Lokkemand insisted their orders were to stay put and for Milo to play eldritch tinker. More than once, Milo had threatened to head off on his own, and Lokkemand had made it clear he would put a bullet in Milo's head if he did. Milo's first time sneaking out had been a test for running off, but the nightwatch and his lack of focus had seen him gathering ingredients for another experiment. Milo had still harbored, out of spite if nothing else, a hope that he'd get a chance to help the Shepherds and hunt down more Questors.

Especially with his secret project having gained crucial ground.

Milo eyed the colonel warily.

"Are you suggesting what I think you are suggesting?" he asked as he stepped to the desk to deposit the remains of his cigarette in the glass.

"That depends," the colonel said, drawing out the tin and fetching another cigarette.

Milo noticed the case remained open, but Jorge hadn't offered yet.

"Depends on what?"

"Depends if you understand what is at stake," Jorge said, cigarette case between them. "Snarl about Lokkemand all you want, but he's not the real enemy."

"I know who my enemies are," Milo said, a defiant edge sharpening his tone. "That's what we are talking about, aren't we?"

Jorge pulled the tin into his lap, his thumb fiddling with the lid.

"That's not precisely what I am talking about," the older man said with forced patience. "You'd best listen carefully."

Milo noted the warning in the colonel's voice, and, checking his temper, he nodded and slid back to lean against the table again.

"Yes, sir."

Jorge stared at him long enough to make Milo feel a tickle of discomfort before raising the hand holding his unlit cigarette. Milo, huffing an impatient sigh as he rose, nicked his thumb and lit the tobacco with a snap.

"Thank you," Jorge said softly as Milo resumed his position against the table.

Jorge took a single bracing toke, then positioned the glowing tip over the glass.

"What I'm talking about is the General Staff," Jorge said, the words coming with a weighty sigh. "The old eagles are finding themselves coming under more and more pressure, and as they do, they are going to squeeze anything they think might keep them in control. Which means the pressure from above is close to crushing everything we could achieve."

Milo frowned, the treasonous implication of the words settling like a weight across his shoulders.

"The General Staff is our enemy?" he asked, fighting the urge to check the shadows.

"Those blundering old warhorses?" Jorge said with a bite to his words that never touched his placid expression. "No, their behavior is a symptom, not the disease."

Milo felt the burden lighten a little. He had no love for the German Empire in general and the General Staff in particular, being a forced conscript under threat of being dissected. Still, he was technically part of the German Army, and being inducted into a war with its entrenched hierarchy compromised at the highest level seemed unwise. Even more so considering the threat of the Guardians.

"So, we are talking about whatever has them under the gun,"

Milo said. "And I'm assuming it's not just the decades-long war effort."

"You are correct in your assumption," Jorge said, the barest hint of approval in his voice.

Milo nodded, then chewed his lip for a second. Lokkemand's sweaty, flushed face loomed in his memory, and Milo remembered a conversation in Afghanistan about changes within the German Army, with men even being willing to defy their orders for charismatic leaders.

"Ritter von Epp," Milo murmured with a low growl. "Him and his cronies?"

The memory of Lokkemand's drunken rant about those within the Army longing to remove *"impure* elements" from among them heated Milo's blood even as it sent sharp spikes of fear up his spine.

"You are on the right track." Jorge nodded, settling into the chair a little deeper. "But you've got the order reversed. Epp is the crony. He's too old to be in the inner circle of what is stirring in Germany. His defiance and grandstanding in Afghanistan are either a pathetic and futile attempt to worm his way in or a reasonably clever ploy to make him sympathetic to those threatening to rise up."

Milo forced down a shiver. The thought of a man like Epp, a man who controlled vast military resources and authority, being a puppet or a stooge for whatever was coming was decidedly chilling.

"Who is the real enemy?" Milo asked, the unspoken "and what do we do about them" hanging in the air with Jorge's lazy curls of smoke.

"I could tell you names that probably mean nothing: Dietrich, Göring, Hess, and others." Jorge sighed. "The important thing is that they are veterans of this war, identifying as the Ewiges Reich. A terrible name, but they are gaining more traction every day. In fact, one of their toadies, a particularly loathsome madman named Röhm, just let a significant number of armed men from the Russian hinterland through German-held territories. Seems they are set on a path for a particular German-friendly but neutral nation."

Milo's eyes narrowed for a moment and then widened, the periwinkle flashing like winter lightning.

"It wouldn't happen to be the one we are residing in at the moment?"

Jorge's smile said everything.

Georgia had been part of the Russian Empire just before its fall, but since the collapse of the empire, the rugged nation had managed to keep its independence, along with a few of its neighbors. The Transcaucasian Federation, as it was called, had managed to be relatively uninvolved and un-harassed for nearly a decade. Part of the reason was that German forces intent on fighting battles elsewhere were granted unmolested passage through the mountainous lands. So long as major military movements did not harass or come near major cities, the peace was kept, though Milo had been here long enough to know that not everyone was as sanguine about the arrangement as the Federation let on.

"Are they some sort of German militia?" Milo asked, wondering at the play being made by a bunch of ideologue warmongers.

"That is what I thought at first," Jorge said, tapping his cigarette ash into the glass. "But the information I have tells me no. With that information also came whispers about the man leading them. Whispers of monstrous sway he holds over his followers. The descriptions of his powers are inhuman."

Milo's pulse quickened.

"You think he's a Questor," Milo said, leaning forward eagerly. "Posing as a human militia leader."

"That or he is human, with help from our Guardian friends," Jorge said, looking down at his nearly spent cigarette. "Either way, he is no good for Georgia, and, I assume, no good for the status quo in Germany. The huge, liver-spotted hands of the General Staff might clench down on Nicht-KAT as they capsize, dragging you to a sterile basement lab in Berlin and me to a firing squad."

Milo once again recalled Lokkemand's terrified and guilt-wracked face.

"That or we all get co-opted by the Ewiges Reich." A low snarl tore across the room that set the hair on the back of Milo's neck on end. The effect was even more pronounced when he realized the angry, bestial noise had emerged from Jorge's thin chest.

"I will see Europe made a wasteland and Germany's name wiped from the record of history," he growled, remembered battle-lust springing up in his worn face. "All that and more to keep such secrets from such men."

Milo stopped himself from pointing out that if the Reich had connections with the Guardians, such secrets as Nicht-KAT had might already be theirs. Jorge didn't seem to be in a debating mood, and Milo didn't want to find out that Jorge had deeper and darker secrets than the world's first wizard.

"Well, then it is not a question," Milo said, stepping away from the table and walking toward Jorge, one hand inside his coat. "You know what you have to do with me."

"Yes?" Jorge asked, giving Milo a long glance out the corner of his eye.

Milo forced his hand to be steady as he reached out and took a cigarette from the open case. Jorge didn't stop him

"Set *De Zauber-Schwartz* loose," Milo said, lighting his cigarette with a snap of azure flame as it hung from his lip. "Stop having me waste my time with faulty baubles and let me do what I do best."

Another crooked smile crept onto Jorge's features.

"Which is?"

Milo sent a plume of smoke over the top of his burning

thumb, setting the smoke alight with a trivial amount of focus. The smoke writhed and burned like coiling cerulean vapors from a dragon's maw before coalescing into leering death's head that blackened and vanished with a sweep of the magus' hand.

"Fight fire with fire." He laughed, a rich dark sound at odds with his scarred young face.

Jorge nodded, the light of fury replaced by brooding glee.

"Will there be anything you need from me?" he asked, depositing his cigarette in the glass.

Milo considered the point for a moment, though he knew it was all theatrics. It was the thing he'd wanted and hoped for since leaving Afghanistan.

"There's a certain fey aristocrat we have in common," Milo said, allowing himself a smile. "I believe she could be vital to the success of the operation."

"I think I might be able to help with that," the colonel said, beginning the laboriously slow climb to his feet. "Assuming she is available, I don't doubt she would be thrilled to work alongside you again. She seemed quite intrigued by you last time we spoke. A new operation would give her another opportunity to indulge her curiosity."

Milo was thankful the cloud of tobacco smoke helped conceal the flush that had come to his cheeks.

"It's not a new operation," he said, his voice rough and throaty. "Just a continuation of what began in Afghanistan, sir."

Now standing, Jorge looked into Milo's face with a strangely paternal glow in his gaze. Wary of such a look, Milo nearly flinched away when the colonel's hand reached out and rested gently against his shoulder.

"Have it your way, son." Jorge beamed as Milo tried not to squirm. "Just remember what I said."

"Which part?" Milo laughed stiffly.

"All of it." Jorge chuckled as he gave Milo's shoulder a squeeze and turned to leave.

Milo sat at his desk, smiling broadly as he went through the contents of the pockets of his coat. He hadn't had a chance to sort through the various ingredients he'd collected on his last late-night escapade, and it was just as well because it seemed his stimulant-soaked brain hadn't been picky.

The ash and soot from the fire of a loving home had many useful properties, but the splinters he'd shaved from nearly half a dozen thresholds were embarrassingly impotent. He also found a sack of petrified pig droppings in the extra-dimensional pocket, which as far as he knew had no use except for being refined into sulfur, which he had plenty of.

There seemed to be even more, including a purse whose contents felt uncomfortably soft in his hands. Given the aura and smell emanating from the container, he wasn't sure he'd ever open that one.

Despite this befuddling chore of discovery, he was still smiling when Ambrose finally ambled into the room.

"I assume you heard all that?" Milo muttered without looking up.

Ambrose grunted an affirmative before shuffling over to the couch against the far wall. He settled onto the seat with a low groan matched by the protest of the furniture beneath him.

"Why lurk outside in the hall for so long?" Milo asked, glancing up with a mischievous twinkle in his eyes. "Didn't fall asleep again, did you?"

Ambrose scowled but decided not to rise to the bait.

"Glad to see you're in a good mood," he said, leaning back and clasping his broad hands across his wide stomach. "But, to answer your question, I was waiting for you to remember you forgot something and run after Jorge to tell him. It lasted so long because, as you know, the colonel is uninterested in hurrying."

Milo stopped his sorting and looked at Ambrose, his smile hardening along the edges.

"What did I forget?" he asked, feeling a twitch in his guts that told him he knew exactly what the big man was talking about.

"Well, besides recommending me for some sort of medal for putting up with you," the big man began his heavy lids sliding to half-mast over his green eyes, "there's the whole issue of your extracurricular research he might want to know about. I mean, I'm glad your little crusade is coming to you, less huffing about for me, you see, but it seems ill-advised to keep from Jorge the reason you're so obsessed with the Guardians."

Milo pushed back from the desk, his good mood in danger of becoming permanently soured.

"If you did hear all that, then you know Jorge doesn't need to know," Milo said with a shrug. "He's a soldier, after all, and aren't soldiers supposed to care only about the mission?"

Ambrose, eyelids so low they might as well have been closed, heaved a great sigh.

"I suppose, but if you have what could be vital intel or a time bomb in your lap, it seems unwise to keep it there without a superior having knowledge of it. I mean, I understand not telling Lokkemand since the man's an ass, but if you can't trust Jorge, we've got bigger problems."

Milo fought the urge to let his gaze slide over to a stone in the study wall where an engraved wooden box sat. Ambrose knew where the box was, but it bothered Milo to even acknowledge its presence except in the process of accessing it. Eyes fixed and voice steady, he regarded Ambrose with forced calm.

"We don't know that we have anything of value," he said evenly as he climbed to his feet and gathered the partially sorted supplies on his desk. "Until we do, there is no need to bother Jorge or anyone else with what we might or might not have."

Ambrose's gaze remained hooded as Milo deposited the

supplies on the table and went back to scrutinizing what was esoterically useful and what was just a curiosity.

"You're the magus." Ambrose shrugged. "I'm just the shuffling assistant."

"Oh, don't pout," Milo said with a groan. "Come on, let me finish sorting this rubbish, and we'll go get something to eat. I've got a lot of catching up to do."

Ambrose's belly gave a low rumble, and the big man had a look of betrayal stamped on his face.

"You're always on his side."

Milo laughed as his pile of discards continued to grow.

"Just because we both know what's best for you." Milo chortled as he twisted around to nod at his bodyguard's stomach. "Now quiet, or I'll mess something up and have to start over."

Ambrose lapsed into silence, gaze downcast for a heartbeat before his eyes swung over to the hiding place in the wall. His hands slid down the slope of his belly to rest in knotted lumps on the tops of his legs.

"You're going to try to talk to her again, aren't you?" he said, his voice low, almost angry.

Milo straightened a little, back stiff, neck tight, too rigid to turn around and face the big man.

"It," Milo said through a clenched jaw. "She's not there anymore, just an impression, an echo."

Ambrose rose from his seat and moved to the doorway.

"When?" he asked while in transit to the portal.

"Tonight," Milo confessed, still fixed in place like an insect on a corkboard. "If I have the strength for the attempt."

Ambrose took up his position at the open doorway, a flat, unapproachable expression settling over his features.

"Don't worry about dinner for me, then," he muttered darkly. "I seem to have lost my appetite."

4

THE CONFESSION

Despite his claim, Ambrose was still munching on a small loaf of dark bread when the witching hour crept up on the slumbering Shatili.

"I thought I was the one who was in a coma," Milo muttered as they made their way into the nether regions of the fortress complex. "You'd never guess it from dinner."

That wasn't necessarily true, but Milo savored the color that rose to the big man's cheeks.

Ambrose muttered something rude-sounding through the bread stuffed into his mouth. His hands were full of supplies and implements Milo had stacked in his arms. Snuffling and grunting, he followed Milo downstairs lined with mossy walls and the smell of old damp. Neither man bothered with a lamp, a candle, or any sort of light. Milo's eyes had been treated with nightsight elixir, and Ambrose's half-angel nature had proven darkness to be no impediment.

It wasn't until they reached the lowest level, bypassing several doors and passages during their descent, that the first light interrupted the utter darkness they'd been walking in.

The raptor-skulled cane shed viridian light over a wide

corridor where iron staples had been driven into the wall to hang manacles from the damp, moss-furred walls. Both staples and manacles were corroded beyond use, but they hung in rusted stillness as a testament to the dark and hopeless times witnessed by the space. Despair dripped from the walls as surely as moisture from the Argun wetted the moss.

The resonance in the room was a strident clamor against Milo's magical senses. Even braced for it, he paused for a moment as he adjusted to the sensation washing over him. The light radiating from above the cane's beak flickered for a second, then flared to painful brilliance before settling to an even glow again.

"Not sure I'll ever get used to that," Milo murmured, his heart coming down from a threadier pace in fits and starts. Drawing his focus from inward to outward, he pressed the witchlight to reach out and caress the sigils carved into the floor and filled with a mixture of ash and silver. They glimmered with a sinister opalescence in the green light, winding in concentric rings of eye-searingly intricate patterns. Satisfied that everything was still in place, Milo fitted the cane into a sconce set in the wall, where it continued to glow.

"Not sure you're supposed to," Ambrose grumbled around a mouthful of bread as he stepped around Milo and carefully deposited his burdens on the floor. "But if you do, let me know."

The big man handed over the wooden box retrieved from the hidden alcove in the study, clearly glad to get some distance from the vessel.

Milo's fingers traced the engravings worked into the box, right-angled versions of the sigils that coiled on the floor in front of him. He could feel the traceries of silver he'd dribbled into each side, a modified version of a warding recipe in *Spectral Ruminations*. The abridged texts he'd been studying since his tutelage among the ghuls had proven to be the only beginning of knowledge rather than the boundary. With not much to do during the claustrophobic winter in Shatili, he'd quickly raced through the codices he had and was soon pushing the limits of the theories and the directives presented. More and more, he had learned magic was an art, even among the seemingly regimented practice of alchemical necromancy. Rules could be bent with ingenuity and fortitude.

The top of the box was sealed by a locked latch worked in heavy pewter. The padlock's keyhole had been filled with molten brass, so the congealed lump denied any attempts to unlock the container.

Milo took the box and set it in the exact center of the concentric rings.

"I still say that you should tell Jorge about this," Ambrose muttered, holding out a bowl full of iron filings. "I mean, what if something she's told us could be useful?"

"It," Milo corrected, scooping out a generous handful of the ferrous dust. "It, not she."

Ambrose rolled his eyes.

"Well, *it* sure looks a lot like *her*," the bodyguard shot back before trading the bowl for the pouch of hearth ash. "And that doesn't change my point."

"We don't know that anything we've heard is even true, much less useful," Milo retorted before he took a pinch of ash and sprinkled it across the filings. "The last thing we need to do is waste the colonel's time."

The iron fractals began to hiss, smoke, and then glow with a forge's heat. Milo let the simmering particles fall from his hand toward the floor, watching as they tumbled around and into one another. By the time they reached the stones, they'd coalesced into a key whose toothy tip still glowed with heat.

Testing first with a light touch before pinching the blackened ring between his thick fingers, Ambrose drew the key up and carefully handed it to Milo, wary of the glowing end.

"I think it has less to do with the colonel's time and more to do with his permission," Ambrose grumbled as he stepped clear.

Milo shook his head but didn't take the time to argue.

Instead, he stepped to the box and pressed the glowing head into the brass-choked lock. There was an instant of resistance, then a bubbling hiss as brass wept from the keyhole and the key began to slide in. Even with the molten metal dribbling across its face to pool on the floor, the ensorcelled box remained unmarred. Sweat sprang to Milo's brow as his spirit strove to unfasten wards under intense pressure without destroying them. The key and lock were ritual instruments, physical manifestations of magical realities, a pantomime for an operation that was metaphysical yet necessary for its success.

The day Milo understood exactly why one needed the other was the day he'd understand things at a much deeper level than he could imagine. For now, though, he had to focus his will and try not to scorch his fingers to the bone at the same time.

Milo felt as much as heard the soft click through the spitting brass as the key drove home. Steeling his mind and body for the next step, he turned the key as he released a single steadying breath.

The pewter lock fell into the pool of brass, the heavy latch flew open, and a nightmare emerged.

Lightless beyond even Milo's magical senses, it was a living shadow given a perverse physicality as it twisted and wrenched itself from the container. Amorphous flesh writhed around warping disjointed bones, refusing to take any shape except that of something straining and raging with overlong limbs and groping digits. The only thing which remained fixed was some semblance of a head, which flopped this way and that while two glowing eyes remained fixed hatefully on Milo as he watched it struggling.

The temperature plummeted, and soon Milo could see his breath forming in front of him in little puffs. A scream like the shearing of a soul pierced the stillness of the dungeon. The air seemed to vibrate with the pent-up malice of the cry as though trembling to bear such hatred.

"BE STILL," Milo commanded in an eldritchly-empowered voice.

Impossibly the horror emerging from the box ceased its straining, and its keening faltered into silence. It swayed slightly, an oscillating torso with an odd number of limbs jutting from a box that could not have held half its mass. The lolling head watched Milo with open hunger, a low cunning glinting in its eyes.

"You come to us again, Milo," the shade burbled in a voice as foul as a septic wound. "Do you think we have anything more to teach you?"

Milo met the taunting glare with a cold, unrelenting stare that bored into the undead specter until it shivered. The magus felt a smile tug at the corners of his mouth; he was either getting better, or the familiar wraith was finally beginning to understand the nature of things.

Milo warned himself not to get cocky even as he raised his chin to glare imperiously at the shade.

"You are the shade of Imrah Marid of Ifreedahm, daughter of Bashlek Ifreedahm," Milo declared, his eye contact not flinching for a second. "I command you to remember what you once were. REMEMBER."

The shade clearly did not appreciate the instruction, flailing at itself with its too numerous limbs with a sob, pinching and clawing in a fit of masochistic defiance before surrendering. Like water taking the form of a vessel, it poured its umbral flesh into the shape of Milo's former teacher.

Only this time, instead of donning Imrah's ghulish form, it emerged from its roiling coils as she had appeared when wearing her human guise.

A small, shapely woman with dark hair and flashing black

eyes had replaced the grotesque creature, but her midsection was painfully pinched in the box, flesh compressed beyond mortal endurance. An ephemeral gown of black gossamer lay lightly over her body, the spectral cloth rippling in an ethereal wind.

"I think you are happy to see me, Milo," she cooed in a voice that was Imrah's yet wasn't, lacking her typical scorn and impatience. "Or perhaps it's the form I've taken."

Milo's gaze remained icy as he reminded himself of what he was looking at and what it wanted. Shades were not souls, only the fractured echoes left by the violent dislocation of death. It was devious, hungry, and desperate, but it was not a true living thing or even an unliving thing. Rather, it was something longing for unlife.

"Shade," Milo said, sending a twitch of irritation across the Imrah-esque face, "I need to know what memories you have that might tell me about Guardians operating in Russia."

"Why should I?" it asked, lip thrusting forward in a pout Imrah would have never deigned to wear. "Come on, Milo, you can't drag me out just to start making demands. Don't I deserve at least some consideration?"

A ticklish feeling in Milo's mind pressured him to give a little, offer a word or two of simple greeting maybe, but he squashed it. The shade was playing on his ingrained interactions, hoping to have him consider it a living thing, a person. That could be fatally dangerous; *Spectral Ruminations* had explained that manifested shades, especially potent ones like Imrah's, could form bonds with the unwary. Those connections resulted in living things wasting away, their vitality drained by an ever-hungry parasite, or perhaps worse, their lives co-opted by an unliving will that took hold when the host was weakest.

The reminders sharpened Milo's focus, and the sigils glittering in the witchlight flared with power.

"Answer the question," he said, his voice low and unyielding.

"Or you go back in the box, and who knows when you'll come back out again?"

He pressed his will on the thing, the blast furnace of his determination washing across it. He was the magus and it was a parasitic memory.

There would be no contest.

The human Imrah disguise ran like wax from a lit candle for a moment, exposing the shriveled ghulish body beneath, all rubbery skin and jagged teeth. Milo glared into the dark eyes that melted into a ghul's bulging orbs and through them to the greedy points of light deep within, which belonged to the shade alone.

REMEMBER

The command was not spoken, but the shade flinched as though struck. Hands that were human except where the flesh had crumbled away to reveal ghul talons flew to its face. Eyes glinting weakly between the shivering claws, it nodded jerkily.

"Yes, yes, YES!" it whined. "There was a Guardian! Many of them! The old forests teamed with Hiisi, who hate men! I knew many who still savored the wild hunts, who still decorated groves with the skins of men and hung the shoes of children above their caves. They were monsters of the oldest order, savages who—"

"No," Milo interjected, cutting off the shuddering recitation. "This would be one who could stand to work with humans, or at least use them."

The shade's sunken gaze lifted above its jagged fingers, wild and terrified.

"They were so awful, taking twisted shapes as they chased the little ones between the trees," it sobbed. "I was so scared when I met them, the air full of blood and howling. And the screaming—always the screaming."

Milo felt a flicker of empathy for the pitiful figure trembling before him, but then his eyes flickered to the sigils shining on the floor.

"Enough of that," he snarled, throwing off the subtle glamour as he bared his teeth in fury. "Tell me something useful, or the box is closed, and I start thinking about which ocean to send you to the bottom of."

To punctuate the point, Milo bent and scooped up the lock from the floor in one fluid motion.

The trembling display held for a second longer, then the shade collapsed on itself to hang limply. Even its eyes fell to the floor in defeat.

"Fine," it croaked in the cold, wicked tongue of the ghuls. "There was one that I knew who won me over to their cause. He understood the truth of what we face. He came down from the north in secret, and when I'd sworn myself to the Guardians, he took me back with him to meet others, including the Hiisi of the First Wood. Last I knew, he was still there doing his work."

Milo heard Ambrose shuffle a step forward in interest, and the magus couldn't deny he felt the same. This was the most coherent the shade had ever been, and it was revealing the most it ever had about Imrah's descent into the fanatical group.

Still eyeing the warding sigils as a reminder to himself, Milo asked his next question in a carefully measured tone.

"How did he know to reach out to you?"

"Rumors and whispers," it replied. "I can't remember if I contacted him or he me, but either way, once it began, I became his pupil, almost his acolyte. He understood that it wasn't going to be as easy as baring our teeth and scaring a few villagers. We needed tools and allies, even among the humans we went to war against. He was the one who gave me the knowledge to seek Kimaris and bind him. he...he—aghhh!"

The shade twisted sharply, the movement so violent and distorting it would have snapped the spine of a living creature. Its ragged arms flew over its head in a warding gesture as it shook and gibbered. Wisps of smoke curled up from its body and hair, and a shriek of blood-chilling intensity tore from its spectral throat.

"IT HURTS! STYX! IBLIS! I BURN! *I BURN!*"

Translucent ghostly flames began to bloom across its form, and the room filled with the faint smell of ash.

"Anything you can do to stop it?" Ambrose called from behind Milo, hands pressed to his ears. "You were finally getting somewhere!"

Milo shook his head as the shade began to flail and scrabble.

This was how all the interrogations ended. Anything that could remind the shade of Kimaris had a chance to connect to the traumatic memories of Imrah's final moments of self-immolation before being crushed and devoured by the gelatinous demon. Once the shade began to burn, any further communication was pointless, the violence of the memory overwhelming everything else.

"REST," he intoned, forcing the frustration out of his mind by raw will as he drove it back into the ensorcelled box. If he interacted with the shade's essence with any strong emotion, there was a chance it could provide an anchor for connection even now.

"It hurts!" it sobbed even as it began to shrink and thin to translucency, drawn inexorably into the vessel. "Milo, please! It hurts so much! Help me, please! *HELP ME!*"

A few more seconds and Milo could see through the shade and into the box. The interior was plain wood enclosed a pitted skull and a few fractured bones, the last remains of Imrah Marid.

"I never could," he said softly as he bent over the box, ignoring the fading image of the ghul's fire-wreathed form. "She never let me."

"What was that?" Ambrose asked.

"Nothing," Milo said flatly.

With an effort both magical and physical, the magus closed the box and replaced the lock.

"Do you think it was true?" Ambrose asked the next morning.

Milo had been too drained to carry on much of a conversation after interrogating the shade. They'd emerged from the depths of the Shatili fortress, thankful the misdirection fetish he'd hung over the dungeon stairs had kept the other occupants ignorant, and headed back to Milo's study. They hid the box again, stored the unused ingredients, and with hardly a word between them, Milo went to bed to endure dark dreams.

Milo had not known pleasant sleep many nights of his short, hard life, and becoming a magus had not improved the quality thus far.

After waking and going through the motions of getting ready for the day, Ambrose came in with breakfast, which the two had on the balcony of Milo's study.

Milo sat munching bacon and considering Ambrose's question as he stared at the green slope of the mountain arm sweeping around Shatili. Despite everything he'd endured, Milo could not deny that Georgia was a beautiful country, especially since the green of spring had taken hold. The land was rugged, with climbing outcrops of rock and steep cliffs in abundance, but it was a living land where wooded valleys nestled between the verdant carpeted slopes. He'd never felt at home anywhere, but he liked to imagine that here among the Greater Caucasus Mountains, he could find a little cabin or village to live for a few quiet years, maybe even a lifetime.

That dream would have to wait until he'd ensured this land wasn't overrun by the Ewiges Reich's cronies.

"I'm not sure how much was true," Milo said at last. "But if there is a possibility that it is, we are dealing with a Guardian higher up the chain of command than Imrah."

Ambrose grunted and took a drink of coffee, then grimaced before eyeing the bottom of his cup in disappointment.

"Which means he's liable to be even more dangerous." The

bodyguard sighed as he lowered his cup. "Probably has a whole stable of demons at his beck and call."

Milo gnawed through the last of his bacon, which was gristlier than he liked, but he savored it all the same. With a final swallow, he frowned upon seeing that Ambrose hadn't procured some other flesh for him to savor. It turned out that magic was a tiring business, and about the only thing that seemed to put him right was meat and lots of it.

"Maybe." Milo grunted, licking grease from his lips, the motion bittersweet in its intensity. "But last I checked, we were veteran demon slayers."

Ambrose gave an incredulous huff as he drew out his pipe and began to pack the bowl with tobacco. "One hellspawn destroyed with pluck and good fortune does not a demon slayer make," he intoned sagely before leaning forward expectantly, pipe stem between his teeth.

"You're telling me you don't have matches?" Milo asked even as he reached inside his coat to nick his thumb.

Ambrose cocked an eyebrow and gave a meaningful look at the tobacco pouch sitting on the small table between them.

"You are telling me you won't want some of my premium tobacco?"

Milo gave a resigned sigh, and with a snap, offered his burning thumb.

After gentle coaxing, the pipe was lit, and Ambrose settled back into his chair.

"I'll be honest, Magus," Ambrose began after sending out a pair of smoke rings to follow each other. "This whole business of chasing Guardians and working with the Shepherds makes me nervous."

Milo nodded but didn't speak as he fetched rolling papers from one of his coat's many internal magical pockets. Ambrose took another draw on his pipe and let it spiral out in an impressive corkscrew before continuing.

"Maybe it's because I've spent my long life fighting wars against men. Men are simple, fragile things, and I know what makes them tick here and here."

His free hand tapped a thick scarred finger to his head and then thumped his chest over his heart.

"But these things, ghuls, fey, demons, and whatever in God names a Hiisi is, they work with different rules and have different plans, schemes, and ways of getting those things done. I guess what I'm trying to say is that I'm not sure how much use an old soldier like me is going to be."

Milo finished rolling his cigarette, then stopped and looked at his bodyguard, puffing on his pipe and staring at the mountains. The ache of regret and powerlessness in the big man's words was palpable enough to strike at Milo's heart, and as he stared, he found it hard to understand. Just to look at Simon Ambrose was to see a man of not only incredible physical prowess but enduring power. Like an old oak or mountain face, Ambrose seemed made to survive beyond mere mortal men, and given his half-angelic nature, he very well might. Yet, it was clear his friend was troubled.

Startled, Milo realized that survival wasn't enough for Ambrose.

The magus had spent his whole life trying to survive, to stave off disaster and see one more day. To him, the power to endure was akin to the ultimate treasure, but now, staring at his century-old bodyguard, he wondered if he hadn't been wrong all this time. Ambrose wasn't afraid of surviving but of what would remain when he did.

Given the power he now wielded, Milo wondered if this was a question he should be asking himself.

His stomach growled, clearly unhappy with his focus on non-gustatory matters.

"You haven't been totally useless thus far," Milo quipped as he tucked the cigarette behind his ear. "But your continued usefulness will wax and wane, depending upon one important task. Really, the entire operation—no, the future of Nicht-KAT and the world of man—may hang upon this singularly important endeavor."

Ambrose glanced up and fixed Milo with an incredulous frown.

"And that task is?" he asked warily.

"Finding some more food," Milo replied as he stood up and grasped his belly. "What are these starvations rations? A growing magus needs his meat!"

Ambrose eyed his lanky frame disapprovingly and, placing the pipe between his teeth, heaved to his feet.

"Come on then." Ambrose chuckled. "I've never been the type to leave a job half-done.

5

____

THE AWAITED

Jorge sent word through encrypted radio signals that Rihyani would be arriving within a week. She would be accompanied by two companions, which Milo expected would be the verdant woman and the bronze giant, her fey comrades from before.

For five days, Milo's world was one of eager, almost painful anticipation combined with mounting anxiety. He suddenly became acutely aware of how the stains on his circulatory system from the nightwatch were slow in fading and how emaciated he looked since the whole debacle. He doubted whether a few days of ravenous eating and vigorous exercise would restore him to something closer to what he'd been, but he was determined to give it his best anyway.

He ate like a sow and sweated like an ox at the plow, engaging in a routine that was one part military calisthenics and the other parts getting bounced around while he had Ambrose teach him a thing or two about fighting. The idea had sprung up after the bodyguard's confession on the balcony, but the moment he'd thought of it, he'd found the idea appealing.

Ambrose was less optimistic.

The big man had first complained that it was fruitless, not

only because Milo was in his words, "hopelessly weedy," but also because he felt Milo should be learning to do magic.

"Why waste time shooting or stabbing when you can kill with a word?" he asked as Milo dragged him down to the courtyard for their first session. "Jorge wants you doing magic, doesn't he?"

"I don't always have the time or ingredients for necromist magic," Milo said, shoving Ambrose ineffectually from behind. He would have had more luck pressing on the walls of the fortress.

"Besides," Milo grumbled, refusing to be deterred, "this is as much about my recovery as learning to fight. Really, I've had more than enough practice."

Ambrose gave an unimpressed grunt.

"That so, eh?"

Milo smiled like a shark scenting blood.

"Yeah," he said, throwing a cocky swagger into his voice as he stopped pushing. "In fact, it will probably be exercise only because I don't imagine there's much I've left to learn about such things."

Ambrose had turned and given Milo a supremely disapproving frown before heaving a sigh and letting it melt into a smile. Milo had won, and they both knew it.

For five days, Ambrose had put Milo through the paces of his eclectic style of training to "end things," as he put it. It was a strange combination of skills training, applied anatomy, mental attunement, and a relentless series of nearly abusive physical challenges. Milo was introduced to ways to kill and maim with his body, blades, and firearms, none of which he mastered, but he was more dangerous for it all the same.

Milo never said anything because he didn't want Ambrose guessing why he had asked him to train him, but the truth was that Milo was coming to understand the considerable breadth of knowledge and expertise Ambrose had. Even as he learned a new way to break an arm, cut an artery, or shoot on the run, he understood that the big man was only revealing a fraction of the prowess he'd developed.

The magus was soon thankful that the big man's skills were not limited to the realm of violence but also encompassed acquisition.

The effort was so intense that whenever Milo wasn't engaged in the regimen, he was either sleeping or eating. By the fourth day, Ambrose had resorted to stealing rations to keep Milo sated and regaining weight on a fatty, protein-rich diet.

Daily Milo felt his strength returning and it was just as well, for the night of the fifth day since Jorge's message the fey arrived.

The pair was in the courtyard, running through a blades drill, folding a closing parry into a diagonal elbow into a draw cut, when Ambrose paused mid-attack. Milo, on sheer opportunistic instinct, sprang forward, feinting the parry before smashing an elbow across the big man's jaw. At that moment, Milo realized every time he'd struck the Nephilim, the blow had been rolled with. Distracted as he was, Ambrose did not bow with the blow, and Milo realized he might as well have struck a brick wall.

Pain shot through his elbow, and the knife tumbled from his numbed grip.

"Damn!" Milo barked before proceeding into a few more picturesque descriptions.

"Quiet," Ambrose muttered distractedly as he cocked his head to one side, squinting.

"Pardon me," Milo grumbled caustically as he bent to retrieve his knife. "Do you hear something?"

Ambrose's brow wrinkled with annoyance, but he didn't respond until somewhere to the west, there was the faintest crackle, like a chorus of tiny thundercracks. Milo saw a few of the soldiers along the walls of the fortress moving to the higher points of the complex equipped with tripod-mounted field glasses, locations dubbed observation posts.

"Is that gunfire?" Milo asked, feeling the hairs on the backs of his arms starting to stand up, his brain racing through scenarios.

Ambrose nodded and moved toward the wall where he'd left the gear and weapons he always kept close at hand.

"Several rifles, and a pistol or two as well," the Nephilim said. "From the sound of it, the fire is one-sided, men firing together with fair discipline and coordination."

Milo wanted to ask how he could tell that from a few muffled pops, but he knew better than to waste time questioning Ambrose about such things.

"People training with firearms?" Milo asked. "A local militia, maybe?"

Ambrose's cocked eyebrow and the frown he gave Milo were clear indications of what he thought of the idea.

"That or someone is under attack," Ambrose growled as he slung his rifle over his shoulder and checked a bandoleer hung with rifle magazines. "And they aren't firing back. You know anyone coming our way that might be a high priority target that wouldn't carry firearms, at least not modern ones?"

Milo had already scooped up his skin-coat and had his hand out for the raptor-crowned cane.

"Rihyani would have ridden the wind, don't you think?" Milo asked, taking up the cane and moving toward the motor pool parked outside the fortress' gate. Ambrose was still tugging things into place as he ambled after his charge, seeming at ease as his big hands worked quickly.

"Maybe they stopped over for a rest, or maybe one of them got wounded by a lucky shot from the ground," Ambrose proposed as he stumped after Milo. "Point is, we need to get there quickly."

Milo was already pelting toward the Rollsy before Ambrose finished his sentence.

The British armored Rolls-Royce had been captured in the fighting in Macedonia some time ago, and by a long winding path, it had found its way into the service of Lokkemand and his entourage. It was hardly an inspiring sight, with a ramshackle aesthetic and a drab paint job of heavy gray. Much of the original armor was gone, replaced by cheap, crudely fabricated pieces in the field, and the armored driving cabin had been decapitated. As such, the driver was exposed from above, and whoever manned the machine gun directly behind the front seat, a venerable water-cooled MG 08, had his whole upper body exposed.

But the engine in the rugged automobile, free of much of the old armored bulk, could roar across the rugged hills to the west better than anything else in the motor pool.

A quicker-thinking sentry on the wall ducked into the guardhouse, having seen the pair run for the Rollsy, and hollered down as Milo climbed into the gunner's nest.

"Keys, Magus!" the soldier cried as he tossed them into the air.

Milo caught them despite the sting of their descent from the top of the fortress wall.

Without delay, he bent and shoved the keys into Ambrose's hand as the Nephilim clambered into the driver's seat.

"We're headed straight west," Milo shouted up, his words almost swallowed in the wakening roar of the Rollsy. "Tell Lokkemand, and I'm sure he'll send a bunch of you after us."

"Very good, sir," he hollered back. "Will do."

Before Milo could say anything more, Ambrose had them tearing across the bridge and racing toward imminent violence.

***

The sun was dying in shades of vermillion and violet as they vaulted over the last hill to the scene of the ambush.

The attackers were so intent on pouring fire into a copse of trees that Milo's and Ambrose's arrival was a shock. The crack of rifle volleys stuttered to a halt as the Rollsy skidded down the hill. Now Milo could see what they were up against. Two staggered lines, each ten strong, had been creeping down the slope, with five-man wings advancing along either flank. They were men in common Georgian dress, chokhas and tall boots, but the rifles in their hands were not local arms. They looked like combat rifles, but none Milo had ever seen.

They'd dominated the field before firing salvo after salvo into the trees where the fey must have been, and despite the pause, they were eager to reassert themselves. He had just enough time to turn the MG 08 on their firing line splayed across the far hill.

The heavy rounds left the short, stocky barrel in a hail of death, stitching a line of rent earth and scattering attackers in its wake. They dove and scrambled into whatever dimples and brush they could find. Milo had only nominally been instructed in the use of the machine gun, and he didn't believe he was going to put them down with one. He just needed their heads down and their return fire scattered.

As though in answer to an unspoken prayer, a bullet zipped through the air to Milo's left, and another rang off the plated forequarter of the Rollsy.

Milo pumped out a few bursts of fire in response, but the results were far less impressive with his targets hunkering down and the vehicle plummeting downhill. A second later, the copse came between him and the attackers.

Milo swung his eyes back to the front with no obvious targets and realized there was no way they were going to get the Rollsy between the close-growing trunks. Ambrose, apparently coming to the same conclusion, swung the vehicle to the left and went thumping along the tree line.

"Do you see them?" Ambrose bellowed over the roar of the engine.

Milo squinted between the trees, searching for the radiant creatures or maybe the dark blotches of their heavy traveling cloaks. Fallen limbs and underbrush whipped by, and they were nearly halfway around the copse and heading toward the enemy when Milo began to wonder if they'd misjudged the situation and the fey weren't here. It still raised the question of why well-armed Georgians were assaulting a patch of trees, but Milo felt the tension mounting in the back of his neck.

Ambrose was going to have to swing them around soon, or they'd plow right under the enemy's sights, and scattered or not, they would be in a much better position to fire down on the open-topped car.

"I can't see 'em," Ambrose shouted, doing his best to alternate between keeping the Rollsy under control and searching the trees.

"Maybe they need a sign," Milo shouted back, letting go of the MG 08 and scooping up his skull-topped cane.

"What?" Ambrose replied, stealing a glance over his shoulder.

"BURN!" he said in reply, and two darts of green witchfire lanced skyward and detonated in twin bursts of stinging light above the treetops.

"Magus, *down!*" Ambrose roared as he swung the car around in a chugging uphill U-turn.

The ambushers' flankers sent a flurry of shots at the Rollsy as Milo did his best to flatten himself inside the gunner's nest. Two rounds clanged off the boot, while the rest buried themselves in the churned earth behind the roaring automobile.

Milo thought about hopping up and swinging the machine gun around, but as he was working himself up to it, he spied something amidst the trees—a shimmer, then a flash of silver light between the blackening trunks in the decaying sunset.

"Milo!" a clear voice rang out, and she strode toward him like an elfin queen in an enchanted wood. The bullets hissing through the air and the roar of Rollsy's laboring engine only made the scene all the more surreal.

"There they are!" Milo shouted, reaching over in his crouch to slap Ambrose's blocky shoulder while the other hand pointed into the wood. "Right there!"

Ambrose twisted to follow Milo's finger, then a terrible humorless smile split his broad face.

"Hold on!" he howled as he whipped the wheel over and they darted between two trees with scant centimeters to spare.

Milo let out a wild whoop of excitement that transformed into a wail of terror as tree after tree leaped into their path and Ambrose yanked the Rollsy over to avoid impact by a hairsbreadth. In some mad see-sawing path, the bodyguard threaded the three-ton vehicle through the needle's eye over and over.

When they finally pulled level with Rihyani in the heart of the copse, Milo felt like his whole body was a series of jellied lumps held together by rubber bands. Limp and nearly boneless, he tumbled free of the vehicle to smack into the loamy ground.

"Somebody call for a rescue?" he groaned, his head lolling upward as Rihyani came toward him.

Her fingers were thin and as strong as tines of steel as she gripped him by his coat and hauled him to his feet.

"My hero!" She laughed and lunged forward to plant a fierce kiss upon his lips.

Milo's body recovered from its flaccid state with remarkable alacrity, and when she finally pulled away her dark lips, he found his feet under him and one arm around her waist.

"That was unexpected," he muttered, wishing he could make a wittier riposte. He felt saying nothing would be worse.

"Quite." The fey contessa grinned ferociously before shoving away from him easily. "Now come on, we're not out of this yet."

Still a little staggered he spun around to see if Ambrose had seen what happened. Unfortunately, Ambrose seemed more concerned about the oncoming soldiers and survival and seemed to decide that such a situation required more than his Gewehr 98 rifle. Half the mountings that bound the machine gun to the Rollsy had been unfastened, but the big man seemed to have run out of patience.

Muscles bunched in like a nest knotted ropes across his

shoulders and arms, and then with a metallic *plink*, the gun came free. A second later, the ammo hopper was ripped free in a similar fashion. Milo gawked at the display of power but was still unsure how he could wield the cumbersome weapon.

"Ambrose?" Milo called tentatively.

"Half a moment," he muttered. More quickly than seemed reasonable, he looped some cabling from the gunner's nest around his neck and the barrel of the gun, then held the MG 08 in his right hand with a belt of brass-cased rounds coiling into the hopper in his left hand.

Ambrose turned to the magus, his face set in a grim frown, not a sign of strain across his frame.

"Yes?"

Milo gaped and then heard Rihyani shouting behind him.

"Just be careful!" Milo shouted and turned back to follow the fey.

"You do the same," the big man growled, then set off in a heavy-footed lope.

Milo would never have called himself an empathetic man, but by God, he felt bad for whoever ran into the Nephilim first.

6

THE MONSTERS

Milo rushed to follow Rihyani but found himself nearly running past where she knelt next to the large trunk of a lightning-split tree.

Next to her, nearly at Milo's eye level even on his knees was the Bronze Colossus, his hands pressing down on the belly of the Green Lady. His fingers were dark with emerald blood, and the air was thick with the scent of crushed lavender.

"She's bleeding," the giant gasped, his herculean features unnaturally bent into numb shock. "Why is she still bleeding?"

The Green Lady's breathing was shallow, and her skin paled more with each heartbeat. More than mere death, Milo felt like he was watching the death of a star or ocean, the eternal fading impossibly but inexorably in front of him.

"Milo," Rihyani said sharply to draw his attention. "Is there anything you can do for her? Our charms of mending aren't working."

"It's cold," the Green Lady sobbed. "So cold. What's happening? Beli, hold me."

Her trembling hands reached toward the metal-skinned titan.

Beli raised a stained hand to stroke her cheek.

"I'm here, my love," he rumbled, his voice choked with despair, before turning accusing eyes to Rihyani and Milo.

"This isn't supposed to happen," he snarled, his words as hot as furnace sparks. "Do something!"

Milo snapped out of the grip of the tragic scene and reached into his coat, snatching up the healing unguent after a second of scrambling.

The Green Lady gasped and shuddered, rivulets of brilliant green liquid running from her lips.

"Milo, hurry," Rihyani pleaded as somewhere out in the distance, the chatter of the MG 08 echoed beyond the trees.

Milo tore the wax seals from the vials with his teeth and knelt near the wounded fey's abdomen.

"Move your hands," Milo instructed, holding the vial at the ready as he drew his focus into a searing point of will.

"You better know what you are doing, ape," the colossus warned, his voice simmering like molten metal. "If your witchery harms her—"

"Beli!" Rihyani snapped, her voice reverberating with wrathful command. "Do as he says."

Beli shot Milo one more warning look before his hand came away.

Milo nearly froze at the sight of so much blood welling, but his burning will cried out to be unleashed. With a sure hand, he pressed down to stretch the wound open wide, drawing a cry of pain from the Green Lady as the other hand emptied the vial into it. Blood clung to the unguent, but driven by his will and the burning essence imbued from Milo's own body in its preparation, it burrowed deep into the wounded flesh.

Like a seed springing to life, it mended and knit flesh together, devouring spare blood and dead meat as it spread. Milo took the gory hem of the fey's garment and swept away the blood pooling on the skin to better watch and impel the unguent to work faster.

Before their very eyes, the wound began to shrink, and the Green Lady's pained whimpers quieted.

"Thank Arawn." Rihyani sighed. "Oh, praises, she's okay."

The wound had shrunk to no more than a pinprick, and Milo felt the urgent threat of his regenerative work overflowing the mended flesh. Like cutting a taut string, his will severed the essence from the ingredients. The backlash of unrooted energies crackled through the magus' body like a live current, and he bit back a scream of pain. As quickly as it had come, it passed.

"Meinir, my heart." Beli sobbed and bent to kiss her forehead before turning to Milo. "Thank you, Magus."

"Glad to help," Milo said, suddenly feeling self-conscious under the giant's earnest attention. "I'm glad I got here in time. Did they shoot her out of the air?"

"I'm not sure what happened," Rihyani said, wincing as a stray bullet cracked off a tree a dozen meters from them. "We were wind-riding as usual, and suddenly we felt the currents turn against us. I still don't understand how it happened, but we knew we had to descend, and as we did, there was a gunshot—"

"Something's wrong!" Beli cried, then Meinir's body arched upward, and a weak cry slipped between her lips, along with more blood. With a lurch of his heart, Milo looked down and saw the wound coming apart like a torn seam, blood flowing freely.

"What is happening!" Rihyani sobbed, darting to the dying fey's side. "Milo, what is happening?"

Milo opened his mouth to answer but then snapped it shut. He didn't know.

Hunkering down, he held a hand over Meinir's wounded belly and felt a pressure, almost a tangible force pressing back. It was like another will, different from the resistance a shade might give, but it was strangely distant like a voice coming from a long way off.

"Magus, explain!" Beli roared, and only an outstretched hand from Rihyani kept him from seizing Milo by his collar. "Why is this happening?"

Milo's mind fractured with a million different theories, terrors, and insecurities. He wasn't a doctor; he barely understood anatomy, and necromist healing was his weakest discipline.

His gaze moved from one fey to the other as the thunderous clatter of a machine gun moved away from them.

"I-I don't know," Milo admitted, holding up his hands hopelessly. "Something is keeping the wound from closing, even forcing it open."

They all stared helplessly at each other until a drawling gravelly voice sounded at Milo's back.

"Hot damn, you can't tell I didn't put her to bed now. That's ten Lincoln skins you owe me, hoss."

Milo's daily dose of omnitongue, an elixir that let him understand all languages, relayed the meaning of the words, even as his ears bore the auditory assault of American English. Milo whirled in time to have the rusted bore of a six-cylinder revolver shoved in his face.

"Easy, partner," warned the ragged voice belonging to the man holding the pistol. "Don't go gettin' yourself killed before I can put some money on it."

Milo nearly choked on the smell of chewing tobacco, cheap whiskey, and oil smoke that seemed to radiate from the man who held the gun on him. He was short and slight, with a rangy bow to his legs and a hawkish face that was so filthy it was hard to know what was stubble and what was dirt crusted across his face. Eyes, jaundiced and bloodshot, met his glare with a wild stare while his mouth was split into a wide grin to display brown teeth and a few flashes of gold.

Milo broke off his glare at the leering face, noting first the worn and drooping cowboy hat and then the cracked and peeling buckskins. Milo stared at the hanging fringe for a second, his mind unwilling to come to grips with what he saw even as he squinted at gnarled hanks dangling along the small man's arm.

"Oh, you like that, hoss." The gunman chuckled, blasting Milo with his malignant breath as he flapped an arm to make the not-fringe dance. "Barked each one of them scalps, a collection of sorts. Every one dead at my hand."

Milo gulped and fought back the bile rising in his throat as he realized the tassels were withered strips of scalp sporting the forelocks of their previous owners. A deep, abiding rage blossomed in his chest.

When a bellow like the bell of the Ares tore through the air, Milo realized he wasn't the only one.

"YOU!" Beli howled as he sprang to his feet, twice the height of the pistol-armed scalp hunter, hands curled into claws that could have encompassed the small man's neck. The fey's usual glowing aura now seethed with fury, and his brass fingers rippled with heat. Milo didn't doubt one touch could sear flesh to the bone.

"I still got one for you, big 'un," the gunslinger spat, whipping another corroded pistol from his belt and leveling it at the approaching fey quicker than seemed humanly possible.

"Beli, no!" Rihyani shouted, throwing herself between the gun and her comrade as the huge fey tried to shoulder past her, his eyes fixed on the small man.

"Please, there's no need for this," a smooth, gentle voice called from amidst the trees. "This doesn't have to end poorly."

A stately man in a pinstripe suit and a matching fedora stepped out from the bole of a tree. He was everything the gunslinger was not: tall, older, impeccably groomed, and looking altogether uncomfortable. In one hand, he held what looked like a very dog-eared book with an unadorned leather binding, while the other fidgeted with something in the pocket of his vest. He stepped closer, eyeing Meinir, who had collapsed, her breathing growing softer and shallower every second. His expression cycled from disgust to amorously curious before settling on a sort of apologetic placidity.

"Damn it, Percy!" the cowboy growled, eyes rolling upward. "Chucklehead spoils everything."

Milo's hand tightened on the raptor cane, drawing on the essence within the polished stone haft.

"Please," the well-dressed Percy implored, almost managing to sound sincere. "No one else has to die."

"Only one more," Beli bellowed and surged forward like a sudden storm.

The gunslinger swiveled both pistols to the charging fey, his movements viper-quick, but Milo, driven by the cane's auxiliary powers, was faster. Both pistols barked into the canopy as Milo swept the cane upward into the gunslinger's outstretched fore-arms. The smaller man barked a curse that was garbled by a broken-voiced giggle as the revolvers tumbled from his nerveless grip.

He twisted back toward Milo, a long, pitted knife appearing in his hand as his perpetual smile widened to maniacal proportions.

"Now this is a proper shindig!" he howled, lunging for Milo.

Mid-leap, Beli crashed into the man like a bronze battering ram. Smoking fingers clamped down with a hiss on ragged buck-skin as momentum carried them both several strides into a broad trunk. The tree shuddered, and Milo was certain the cowboy was broken in two by the impact, but a wild, blood-chilling cry announced the opposite. The cowboy had somehow twisted his way out of Beli's smoldering grip and was now astride the huge fey's back, plunging the rusty blade into the broad bronze back he rode. Milo would have thought the metallic flesh of the giant proof against the dilapidated knife, but it punched through, leaving a ragged, corroded wound that wept black ash.

Milo sprang forward, thinking to swat the clinging cowboy off Beli's back with one magically enhanced swipe of his cane.

"Milo!" Rihyani shouted behind him. He felt a sudden pressure at the back of his head, and the air filled with sparkling motes. His body pitched forward and hit the ground as the forest faded and the motes expanded into silvery clouds that hung in front of his eyes. The sounds of Beli's and the cowboy's struggle became distant and forgettable. He thought about rolling over and seeing what had brought about this remarkable change, but at the moment, it all seemed incredibly uninteresting. Better to wait for things to sort themselves out.

He was enjoying watching the beautiful clouds, after all.

He heard Rihyani cry in outrage somewhere closer than the rest of the fighting, but then there was the distinctive mechanical click of a pistol cocking.

"Have no fear, dear lady," he heard Percy saying. "The blow was learned from an ancient Tibetan scroll. The young man will be fine so long as you don't do anything foolish. Just allow those two to settle their differences without interruption, and I will see your human servitor revives without any permanent damage."

Milo felt something hot and sharp pressing in his mind, something that demanded to be noticed, but the mists were so beautiful and everything else was so far away.

"I'm going to pluck the eyes from your skull," Rihyani snarled, her voice throaty and bestial. "Then I'll whisper a charm so they can bear witness to the terrible things I will do to the rest of you."

"Madame, not one step closer," the fancy man warned in an admirably steady voice. "One more, and it won't much matter what you do to me as far as this fellow is concerned. He'll be dead, and then you will have to contend with my compatriot."

As though in answer, the cowboy threw up a strained holler of triumph, and there was a tremendous crashing sound. The painful point in Milo's mind, which he finally realized was his will, began to burn away the discombobulating clouds, his sight and soundness of mind returning by degrees.

Milo could make out the shape of Percy standing over him, a pistol held right above his face.

"Ha-ha, hot damn!" the cowboy crowed somewhere beyond the looming barrel that eclipsed Milo's vision. "Two for one! Now, this is a good day!"

Another carnivorous snarl issued from Rihyani, but Percy demonstratively leaned a little closer to Milo.

"The worst of this is almost over," he assured her, his voice like that of a doctor consoling a fussy patient. "Just please, don't do anything rash."

Milo's hand was resting on his cane, and he slowly curled his fingers around the polished stone haft. Keeping his eyes half-lidded, he slid his gaze to Rihyani, who was in a half-crouch. Milo almost didn't recognize her with her face twisted by rage. He wasn't sure, but it looked like her teeth had become fangs.

"Your turn's comin' next, darlin'," the cowboy muttered as he busied himself with something Milo couldn't see. "Don't you worry your pretty little head about that."

"Ezekiel Boucher!" the well-dressed man snapped in his first show of temper. "Bad enough I must tolerate your deplorable habits, but you are now putting our operation in jeopardy. Get on with it."

"Good ol' *Mister* Astor, dishing on a man in his moment of consummation, no less!"

"Now, Zeke!"

"Yankee spoilsport."

Milo slid his eyes over and could just make out the cowboy, Ezekiel, bending the toppled hulk of Beli's bronze body. The corroded black wounds dotting his bowed muscular back were heartbreakingly numerous. It hadn't been a clean death, and given what Ezekiel seemed to be doing, even the fallen fey's death was not without the rending touch of the pitted knife.

Milo turned the cane ever so slightly in his hand, the raptor's sockets now at the proper angle.

"You'll pay for this!" Rihyani growled, edging a little closer, every muscle coiling for a spring.

"Madame, this is getting tedious." Mr. Percy Astor sighed. "I understand this all seems in bad taste, but I must insist your stop threa—"

BURN

Milo's command sent two darts of burning energy lancing at Percy, but Milo had misjudged the angle. Instead of striking the man in the chest and ending him in an immolating burst, both darts grazed the man's gun hand and then blasted his shoulder. Superheated by the sorcerous flames, several rounds in the pistol went off at once.

Only luck and the enchanted resilience woven into the black cloak kept Milo from being perforated by the wild eruption of rounds and metal shrapnel that filled the air. The suddenly less well-dressed man was not so lucky, tumbling backward as he held up his mangled hand in a ravaged sleeve. He stared at the ruined flesh and gave a shrill scream even as Milo climbed to his feet.

"Percy!" Ezekiel croaked in genuine concern even as he leapt over Beli's body, knife in hand.

Milo spun to face the man, but for the second time, a fey beat him to the punch. Like a lioness, Rihyani sprang forward, covering an inhuman distance as she sailed toward Zeke, fingers stretched into ivory sickles. The fiendishly quick scalp hunter slipped to the side of her impaling pounce, but not to be denied, the unleashed contessa raked her talons across his face and shoulder.

Unnaturally dark blood welled up in the wounds, slow and gummy, made more horrible by the crazed grin that stretched across the man's face. He whipped the knife around as she flew past but only managed to shear through her traveling cloak.

Rihyani landed on all fours and bounded to her feet with liquid grace as she whirled to face Ezekiel's advance.

"Get Meinir to the car!" she snarled through a mouthful of what most certainly were needle-sharp fangs. "Now, Milo! Please!"

Milo nearly defied the instruction, leveling his cane to blast the monstrous scalp hunter, but in a blink of an eye, he and Rihyani were engaged in a lightning-fast exchange of darting swipes and nimble dodges. There was no way he could be certain he wouldn't hit her, so with a frustrated growl, he spun and made for the Green Lady lying on the ground behind them.

Even as he bent to scoop her up, no easy feat since she was taller than him, he knew she was dead. Her features were locked in a rictus of agony, but no breath stirred her chest, and the emerald blood on her body had grown thick and tacky. A tremor of rage and frustration threatened to shake him to pieces, but with a brutal effort of will, he shoved it from his mind.

Grunting and huffing, he heaved upward with Meinir draped across his arms, feeling the muscles of his back scream in protest. Righting himself after a misstep almost toppled him and the dead fey, he took off at a jog before a sharp cry made him swing heavily around.

Rihyani was slashing savagely with one hand, but the other hung at her side, pale blood seeping from a gash across her shoulder.

Ezekiel kept clear of the sweeping claws even as he slowly advanced, tossing the knife from hand to hand playfully as he chuckled.

"Three little faeries in one evenin'," he cooed in a sickeningly tender voice. "Oh, I'm a lucky, lucky boy."

Milo looked down at Meinir's limp form, imagining the same agonized death mask on Rihyani's silver face. A deep, tempestuous rage came over him, and the world shrank to the path that led straight to the back of the scalp hunter's skull.

Placing Meinir at his feet, he started advancing, cane in both hands like a pick hungry to bite deep. He made it two steps before his tunnel vision exploded with pain as something sharp bit into his calf.

Percy, creeping on his belly unnoticed, had buried an ornate dagger in Milo's calf and twisted it cruelly even as he glared hatefully up into the magus' face.

Righteous fury keeping him upright, Milo jerked his leg away, the knife still buried in the meat of his calf, and brought the cane down on Percy's upturned face. The abused man slumped to the ground bonelessly, a deep gash across his forehead.

Milo might have delivered the fatal stroke then and there, but another cry from Rihyani drew his attention. The contessa, a second slash across her arm now, was scrambling back from Ezekiel, snapping her fangs at him but clearly weakening. The scalp-hunter followed her as she lurched behind Beli's fallen form.

Spitting curses through the agony in his leg, Milo threw himself after her. The dagger still in his flesh gouged and tore with each step, so blind with pain and rage, Milo threw himself over Beli's body to smash his shoulder into Ezekiel.

The maniacal cowboy tumbled head over heels, his hat flying from his head and the scalp fringe tangling. It was all Milo could do to keep his feet, his limbs trembling as he gripped his cane with unsteady hands. The world swam for a second, and at that moment, Ezekiel Boucher had found his feet and advanced, waving his bloody knife in front of him teasingly. The strangled purple of the sunset glinted like a bruise across his thinning pate. His smile was transcendentally terrifying and perversely suggestive.

"Oh, boy, it's been a while since I barked a dude." He wet his lips with a craggy tongue. "But don't you worry, kid, Uncle Zeke is going to take his time with you. I'm not going to take a little bit off the top, oh no, sweetie, never. I'm going to peel you clean and do it just right so you're still breathing when I show you every inch of your own hide."

Milo wished he could draw his focus to blast the sadistic fiend, but the knife was still buried in his leg, and the pain was making it hard to stay conscious, much less do magic. What wouldn't he have given to have remembered to put his service pistol on his hip before he'd rushed off to be heroic!

"The only question is do you want me to start at the bottom," Ezekiel purred, gesturing at Milo's feet before rising to eye his scalp lasciviously, "or go with the classic top?"

The magus tightened his grip on his cane. There was no way he could beat the madman, but he would go down swinging.

"If you've got to start somewhere, why not the ears?" he quipped, forcing a smile despite the agony in his leg. "I've never been scalped, but I can't imagine it's worse than listening to you a second longer."

"Ohhh," Zeke groaned with unseemly gusto. "Now I've got to start with your tongue and save your ears for last. It's going to take some work, but you're worth it, kid."

Milo drew back for a swing as Ezekiel made what would most certainly have been the fatal slash had an empty ammo hopper not smashed into the cowboy's chest.

Milo's head whipped around to see Ambrose pounding toward Ezekiel.

"Again?" Ezekiel shrieked wetly as he dragged himself out from under the heavy metal bin. There was something wrong with his chest, one part of it sunken and unwilling to follow the rhythm of the other side.

Milo winced at the sight, but he had little time to dwell on the man's injuries as Ambrose leaped forward to inflict new ones.

Ezekiel tried to indulge in more of his taunting, but he hardly had formed the first words before the big man's fist lashed out and cracked across his jaw. To the small man's credit, though he rocked with the blow, he swung back to spit a mouthful of blood and resume his mad smile.

"Now, this is going to be one hell of a fight!" he cackled as he fluttered the blade in front of him again.

"No," Ambrose said in a flat, icy voice, "it won't."

As Milo had known since the first time he'd met him, Simon Ambrose was a man who didn't need to lie.

Ezekiel was fast, vicious, and had already proven his knife work was lethally proficient even against a giant like Beli, but none of that was enough. Ambrose didn't seem to be moving fast so much as he knew exactly where he did and didn't want to be. Three slashes and one thrust passed within inches of his skin, Ambrose letting them slide by as his burning green eyes remained fixed on the maniacal scalp hunter, who had begun to giggle.

The fifth strike was never finished as Ambrose, deciding he had the measure of his opponent, grabbed Ezekiel's wrist in one hand. Milo knew what was coming but couldn't tear his eyes away as Ambrose gave a quick twist and bones snapped like wet kindling in a fire.

Ezekiel's tittering swelled into breathless hooting as the knife fell from his suddenly limp grip.

What followed next was the quickest and most complete ruination of a man he'd ever seen, which the Nephilim did with nothing but his bare hands. His rifle and bayonet remained fixed and the sword on the big man's belt remained sheathed in utter contempt of Ambrose's opponent.

A change of grip, one sharp tug, and the cowboy's shoulder separated with a hollow pop. Then one shuffling series of steps and Ambrose launched two stomping kicks, one into the back of each knee, and there were more sickening sounds of tendons parting.

Ezekiel fell flat on the ground, only one hale limb left to clutch at the loamy ground as the other three twitched pitifully. The fit of hysterical laughter was approaching a crescendo.

"HAHAHAHA!" On and on he screamed, his voice growing more and more hoarse.

Ambrose frowned at his broken foe before stomping down with his heavy boot. This time Milo did look away as the laughter finally ended with a wet crunch.

He spied the knife still jutting from his calf, and remembered he was in agony. The world wobbled, and he didn't have the strength to fight the quavering call of the earth. He sank down with enough presence of mind not to let his descent drive the knife deeper into his flesh.

By reflex, his fingers reached out and brushed the hilt, but that brief touch made his stomach lurch into his throat, and the world was swallowed in a static crackle of obliviating pain.

When he came to, Ambrose was crouching next to him, a bandage in one hand and the strap of his Gewehr in the other.

"Here," the big man said a second before he shoved the leather strap between Milo's teeth. "This is going to hurt."

"Whuf iz?" Milo choked out around the taste of tanned cowhide, then Ambrose tugged the knife free.

Milo was a man experienced with pain; it might not have been the worst he'd ever felt, but it was in the running for a place on the podium.

His teeth drove into leather, his scream choked by the tooth-sparing gag, and then it was all he could do to keep breathing. He felt the big man at work, binding up the wound, cruelly and carefully making sure each wrap and twist of the dressing was cinched tight.

"Up on your feet." Ambrose grunted and gripped Milo by the elbow.

Despite every expectation, a moment later, Milo was on his feet. He leaned on his cane heavily and swore in a jagged string of incoherent profanity, but he knew he could force himself to make it to the Rollsy. Swiping sweat and tears from his face, Milo turned and was happy to see that Ambrose was binding Rihyani's wounds.

It was also a relief to see that she had the strength to argue with him, though her voice was faint and soft.

"No, not me," she wheezed, raising one pale arm to point at Meinir and then Beli. "They need your help."

Ambrose ignored the entreaty and two more as Milo limped over and awkwardly squatted next to the contessa to take her pointing fingers in the hand not clutching his cane.

"Rihyani," he croaked, pausing for a heartbeat when his voice sounded raw in his own ears. "I'm sorry, but there's nothing we can do."

Rihyani's gaze swung to him, and for an instant, Milo feared she would sink her fangs into his face as her fingers dug into his hand.

"This shouldn't happen," she sobbed, a fierce light shining in her eyes. "This can't."

'It did." Ambrose huffed as he tugged the bandages tight, drawing a cry of pain from the contessa as she let go of Milo's hand. The magus stared at five dots of blood where the fey's nails had bitten into his flesh, thankful she'd kept herself from sprouting the wicked talons from before.

"Right now, we need to get out of here," the big man added.

The shadows had deepened in the copse of trees to the point that Milo was finding it hard to see beyond the trees to the hills. The paranoid itch of being exposed to the enemy spread from the back of Milo's head to nestle between his shoulder blades. He didn't dare to hope that Ambrose had managed to kill or drive off all the ambushers. In truth, there could be enemy reinforcements closing off their retreat right now.

He felt the tightness in his wounded leg and saw the bandages on Rihyani already growing damp with her pale blood. They wouldn't survive much longer if they didn't get moving.

"Carry her and let's get to the Rollsy," Milo said before rising with a heavy grunt. "Lokkemand should be on his way, so let's hope to God we can outrun the bastards long enough to reach friendly forces."

"We should bring their bodies," Rihyani said, obviously taking great pains to keep from sounding too desperate. "Their clan will wish to perform the rites, and—"

A trunk less than a meter from Ambrose sent up a shower of splinters an eyeblink before the report of a rifle was heard.

They were out of time.

"Their clans will have to understand that we'll come back for them," Milo hissed through clenched teeth. "Ambrose, let's move."

Ambrose scooped Rihyani up as though she weighed no more than the cloak she was wearing.

Bleeding, limping, and ducking each crack of rifles in the growing dark, the trio made their way between the trees to the patiently idling Rollsy. A second later, the engine growled and Ambrose wove through the trees to thread a course back up the hill and toward Shatili.

7

THE HERESY

The Rollsy gobbled up the miles as the last of the daylight was swallowed by the horizon and the countryside became a series of undulating shades of black.

Thankfully, none of those in the vehicle required visual assistance, though Milo did have to fetch the nightsight along with more healing unguent for his leg. As he applied the former, shaking the distortions from his eyes, he looked at Rihyani in the back of the Rollsy. Her bandages were beginning to seep blood, and Milo wondered even with his leg throbbing abominably if he should work on her first, but then he remembered the failure with Meinir.

Had he made things worse by attempting to save her? There had been so much blood; Milo was no trained doctor, but it had seemed to do something, if only for a minute or so. Was it because she was fey, or did it have something to do with her attacker? Something about Ezekiel Boucher had struck Milo as unnatural, and it was not the unnerving laughter or bloodlust. As a budding magus, Milo was learning that there were clues and truths that could be discerned but not by anything as pedestrian as the five senses.

Remembering the deceased cowboy sent a shiver down Milo's spine, but then the car thumped over a section of pitted land and Milo's leg bounced against the bed of the truck.

Another mind-throttling surge of pain sprang up from his leg and the immediate course of action resolved itself. If Milo didn't do something about it, he wasn't going to be any good to anyone very soon.

Wincing and blinking back tears as he unwound the dressing, Milo finally had the clearance he needed to pour in the unguent. Steeling his mind and soul against the pain that tried to distract him, he compelled the unguent to work and soon felt the stinging itch of flesh mending. He went slow, careful lest the regenerative create a distended tumor or jar his focus to create some other even worse side effect.

The wound began to close as they rolled on, their headlights off as Ambrose used whatever supernatural senses he possessed to steer them across the countryside

They very nearly plowed into Lokkemand's patrol, which came rolling up along the crest where it slid alongside the Argun and thus toward Shatili. Milo had unclenched his focus and dissipated the last of the unguent as the light of many headlamps broke over the Rollsy like a false dawn.

Ambrose swore and swung over to the side, sending Milo scooting across the bed to fetch up next to Rihyani. Only his outstretched hands kept him from losing his teeth, but his momentum still saw the wind knocked from him. He sank down to the bed, gaping like a landed fish as he looked at Rihyani's downturned face. Her skin was ashen and almost translucent enough that he thought he could see the layers shifting as her lips parted in a weak smile.

"You don't look so good, Milo," she said, her voice barely audible above the trembling growl of the engine. "Maybe you should lie down and catch your breath."

Milo forced enough air into his stubborn lungs to manage a wheezing laugh.

"Speak for yourself, my lady," he got out as he struggled to his feet.

"I'm just a little tired." She gave him a wink. "Had a long trip to see a good friend, you know."

Even with his entire abdomen determined to never breathe again and his limbs trembling as he favored his recently mended leg, Milo felt that staring at her face was something he could do forever. It plucked his shrunken heart like the first note of spring, taunting and teasing a gnarled tree to consider awakening. It was so unfamiliar it seemed painful, but he knew somewhere in the root of him he couldn't deny the siren song, not forever.

Then her wine-dark eyes with their piercing golden pupils rolled upward as her whole body shivered. A soft groan escaped her gray lips, and her fingers groped her wounded shoulder. Pools of her pale blood had formed under her on the floorboards.

If his heart ever wanted to hear that tune, he needed to get her help and quickly.

"Lokkemand!" Milo barked as he stood in the bed of the Rollsy. "Captain Lokkemand!"

There was the protesting squeal of a heavy door swinging on ill-maintained hinges, then the clank of that door on an armored hull.

"Volkohne, report," Lokkemand's voice instructed coolly from behind a large set of headlamps.

Milo hated how calm and confident the man sounded, even though somewhere in the back of his mind, he knew it was a good thing.

"The contessa and her companions were ambushed by Georgians and two Americans," Milo shouted back, trying to force his voice to be steady but not succeeding. "The contessa is wounded and needs immediate medical attention."

"The companions?" the captain asked, his voice neutral and unassuming.

"Dead," Milo reported stiffly, unable to ignore the soft sob that came from Rihyani at the proclamation. "Killed by the Americans."

There was a pause, then Lokkemand's voice rang out, steady and sure.

"How was the enemy equipped?"

Milo faltered as he thought of how to describe the Americans, but Ambrose piped up readily.

"Small arms only, sir," the big man reported. "The Georgians were probably just a militia turned mercenary. Fair shots and they knew the ground, but they weren't organized or motivated to face hardened opposition."

"The Americans?" Lokkemand asked.

"Dead or wishing they were," Ambrose said confidently. "Left them in a small copse of trees about ten miles west of our position with the bodies of the contessa's companions and whatever is left of the Georgians, which is shy of a dozen by my count."

Milo couldn't keep from giving Ambrose an impressed look. He'd single-handedly reduced the enemy numbers by half and had still found time to save Milo and Rihyani from the Americans.

"Any clue as to the enemy objective?" Lokkemand asked. In response, Ambrose shrugged and threw a glance at Milo.

"Umm, p-possibly the capture of the contessa," Milo stuttered lamely, trying to replay and interpret the events in his head. "Not entirely sure, Captain."

"Any signs of pursuit?"

"No, sir," Milo said with a shake of his head after looking over his shoulder to make sure he wasn't being proven a liar.

Milo could almost see Lokkemand give a thoughtful nod before straightening and issuing his orders in crisp, smooth commands

"Brodden's vehicle escorts the magus and sees that the contessa is tended to. The rest of you, adjusted pattern *Roth Ritter*. We sweep wide around the last confirmed point of contact and approach from the east."

There was a quick chorus of confirmations from the men in the other vehicles, then one of them peeled off from the formation and executed a three-point turn to head back to Shatili and the fortress. Ambrose followed, almost as though he might nudge the vehicle along with the Rollsy's jutting nose.

"We'll retrieve the contessa's companions," Lokkemand shouted before turning back to address his soldiers. "Maintain fire discipline out there. The last thing I need to do is pay to replace some shepherd's goats."

"I don't understand," Ambrose said as they carried Rihyani into Milo's study. "Why can't you just rub one of your potions on her or something?"

Brodden the medic strode alongside Rihyani, working to apply a tourniquet as they moved into the room. Seeing an open table, he barked an instruction that she be laid on it.

"I tried that with Meinir," Milo said as they eased the fey's limp form onto the table. "It worked for a second, then the wound opened again. I think it might have made things worse."

"Is it because she was fey?" Ambrose asked as they stepped over to observe Brodden as his hands worked with crisp professional rapidity.

"I'm not sure, but Rihyani acted surprised when she started bleeding again," Milo said, trying to force his brain to work but only managing to stare helplessly at Brodden's pink-stained hands. "Really, they all kept asking why it was happening, almost like they were surprised she had been hurt at all."

Ambrose and Milo both winced as Brodden tightened the

tourniquet, drawing a soft but distinct moan of pain from Rihyani.

"One of you with a strong stomach, get over here," the medic directed as he held Rihyani's arm up in the air.

Ambrose was quicker to step forward and was soon holding the contessa's arm aloft while Brodden worked some sterile packing into the wounds. Milo moved closer to watch, though his mind was preoccupied with possible adjustments he could make to the formula so he could try his healing unguents again.

"She seems close enough to human," the medic said as he worked. "So I'm assuming that the amount of blood she's lost is as dangerous to her as it would be to a human."

Ambrose nodded with a sigh as Brodden reached out and grabbed Milo, who started but didn't resist as his hands were led to press against the packing.

"What does that mean?" Milo asked, staring into Rihyani's face. Her eyes were shut and seemed sunken into her face, which they had not previously been.

Milo felt an icy talon of fear digging through his guts, searching for his heart.

Was it already too late?

"Means she needs blood," Brodden said, wiping sweat from his forehead with a forearm while his other hand plunged into his bag. "Plenty of blood if she's going to last much longer."

"Take mine," Milo said without pause as the medic dragged out a series of tubes and an arcane set of steel devices. "Take however much you need."

"It's not like books and radio programs," Brodden growled as he set about assembling and checking the equipment for the transfusion. "If I give her the wrong type of blood, it could kill her as surely as not giving her any, and seeing as she's not human, I doubt we're going to be able to hook you up and hope for the best."

Milo's fear kindled to a frustration that sharpened his tongue into a flailing weapon.

"Then why are you wasting time getting that wretched thing out?" he demanded with a snarl.

"Because I'm a medic, damn it!" Brodden shot back. "I'm doing what I know how to and hoping someone's going to tell me they've got a stash of faerie blood in this weird workshop of yours."

Ambrose raised a hand to give Milo's trembling shoulder a steadying squeeze.

"Got anything like that, Magus?" he asked, his voice steady and soothing like a man seeking to calm a skittish horse. "Anything that could help?"

Milo almost threw off the hand and screamed in the big man's face for the stupid temerity of the question. He almost raved at the idiocy of thinking he kept bottles of fey blood for just such an occasion.

But he stood there silently, mouth moving in a string of unvoiced half-formed words as his mind hit upon something that *could* help. The healing unguents had sought to regenerate and bind flesh, and to his mind, they had been violently rejected by either fey physiology or something in the wound created by Ezekiel Boucher, but what if it was something where the magical process had ceased and was just, from all points of view, blood? It wouldn't heal Rihyani like his unguents, but it might give them time.

"I don't have fey blood on hand," Milo said, his eyes searching the shelf behind his desk for his copy of *Transitional States: Transmogrified Truths of Matter Living or Otherwise*. "But I might have a way to make some."

Not for the first time, Milo wondered if the dreaded ghul scholars who'd penned the works he studied ever thought a human would come along and break what constituted the few taboos of their kind.

For reasons both practical and similar, the ghuls had strict injunctions against using the blood of the living in their magics, especially a necromist performing alchemy. The fact that Milo, in refusing to use human remains, used his own blood to power his works was a smack in the face of everything the ghuls held sacred. Using his blood magic to pervert an alchemical formula into making blood now seemed comically transgressive.

He hoped he was going to live long enough to be able to gloat the next time he met one of those depraved troglodytes.

"You sure this won't kill you?" Ambrose asked for the third time since Milo had rushed through the rough outline of what he was going to do.

"No," Milo repeated, also for the third time as he ground a pungent mixture of herbs, preserved amphibian extracts, and his own blood. "I'm not, but we don't have time for me to be sure."

"You really don't," Brodden said as he hovered over Rihyani, his face a grim mask. "She's hanging on by sheer willpower at this point."

"You're saying this might not even save her?" the big man asked, his eyes working a jagged triangle between the medic, the fey, and the magus.

"I'm saying we do this," Milo cut in before Brodden could answer. "And that's the final word."

Ambrose opened his mouth to argue, but his jaws clamped shut with a snap.

Milo checked the consistency of the contents of the bowl, not only physically but through his probing magical senses, then checked his text.

It was two parts daring and one part foolishness, bending the theory the way he was, and it involved more than a few intuitive leaps, but one look at Rihyani's listless body on his workbench told him all he needed to know. He was going to make her blood or die trying. Everything from here on out was a consequence playing out.

"Are you ready with that thing?" Milo asked as he approached with his elixir.

"I suppose." The medic shrugged and held up a long needle connected to a strand of tubing that wound back to the bizarre arrangement of metal that Milo had a hard time believing was not magical. "Are you?"

"Almost," Milo said, and he stepped over to Rihyani.

Her wounds had slowed to a trickle, but that trickle still stained the packed bandages. With a muttered apology, Milo squeezed the bandage to get a few drops of blood from the fabric that he flicked into the bowl. Though not apparent to anyone else in the room, Milo felt the ingredients align metaphysically, almost snapping into place with a ripple of magical pressure.

"That's got to be a good sign," he told himself before tilting back his head and downing the mixture.

Milo felt the magical matrix bound up in the ingredients slide down his gullet and diffuse as it went. Magic was not science, though necromantic alchemy came the closest in comparison, and gestures meant things. The act of ingestion wasn't about digestion so much as reception, willingly partaking so that the power imbibed could work itself into a welcoming host.

And work it did.

Milo's body spasmed as the power poured through his veins and arteries.

"Now!" Milo gasped as he sank into a chair next to the workbench. "Quickly."

Brodden slid the needle in and then activated a pump, and within seconds, a stream of living fluid was spiraling through the tubes and headed to the needle already buried in Rihyani's arm. The vitae was a pale shade of pink.

"It worked," Ambrose murmured, then frowned as he stared at Milo's face. "What's wrong?"

"I'm trying to control it," Milo growled, sweat running from his brow as he wrestled with the catalyzing forces inside of him. "Changing what's going out without changing all of it and killing me."

Ambrose swore, a long and potent assemblage of profanity in a particularly florid French dialect.

"How much does she need?" the big man asked Brodden, who was busy overseeing the technical aspects of the transfusion.

"As much, ugh, as much as I can give her," Milo hissed between gritted teeth, which became a strained, defiant smile as Ambrose glared down at him.

"Don't be stupid," the bodyguard spat even as his eyes softened at the sight of his ward's pained expression.

"Too late to turn back now." Milo laughed and held onto the arms of his chair in a knuckle-popping grip. "Now, if you w-will excuse me, I need…oh, God…to manage a complex alchemical reaction while not dying."

8

THE WOUND

Milo awoke with a start on his bed, clawing at his arm frantically. He stopped when he realized the vampiric eel, a resurrected casualty from a bygone alchemical project, was not in fact affixed to his arm as he'd just been dreaming.

"You'll make a mess of your bandage," Ambrose growled around the pipe between his teeth from the spot near the balcony where he slouched.

Milo had indeed made a mess of the bandages around his arm, so much so that he found his fingers entangled in the wrappings he'd wrenched free. As he tugged his fingers loose from the snaring fabric, he saw the puckered mouth of the puncture marking where the transfusion needle had been sunk into his arm.

"How long was I out?" he asked in a numb mutter as he decided to unravel the linen on his arm. The wound seemed sound and unlikely to reopen.

"For the past twelve hours." The big man puffed with a gust of pipe smoke. "Brodden demanded you stop after giving what he guessed was three pints, and forcibly cut you off after nearly four. I gave you a double dose of the restorative and brought you here. They've moved her to a separate room that's become a makeshift infirmary."

Milo stared at the scabbed-over red wound as he recollected the events of the night and early morning at Ambrose's prompting. It had been like holding onto a cliff's edge by his fingernails the whole time, but as the blood flowed from his veins into Rihyani, he'd drawn strength from knowing that he was doing everything in his power to save her. When the needle had come out and he'd released the energies of the spell into the ether, it was an almost pleasurable feeling, followed by utter exhaustion.

Milo's stomach rumbled grumpily at the debt he'd run up with all his heroics.

"Is she showing signs of recovery?" Milo asked, unwilling to hope that she was on the mend.

Ambrose frowned and then reached over the balcony to tap out his pipe. The stretching silence made Milo shudder, and he reflexively pulled the covers up, performing the necessary mental gymnastics to convince himself it was the blood loss that was making him act this way.

"She's not dying." Ambrose sighed as he pocketed his pipe. "But all the same, her wounds aren't healing."

"What does that mean?" Milo asked, willing his teeth not to chatter as he shivered.

Ambrose rose to his feet and shrugged.

"Exactly what I said; her wounds aren't healing," he said, not sounding angry so much as frustrated. "We've got the bleeding down to barely a trickle, through pressure and some clever needlework by Brodden. After twelve hours, her body should be showing some signs of clotting, but as far as we can tell, it isn't."

Milo started, trying not to let an overarching wave of despair spread over him.

"The truth is that she shouldn't have lost as much blood as she did from those wounds." Ambrose's gaze slid to the floor, and he brushed the fingers of one hand over the knuckles of the other hand. "The cuts were thin and pretty shallow, and they don't seem to have hit any major arteries. It doesn't make sense."

At those words, Milo felt a prickling along the skin of his arms and the back of his neck.

"Magic," he breathed. "The Americans—that maniac Ezekiel. He must have had something or known some way."

Ambrose froze, his eyes narrowing as he stared at Milo.

"You mean, you aren't the only wizard?"

The question struck Milo harder and deeper than he would have imagined.

He knew that it was entirely possible, even probable that there would be others, but recognizing that he might have met another human who could perform magic shook him all the same. His unique and even privileged, though weighty, position suddenly felt precarious in a way he wasn't prepared for. Milo had only been a wizard, the world's first, for a short time, but it seemed that his short furlough had indelibly marked him to assume, at least subconsciously, that it would always be so.

What had Ezekiel Boucher learned that Milo hadn't? What creature had shared its dark arts with the despicable man so that he could inflict wounds that denied healing both magical and mundane?

He can't tell you, now can he? Milo thought, welcoming the memory of the madman's final moments. Milo told himself it was his well-honed survival instincts that could gauge the utter depravity of a man like Ezekiel. However, he imagined even a half-witted rube could have spent one minute with the American and understood him to be reprobate of the lowest order.

"Maybe I wasn't the only one," Milo said with a meaningful glance at Ambrose's boots. "Before he met you, that is."

Ambrose looked down, and a sudden grim smile spread across his face.

"I don't often take pleasure in killing a man," Ambrose said, his voice lower and thicker, "but I'm not going to pretend that ending that monster wasn't satisfying."

Milo nodded, agreeing that if anyone had deserved such an end, it was the scalp-hunting American. The sight of him gleefully hoisting the trophy carved from the fallen Beli was something that would not leave the dark and bitter corners of his mind any time soon. The way the wounds had seemed fouled and corroded on the dead titan had seemed like a greater insult than the injuries.

Milo straightened, his mind struggling to accelerate despite his hunger and fatigue.

"Where are Beli's and Meinir's bodies?" he asked, throwing off the covers and climbing hastily if unsteadily to his feet. "If I can examine their wounds, maybe take samples, I might be able to figure out what is wrong with Rihyani."

Reverse-engineering magic, especially magic he was unfamiliar with, was doubtful, but not impossible. He wasn't sure about the burial customs of fey, but he was sure that both of the contessa's companions would have been glad to not have their deaths be in vain.

Ambrose blinked at Milo as the magus retrieved his coat from the foot of the bed, straightening as he slid it on.

"Where are the bodies?" Milo asked again, testing his repaired leg, thankful for only a hint of stiffness.

"They weren't there when Lokkemand and crew got there." Ambrose sighed. "The fey bodies and the Americans. Seems like the Georgians scooped up everything before getting out of there. Lokkemand said they didn't make contact with the enemy after two wide sweeps of the area."

Milo ground his teeth in frustration. Nothing could be easy, could it?

"Damn! Where is Lokkemand?"

"In his office," Ambrose answered, his frown deepening. "Wait, why couldn't you take samples from Rihyani?"

"I could," Milo acknowledged, moving toward the door. "But since we think it is actively malignant magic, it could react badly to my magic."

"Your blood-changing bit didn't seem to bother it," the big man pointed out as he followed Milo into the corridor. The fortress at Shatili was a venerable military structure, designed so that even when enemies breached the exterior walls, defenders could mount a strong opposition. The hallways were tight passages where only one man could pass easily, so Ambrose was forced to follow as the magus stalked toward Lokkemand's office at the center of the complex.

"The magic had already happened by the time the blood reached her," Milo explained. "Whatever is doing this to her wouldn't have sensed the magic I was using because it was done, inert, finished."

Ambrose's brows knit as they hustled into the heart of the complex.

"When will she need more blood?" Milo asked.

"Not sure. Maybe a day or two," Ambrose confessed as they rounded a corner and came within sight of the small antechamber that led to the captain's room. A soldier stood guard in the room, which was furnished with a small rug and a wooden chair, as though Lokkemand expected that his appointments might need a place to sit while they waited for him.

"I should be able to give again," Milo muttered mostly to himself.

"Not sure that's how it—" Ambrose began as they moved into the antechamber before Milo cut him off.

"Magic," Milo interjected before turning to the straightening soldier in front of the door. "I need to see Captain Lokkemand. Is he in?"

The soldier, who would have been classically handsome with his strong chin and dark, lively eyes if not for a crooked nose and a goat-toothed mouth, eyed Milo. What was possibly habitual defiance seemed ready to creep into his stance until he met Milo's pale eyes. Whatever he saw gave him pause.

"Yes," he replied with the slightest nod.

"Yes, *sir*," Milo snapped. He still wasn't sure of his position, but he'd been given the black coat of an officer, so not acting like he was an officer confused the men.

"Yes, sir," the guard replied with only a little sullenness in his voice. "But he said he was drafting a report or something. He instructed me to not let him be interrupted, sir."

"I'm afraid this can't wait for paperwork," Milo said, straightening a little to leverage his greater height. "Open the door, or get out of my way so I can."

The soldier stared at Milo for a second, his eyes searching the wizard's, then, uncomfortable with what he saw, they dropped to Milo's shoulders and the black coat covering them. That seemed to seal the deal, and with a muttered apology, he opened the door, stepping aside to let Milo pass as he began his speaking.

"I'm sorry to disturb you, Cap—"

"But certain things can't wait," Milo interrupted, sweeping past the soldier. Ambrose ambled after in his wake.

Lokkemand sat at the far end of what might have been the castellan's war room, a square apartment where rustic tables were pushed together in a large rectangle. Lokkemand's files, maps, and various other forms of paperwork were spread across the tables, obviously possessing some order that was unclear to anyone except the captain. Lokkemand was standing over the maps, arms crossed with his chin in one hand. He did not appear surprised or put out by Milo's sudden arrival.

"Thank you, Dieter," he said with a nod. "You can go."

With a relieved sigh, Dieter retreated, closing the door behind him.

"Magus," Lokkemand said, turning his gaze back to his maps. "What can I do for you?"

"Captain, Ambrose told me you didn't recover any of the

bodies from the battle site," Milo began. "Did you find anything else there? Anything in the copse of trees or around there?"

Lokkemand bobbed his head and without a word, he walked over to his desk at the head of the assembled tables.

"We found these," he said as he drew out a thick envelope and shook out its contents. "When the men found them, I wasn't sure if they had anything to do with those who attacked the contessa, but it seemed remiss not to bring them in."

The captain flipped open the unsealed top of the envelope and dumped its contents onto the desk. The first thing to emerge was a twist of hair attached to some shriveled leather that fluttered feather-like down onto the desk. Milo's mind flashed back to Ezekiel holding up the sawn-off section of Beli's scalp and Ambrose's boot descending on that grinning face.

Almost as though to make the point, the second item fell out, thunking point-first into Lokkemand's desk. Its pitted surface still crusted with blood and flecks of hair, Ezekiel's knife stood defiantly upright before them.

"Didn't feel the need to mention that?" Ambrose asked tartly.

"You asked about bodies," Lokkemand replied coolly. "And the second you heard there were none, you were off. I wasn't going to chase you down. I figured once your ward was up and about, someone would come looking."

The two men exchanged glares before Lokkemand, as was almost customary now, looked away as though suddenly very bored.

"Fair enough," Ambrose grumbled as he nodded, turning to Milo. "That might do the trick, eh?"

"Yeah." Milo swallowed, his mouth suddenly dry. "That might work."

He was having a hard time not staring at the weapon, something inside him twisting at the thought of touching the horn handle. Milo tried to tell himself he was being foolish, that it was a simple piece of metal and bone fastened together, but he remembered Jorge and Imrah's shade talking about the one who could be using men to do his dirty work. If he was dealing with a Guardian and therefore magic, it was possible the knife was far more dangerous than a simple piece of metal.

Was this his handiwork, the Guardian who'd recruited Imrah? Was Ezekiel Boucher one of those fanatical followers? The man had seemed insane enough for such things.

The more Milo thought about it, the more he was certain that was what they were dealing with.

"I'm judging from your reaction that these are significant," Lokkemand said with a sweeping gesture toward his desk. "Will they help you identify the ambusher or assist the recovery of the contessa?"

"Both," Milo said, dragging his eyes from the knife to meet the captain's face. "Thank you, sir."

Lokkemand's eyes darted between Milo and the knife before he stooped to sweep the scalp and slide the blade into the envelope.

"I'm glad to hear it," he said, holding out the envelope for Milo to take. "We need to resolve this business as soon as possible. Our operation is about to become active, and I need you focused on the task at hand."

"Our operation, sir?" Milo asked as he stepped forward and took the envelope. He tried to tell himself the uncomfortable and beguiling tingle he felt upon taking it was a function of his fatigue and hunger.

Lokkemand narrowed his eyes at Milo, then looked at Ambrose.

"Did he suffer a blow to the head or something?"

"More tired and hungry than anything else, I expect." Ambrose grunted noncommittally. "He sorts himself out just fine, though."

Milo found himself looking between the two men as he stood there gingerly holding the envelope.

"What are you two talking about?"

"The operation, Magus," Ambrose prompted, which Milo was certain he thought was helpful. "The bit about taking out the bad men heading this way from Russia."

"Oh, that," Milo said, almost relieved that he wasn't the one falling behind. "We're already there, aren't we? I mean, a guerrilla force waylays the fey, and we find one of them in possession of magical paraphernalia. Seems pretty clear to me."

Ambrose opened his mouth and then fell silent, digesting the words, while Lokkemand shook his head and pointed at the maps and reports on the tables.

"I'm almost certain those actors were a third party," the captain said firmly. "That or perhaps they are operating as a vanguard for a much larger force, which is what you need to be preparing for right now. Didn't you say they were Americans?"

Milo felt a familiar tension in the back of his mind and across his skin as he responded to Lokkemand, unable to keep the heat from his voice.

"They could have been posing as Americans, or maybe the mind-twisting Guardian picked up a few American operatives." Milo shrugged as though it was settled so simply. "Either way, it doesn't matter. I need to figure out how to help Rihyani first, sir."

Lokkemand bristled a little and gave a fractional snarl of irritation.

"I think you need to spend less time concerned about the fey and more time concerned with the mission Jorge gave you."

"I'm not a scout or a *jaeger*, sir," Milo shot back. "The most dangerous of the two Americans is dead and the other could be also, but either way, they are in retreat. If you are so worried about them, you should start patrolling the countryside to finish off stragglers or find a new target and leave me to look after Rihyani, *sir*. When you have something real for me to worry about, maybe I'll give it my due attention."

Ambrose's hand settled on Milo's shoulder and he led him toward the door.

"I think the magus needs a little more rest and a lot more food," the bodyguard stated as Lokkemand bristled.

"Quite," the captain replied curtly. "See him put in good order and soon because we'll need him fighting fit when the time comes."

Milo turned to argue but Ambrose didn't give him an option, driving him onward like a small boat before a massive wave.

"What's that, Magus?" the big man called in a booming voice as he raised a free hand to his ear. "Sorry, I can't hear you over the sound of your growling stomach."

"Just what the hell was that?" Milo asked, forcing down another mouthful of seasoned lamb before taking an embarrassingly large bite from a slice of black bread.

It wasn't the fatted calf, but it seemed Ambrose had somehow encouraged the quartermaster to provide a veritable feast for the recovering magus.

Ambrose had quickly ushered Milo down to the mess hall on the ground floor and placed him at the waiting table where a large lump of goat cheese and a whole loaf of black bread sat. After he needlessly instructed Milo to eat, Ambrose had vanished for a moment, before returning with enough lamb to put even the magus' ravenous appetite to bed.

His hunger roused to an unbearable intensity by the sudden profusion of edibles, he'd stuffed himself for several minutes before he had the presence of mind to remember he was angry at both his bodyguard and the captain.

In fact, the bewildering idea that both seemed dead-set against his sound advice had been so bemusing, he'd needed a few more minutes and several more mouthfuls to compose his thoughts.

"Since when do you take up with Lokkemand?"

Ambrose, standing on the opposite side of the table with a jug of water and a cup he was filling, looked almost offended.

"Take up with?" he asked, slapping the cup down and sliding it to Milo, sloshing water on the table. "I wouldn't call it that. More like keeping a tired and naïve man from making a fool of himself. Lokkemand was inconsequential in that equation."

"Naïve?" Milo said after washing down his last bite with a slug of water. "What in all our time makes you think I'm naïve?"

Ambrose scowled as one of his eyebrows cocked up.

"You know, it is exhausting, trying to find ways not to believe you are just stupid."

Milo choked on a hunk of bread and cheese as much as the insult, coughing and hacking for a bit before he could retort.

"I'm stupid?" he croaked, jabbing his chest for emphasis, forgetting he still had a greasy hunk of lamb in his hand. "I'm not the one letting enemy forces get away with valuable intelligence and friendly remains. That's Lokkemand, remember?"

"Take a drink already," Ambrose growled irritably as he bent and refilled Milo's glass, his brow knitted in thought. "You sound awful."

"Must be from all the time spent with you," Milo quipped as he raised his cup to comply. "All that smoking and carousing. You're a bad influence on the younger —*much* younger —generation."

Admittedly, it wasn't his sharpest bit of humor, but in the realm of friendship, the laughs and barbs flow easily, so it was unsettling to Milo when he realized that neither chuckling nor a stinging retort was quick in coming. Milo looked up from his drink to see Ambrose staring at him, brow bunched as it had been in Lokkemand's office earlier.

"I've been thinking about what you said on the balcony,"

Ambrose said, slowly at first but warming to his point quickly. "You said I had something to offer you still. I'm beginning to believe that you might be right, but it's nothing to do with fighting. Rather, I think it has more to do with imparting wisdom and insight that you as a young man don't have."

Milo stared at Ambrose, then carefully placed a hunk of meat back in the bowl and licked the grease from his fingers. He pushed the plate of cheese and bread away next and set his elbows on the table, fingers intertwined in front of him. Ambrose watched it all in silence, his expression unreadable.

"All right then," Milo said in a dangerously soft tone. "Tell me. I'm listening."

Ambrose looked unsure, but he shook off the anxiousness like a bear shaking water from its pelt as he set the jug down. His pawlike hands settled on the table as his head slung forward between his expansive shoulders so he and Milo were nearly eye to eye.

"You're scared," he rumbled. "Worse, you're too scared to admit you're scared."

Milo met his gaze, felt the pressure building between them, then slowly and deliberately picked up his cup without letting his eyes wander.

"Do tell," he replied frostily before taking a small sip of water. "What am I afraid of?"

He wanted to lash out, but he knew that would confirm to his bodyguard that he was unstable because of his supposed fear.

"You're afraid you aren't the only wizard," Ambrose said, refusing to look anywhere except directly into Milo's eyes. "You're scared there are others, and that means you might be the lesser wizard, the inferior one."

Milo felt the urge to look away and squirm just a little.

"Doesn't the idea of another wizard, one working for the enemy, concern you?" Milo asked smoothly to cover the internal shifting he felt. He told himself he had to keep being rational, and everyone would follow suit eventually.

"Concern, maybe," Ambrose admitted with a slow bob of his head. "But not so much that I'm going to deny what is right in front of my face."

Milo couldn't keep a short, sharp laugh from cutting between his teeth.

"Oh, really?" he said, chuckling without a hint of humor. "And what is right in front of me?"

"The threat isn't over," Ambrose said, each word coming slow and heavy from his lips. "The Americans weren't the ones Jorge was worried about, and we need to think about what that means for you, for the operation, and for Rihyani."

Milo felt something hot and angry building in his chest.

"What do you mean, for Rihyani?"

Ambrose wasn't quick to answer, the anxiousness creeping back into his eyes as he rose from where he perched on the table.

"I'm not saying it's easy," Ambrose began. "I'm just saying we can't have you going off the deep end trying to save her. We've got other problems, big ones, headed our way."

Milo felt a twist in his chest as the implication of what Ambrose was suggesting began to sink in.

"You want me to let her die," Milo muttered, disbelieving.

"Now that's not what I said," Ambrose began, but Milo shoved away from the table hard enough to make the bench bark across the stone floor.

"You'd rather me focus on preparing for some enemy that may or may not be coming," Milo growled as he rose slowly to his feet, "than spend my time trying to save the woman who is responsible for saving both of our lives and who came here to help us because we asked her to!"

Ambrose crossed his arms over his massive chest and scowled.

"First, I'm not saying you can't try or even that I could stop you from trying," the big man retorted, his voice sinking lower, softer, and yet somehow more powerful. "But you nearly killed yourself trying to figure out formulas for Jorge. We don't have time for you to be out for a week again, trying to save her."

Milo could see his concern, and part of him even acknowledged it was a fair point, but his temper was up and he was standing angrily across the table, so he wasn't about to back down just yet.

He sneered. "Anything else?"

"Second," Ambrose growled, his hands curling into mallet-sized fists. "These aren't weather predictions you can shrug off. The Americans weren't the real threat, and pretending that things are ready to wrap up is setting yourself and everyone else up for a hard fall. Like it or not, Lokkemand may be the commanding officer, but you're the one leading this operation. You need to think bigger, bigger than Rihyani. You bleed yourself dry and wreck yourself trying to save her, then this all falls apart."

Again, Milo could see Ambrose's point, but there was something his anger and will could find traction on, and he went after it with zeal.

"Why do you think I need to save her, huh?" Milo asked, pointing toward his study where the stricken fey now lay. "You think it's because she's beautiful and I have some childish feelings for her?"

Ambrose looked ready to fire back but caught himself with his mouth opening and shutting. He let out a spluttering sigh and ran a hand over his face.

"Are you telling me that isn't the case?" he asked with deliberate calm.

"I'm telling you it is more than that," Milo replied, leaning forward so Ambrose could look deep into his eyes. "I'm telling you I'm thinking bigger, much bigger, and yet smaller."

Ambrose narrowed his eyes and shook his head.

"Start making sense, or I am going to have Brodden check you over for a head injury."

Milo felt his anger cool at the bemused look on the big man's face, even as he warmed to his subject.

"The bigger picture here is not that a bunch of armed men is moving around Georgia," he explained. "It's the Great War, after all, and that's been normal for decades. No, the bigger issue is that we are dealing with intervention and manipulation by supernatural forces into this ugly, bloody mess."

"By which you mean, besides you, the Shepherds and the Guardians?" asked Ambrose, cocking his head to one side.

"Exactly," Milo agreed. "We are certain the Guardians mean all humans harm, while the Shepherds mean to help at least some of us, right? And we're fairly certain that unless something drastic happens in this war, it will keep dragging on as it has for the last twenty years. The drastic thing is either the Guardians or the Shepherds. The Guardians have already chosen to side with, or at least manipulate, bastards like Epp and others."

"Which is precisely why you need to be focusing on preparing for them. You know, arming up and resting up?"

"All the preparation in the world won't do me much good if I don't have a guide," Milo explained, forcing the words through gritted teeth. "There's still so much I don't know. You say I'm scared of being an inferior magus. Sure, I guess that is true, but I'm not nearly as scared of that as I am of not knowing what I can do to stop the Guardians. For that, I need the Shepherds, and last I checked, the contessa is the only Shepherd we know."

Ambrose began to nod.

"So, having her come here wasn't just a bribe from Jorge, and you saving her isn't just an act of desperate romance?"

Milo gaped at his bodyguard.

"Is that what you both thought this all was?" Milo asked, appalled. "Some sort of schoolboy crush?"

Ambrose shrugged, his cheeks coloring a little.

"You have to remember something, Magus," he said, scratching his whiskery cheek. "To us hoary old veterans, you look half a step past being a snot-nosed brat, yet we all know you've got the keys to the kingdom, as it were. I think sometimes we forget there's more meat than milk running through you."

Milo shook his head slowly, and then, looking at the reminder of his food, decided he'd calmed down enough he could do with a little more lamb.

"Given what you feed me," he said before stuffing the cooling chunk of flesh between his teeth, "you've got no one to blame but yourself."

"I suppose so," Ambrose said, his eyes twinkling as he watched Milo. "You never explained the smaller thing."

"Huh?" Milo asked as he filled his cup.

"You said you were thinking bigger and smaller," Ambrose said. "You explained the bigger, now what about the smaller?"

"Oh." Milo grunted as he gulped down a mouthful of water. "What I meant is that when it comes down to it, even though the *smaller* thing is to worry about the damsel in distress, that doesn't stop it from being the right thing. In fact, I'm beginning to wonder if it's the only thing any of us can do and still be something like decent humans."

"So, here you get to be a decent human and take care of the big picture?"

"I'm sure hoping." Milo took one last bite.

"I guess if you're wrong, it'll be too late," Ambrose mused. "And at least you'll have tried being decent."

Milo nodded somberly.

"That's the idea."

9

THE HEX

"Nothing," Milo snarled, throwing the codex on top of the others. *"Nothing!"*

He stalked away from his desk then walked back to snatch up the opened envelope they'd retrieved from Lokkemand. Milo's hand slid inside, and his fingers rested on the bone handle as Ambrose watched him from a chair he'd dragged over to the door. It was the third time Milo had magically "inspected" the knife, but each time made Milo's hands trembled as he opened his senses to what lay beyond the physical.

The knife was possessed of magic, Milo was certain, but it was unlike anything he'd ever encountered. Energies simmered within it, but they were not the raw essence Milo had learned to manipulate. It was too active for that, possessing a nature that he at first compared to shades, but it was both more and less than that. It seemed to have a will or life of its own, where shades only had impressions and echoes of original lives, but the life and will was unidirectional, a myopic focus, unlike anything Milo knew in life.

And that focus was ruin.

Milo could feel the corruptive, gnawing potency seething hot and tight within the crude material of the knife like an infection in a swollen wound. Having felt it, Milo grasped the corroded punctures in Beli's skin and the unhealing wounds on Rihyani's arm. When flowing freely, such magical energies would lodge themselves in wounded flesh and render it as impotent and lifeless as salted earth.

But it didn't flow freely, not now.

It was present but seemingly inactive, and even stranger, it didn't seem to respond to Milo's metaphysical probing. When he had first opened himself to inspect the blade and felt the potent conscious energies within, he'd withdrawn quickly, fearing it would try to infect him, maybe even form a bond like a shade. Yet, that hadn't happened. The magical presence in the knife stayed within the confines of the weapon, seemingly oblivious or uninterested in Milo's mind or his power observing it. Oddly, when he pressed as deep as he dared against the skein of the magic, he felt as though it was waiting like an expectant hound at the door.

When its master returned, it would spring to its unkind work, but until then, it waited, death roiling invisibly under the surface.

A fresh inspection revealed nothing new, and Milo let the envelope and its infuriating burden slide to the table.

"Is there some sort of experiment you could run on it?" Ambrose asked after giving Milo a heartbeat or two to stew in his deepening despair. "You know, exposing it to different ingredients or elixirs or whatever else, to show something."

Milo shook his head and then threw it back to rake his fingers through his hair.

"I could expose it to everything in my lab," he said, trying to keep his voice level and failing. "But there is no guarantee it will do anything I could understand, and there is a very real possibility it could touch off some sort of magical meltdown."

"What would happen if you set that off?" Ambrose asked, eyeing the knife suspiciously.

"Anything from destroying the knife to setting off some sort of magical backlash that could kill me and possibly others," Milo said, glaring down at his suddenly useless pile of codices.

When he'd first been given the texts, they had seemed like such a treasure trove of knowledge, but now it seemed like the treasure was in a currency that could not buy him the answers he needed. He needed a translator, someone who could show him where the connection was to his experience and this new magic. A guide or a teacher.

Milo's eyes wandered to the hidden resting place for Imrah's remains.

"Ambrose," Milo began, moving to the door to check that no one was passing through.

Ambrose had followed Milo's gaze before he'd gone to check the hall, and he stood up from his seat sharply.

"Are you certain that's a good idea?" he asked, his tone making it quite clear what he thought about the situation. "It's pretty taxing, and you still are going to need to get bled for the contessa soon. I'm not sure we have enough restorative."

"This isn't necromist work," Milo said, stepping back from the door, satisfied they had the necessary privacy. "I don't have the breadth of knowledge. I can't even guess what this is."

Ambrose shuffled to the concealing stone but stopped short of fetching the box.

"But if it isn't necro-whatsit, what use is she going to be?" the big man asked with a scowl. "Isn't that the only kind of magic her kind does?"

"True," Milo said, nodding as he dragged out the box where they kept most of the necessary materials for managing the shade. "But she has lived in the world of the supernatural longer, and she could probably recognize what is going on, maybe give us a direction to go for finding answers."

Ambrose's mustache bristled and gave a fretful waggle.

"All right," he surrendered, his face downcast. "But for the record, I think it is a dangerous waste of time."

REMEMBER

The word was intoned, the tortured transformation occurred, and Milo stood in front of Imrah's shade, now a patchwork of human and ghulish flesh held together by rippling strings of shadow.

"Oh, *Milo*," it cooed in a layered voice that was human and ghul tongues speaking together. "I *knew* you would return to me."

"Enough of that," Milo instructed, the words driven by simple confidence rather than magical will. "Speak plainly, or you are going back in the box."

He stared directly into the shade's eyes as if it were a cur that needed chastening. He needed to convince the shade in whatever capacity it could understand that he was in control. It couldn't know how desperately he needed its help, or else it would use its low cunning to extract something from him, and Milo was scared to admit to himself how much he would sacrifice.

"*Very well*," came the petulant groan, and the specter imploded with a hiss of tightening strings.

A second later, the collapsed fold burst open, and Imrah's human guise emerged from the waist up like a gory fresh blossom.

"Does this suit you better, *master?*' the shade asked as it trailed fingers through the crimson fluid that coated its hallucinatory flesh.

"I'm growing bored." Milo sighed and bent to pick up the lock in front of him. "Maybe we can talk when you are in a more serious mood."

"NO!"

The shade's cry had a desperate, piercing note that made

Ambrose wince and shuffle a bit, but Milo only paused, his fingers hovering over the lock.

"If you want to have your time out of the box," he began matter-of-factly as though speaking to a rather slow child, "you need to behave correctly while you are out."

The shade's gleaming eyes tried to burrow into Milo's gaze but found no purchase in the glassy surface of his pale blue eyes. It may as well have tried gouging an iceberg with a teaspoon.

"I'm sorry," the shade muttered softly. "It was worth a shot."

Milo gave the wraith a long, sardonic stare until it flinched.

"No more warnings," Milo told it, praying he wasn't painting himself into a corner with all this tough talk. "Behave yourself, or I'll have your remains sent to the bazaar in Ifreedahm to be ground up for essence. I imagine you would fetch a pretty penny."

The shade drooped slightly, looking up with teary eyes, but upon seeing Milo's face, the tears dried with incredible speed.

"As you wish."

Milo sensed an undercurrent of sinister will behind the obedience, but for now, he was glad she wasn't testing the limits he knew he wouldn't keep to.

"Good," Milo said and held out his hand behind him.

Stepping reluctantly forward, Ambrose opened the envelope and placed the knife in Milo's hand before backing away once more.

"Have you brought me a gift?" the shade asked, leaning forward so her blood-soaked hair dripped phantasmal blood on the dungeon floor. "Or is this something even more precious than a gift for your old teacher?"

Milo remained unmoving, glaring until the specter of Imrah leaned back, after which he held the knife out for a visual inspection.

"This knife was used in the murder of two fey, and it clearly has magical properties," Milo explained. "But it is not necromistry. I need to know as much as Imrah knew about what it might be."

The shade's gaze had remained fixed on Milo's face, a wide smile spreading from human teeth to the overlapping fangs of the ghul.

"I see, I see," it purred, still refusing to even look at the blade. "Dead fey? Not easy to do. Is that smoke-sucking strumpet one of the two? Is this a quest for vengeance? Are you on a quest to avenge your slain lover?"

The words rolled out of the shade's throat with an unctuous timbre that roused Milo's anger, and when his command came, it seared the wraith-like flame.

LOOK

REMEMBER

There was an instant of resistance, but the shade's pseudo-will snapped beneath the driving piston of Milo's command. Its head twisted around, and its eyes wrenched wide open to look at the knife. Milo could feel something shifting within the slippery phantom as deeper recesses of echoes and their fractured memories bubbled up to the surface like the last gasps of a drowning man. Milo held the shade through will alone until he felt its essence heavy with congealing memories.

"Enough!" it cried. "I remember! I remember! Please! Enough!"

Milo released his command and watched as the shade clutched its skull, swelling like a balloon until the locks of bloody hair were stretched over a grotesque bulb.

"What did she know?" Milo asked, channeling Lokkemand's utter and certain command.

The shade's neck bowed under its immense, wobbling head, struggling to raise a hateful glare to meet Milo's gaze. Its fingers trembled over bulging veins on its distended skull as though trying to come to grips with what had happened to, its bitter stare never leaving Milo's unflinching gaze.

"The blade is curzed," the specter hissed through a scraping thicket of fangs. "It'z been touched by a dark hex."

Milo didn't allow his determined expression to so much as flinch as he slid a glance to the blade and back to the shade.

"Curse? Hex?" Milo mused. "I haven't read about anything like that in the texts."

"Becauze it is not ghul magic," Imrah's echo snarled, the very effort of speaking the memories seeming to be accomplished only with significant discomfort.

Milo couldn't keep the eagerness from his voice as he leaned forward.

"What sort of magic is it?"

"Err! Wretch…agh! Wretched fey witchery! Ahhh! It hurtz!" the shade gasped, squeezing its skull until the flesh was dimpled and he could see tiny rivulets of glittering ectoplasm leaking between its fingers.

Milo frowned at the shade's behavior, sensing an undercurrent of movement, like a loose thread being jerked fiercely. Could some of the memories be potent enough, dangerous enough, that clear remembrance put the shade in danger of losing cohesion?

Milo wasn't sure, but that uncertainty made him wary of pushing much further.

He knew it was fey magic, a hex, or a curse, and that would mean he would need someone to tell him about their magics. It seemed a cruel irony that the very one he was saving was the very one he could trust to give him advice on how to handle this curse, but then again, Milo remembered he was Russian, and expatriate or not, cruel irony was par for the course.

"How do we undo the knife's curse?" he pressed, his words coming out fast as he watched the shade digging fingers deeper into the pulsing skull, gouging past the first knuckle.

"Kn-knife izn't, ugh, c-curzed," it moaned. "The hex is the owner'z. Knife iz hiz, zo-erkh! Zo knife touched by curze —AHHH!"

The last utterance became a shrill scream, and a silvery seam began to form along the crown of its skull. Ectoplasm leaked freely, and Milo felt flashes of essence dissipating into the aether. The shade was coming apart from the weight of the memories; there could be no doubt now.

"I think it's time to wrap this up," Ambrose suggested at Milo's shoulder, his voice brittle with horror and disgust.

"If Ezekiel is dead, why is his knife still carrying his curse?" Milo asked, partly of Imrah's shade and partly of Ambrose. "If he's the one who's cursed, and the knife is cursed because of him, it follows that if he is dead, this hex should be lifted."

The shade didn't answer except to gasp and give a series of mewling screams, as hideous as they were pitiful.

"Either way, I don't think we are getting anything more from her." Ambrose pointed at the widening gap in the shade's head. Inside the wound, past the ragged ectoplasm-leaking edge, Milo saw the trembling darkness of the shade's essence made manifest. Staring at it, he felt the fragile energies beginning to shake apart in psychic tremors of growing intensity.

Milo bit back the furious questions demanding to pour forth and snatched up the lock.

REST

A few moments later, the shade was bound and recovering in its box, and Milo stood with both palms against the growing ache in his skull. He told himself they weren't sympathy pains, but the voice in his head was not entirely convincing. He wondered, not for the first or last time, why he couldn't be as good at lying to himself as he was at lying to other people.

"Well," Ambrose said, gingerly scooping up the supplies, "we've got part of the puzzle."

"Yes, we do." Milo heaved a sigh and gave up his feeble attempts at forcing the tension back. "And I'm pretty sure I know where we are going to get the next piece."

"Really? Where?"

Milo fought back the sick feeling in his stomach at what lay ahead.

"Doing something I'm going to hate even more than this," he groaned. "Let's hope I get better results from the next person I have to ask."

Ambrose paused as he bent to pick up the box with Imrah's remains.

"You're not saying what I think you are." Incredulity sharpened his words. "You can't be."

Milo shook his head and headed out of the dungeon. He suddenly felt more tired than he had that morning when the nightwatch was wearing off, except this was fatigue of the soul rather than the body.

"I didn't say it was a good idea," he muttered as he slowly began to mount the steps that would take him out of the darkness. "Just the only one I've got."

The elixir was in his hand as he stood over her, but his whole body seemed locked in place by some paralytic. His heart hammered in his ears, and between the throbbing beats, he could hear his breath rasping horridly loud.

"We don't have to do this," Ambrose said at his shoulder, his deep voice seeming sudden and alien against the clamor of Milo's body.

"What are our other options?" the magus asked, certain he knew the unsatisfactory answer.

"We could wait and see if Jorge has any more fey contacts," Ambrose said, sounding less than convinced. "Maybe one of them can get here before she's too far gone."

Milo looked at the contessa, noting her silvery glow and the dull sheen that could be explained as a trick of the light. Her skin was gray and loose around her long form as though she was withering from within, which given that she was constantly losing blood wasn't far from the truth.

"Does she look like she can wait?" Milo asked, the question broken but without malice or anger. "You heard Brodden say it was a miracle she was holding on, and even if we can keep up the transfusions, the efforts to keep the bleeding under control are going to start having lasting effects if they haven't already."

Ambrose wanted to argue, but his eyes were downcast as he looked at the fallen fey with welling sadness.

"I assume she's too weak for an amputation?" the big man asked, eyeing the pink-stained bandages across her shoulder.

Milo nodded.

"She'd be dead before they could even start to close things up."

Ambrose swore softly in French and sucked his teeth as he scratched his chin.

"And none of your magic can fix her up?" Ambrose's expression said he knew the answer before Milo gave it.

"Besides changing my blood, everything else has magic interacting with the wound," Milo explained. "That triggers the curse that pulls it apart, and pulling it apart like that means it could do more damage. Even if it doesn't do more damage, it will use more of my energy and ingredients, and thus I will be less able to do anything useful if and when we do have something we can do."

"So, this is it, then." Ambrose's massive shoulders drooped in a way that might have been comical had it not been for the circumstances.

"Like I said," Milo murmured, raising one hand to the stopper on the vial, "not a good idea, but the only one I've got."

Ambrose nodded. "Should I wake Brodden up?"

In true veteran fashion, the medic had collapsed into sleep the second the two of them arrived. The steady sawing of his gentle snores was the only thing that confirmed the lump on the cot opposite Rihyani's wasn't a bundle of old laundry.

"No," Milo said softly. "Let him sleep. If things go wrong, he'll know soon enough."

Milo remembered the man's bloodshot eyes and harrowed face and made a mental note to do something for him, however this turned out. Ambrose would probably know what to do and could see it done.

"Dear God," Milo whispered, the word sounding like an entreaty instead of a curse, "let this work."

He removed the stopper, gently opened Rihyani's mouth, and slowly poured the nightwatch down her throat as he impelled the ingredients with essence from a razored thumb.

As predicted, the elixir took some time to work. Rihyani's eyes fluttered teasingly as her limbs trembled and her fingers twitched. Milo could feel Ambrose's gaze shifting from the fey to himself and back, checking to see if anything the contessa had done was a good or bad sign. He could have told him that he had no idea if any of it was a good or bad sign, that he was flying blind, but he had a feeling Ambrose already knew that.

Milo watched silently, half-remembered prayers overheard in his youth going up with every twitch. He'd seen demons and he walked with a half-angel, so it wasn't beyond hope that someone was listening, though in Milo's experience, fathers and mothers, divine or otherwise, were never around when they were needed.

That thought, one thorny musing amongst a field of bitter brambles, dug deep into the prayers. The entreaties became pleadings, became demands, became accusations. Gradually, as his eyes bored into Rihyani's supine form, he saw through her to the flow of essence he'd issued into her, which sparked and tickled along chords of magical power suffusing her frame. His will and fury stoked by his prayers-turned-condemnations lashed at the essence, driving it onward.

God was not here, but Milo the Magus was, and he would be damned if he let this fail.

"Milo!" Rihyani cried, and Milo's eyes focused on crude matter once more.

The fey's body was sinking down from a cruel imitation of ecstasy's arch, her limbs still trembling.

"Milo," she murmured softly, one hand reaching out to him feebly. "You hurt me."

Milo, blinking and wondering at the wetness upon his cheek, met her searching wine-dark eyes and nearly gasped at the sadness rippling behind those golden pupils. Pain he had expected, anger he had accepted, but sadness struck him where he was unhardened and unguarded.

"I'm sorry," he said, deflating as his guilt sucked the bile from him and left him aching. "I needed you to wake up."

"All for the best, *chéri*," Ambrose said in a steady, soothing voice.

The sadness still swimming in Rihyani's eyes told him that neither of them was afforded the ignorant innocence of the bodyguard. Milo inwardly cursed himself for letting his emotions, and such powerful and bitter emotions at that, interfere with his magic.

As she stared up at him, Milo felt the urge to run and hide like a child, such was his shame, but then a shudder wracked her body, and he realized what was happening. He was making it about him again, and it was costing them time they didn't have.

"The cowboy, Ezekiel, was hexed," Milo began, his words coming clean and fast. "The knife was cursed too, so your wounds are cursed. That's why my magic can't heal them and they won't mend on their own."

Rihyani seemed to be struggling to maintain focus, her gaze drifting, but as he finished speaking, she began to nod.

"A Death Hex," she whispered, and her eyes slid to half-mast. "We should have known. Should have und...understood..."

The words slid out, then the contessa lost the understanding of where she was, her head lolling one way and then the other.

Milo hadn't expected her to burn through this much of the elixir this fast.

He dropped down and took the hand he'd been too ashamed to hold before. Her skin was cold to the touch and rolled freely over the delicate bones of her hands.

"Rihyani," he called, hating how weak he sounded. "Please, can you break the hex?"

Her head stopped rolling and she looked at him, her lips spreading into a glorious sleepy smile.

"No." She sighed, her eyes drooping a little lower. "But you can."

Milo's fingers tightened around hers as though by his grip, he could keep her from succumbing to the trauma-induced slumber.

"How, Rihyani?" he pleaded. "Tell me how."

With what must have been the last of her strength, she drew Milo closer to her.

"*Tsminda Sameba*," she whispered. "Go there."

Milo's heart sank. He didn't know where Tsminda Sameba was, but he knew every town and landmark within a day's travel. If it were farther than that, what hope could there be that she would last that long?

"Rihyani, we don't have time for that," he implored, his heart sinking. "You are dying."

Rihyani shook her head.

"I've strength enough to wait for you," she muttered softly. "Climb to Tsminda Sameba and ask to meet the marquis."

Milo pulled back so he could look at her face, his heart beginning to beat in his ears as he felt the magic weakening in her and her grip on his hand loosening.

"The marquis?" Milo asked, the questions springing from his tongue before he had time to even consider them. "Who is that? A fey? Will he help me, teach me how to break the curse?"

Rihyani's eyes were closed now, but her smile was even more

brilliant, as though transported by whatever she saw behind her eyelids.

"He won't want to," she said, a laugh she didn't have the strength for dancing behind her words. "You'll have to make him see."

"See what?" Milo demanded even as he felt her slipping away. Ambrose's big hand descended on his shoulder.

"Easy, Magus," the big man muttered thickly. "Easy."

"See what?" Milo repeated miserably.

But Rihyani was unconscious once more, fresh blood seeping from her bandages.

THE TRUTH

"Not that I mind you taking a concern outside your study," Lokkemand called sharply as he strode into his office, heels snapping on the stone floor. "But I do prefer it when subordinates ask to enter my office rather than assume the privilege."

Milo straightened from gazing over Ambrose's shoulder as he sketched out a rough imitation of the map before him. Goat-toothed Dieter watched, helpless and befuddled, from the door until Lokkemand firmly shut it. It wasn't a slam, but it was hard enough to punctuate his entrance.

"Do you care to explain to me exactly what it is you are doing?" he asked in a tone that made it very clear it was a courtesy. "Or do you want me to start filling in the blanks?"

"We needed a map," Milo replied simply, eliciting a distracted snort of amusement from Ambrose. Milo's gaze slid back down to the maps once again.

"Obviously," Lokkemand replied in flat disgust. "Perhaps I should have been more specific. Where do you plan to go that would require you to acquire a map?"

"Just about done," Ambrose muttered, his gaze sliding between his map and the one on the table. "

"Volkohne?" Lokkemand demanded, his voice dropping to a low growl.

"Tsminda Sameba, sir," Milo said as he met Lokkemand's glare. "Took us a bit, but we found it. Seems it's an old church on the slopes of Mount Kazbek."

"Kazbek," Lokkemand repeated, and Milo could practically hear the files being shuffled behind Lokkemand's gray eyes. "That's in the Khevi province, nearly two days travel from here."

"I think I've got it down to a day and a half if we use the Rollsy and these routes are cleared out," Ambrose said as he straightened, his map held out at arm's length for a final inspection.

"Is this where the guerrilla force is going to be?" Lokkemand asked, his tone hopeful despite the incredulous scowl on his face. "I heard from some mutterings that you've been engaging in your own methods of reconnaissance."

Milo and Ambrose shared an uneasy look. They'd always assumed their efforts were wilfully ignored by the soldiers in Shatili, and even more so when they attempted secrecy. The fact that their investigations, however vaguely observed, were known to the men was a shock.

Both men lapsed into silence, alternating between looking at each other and the captain.

"You didn't seriously think I wouldn't keep tabs on you?" Lokkemand barked with a sharp, mocking laugh.

The magus' and the bodyguard's silence offered a clear answer, but it was not appreciated by the captain. His eyes blazed with outrage as both hands tightened into fists.

Milo struggled to meet the man's gaze as he loomed huge, trembling with righteous indignation.

"I know both of you don't think highly of me, but I am an intelligence officer, for God's sake! Give me a little credit!"

Again, neither spoke. Milo stole a glance at Ambrose, who, as usual when dealing with Lokkemand, wore an expression of boredom. Milo was certain this did nothing to improve the captain's mood.

"So, this has nothing to do with your actual mission?" Lokkemand spat the question out like it offended his tongue. "Even with food in your belly and time to get your head on straight, you are still chasing miracle cures. Now I find out that you are going to run across the country because you broke into my office."

"Dieter let us in," Milo began, and Lokkemand's fist came down on the table like a mallet.

"Dieter be damned!" the captain bellowed, taking one long step to loom over Milo. "You think you can do whatever you want, do you? This is the Army, Volkohne, not some back-alley gang, and discipline will be observed! I have orders, you have orders, and by the Kaiser and Almighty God, you are going to start acting like it!"

Milo met the captain's glower, his unease giving way to growing defiance, warmed by an indignant fire in his belly

"If the fey dies, you are going to be a soldier and take it in stride. Do you understand?" Lokkemand hissed as he bent so he and Milo were nose to nose. "I'm through indulging in your petulant romanticism. If you hadn't noticed, there is a war going on, and it's a lot bigger than whatever you're hoping to get out of that faerie tart."

The corner of Milo's mouth curled up to form a disdainful snarl. So far, he had not wanted to engage out of some unfamiliar sense of guilt, but at the callous mention of Rihyani's death, that guilt evaporated.

"You idiot," Milo snarled. "You petty, jealous moron!"

Lokkemand reared back at the venom of the words. Even Ambrose's eyes widened in surprise at the sudden vitriolic retort.

"What did you j—" Lokkemand shouted, but Milo thrust his face upward as he set in like a dog with a bone.

"You don't even see it, do you? Bitter and blind, you don't see that it isn't just about Rihyani, though God knows that should be enough. You claim to be an intelligence officer, but you need me to put the pieces together for you."

"You arrogant little—"

"I'm not finished!" Milo roared. a bass note of magical potency underpinning the declaration. "I need information, expertise, and knowledge to fight the kind of fight we are going to face. Rihyani represents that, but it isn't just her or even other fey, but the Shepherds who are going to be our best bet for taking on the Guardians and the Reich. That being the case, it seems a piss-poor decision to let their friendliest agent die when we could save her, doesn't it?"

Lokkemand's jaw worked as he ground angry retorts into furious silence.

"I'm going to that mountain, and I'm not coming back until I've got something to save her," Milo pronounced before turning to Ambrose and jerking a thumb toward the exit. "Come on. I've got to bleed one more time, and you've got to prepare for a trip."

Ambrose, his face flushing under the burden of bewildered respect, nodded and tucked the map under his arm as they moved toward the door.

Milo felt Lokkemand tense at his back, his body coiling to spring. The magus was more relieved than he cared to admit that in the end, Lokkemand decided against it. That was a fight no one would have won.

"The enemy is expected in three days' time," Lokkemand said, his voice as hard and sharp as a chisel's edge. "You are putting everything at risk. Everything."

"I can live with that," Milo spat as he yanked the door open, sending Dieter scrambling to get out of the way. "I guess you'll have to also."

"I'm within my rights to stop you," Lokkemand warned, his voice sullen and dangerous. "I could have both of you shot right here right now and that fey dumped into the river to become someone else's problem. It would take one word, Volkohne. One word."

Milo paused in the doorway, the cane in his hands giving the briefest flicker of witchfire.

"Then say the word," Milo challenged, his eyes fixed on the room beyond. "*Captain.*"

His words hung upon the trembling air.

A few fragile seconds more and Milo nodded and walked out of the office, Ambrose right behind him, one hand still resting on the knife at his belt.

"You think she'll be okay here?" Ambrose asked, casting a concerned glance at Rihyani's recumbent form. "I mean, after everything Lokkemand said?"

"What did Lokkemand say?" Brodden asked as he finished bandaging Milo's arm.

Two and a half more pints of blood.

"Don't worry about it," Milo grumbled as he rose from his seat next to her cot. "And yes, Ambrose, I think she'll be fine."

Milo wobbled for an instant, and both bodyguard and medic shot out a hand to steady him. The magus waved them off as he righted himself, surreptitiously leaning on his cane and taking the smallest sip of supernatural strength from it.

"You need to rest and refuel," Brodden said, looking Milo over and shaking his head. "I know you've got that magic business to help, but in less than forty-eight hours, you've given the equivalent of a human body's entire blood supply. It can't be good for you."

Milo patted the man on the shoulder and gave what he hoped was a reassuring smile.

"Don't worry. I'll have nearly two days to do nothing but sleep, eat, and whine at my nurse."

"A day and a half," Ambrose corrected. "And the second you complain about my bedside manner, I'm throwing you in the trunk."

Brodden snapped a look at the two, dragging a hand over his haggard face.

"When they told me I had signed on for Nicht-KAT duty, I expected things to be different," the medic muttered as he started cleaning the transfusion kit. "The truth is that in some ways, it's been both better and worse than I ever thought it would be."

"Didn't exactly think serving the Fatherland would involve swapping blood with faeries, eh?" Ambrose asked with a chuckle.

"A patient's a patient," Brodden stated. "Sure, pink blood and all is a little off-putting, but the rest of it is pretty familiar."

"Then what part is throwing you off?" Milo asked with a yawn. He was suddenly looking forward to taking the restorative and hunkering down in the cab of the Rollsy.

"Honestly?" Brodden asked, his gaze sliding between the men, seeming to size each of them up.

"Of course, honestly." Milo laughed, but the sound died on his lips as understanding dawned on him. "O-oh, you mean us?"

Brodden nodded slowly, weight shifting cautiously to his back foot.

"Yeah," he said softly, his eyes narrowing even as his tone edged toward an apology. "Fact is, we, meaning the other grunts like me on this detail, we're used to some friction between NCOs and COs, and even rivalries between officers, sure, but this is something different."

The magus nodded before he realized what he was doing, the medic professing something Milo had felt since donning the black greatcoat. A dissonance, an uncertainty, and not only in himself.

Brodden took a deep breath,

"We came expecting to face strange things, but I expect most of us thought the backbone of our time in the army, duty, chain of command, order, wouldn't be the thing to change. You two are walking, talking deviations from that."

Ambrose shot Milo a look, mustache bristling as he formed a retort, but Milo gave a slight shake of his head. Brodden carried on, either not noticing or not caring what had passed between the two men.

"Neither of you has a real rank, but you're not civilians," Brodden said with a shake of his head. "You defy orders and aren't punished for it, and when a high-ranking officer shows up, he barely has time to notice your superior officer before having a chat with a former conscript wearing the black."

Milo felt the urge to bristle rising, but a combination of curiosity and fatigue shut down the impulse.

"We all have to wonder if you're the one running the show, but we don't even know what the show is." Brodden shrugged. "You whisper together and steal supplies, then disappear, only to come back and fill the nights with screams and the smell of sulfur and smoke."

Milo took a deep breath, his mind filling with the realization of how the horrors and marvels of his new reality might look to common men, many not so different from him. He had to admit that he'd not given them much thought, and he'd never seriously considered what they thought of him.

"We've all been doing this long enough that we're used to not knowing the reasons we've got to fight and die," the medic said with a grim smile. "But with everything else we count on going out the window, maybe we just need to know what it is we're trying to do."

Milo knew the answer, but for a second it hung on his tongue, seeming like something more fantastical, more impossible than even talk of faeries and curses. Ambrose, seeing the conflict in Milo's eyes, made to answer, to guard, but again Milo warded him off with a look.

Brodden, faithful to his patient despite everything, at least deserved the truth.

"I'm trying to end the War," Milo said.

To his relief, Brodden didn't laugh or sneer. He stared, eyes narrowed, waiting.

"I found out I can do magic, and now I'm trying to use that magic to end the War," Milo explained.

"You mean to win it?" Brodden asked, eyes still narrowed.

"If that's what it takes," the magus said, his gaze unwavering. "No matter what, it's got to end, but to have hope for any of this, I need help, and for that, I need her. She's fighting to help stop the War too."

Brodden looked down at the fey, his face flat and unresponsive even as his eyes revealed a riot of feelings.

"So right now, all of this," Brodden continued, not looking up. "It's to help a fellow soldier, then."

Milo felt a smile creeping across his face.

"I suppose that's the truth."

11

THE SCARS

The wind was on fire.

He could smell it, could hear it, and when he finally had the courage to open his eyes, he could see it.

Cinders trailing tails of stinging flame moved like a swarm of locusts, flying up and out over the street to slither across the rooftops. Some of the hellish sprites caught amidst the snowy crevices, winking out, but others found drier homes where they could nest and start colonies of flame. These colonies soon gnawed deep enough that they were sending up their own infernal offspring to reinforce the burning pestilence roiling through the air.

The wind continued to burn, and he watched it ravish the City.

But where is this?

The question struck his mind like a hammer, and the whole world rippled, even his body. He wondered if the firestorm had asked the question, and a sudden fear gripped him. If he did not answer, would the storm take him away?

"The City!" he cried out in his small voice.

His fingers tightened around the blanket in his hand, but he didn't put it in his mouth like he wanted to. Momma had said he was too old for that sort of thing, so as bravely as he could, he stood and watched the storm, waiting for another question.

Where is Momma?

The last word came out strangely, as though the storm was unfamiliar with the word. He supposed that storms did not have mommas, so it made a sort of sense.

"I don't know," he said, and the utterance of the words made his throat tight and his chest flutter. He felt his eyes doing another thing Momma told him he was too old for.

"Sorry." He sniffed as he ground his blanket against his treacherous eyes. "I don't know."

The storm did not speak again, but he felt heat against his back. Looking back and up, he saw that the building he sheltered beneath was now burning. One of the windows on the second floor burst into a cloud of brilliant razors that fell twinkling on the street just a few steps from him. His bare feet itched and ached at the thought of walking that way.

Black smoke belched from the shattered window, and he knew it was time to go.

Stepping down from the house, he heard two more windows break, and the roar of the flames within almost drowned out the chiming tune of glass shattering behind him.

He made it several steps before realizing he didn't know where he was going. He looked back down the street and saw that the house he'd been in front of had spread its fiery infection to its neighbors. Snow-covered roofs sent up clouds of steam that were blotted out by black smoke. Windows shattered and doors cracked as the infection consumed more of its victim.

He looked back up to the storm again, red and vast above him.

"Where do I go?" he pleaded. "I'm lost."

Again, saying the words prompted his eyes to betray him, and he was obliged to mop his face.

The storm did not answer in a voice he understood, continuing its crackling howl, but he heard something that made him turn back to where he'd come.

There were screams and snorts and shouts, and for a moment, his eyes could make no sense of what he saw. Shapes emerged from the corridor of flame that had become the street behind him, their gait wrong and ungainly as they moved with incredible speed. They seemed to be made from smoke, they were so dark and swift, but at the ends of their outstretched limbs were angry flickering stars. The closer they drew, the more he could hear of their hooves striking the cobbles and the more he understood their harsh, baying voices, but the less he could see of them, their forms wavering and running together. He realized that his eyes had played Judas once more, and by the time he'd swept the obscuring tears away, it was too late.

They were bearing down on him, and from where he stood on the street, he couldn't avoid them.

"Bolshevik whelp!" "Red brat!" "Traitor-spawn!"

Stamping hooves and stars at the end of hard sticks swept around and over him, a new storm to bear. He scrambled and shrieked in fear, but there was nowhere to go. He glimpsed their faces over him, stark white faces streaked with soot, with eyes burning like the storm.

A hot, hairy flank bludgeoned him to the ground, and one of the stars was thrust toward him.

He felt the heat, but at the same time, he felt hands, small but strong, drag him up and away. He was on his feet as an equine scream, chillingly familiar, rent the air. The hands were pushing him now, moving him forward. The next scream was distinctly mannish, and there were loud impacts that made his body shake hearing them. He tried to look around to see what was happening, but the hands kept him moving, off the street and between two houses that had not yet succumbed to the storm's infectious presence.

He'd lost his blanket somewhere along the way, and without

thinking, made to go back and look for it, but the hands slammed him against the alley wall.

"What are you doing?" hissed a voice that wasn't a man's but wasn't a boy's either. "Do you want to die?"

He blinked and saw the face of a boy, a much older boy, glaring down at him with dark, angry eyes. Even with the eyes blazing, he recognized the boy's face as very handsome, even beautiful. It took him a moment of staring to realize that the hands that held him and the beautiful, angry face that watched him belonged to the same person. He felt silly and scared all at once, and that made it even harder to respond.

"Are you just stupid?" the boy demanded, and somehow the words made it clear he wasn't so much older. Maybe not the words, the way the beautiful boy said them.

"What's your name?" he managed to squeak out as the older boy let him go.

"Roland," the boy said, his face losing some of the anger. "What's *your* name?"

"Milo," he replied, then he felt something hard and unforgiving in his throat. "And I'm lost, and I don't know where Momma is."

He hated himself for the tears that were running down his face, hated how disappointed Momma would be, even hated how the older boy didn't get mad at him for being a baby, only looked sadder and more scared.

"Hey." The older boy sniffed, looking away as a palm drug across those burning eyes. "We need to move. They might look for us."

He peered at the beautiful boy who was trying to pretend he wasn't crying too and decided that the boy wasn't that much older after all. Bigger, yes, braver, certainly, but not that much older. Somehow that made him feel closer to the boy, warmer. He decided then and there to trust him.

He took one of the strong hands that had saved him in the

hand that had held his blanket, and there was no effort to shake him off. They were friends now.

"Where are we going?" he asked.

"I don't know," Roland answered. "But we stick together, okay?"

"Okay."

So, this was how it started?

Within the alley, the presence of the storm seemed diminished, and he realized the voice couldn't be the storm. It was too cold, too small, and too close, seeming to come from just over his shoulder.

The storm was an angry god. This voice belonged to the things creeping under beds or inside closets.

Still holding Roland's hand, he turned and looked at where the voice had to be.

He saw nothing but a brick wall, but as he stared, the hairs on the back of his neck prickled, and his eyes opened to the space between spaces, past the remembered bricks.

Gleaming eyes winked over a mouth full of fangs.

Milo woke with a start and promptly struck his head on something hard, knocking the recollection of the dream from his mind.

Emitting the most incendiary profanity in his repertoire, he slumped back to the bed of the Rollsy. He glared up at the underside of the metal lip framing the armored bed while rubbing the knot forming on the top of his head gently. He'd attempted to bed down in the cab, but the armor-encased cockpit had proven singularly uncomfortable. In the end, he'd clambered back into the bed and fallen fast asleep. As he slept away the miles and the restorative regenerated his depleted blood, somehow during his slumber, he'd managed to slide up against the front.

For some time, he stared up at the offending lip until he realized there was a distinct lack in the ambiance. The chugging rumble of the Rollsy's engine was gone, as was the slight but distinct vibration that coursed through the frame of the vehicle. They hadn't just stopped; the engine was off.

Still muttering curses, he pressed against the truck and slid back to blink up at the brilliant blue sky of a clear spring morning. Propping himself up on his elbows, he saw the rising peaks of the mountains, white-frosted crests emerging from the rippling waves of green that swept across the horizon.

Again, Milo felt something stir in his chest, something which cried out, "Yes!" He wished for nothing more than to climb a peak and never come back down.

Then his head throbbed, and he coughed as his painfully dry throat reminded him of the restorative's desiccating effect. The dull, painful grip of reality returned him to the immediate situation. With a snarl and an arm thrown over the side of the truck bed, he clambered onto his feet and looked around.

For an instant, his heart seized at the sight of the empty cab, but a frantic sweep revealed Ambrose's location and reason for stopping. The instant he spotted him, Milo was torn between crying out in shocked disgust or deprecating laughter, but since his throat was dry, only a soft croaking cough came out.

The bodyguard stood a dozen strides or so from the Rollsy on the other side of a small mountain stream which burbled so softly Milo only heard it once he knew what to listen for. The big man's clothes were stretched out next to the stream on some large stones, while their owner stood a stride away, relieving himself against a mossy boulder. Ambrose was nude and had clearly just finished washing in the stream, his great lumpy body glistening as he dried in the cool air. Auburn hair plastered to his head, he leaned back, savoring the fluid expulsion, one hand aiming while the other raked and scratched his markedly paler backside.

In the stillness of the scene, Milo could hear Ambrose talking softly in French. Milo realized he didn't understand because it had been too long since he took the elixir allowing him to understand all languages.

All the same, Milo held very still for a moment in a desperate attempt not to be noticed.

It wasn't his nakedness or that Ambrose was talking to himself that sparked Milo's desire to remain unnoticed, but that watching Ambrose like this was perhaps the only time Milo could see Ambrose with his guard down, or at least as close as the old soldier got. Even without a stitch of clothing on, the Gewehr and belted sword hung from one rocklike shoulder.

Quietly as he could, Milo fetched the elixir of tongues from his coat and administered the necessary salve to his ears. Ambrose's words attached to their relevant meanings as he began to slide the small tin disk back into his coat.

"Not sure, either way," the big man muttered as he rolled his shoulders in a vigorous stretch before shaking out the last of his effluent. "But I do know the boy's only going to get more dangerous as things go on. I'm going to need your help knowing what's what—"

Klink!

His attention divided between Ambrose and being stealthy, Milo hadn't noticed he was putting the salve tin in the wrong pocket, and it struck the glass vials kept there. Before Milo had time to register all of this properly, Ambrose spun, the Gewehr appearing in his hands.

Reflexively, Milo threw up both hands, dropping the tin in the process, raising further clamor as it clattered on the bed.

There was a single second where Milo felt what hundreds of men must have felt throughout the last century before the Nephilim ended them with a shot, but the moment passed in a single heavy heartbeat. Then Ambrose thumped the rifle butt on the ground.

"You need to be careful about sneaking up on folk, Magus," Ambrose muttered, resting a shoulder against the barrel of the rifle. "Could lead to messy consequences."

"Not sure which I'm more afraid of," Milo confessed, hand still raised. "The weapon in your hand now, or the one you were holding a second ago."

Ambrose threw back his head and trumpeted a bawling laugh that echoed up the slopes and back. He rocked back, leveraging the rifle in one hand while slapping his bulging, thickly thewed stomach with the other.

"Best hope it never comes to that." He snorted before hoisting the rifle over his shoulder. "Wouldn't want to be on the receiving end of either."

"Don't suppose I would," Milo said as he slowly lowered his hands. "Now, do you plan to arrive at the church like that, or can we get on our way?"

Ambrose chuckled as he looked himself over, then strode toward his clothes.

"Suppose no one's virtue is at risk." The big man chuckled. "But I'd hate to be the cause of some nun's broken vows all the same."

Ambrose scooped up his clothes and trundled across the stream to the Rollsy. He tossed the garments halfway over the cab door for a quick inspection. This close, Milo saw the vast network of scars covering the big man's flesh. Self-conscious in his staring but unable to look away, Milo assessed that there didn't seem to be a place on the man that was not a finger length away from three or four other scars. They were varied as well, from the dark, cloven lines of slashes to the raised keloidal scars of burns. Some rolled and shifted with his muscular bulk, while others seemed fixed deep in his flesh, so they barely moved.

"You live long enough like I have, you collect some souvenirs," Ambrose said without looking up from inspecting a hole in the leg of his trousers. "A few fun stories among them, but most are stories of being a fool or unlucky."

Milo looked away, embarrassed to have been caught scrutinizing the man so blatantly. Then a thought occurred to him, and curiosity overcame his shame.

"But when you came back from Kimaris killing you, you healed everything," Milo said, pointing at Ambrose's face. "You didn't just grow back the essential parts. You don't even have scars from it."

"What's with all the other decorations?" Ambrose offered.

Milo nodded as his eyes charted a path between a puckered scar on the big man's belly through to a matching scar in the back.

"As far as I can tell, which isn't much, mind you," Ambrose began as he pulled his undershirt on. "When I do the whole die-and-come-back bit, I get put back together just as I was before the thing that killed me happened. Everything that came before and everything that comes after, so long as it doesn't drop me, stays."

Milo nodded and took one last look at the ragged seam of scar tissue above the clavicle and a circular scar that must have been a gunshot wound under the arm. Those and over a hundred others were wounds that Ambrose had survived.

"Any of them still bother you," Milo asked.

Ambrose nodded as he carried on the business of getting dressed.

"A few," he muttered as he tugged on his trousers. "I've learned to live with the aches and pains. Some of them even help me know when I'm hurt because if I can't feel them sawing on my nerves, I know I must be in bad shape."

"To live is to know pain," Milo mumbled. "Only the dead know peace."

"Cute." Ambrose sniffed. "Especially given you know that's not always the case."

Milo felt an odd chill and shook his head to dispel the thought of glinting eyes and teeth.

"Maybe." He turned his eyes to the western horizon. There was nothing but the green-skinned Caucasus Mountains in spring, but Milo knew that somewhere beyond one of those rises was Tsminda Sameba, a church that Rihyani had said would help save her.

"How much longer?" he asked, turning back as Ambrose was buttoning up his collar.

"Another eight hours," the bodyguard said as he ambled toward the back of the bed, where fuel cans had been arranged and bound by a length of rope. "Maybe less. We've made fairly good time, considering there is nothing like a decent paved road in this country."

Milo gave a low whistle when he realized that meant he'd been asleep for nearly twenty-four hours. He supposed that explained why he was refreshed if a little sore. Looking down at the Nephilim, he found himself thankful that it seemed the half-angel viewed sleep as recreational interest, enjoyed when possible but hardly necessary.

Ambrose, having clambered up to grab two fuel cans, gave a strong sniff, then swung a frown toward Milo.

"Seeing as we're having such a good time," he said in an exaggeratedly delicate tone, "maybe you'd like to take advantage of the stream over there too."

Milo squinted at the bodyguard, who grinned sheepishly back as the magus bent his head to take a quick smell. What greeted him was striking enough that without another word, he hopped down from the bed and began shedding clothes as he made for the stream.

The stream was clean, clear, and heart-stoppingly cold. With a gasp, he felt his skin erupt in gooseflesh. Despite the initial shock, it felt good to rinse away the days of sweat, blood, and other strong scents that had accumulated on his person. At its deepest, the stream only came up to his knees, so Milo had to stoop and plunge his shivering arms in to draw out water in cupped hands.

He'd slapped a double handful across his face when he noticed Ambrose had approached a bar of soap in one hand and a small towel in the other.

"Thanks," Milo said, taking the soap and starting a lather on his chest and underarms.

"No problem," Ambrose muttered, his gaze roving across Milo's chest and shoulders before he pointed at a crudely tattooed cottage resting on a taloned foot on Milo's left arm. "Any of those still give you trouble?"

Milo looked at his own tapestry of old wounds and ink, each a bittersweet memory. He remembered the days when he believed he was part of a band of brothers, when he'd felt they were bound together in a pact of defiant hope. For all the hurt and fear that had come after, he couldn't help but see the old marks and remember the few good times in his short, ugly life.

Then his eyes settled on the skull on an orthodox cross on his wrist, and he felt a sharp, hot sting in his chest. Nostalgia became bitter ash at the back of his throat, and he spat into the stream.

"A few," he muttered and went back to washing.

12

THE UNLIKELY

Tsminda Sameba was a romantic's phantasm, sprung from canvas into the real world.

Sitting atop a high hill before the steep slopes of Mount Kazbek, its steeple and separate belltower made it look as though it was a gatehouse perched before the arduous trek to the white-headed peak. The track up to the church wound a penitent's grueling path in a series of switchbacks and a final looping spiral to the courtyard of the church. This final run around the church was dotted with votive alcoves crowned with crosses, clutching icons to their stony bosoms. The entirety of the scene left both men muted in wonder and trepidation as the Rollsy chugged up to the courtyard. A wall of stacked stones ran alongside the courtyard channeling foot traffic, if there had been any, from the courtyard to a smaller stone-paved platform that led to the church doors.

A black-garbed man built like a low-slung ox stomped out of the church doors, waving his hands furiously at them as he skirted along the wall.

"You didn't tell me you had family here," Milo quipped as the Rollsy slowed to a stop.

"You noticed the tell-tale family coloration, did you?" Ambrose chuckled as the man came storming up to the cab, black beard bristling as his dark eyes glowered furiously at both of them.

"This is no place for soldiers!" he shouted, only partially out of anger since the wind and the Rollsy engine made a conversational tone impossible. "Turn this car around and head back down the way you came."

The man planted himself firmly in front of Milo's door, arms crossed over his broad chest. Milo couldn't open the door without hitting the man, which he assumed was precisely the idea.

"Hardly hospitable, Father," Ambrose called in Russian, turning off the engine as he half-rose in his seat to face the irate man. "What about a little Christian charity for weary travelers?"

"Not priest, deacon," the man said in broken Russian. "Need things to go village now!"

With a jab of his finger, he pointed down the hill at the village of Gergeti, which Ambrose and Milo had been keen to avoid lest their presence cause a stir. A few men dressed like German soldiers might lead people to assume a German force was moving through the area, and while the agreement between Germany and Georgia had held thus far, Milo's errand was too important to take chances.

"Deacon." Milo spoke up, the elixir he'd learned in Ifreedahm granting him the ability to be understood in any language the hearer spoke. "We don't mean to intrude, but we are looking for someone. A word, and we'll be on our way."

The deacon turned to Milo, bushy eyebrows raised in surprise as he looked the magus up and down.

"There is no one here but the priest, me, and one another deacon," he said, curiosity stealing some of his bluster. "We have no business with soldiers, so you must be in the wrong place. If you are really looking for someone, you would be better off talking to those in the village. Please, go back down now."

"We aren't soldiers," Milo said as he stood up and swung one lanky leg over the cab door. "And we'll be off as soon as we can. We need to ask about someone and have you or the priest point us in the right direction."

The deacon eyed the magus warily but took a single step back so Milo could dismount without standing nose to nose with him.

"Tell me who you are looking for, and I'll tell you if I have anything to say," he declared with a shrug of his shoulders. Despite his attempt at unruffled control, Milo didn't miss how the man eyed Ambrose's Gewehr.

"We were sent by the contessa," Milo said, meeting the burning eyes under the man's beetled brows. "She told us to come here and ask to see the marquis."

The deacon stood for a long time, staring at Milo as the wind whipped across the worn paving stones of the courtyard. Milo held the man's gaze, fighting the sudden and dominating urge to scratch his nose as the faintest smell of incense reached his nostrils. Behind him, the Rollsy creaked as Ambrose shifted impatiently in the cab.

"Wait here," the deacon said before turning on his heel and walking back to the church.

With a relieved grunt, Ambrose threw himself out of the cab and set about stretching his back as he eyed the double doors and the paned windows above. The stones were centuries old and looked it, their surfaces pitted and chinked. Despite this, though, he could easily pick out the details and decorations graven there. Standing in its presence was like standing before a sleeping titan whose foundations rested beyond the ken of time, even though intellectually, both men knew the place couldn't have been more than five hundred years old.

"What do you think the odds are someone starts shooting us while we stand here?" Ambrose asked, throwing a quick look around the area. "If it was me, I'd also have put a sharpshooter over in that belltower to hit from two different angles."

Milo eyed the belltower that stood separate from the church, a rounded tower where open archways would project sound and serve as excellent sniper nests.

"That is assuming these are a batch of militant priests stockpiling for some ill-fated crusade," Milo said as he silently told himself to stop searching the belltower for the glint of sunlight on a scope. "Not a bunch of surly old hermits using the religion as an excuse to hide from a world that's never done anyone any favors."

Ambrose clucked his tongue and gave his head a wag.

"I'll admit that mine sounds paranoid," he said, shuffling behind the cover of the Rollsy's armored hood. "Yet somehow yours is even sadder."

Milo shrugged and defiantly stayed where he was, scuffing a boot against a paving stone.

"It's a gift," he muttered and looked up as he heard the groan of the church doors swinging open.

"What, being wrong?" Ambrose grunted as he nodded at the deacon, who was returning with another man in black, both carrying rifles.

Milo planted the cane in front of him and controlled the urge to lash out in waves of crackling green fire. He imagined that if the men had intended to shoot him, they would have done so from the cover of the door. This was a show of force, demonstrating that they were armed and weren't afraid to use those weapons on soldiers if need be. At least that was the show they were putting on.

Milo put on his best ingratiating smile and held up his hands in a slow, easy manner.

"Good deacon, there is no need for—"

The ox-shouldered deacon's rifle thundered, and Milo winced as he heard the shot zip over his head.

Milo realized that perhaps this wasn't as much of a show as a demonstration.

"How do you know of the marquis?" the deacon growled as he chambered another round.

Milo looked at the two men, searching for how to explain.

The other man in black was slighter, taller, and older, with a gray beard on a face that seemed graven in stone. A look into his flinty black eyes told Milo that one wrong move and he wouldn't be firing warning shots. Surreptitiously following the man's aim, Milo could tell the man's rifle was trained on Ambrose on the other side of the Rollsy. Milo didn't doubt his bodyguard was hunkered down with his own rifle trained over Milo's shoulder. As unyielding as the men seemed, Milo didn't doubt Ambrose could drop both of them in short order.

The only problem was, Milo was between them and thus lethally exposed.

"A friend of mine, the contessa. Remember?" Milo asked, his words coming out slowly because he wanted to keep his voice from shaking. "She is hurt and needs help. She sent me to find the marquis here. That's truly all I know."

The priests shared a look, and Milo got the feeling his life hung in the balance. Then the older man nodded, and Milo was convinced he saw them relax slightly, even though neither man lowered their weapon.

"This contessa. She is not like other women, then?" the black-bearded deacon asked, giving Milo a measured look.

Milo nodded emphatically and forced a smile.

"Not unless other women can ride the wind or disappear with the snap of the fingers," he said with a forced laugh.

Again, the two men shared a quick look, and to Milo's immense relief, they lowered their rifles to rest across their bodies.

"You may enter and talk to the priest," the elder deacon said in a raw, watery voice. "But you will not bring weapons into the church."

Milo looked over his shoulder at Ambrose for the first time and saw that the big man still had his rifle trained on the men.

"What do you think?" Milo asked quietly so that only Ambrose could hear him over the wind. "You want to stay out here while I go inside? Keep an eye on these two."

Ambrose squinted down the length of the barrel, some internal calculation swimming in his head before he sighed and took the butt from his shoulder.

"No." He grunted before sliding his weapon into the driver's seat with a petulant huff. "Who knows what's in there? These bumpkins better not fiddle with my Gewehr. I just finished some adjustments, and I don't want them tampered with."

Milo shook his head.

"You're worried more about leaving the gun out here than going in unarmed?" he asked incredulously as he took the pistol from his belt and deposited it on the passenger seat of the cab.

"I'm never totally unarmed," Ambrose said and gave his knuckles a crack.

"No, I don't suppose so," Milo muttered and raised his cane to his forehead in jaunty salute. "Now come on, let's go talk to a priest about pixie problems."

***

Reverend Father Akaki Zoidze was a small man with deeply lined skin the texture and color of old leather. The folds in his face hid his eyes beneath the sagging weight of wrinkles. On seeing the man, Milo had attempted to brace himself and set aside his typical irritation with the elderly. Milo had come to associate advanced age with a vague, muddled response to life, expecting most who lived to such an age to be either bemusedly good-natured or distractingly cantankerous. In the Wassenhaus, he'd known the nonsensical ire of the latter and the uncomfortable affections of the former and had since decided he did not have much time for either.

For better or worse, the priest was neither of these, seeming instead to be a man who was acutely aware of everything around him and therefore acutely displeased.

"Deacon Saba, the lumbering dolt," he hissed between the few teeth that remained in his mouth, "should have shot you at the door. It would have been kinder than anything I have to say to you, young pagan."

"Pagan?" Milo asked, unable to stop himself. "That's an interesting insult. I'm not sure it's accurate, either."

The priest gave a hacking exhalation that took Milo some time to recognize as a laugh.

"What else would you call a young fool dressed like a soldier who comes looking for heathen gods?"

Milo frowned, wondering if he needed to reassess his estimation of the priest's faculties.

"I'm not sure I understand, Father," Milo said, attempting to strike a gentler tone. "We were sent to look for the marquis. I'm not sure gods, heathen or otherwise, were part of that."

The next bark of laughter could have been a muddled cough, and the small, shriveled man shook his head hard enough to make his jowls swing.

"Disaster is the companion of the aimless traveler." Milo assumed it was a proverb. "Yes, the Marquis of Veils is one of the names he wears among his Dobilni kin, but it is not the only one. Among the superstitious fools down in Gergeti and other small hamlets, he is whispered to be Ochopintre, the wooded god of the hunt, or some other petty deity for savages to make bloody offerings to."

Milo blinked and exchanged looks with Ambrose.

"How does a priest know about all this?" Milo asked, the words coming out blunt and terse, but as such honest.

"Why would a priest not know the superstitions of the ignorant fools he serves?" Father Zoidze asked, thrusting a stubbled gray chin at Milo. "To save their souls, you must know what holds their hearts, and on this God-cursed mountain, that Dobilni with divine aspirations has had these ingrates in the palm of his hand. Sixty years ministering to them, and in all that time, only those two idiot deacons to show for it!"

The priest rocked back in his chair and crossed his arms as though suddenly cold, looking more shrunken and mean for the change.

"Ochopintre still gets his sacrifices, and I still get to see the heathen on Sunday, half-asleep in the pews from their late-night revels," he spat before his seamed face molded into a frown that he leveled at Milo. "Is that what you've come for then, to make a red offering on one of his stones in the valley?"

Milo paused for a moment, unsure of what to say. The bitter old man seemed to be no friend to the marquis but didn't seem opposed to talking about him.

"We need to contact him," Milo said, choosing his words carefully. "Our friend the contessa is in need of his assistance."

"Contessa?" The old man sniffed. "One of the slatternly females of the wicked Dobilni, no doubt."

"Yes." Milo nodded, assuming that "Dobilni" was analogous to fey. His elixir translated well, but sometimes the proper names of things could trip it up.

"It makes sense that she would send you here," the priest muttered, rocking slightly as he tightened his grip around himself. "God must know my sins need further penance."

Again, Milo stole a glance at Ambrose, who simply shrugged. He remembered that Ambrose didn't speak Georgian, so was at best reading the priest's body language.

"Listen!" Father Zoidze said sharply, drawing Milo's attention back to him. The priest's brows were raised, and Milo got his first and only look at the man's startlingly brilliant blue eyes.

"If you are seeking the marquis, you are going to need a map," he growled and reached inside his desk to produce a small sheet of parchment and a quill writing set. "If you get out of here quick enough, you may be able to reach it as the sun is setting because the passage to his home is most easily seen at sunrise and sunset. You'll be able to tell by the mists, I expect."

The old man began to scratch on the parchment in short spidery strokes.

"Not to be ungrateful," Milo began, unsure of how to phrase his concern, "but you seem awfully helpful in finding the marquis when you clearly don't like him."

"Is that supposed to be a question?" Father Zoidze asked without looking up.

"If you hate him so much, why tell people how to find him?" Milo asked. "Why help the Dobilni?"

The old man frowned down at his hastily scrawled map, the quill poised for another dip in the ink.

"It's the deal we struck," he said softly. "A long time ago."

A few more scratches of the quill and the map was done.

"Take it and go," Father Zoidze muttered as he held it out to Milo. "I'll pray you renounce your wicked ways, but I doubt it will do much good. If you're already this far down the Devil's path, there seems little hope for any of us."

Milo took the map and looked it over. It was crude, but he could clearly see the church and trace a route along the mountainside to a narrow valley filled with sentinel pines.

"Thank you," Milo said and made to rise.

The priest's hand shot out, snaring Milo's wrist with surprising strength.

Milo felt Ambrose surge up behind him, but he waved him away with his free hand. Something in the old man's grip told Milo this wasn't a threat but a plea.

"Dealing with their kind never ends well, my son," Father

Zoidze said in a husky whisper. "Whatever your aims, however noble, just remember that. Take it from someone who knows."

With that, the old man released Milo, sank back down behind his desk, and would say no more.

***

Milo and Ambrose were a half-dozen strides from the church doors when Ambrose grabbed Milo by the shoulders and bore him to the ground. Both men hit the stone floor together, and quick as thought, the bodyguard had them rolling behind a wide stone column resplendent with iconography.

"What the—" Milo snarled before Ambrose's paw slapped over his mouth.

"Trouble," the big man growled in the magus' ear, then shuffled to make himself as narrow as possible behind the pillar, which was no small task.

A heartbeat later, the doors to the church banged open, and they could hear the scuff of many feet on the stones as the bearded deacon, Saba, bellowed his protest.

"How dare you! This is a house of God!" the deacon bellowed as he came up behind the crowd entering the church. "Leave now!"

"I'm terribly sorry to inconvenience you, Deacon, but we have business with some of your new parishioners," a familiar voice replied in smooth Georgian. "As soon as we have a brief conversation with them, we will no longer darken your door."

Hunkered behind the pillar, Milo and Ambrose watched as Percy Astor, now clad in a gray silk suit and matching Homburg, strode by with a cadre of the Georgian mercenaries in dark chokhas. The two men pressed against the pillar as the party strode by and Deacon Saba tried to push his way to the front. Milo allowed himself a petty smile when he saw the stitches on the side of Percy's face where Milo had struck him with his cane, along with his left hand swaddled in heavy bandages.

He was so enjoying the sight, Ambrose had to haul him farther back behind the pillar, but not before Milo caught a glimpse of the opposite wall. There was a cavity in the wall, a miniature shrine where icons, some in frames, some painted directly onto the stones, were on display. There were places for votive candles, but the light spilling across the space came from a large open window less than two meters off the ground.

The encounter between the unlucky deacon and the American continued as Milo pressed his back against the pillar and took a steadying breath. He checked to make sure the attention of the intruders was upon Saba and saw that the other deacon had arrived, rifle in hand.

"No, Iacob!" Saba cried, trying to step between his fellow churchman and the half-dozen men who raised their weapons in response, a collection of stocky carbines.

"Leave now!" Iacob shouted hoarsely, and to the man's credit, his hands and voice were both steady.

"Please don't make this any worse than it has to be," Percy said with a note of distracted irritation rankling his smooth intonation. "This can be resolved quickly if you would list—"

"This is a house of God!" Saba practically wailed. "Go outside, then we can talk!"

The mercenaries flinched at the outburst. Milo was certain shots were about to be fired, but miraculously, everyone stayed their hand for a moment.

Milo decided they needed to get out of here before the bullets started flying, and there was no better time than now.

"Follow me," he hissed into Ambrose's ear, and, knowing it would be pointless to steal another look, darted over to the alcove.

"Leave now," Iacob repeated, and there was something final in his voice. Milo wasn't the only one who heard it.

Under the gaze of saints and patriarchs, they scuttled beneath the window as the thunder of six carbines firing filled the church. Both men froze for a second, convinced the shots were meant for them, but when no rounds chewed the stone, and when Saba's dismayed scream chased the echo of the shots, they understood the truth.

"Why does no one ever listen to me?" Percy muttered, and there was a brief rustle of cloth.

"*MURDERERS! TRAITORS! GOD DAMN YOU!*" Saba howled, his voice cracking with the impotent fury coursing through him as he collapsed into heavy sobs.

"Hardly language for church," Percy chided. There was the click of a hammer being cocked, and the bark of a pistol silenced Saba's weeping. "Though I suppose you might be right on that last point."

Fury, caustic in Milo's chest, rose into his throat. He growled a curse, and the raptor skull's sockets glowed with sympathetic flames. The churchmen were sour old fools, but they didn't deserve this. Not on their behalf.

Milo was halfway out of the shrine's alcove when Ambrose grabbed him and dragged him back under the window. Milo tried to pull free, but the Nephilim's strength and leverage were undeniable as he held Milo long enough to draw his eyes.

"No weapons," Ambrose mouthed, gesturing with an empty hand. "Too many."

Milo ground his teeth, swallowing the rage like bitter bile. Ambrose was right; they weren't going to be any good if they got themselves killed. Silently, he swore that one day, Percy Astor was going to pay.

"Search the place," Percy called to his mercenaries. "Bring the priest to me for interrogation, but I imagine he will be as useless as those poor deacons."

Ambrose was already hoisting Milo up to the open window when they heard the tramp of boots.

"Do be quick about it," Mr. Astor called after his goons. "If my compatriot gets bored, he's apt to start burning things down, and it would be a shame to deface so picturesque a place."

Milo swung himself over the window and discovered that the ground outside the church was significantly lower than the floor inside the church. He had enough time to register that in a surge of panic before he struck that ground hard.

Stars detonated inside Milo's head, and only reflex had him rolling away, thus avoiding Ambrose's descent. The big man took the fall in stride and had hauled Milo to his feet before he'd managed to force his winded lungs to take another breath.

They were standing on the grassy soil ringing the base of the church, only a few steps away from the paved walkway that wound about the building and connected it to the belltower.

"Belltower," Ambrose suggested in a low voice as he searched the grounds for mercenaries. "We scamper down the outside and see if we can make a break for the Rollsy."

Milo nodded, still fighting to breathe consistently, much less speak.

There were no apparent enemies outside, but Milo expected that was because this side of the church was farthest from the courtyard. The wind howled across the hilltop, but he was certain he heard the rumble of idling vehicles. Even if the Americans had gathered more mercenaries, those that had attacked Rihyani and company had numbered nearly a thirty, so half as many men could be expected by the vehicles. Then there was whatever new deviant companion Percy had acquired that liked to burn things. An American, maybe? Setting things on fire seemed to Milo a very American sort of thing.

They made it to the belltower and clambered down its rough-hewn side without incident, and both men heaved a sigh of relief.

"If those bastards have touched my rifle..." Ambrose hissed acidly as they crept along the base of the belltower toward the courtyard where they'd left the Rollsy.

"Glad your mind is on the task at hand," Milo muttered.

They reached the corner of the belltower, and Milo peered around to assess the situation.

He silently swore and pulled back, then shuffled over to let Ambrose steal a glance. Ambrose gave his own curse and slid back to exchange unsure glances with Milo.

The courtyard was crowded with three squat canvas-backed trucks, which blocked the view of the Rollsy and everything else, for that matter. There was a driver in each truck, but that left at least a few mercenaries unaccounted for. Both men stood, pressed flat against the belltower, thinking and listening, but the only sound to be heard was the whine of the wind, underpinned by the growl of the truck engines.

Milo's mind raced as his fingers darted into the various pockets of his coat, nervous energy leaving him double- or triple-checking the paraphernalia on his person. He had a plan forming, but it all depended on him having…

His fingers brushed three corked vials, and his face broke into a wicked grin.

He drew out the first vial from the extra-dimensional pocket woven into his coat, giving the long glass tube a little shake that set the black grit within to twinkling with unnatural light.

Ambrose saw what Milo had produced, and he gave an approving nod.

"I've got a plan," Milo said, his voice loud enough to be heard over the keening wind.

The men sitting behind the wheels of the trucks didn't have a chance to understand their peril until it was far too late. Like their companions tearing through Gergeti Trinity Church, they were all veteran fighters, men of the mountains who'd made their living fighting foreign powers who sought to dominate their homeland and occasionally taking work with those willing to make generous contributions to their cause. Hammered relentlessly upon the anvil of life, they were hard men, willing to do hard things.

They'd fought Russians and they'd fought Ottomans and now the Germans, and to them, one foreigner was pretty much the same as the next when it came to fighting and dying, slight variations in tactics and plunder notwithstanding. The fact was, they were experienced at guerrilla warfare and had faced "superior" forces in the past.

Yet, they'd never faced a necromist, and so were singularly unprepared when coils of black sand began to slither under their vehicles.

Only one of the drivers, the one parked closest to the ramshackle German vehicle, noticed the flicker of movement out of the corner of his eye, but he quickly dismissed it. He chalked it up to the wind kicking up a little dervish, gone as soon as you realized it was there. After all, professional freedom fighter or not, he had other things on his mind.

The business with the Americans had been more dangerous than expected, and when their platoon's commanding officer had threatened to abandon the Americans, they'd doubled the offered fee, including the pay of those slain. Seeing as this driver had two cousins among the dead, this turn of events struck him as significant. The one man who might have done something was too busy trying to plan what percent would be fair to give to the men's families and what percent to keep for himself to pay real attention to the trickle of glittering black that slid under his vehicle.

He was still trying to work out percentages in his head when a ribbon of congealing midnight slithered up the side of his truck, lanced through the door window, and tore out his throat like the other two drivers.

The shattering of glass could be heard even over the hellish wind, and it drew the attention of the men standing watch at the church door and by the Rollsy. As one, they turned, and after giving a chorus of piercing whistles, they slunk back toward the vehicles, rifles ready.

Seeing their fellows slumped in their seats, windows shattered, they took positions along the wall bordering the church, eyes searching for snipers. That ensured they had nowhere to run when Ambrose and Milo sprang on them.

Ambrose leaped on the first man, delivering a single punch that shattered the man's jaw and left him senseless. Milo hit the man behind the first with a magically enhanced stroke of his cane that left him poleaxed. The last man had only enough time to open his mouth for a scream before his cries were suffocated by a blast of witchfire that instantly immolated everything from the shoulder up.

"Grab a carbine," Ambrose growled as he snatched up the first two men's strange firearms.

Milo complied, taking half a moment to wonder about the solidly built weapons' shorter barrel and the strange case for its ammunition. A quick glance showed labels and markings in English. The rifles must have been new American designs, which explained the impressive firepower the mercenaries had put out during their ambush.

Milo raised his head from inspecting the weapon to see if anyone was coming from inside the church, but it seemed those within had not been alerted.

"Ready when you are," Ambrose whispered hoarsely, one carbine in hand, the other slung over his shoulder.

Milo nodded, and they both made a run for the Rollsy, which they could now see standing at the end of the formation of trucks.

"Let's try and ease out of here," Ambrose said as they both skidded to a stop and began to clamber up the sides of the vehicle.

A ragged figure rose from where it had been lying in the cab, a rust-flecked revolver in each hand, leveled at Milo and Ambrose's temples.

"Now, now, boys," Ezekiel Boucher said with a slow, chiding cluck of his tongue. "You ought to know by now, ain't nothing easy in this line o' work."

13

THE HARRIERS

Milo and Ambrose froze, transfixed by the black basilisk stares of the pistols' barrels as they hung onto the sides of the Rollsy's cab.

"Didn't figure you'd be seein' ol' Zeke this side o' Hell, now did you?"

Milo glimpsed the base pleasure shining in the scalp hunter's eyes and felt a welcome and defiant anger blooming in his chest. He forced a fierce smile onto his face and tore his eyes away from the pistols' menacing gravity to meet the cowboy's gaze. The same wild stare waited there, more jaundiced and bloodshot than before.

"Am I supposed to be impressed?" he snarled at the man through bared teeth as his will sent out a rallying cry. Now he needed to stay alive until they arrived.

"You think you cornered the market on death, *cowboy*?"

As the jeer slid from his tongue, a voice in the back of his mind screamed that he'd gone too far and the end was nigh. To Milo's utter shock, something that might have been fearful confusion crept into Ezekiel's eyes before he threw back his head and gave that mad cackle that never quite touched his bloodshot eyes.

"You've got gumption, I'll give you that, partner." Ezekiel giggled and gave Milo a wink as he pressed the revolver against the magus' forehead. "It's been a while since I scalped one of my own kind, but you two make the cut. How does that sound?"

A growl that must have been felt in the tectonic plates rumbled in Ambrose's chest.

"Sounds like you already forgot what happened last time," the big man said in a tone so cold Milo felt a chill shimmy up and down his spine. "Take what's coming like a man, and I might leave pieces big enough to find."

The scalp hunter's smile widened until Milo was certain the man's face had stretched like taffy to accommodate the expression.

"W-eh-eh-ell, listen to the pair o' you!" He chortled, leaning against the seat, both pistols' aim remaining true. "Regular pair o' comedians! You keep this up much longer, and I'm goin' to be laughin' too hard to put you down clean! Ha-ha, might end up taking me hours, I'll be laughin' so hard."

In Milo's peripheral vision, he caught the sable glint, and his smile in the face of Ezekiel's threats was suddenly less forced.

"Not so sure about that, *partner*," Milo said with mock solemnity. "I've got a feeling you're going to get bored with our act real soon."

"Hehehe...why...hehe...why's that?"

Milo threw Ambrose a wink before meeting Ezekiel's eyes with a grave expression.

"Our acts always have the same punchline."

Three ribbons of shimmering black sand lashed out from the back of the Rollsy, twisting mid-flight into a shadowy semblance of thorny vines. Two of the tendrils went for the cowboy's hands, ripping the guns into the air in a spray of lacerating particles. The third tendril coiled around Ezekiel's neck and yanked violently backward, man and si'lat tumbling into the empty gun nest.

Milo and Ambrose leaped into the cab, Ambrose rushing to get the vehicle started while Milo scrambled to follow the gurgling cowboy. His will called the two si'lat from battering the two revolvers across the courtyard to attend him as he surveyed Ezekiel Boucher's struggle.

Still managing to force a choked, viscous laugh as the jagged black vine twisted and ripped at his throat, the cowboy never stopped thrashing and kicking. The heels of his peeling split-sided boots rang off the sides of the gunner's station, a violent staccato beat. Bright arterial blood sprayed across the metal deck and was promptly smeared this way and that as Ezekiel continued to twist and squirm.

His thorn-ravaged fingers raked through the si'lat ineffectually, then somehow, he wrenched his chin low enough to bite down on a mouthful of black sand with stained teeth.

Milo reeled as he felt his connection with the shade-animated construct snap like a taut wire.

Swearing and batting ineffectually at the spots flickering across his vision, Milo's mind loosed the two other si'lat. Cutting the air with a serpentine hiss, the vicious constructs flew down on the cowboy in a whirling, scouring cloud of black razors.

The Rollsy's engine roared, and Milo felt the vehicle lurch underneath him with a snarl of gears engaging. His hands shot out to brace himself on the lip of the nest, and he was thrown halfway into the nest. One knee of his trousers soaking in Ezekiel's blood on the metal-plated deck, Milo found himself within arm's reach of the bloodied man, who tore at the black grit slashing back and forth across his body. As Milo struggled to stand, he felt a tremble in his magical awareness.

As impossible as it seemed, the cowboy's raking fingers and snapping teeth were in fact draining and wounding the si'lat.

Milo had once emptied a pistol into a si'lat, and it had no effect on the creature. It had required magical fire to destroy it. It made no sense that the scalp hunter's bare teeth could inflict such damage, but then Milo remembered the curse. Some aspect of it must have made anything he used to inflict violence exceptionally potent, even in the realm of the metaphysical.

The Rollsy swung into reverse, and Milo was thrown to one side as he watched Ezekiel struggle with the weakening si'lat. The cowboy, despite his wounds, showed no signs of faltering, and Milo realized he had seconds before his constructs came apart like the last one.

Still gripping the lip of the gun nest, Milo recalled the si'lat, then threw his body into a thrusting frontal kick.

Ezekiel, reaching to tear at the retreating clouds of grit, took Milo's foot square in the chest and went rolling head over heels into the bed of the Rollsy. He landed flat on his back with a dull thump, his head pointed toward the rear of the vehicle less than a foot from the fuel cans strapped there. With an almost boneless litheness, he rolled to his feet, a blood-soaked specter with a smile that gaped like a knife wound. Bulging eyes swept over Milo, and then the scalp hunter's nostrils flared in a series of exaggerated sniffs.

"Ha-ha, there it is," he crowed. "You *do* have my knife! Told Percy I could smell it. Good thing, since I'm going to need it."

He then spread his arms so Milo could appreciate the scalps dangling from his slashed, gory buckskin.

Both men braced themselves as the Rollsy began to accelerate, ready to bear them out of the courtyard and down the looping track. Ezekiel turned his crouch into a spring, and Milo only had a heartbeat to react.

"Here's the punchline!" he roared as he swung his cane up.

BURN

The skull yawned wide to vomit witchfire and the blast caught Ezekiel mid-spring, unnatural heat and the eldritch force driving him down and back. There was a bell-like clang as his burning body rebounded off the strapped-in fuel cans, then he was bouncing behind them as the Rollsy pulled away. Milo nearly gave a whoop of victory as he watched the flames lick over Ezekiel's shrinking form, but then his mind registered what his eyes had already seen.

Emerald flames clung to the fuel cans strapped to the bed.

Seeing no other choice, Milo launched the mangled si'lat at the straps, their jagged forms ripping through with ease. Another command and the animated clouds of black sand hoisted the cooking canisters up and over the tailgate just in time.

The fuel canisters struck the paving stones of the courtyard entrance as the Rollsy flew onto the track, detonating in a cascade of natural and supernatural flame. Milo twisted away from the heat of the blast as his ears rang with the auditory assault of the detonation. The si'lat were not so lucky, hanging at the end of the tailgate, their abused essence matrices shattering under waves of heat and raw force.

When Milo looked at the mass of twisted metal and burning fuel in their wake, he breathed a sigh of relief he couldn't hear because of his explosion-abused ears. The sigh caught when he saw a smoldering figure rise from the ground. One hand waved jauntily at them while the other slapped the clinging flames with a filthy, drooping cowboy hat.

"HAHAHA! Don't worry!" Ezekiel hollered after them, his voice fading on the wind. "I'll be seein' you boys real soon!"

"Is he one of you?" Milo asked as he slid into the cab's passenger seat. "Is he a Nephilim?"

Ambrose kept his eyes forward as they carved down the winding track, hands clenched on the wheel.

"I don't know," he shouted back to be heard over the wind and the chugging engine. "I don't think so."

Milo craned his neck to look over his shoulder. So far, there were no signs of pursuit, but he didn't imagine that would last.

"We thought you killed him," Milo said, pointing at Ambrose and then putting the same hand on his own chest. "I hit him hard enough to kill him three times over."

Ambrose shook his head, and Milo saw his huge hands tighten on the wheel.

"But he didn't stay that way, I know!" he growled, then he swung his head to one side, eyes narrowed. "Hold on, this is going to be rough!"

Milo latched a white-knuckle grip on the dashboard and door as the Rollsy swung hard left and began to rumble down the unformed slope.

"W-what the H-h-hell!" Milo screamed. His bones were about to rattle free from their jarring descent.

"Need to avoid the switchbacks," Ambrose shouted back, then raised a hand where Zoidze's map lay crumpled. "And this cuts a clearer path to where we're headed. Just hold on and shut up!"

Milo could not shut up. He was too busy screaming in terror as Ambrose took them on a course that was one part high-speed off-roading and one part slalom, using an armored vehicle instead of skis. They rode the razor edge of rapid descent and flat-out plummeted for what felt like hours as Ambrose tacked and pitched the Rollsy like a boat in a storm. More than once, it seemed impossible for them to not go plunging off some ridge-line or plow into a rocky outcropping, but each time, the big man managed to skate by with a clearance of mere centimeters.

The last dive onto relatively level ground bounced the Rollsy hard enough that it knocked the wind out of Milo, leaving him gasping like a landed fish. Milo fought to force air into his lungs for several seconds before he realized that they were rolling along at an almost leisurely pace.

"See?" Ambrose muttered as he squinted at the map. "Nothing to worry about."

Milo, his muscles still spasming from the strain of the descent, sat staring and twitching at his bodyguard.

"Next time you find a short cut," Milo said slowly, hoping the hammering in his chest would slow down soon, "just say no."

Ambrose frowned at Milo, shaking his head ruefully.

"Do you know how many people could have made it down that slope alive, much less with their vehicle in one piece?"

Milo stood up a little in his seat to look back up the hill, which might have been called a mountain had it not stood in the shadow of Mount Kazbek.

"Just because you can do something, it doesn't mean you should." Milo grunted and slumped back down to nod at the map. "You got that figured out yet?"

Ambrose nodded but had reached down under the seat to pull out his copy of Lokkemand's maps. The Rollsy continued to crawl along as somewhere up above, there was the distant rumble of large engines and the squeal of brakes.

"What's wrong?" Milo asked, not bothering to keep the anxiety out of his voice. "Why aren't we speeding toward the marquis?"

Ambrose was alternating between the two maps, brows furrowed as his mouth worked at forming words he never got around to speaking.

"Ambrose?" Milo prompted, about ready to give the big man a shake of the shoulder when he threw both maps down on the seat between them and laid his boot into the accelerator.

"Just hope that old priest knows what he's about," Ambrose growled over the rising roar of the engines. "He's got us heading into a wooded vale with a river, but according to Lokkemand's map, that gorge doesn't have a forest or a river. It's just a bare gorge."

Milo picked up the maps, more to feel involved in the process than to check Ambrose's map skills. If he said things didn't match up, they didn't.

"It's the only lead we've got," Milo said as he frowned down at the maps. "And we can't expect that Zoidze hasn't given them the same information. The Americans could be heading there the same as us. That cannot happen."

Ambrose nodded and turned back to the road for a moment before swinging his gaze back to Milo.

"About the cowboy," he began, mustache wriggling like it always did when he was searching for words. "I don't think, or my best guess is, that he isn't a Nephilim like me."

Milo sighed and slumped a little deeper into his seat.

He'd expected as much, though he couldn't have explained why he'd intuited the same. Perhaps it was something about the utter difference between the two men. Ambrose seemed awkward, even bumbling, as he ambled about daily tasks, but in battle, he was a force of nature moving with a speed, sureness, and strength that could turn the tide of a fight in an instant. Even if Milo hadn't known Ambrose to be half-angelic, he would have known he was inherently potent and glorious after seeing the man at war. Even if Ambrose had been a villain and used his prowess for evil, it would have been a grand and spectacular sort of violence, the kind to cow cities and break armies.

Ezekiel Boucher was nothing like that.

Dangerous, extremely so, but it was all quickness, low cunning, and viciousness. It was a murderer's way of violence— not the sort to rally allies and intimidate foes, but something which would seem cheap even to allies and abominable to the enemy. A man that rotten, and Milo wasn't just thinking of the scalp hunter's hygiene, couldn't be heroic or tyrannical even if he wanted to.

That meant he was some other sort of dangerous being who was nigh impossible to kill, which currently was the last thing Milo needed on his list of concerns.

"What is he?" Milo groaned as he looked out and saw the sun sinking toward the mountainous horizon.

"Cursed," Ambrose said with a shrug. "That's about all we know about him."

Being reminded of the curse brought the hexed knife to mind, and Milo felt where the knife lay in his coat pocket in a wrapping of greased leather.

"He said he could smell the knife on me," Milo said, his skin crawling as he felt the blade through the fabric and hide. "I wonder if the curse has some kind of connection that he can track?"

Ambrose gave Milo a sidelong look that told him the thought was not a comforting one.

"You could pitch it," Ambrose suggested, thrusting a chin to the rocky slope to their left. "Wing it hard enough, and you could send them down into that ravine sniffing for us."

"I wish I could," Milo murmured honestly. "But I need to make sure the marquis knows what kind of curse we are working with, and the best way I know to do that is by making sure we have something carrying the curse with us."

Ambrose nodded, but his face was twisted like he'd smelled something foul.

"I suppose," he agreed, shaking his head. "We'll have to hope we aren't bringing too much trouble to this marquis' door. Not sure about the fey, but most people don't take kindly to strangers showing up uninvited and making a mess."

"I agree, but once again, what other choice do we have?" Milo asked, and since both knew the answer, they shared a weary shrug and lapsed into silence. As the miles rolled beneath them, there was only the chug of the engine and the keening of the wind to fill the stillness.

The red sky was deepening into the first shades of a bruise when they crested a hill and looked down into a rocky gorge.

"This should be it," Ambrose grumbled as he brought the Rollsy to a halt. "But I don't see any trees or rivers, do you?"

Milo squinted down into the barren cleft between climbing slopes, trying desperately to fight the rising panic in his chest. There were signs that a small stream had wound between the tumble of rock, but the pebbled ground was dry, and the typical green of the springtime Caucasus was only a mangy patchwork. Milo wasn't certain a single tree could survive amongst the parched boulders, much less a wood.

But the priest had seemed so certain, so sure.

"What do you want to do?" Ambrose asked, looking at Milo, his expression grim.

It was doubtful that Rihyani would last long enough for them to get back as it was. If they retreated to Shatili and tried to form a new plan, they knew they would be returning to watch her die.

"Let's get down there." Milo sighed, shaking his head at the lunacy of the direction. "Maybe we can find something to help us figure out what happened to the marquis' valley. Maybe they left some sign."

Milo didn't have to look at Ambrose to know he was staring at him pityingly.

"Okay, Magus," Ambrose said. "But don't get your hopes…"

Ambrose's voice trailed off, his head cocking to one side. His expression darkened to a vicious scowl.

"They're coming," he snarled, throwing the Rollsy into gear.

Milo stood up and looked behind them, and then swore ferociously as he spotted two of the canvas-backed trucks rolling over the hills toward their position.

"Hold on," Ambrose warned, and they plunged toward the mouth of the gorge.

Milo looked ahead and dared to hope that there among the boulders, the smaller, narrower Rollsy would have a chance to take a path the trucks could not. Considering he'd managed to lose all their fuel, that was about the only hope they had of evading the Americans and their goons. An extended chase was out of the question.

Milo mentally urged the Rollsy to move faster, and as they neared the gorge, he imagined they had begun to move so fast that the air rippled around them. A moment later, he was sure it wasn't his imagination, but a real distortion in the air.

"Milo?" Ambrose called, an anxious edge in his voice.

"I have no idea," Milo confessed at the top of his lungs as they plowed on. The entire gorge wobbled and flexed like water before their eyes.

Then, as if emerging from underwater, they roared into a wooded vale where the dying sun lit the mist beneath the boughs on fire.

Ambrose swore as he looked around in utter wonder at the soaring evergreens standing sentinel over the vale, each taller than any tree he'd ever seen. The gorge wasn't only verdant but also larger, wider, and deeper than he would have thought possible.

Both men gawked, for a moment forgetting they were being pursued by violent men in a flash of childlike wonder.

Then they realized that they were racing at breakneck speed toward a wall of trees.

14

THE SACRIFICE

Ambrose swore and sawed the wheel with reckless abandon.

The Rollsy began to slide sideways, throwing up a sheet of water as it skidded through the shallows of a pebbled riverbank that hadn't been there moments ago. Ambrose bellowed several colorful curses in French as the Rollsy refused to respond. The drag of the water and the tires plowing through sand robbed them of some momentum, but not enough as the vehicle skidded free of the shore and slung around toward a towering pine. Milo braced for the impact as the barked column consumed his view of the world.

The Rollsy hit the tree broadside, crumpling the armored flank on Milo's side in a sense-blasting crash.

There were a low hiss and several heavy clunks beneath the hood of the vehicle, and the engine died with a dull clinking sputter. For a moment, nothing stirred in the wood except the languid curls of mist and the soft burbles of the gentle river. The entire mouth of the vale seemed to be holding its breath after the violence of the impact, waiting in trepidation for something to stir in the wreckage.

Ambrose was first, slumping in his seat after unpeeling his

hands from the wheel with a groan. He looked at Milo, saw the steady rise and fall of the magus' chest; there was cause to be hopeful he would wake soon. He gave a low sigh and slowly squirmed around to fetch his discarded weapons from the back of the cab.

Milo woke with a start a few seconds later and then gave a grunt as he twisted his head to elicit several loud pops. His body was stiff and unsteady, but he found himself thankful as he looked down and saw the buckled-in door. His unmolested leg lay less than a finger's breadth from where the metal had imploded into the cab, rending through the cushion of the seat.

"That could have been worse," Milo hissed as he forced his sore body to move, shuffling clear of the collapsed door.

"We need to get into the trees," Ambrose said as he made to swing out of the cab. "If we could get through, there's no reason that they can't follow us here."

As though in affirmation, the rumble of engines sounded from where they'd come. They weren't coming as fast, but there was no mistaking that they were indeed coming down into the valley. Milo let a hand stray to the knife in his coat and wondered if it would be better to toss it into the river. He considered coming before the marquis empty-handed, but then he thought about the trucks rolling in with Ezekiel, and he imagined dragging the monstrous man before the marquis.

Why settle for the hexed knife when the recipient of the curse was right there?

Milo sprang out of the Rollsy and scuttled over to Ambrose, who busied himself checking his weapons and ammunition. His Gewehr and bandoleer were nowhere to be seen, but one of the stocky carbines was over his shoulder, and he was busy yanking the oddly layered magazines out of the other two carbines and stuffing the reloads into his pockets.

"It's our turn to do the ambushing," Milo said, pointing with his cane out of the vale, where the sound of the trucks was growing ever louder. "I need you to help me pull it off."

Ambrose frowned as his gaze swept across the vale, and he turned in a small, shuffling circle. He sighted down the carbine barrel at the mouth of the vale, mustache twitching, then looked back among the mist-swathed trees. Milo didn't need the big man to say anything to tell him he didn't like the setup, but the engines revved, and a bloodthirsty "YEEHAW!" echoed around them.

"They have us outnumbered," Ambrose noted flatly. "And we know as much about this terrain as they do."

"Sure." Milo shrugged and threw his best devil-may-care smile. "But we've got something that evens all that out."

Ambrose's brows knitted as he gave Milo a bemused look.

"Magic?" he asked, his head tilting to one side.

"Not a bad guess." Milo grinned. "But I was talking about you, my avenging angel."

To punctuate the point, Milo punched the big man's shoulder, which turned out to be as good an idea as punching the tree that had nearly smashed the Rollsy. Milo shook his tingling fingers as Ambrose rolled his eyes.

"One other thing," Milo said, the smile dropping as he continued to shake out his hand. "We'll be taking the cowboy captive, so you're going to have to hold off on your promise to chop him to bits."

Ambrose looked unhappier about that caveat than anything Milo had suggested thus far. Head shaking, he turned toward the trees and unslung the stolen rifle from his shoulder.

"Come on." Ambrose set off toward the woods, moving as quickly as he dared over the obscured ground.

Before turning to follow, Milo drew out the knife, still in its bag leather bag, hefting it in his hand.

"Sniff this out," he spat and sent the knife tumbling end over end into the river.

Behind him, he heard the engines baying, and he stole a glance over his shoulder to see a pair of headlights glowing in the enchanted fog. Milo looked back at the forest, where Ambrose had shuffled behind a colossal tree trunk. The purple of evening had settled over the valley, and as it deepened before his eyes, Milo felt a tingle of fear. The woods exuded a sinister, primordial aura, and Milo remembered Imrah's shade telling him of horrors hanging bones and skin from the trees.

"Just remember I'm on your side," he whispered as he loped between the trees.

The mist swallowed them, a strange, almost perverse amniotic experience.

The air was close and moist, and everything seemed to press in around them. Sounds, strange calls, and croaks that came from no animal humans had ever heard of echoed and warbled on the watery air. The weight of the trees bore down on them, and both were soon crouching under the subconscious pressure.

Ambrose's gaze swept left and right, searching for a suitable spot to stage their ambush, but the deeper they went, the closer the trees seemed to be. Soon there was nothing to do but shuffle down the narrow path between looming trunks and drooping branches. Twice they stopped dead when something long and pale darted across the path, but each time neither could remember what they'd seen and despite several seconds' pause, there was no sign of the creature returning.

After a few minutes, Milo was certain he'd made a terrible mistake suggesting they try to ambush their pursuers, and he almost asked Ambrose if they were lost and needed to retrace their steps. Then silvery light shone in front of them, and without a word between them, they both quickened their pace to escape the oppression of that arboreal corridor. Just before they burst from under the trees, Milo could have sworn that he could hear them creaking as though tightening around them.

They emerged in a small glade, where a series of six tall stones, three to a side, flanked a moss-speckled patch of flagstones. The rough-hewn obelisks were covered in thickly daubed and crudely depicted eyes marked with blinding slashes. In the moon-cast shadows of the stones, they saw bones through which grew thick vines.

Milo fought back a shiver.

"So," Ambrose said, looking around the glade but avoiding the standing stones. "This will work better than anything else. I expect they'll have to come the same way we did, which means that they'll probably rush in here, either because they're on our trail or they just want to get out of the woods."

Milo nodded, then looked back the way they'd come. The shadowed path was dark and narrow, certainly, but on this side, the terror they'd both felt could only be explained by the pervasive magic Milo felt coursing through the air. It was not just the tingling, but he most certainly felt something stirring around them, almost like a vast, sleepy presence yawning. Inside the tunnel of trees, they'd felt the weight of its half-awake stare, dull but terrible.

"Which means I'm going to be at their backs," Ambrose explained, pointing at a shallow gap in the trees by the glade entrance. "This rifle seemed potent enough when the mercenaries were using them, so I should be able to drop a few of them. I expect when they turn around to return fire, you can step in. Figure you can roast a few of them, Magus?"

The question woke Milo out of his enraptured staring, and his brain scrambled to recollect what his ears had been hearing.

"Um, uh, yeah," Milo said, trying to shake off the feeling of that huge presence bending low to squint at him. "So, where do I need to be?"

Ambrose scratched his cheek.

"Somewhere with solid enough cover that I don't have to worry about a stray shot hitting you," Ambrose told him, slowly dragging his eyes over to the standing stones. "One of those would fit the bill if you could stand it."

Milo looked at the adorned heathen stones and the bones splayed at their feet and found himself hesitating. He tried to tell himself that after his time among the ghuls of Ifreedahm, this was a simple thing, but the supernatural presence that settled over him had rendered everything about the vale menacing.

But Milo had spent his entire life fighting scared, and ominous homicidal forest or no, he wasn't about to back down from a couple of painted rocks.

"Yeah," he almost growled, his lips curling back from his teeth. "I can do that. Just make sure you keep your head down when I start the cookout."

Milo looked over and saw Ambrose smiling at him.

"You almost make me believe this isn't a bad idea." He chuckled before moving toward his hiding spot.

"You're saying this might work?" Milo called over his shoulder as he marched determinedly toward the row of stones.

"Let's not get ahead of ourselves," the big man replied without looking back.

Milo carefully maneuvered his feet around the bones as he glanced around the standing stone. Then the mercenaries filed into the glade.

The first three emerged with their rifles at their shoulders, sweeping left and right, their bodies illuminated in uncommonly bright moonlight.

Even from this distance, Milo could see the men were unsettled, their movements jerky, eyes bulging. When nothing immediately sprang at them, they motioned back down the forest path.

There were sounds of more men coming while the vanguard held their position, doing their best to stay on guard while avoiding the sight of the standing stones.

Standing close to the stones, his nostrils full of the smell of rot and old earth, Milo understood the feeling.

Watching the mercenaries, something like pity rose up in the magus' chest as he imagined being one of the poor wretches, no doubt roped into the job with promises and threats or both, now seeing their numbers whittled down to half a dozen or so frightened men who were so far out of their depth it ceased to be funny. Milo wanted to hate them because hating them made everything easier, but he couldn't manage it.

Luckily for him, a voice he did hate sounded from the forest path.

"Tell this yellow saddle-sore he best get back to his job," Ezekiel Boucher snarled, a hint of a giggle in the back of his throat. "I'd hate to have to remind 'im how to settle a negotiation."

"Please, Mr. Boucher," Percy Astor said with forced patience as they emerged into the glade. "I trust you to handle certain portions of our operation. I ask you to let me handle my portion without interference."

Ezekiel came into the glade, Ambrose's Gewehr in his hands. To Milo's supreme irritation, there wasn't a burn on the cowboy or his grotesque outfit. Milo still wanted to end the curse to save Rihyani, but he had a new secondary objective for seeing the magic undone: to hurt Ezekiel Boucher.

"Captain Saakadze," Percy said in Georgian as he followed the scalp hunter out. The captain was a fiercely mustachioed man in a black chokha, hot on his heels. "I can understand your trepidation at the progression of events, but that is why we agreed to pay you a very handsome sum, including for those unfortunate enough to have lost their lives in this endeavor."

The man in the chokha who must have been Captain

Saakadze shook his head hard enough to make the tips of his mustache waggle.

"It is not a matter of money," the mercenary commander declared in a sharp tone that softened as he snatched a nervous glance around the glade. "All the money in the world is of no use if we are all dead. You don't know the stories they tell of this vale."

Astor and Ezekiel paused and shared a look Milo couldn't read from his hiding spot. Both men turned to Saakadze, their posture almost eager.

"What stories?" Percy demanded.

Saakadze balked under their combined scrutiny, his weathered features paling before he gathered himself. Straightening and clearing his throat to speak matter-of-factly, he managed to meet both men's eyes.

"The Lost Vale is a warning to rebellious children and a ghost story," the commander said, his face coloring at the admission, which was all the more striking for how pale he'd been. "Runaway brides disappear when they go to the Dobilni that live within the vale or invading armies being led into the Vale to never again emerge except as wails of dying men."

"You're telling us this now?" Ezekiel snorted, a titter at the back of his throat. "When we're already in here? Sounds like too little, too late, partner?"

Saakadze didn't bother to hide his disgust for the scalp hunter.

"I thought they were just stories!" he growled, hands tightening on his carbine. "It wasn't until the gorge turned into this place that I realized what was happening, and then you were racing off to chase them!"

Ezekiel spat at the commander's feet but turned to Percy, lifting the brim of his hat with a thumb.

"You figure those pixie lovers went to ground because they

got friends here?" Ezekiel asked before throwing a look over his shoulder at the standing stones.

Mr. Astor nodded as he gingerly massaged his bandaged hand.

"There is more than a good chance," Percy said, his voice dropping so Milo strained to hear each word. "Which would make pursuing them further highly inadvisable."

Milo silently swore as he felt the moment slipping away.

The three mercenaries running point were in sight of Ambrose's position, but the rest were too far back. Having thrown the knife away, they needed to take Ezekiel, but if they pulled back, there was no reason to think they'd have a better shot, and they didn't have time to track him down again. They needed to give them a reason to move into the glade.

"Making a bad idea worse." Milo sighed and then stepped out from behind the standing stone.

The raptor skull crackled with unnatural fire in anticipation of Milo's will, and the sight caused the mercenaries to falter and gasp.

BURN

Two bolts lanced out from the sockets, dazzling the mercenaries' eyes with the sudden, fierce light that went hissing over their heads. Milo had been aiming for Ezekiel, but the fiery darts missed him by scant centimeters as he twisted away and dived for a tree. Return fire from the mercenaries was spotty at first. Two shots went wide into the forest, while a third kicked up earth a few meters from Milo's foot. More shots came, but the magus had ducked behind the standing stone, though he tried not to flinch and wince when he heard rounds whining away into the dark after striking the shielding stone.

"I told you!" Ezekiel howled from his arboreal cover. "The gangly one's a conjurer!"

"Must be the staff," Percy hissed venomously. In answer, Milo swung around and loosed another pair of bolts, which Percy only avoided by falling flat as soon as he appeared. Milo was chased back into cover by a much more accurate volley of fire, one shot zipping close enough to crease the arm of his coat.

A very undignified curse escaped Percy Astor's lips as he scrambled on his belly to hide behind his own tree. He drew out his pistol and then raised his voice to an imperious shout.

"The one in the black coat must be taken alive. Do you hear me? Alive!"

"Are you mad?" Captain Saakadze cried.

"Get the rear guard up here," Ezekiel called as he swung forward to fire the Gewehr before Milo could emerge for another blast of witchfire. "And keep an eye out for the fat one."

The resignation in Captain Saakadze's voice was palpable, but he shouted back down the forest path, and Milo heard the rush of feet coming down toward the glade between the crackle of suppressive fire hammering at the stone.

Soon they'd have enough to flank his position, coming at him from too many angles to counter them all at once. He needed to give Ambrose a better shot before that.

Steeling his nerves, Milo willed the beak open and darted to the other side of the stone to spray a torrent of green flame. He expected it would be a distraction, an impotent show of force before he raced back to the second stone in his row. As it was, one of the mercenaries had advanced several strides since opening fire.

The belch of flame bowled him back and set him alight.

He didn't even have time to scream as Milo's sudden appearance filled his startled lungs with hungry flames. His body spasmed on the ground, and a single round from his carbine flew off into the dark. Whether the shot came from the superheated metal or an expiring twitch, Milo never knew.

Milo continued the sweep of the flame and caught another advancing mercenary, but the man was farther from the blast, so only one side of him kindled. To Milo's horror, the man screamed but did not go down as flames licked his body. The magus was ducking back behind the standing stone when the burning man let out a blood-chilling shriek and charged Milo, firing from the hip as he went.

None of the mad shots struck home, but that didn't deter the flaming mercenary, who gripped his smoldering gun like a club and launched himself at the magus. His body reacting before his mind could calculate a response, Milo turned the wild swing aside with his cane, just as Ambrose had shown him, and then snapped the shaft of the cane up and across. The blow took the pain-maddened man across the unburned side of his face, resulting in a spray of blood and teeth.

Reflexively Milo swept the cane down hard on the man's exposed wrists, sending the carbine-cudgel tumbling among the vine-wrapped bones. Snarling and spitting crimson froth, the mercenary lunged at Milo to trap him in a fiery embrace, but the magus pivoted back. The man stumbled, and with the moment of respite, Milo drew on the potency of the staff.

The burning man rose as Milo swept the cane out in a two-handed stroke. The stone shaft connected with the man's neck, shattering vertebrae, but its arc would not be denied as it drove his flaming head to crash into the standing stone. There was a sickening, squelching crack as the man's head deformed against the stone.

The slashed eyes stenciled across the stone seemed to glint as though each had received a fresh spattering of blood, and Milo felt the magical presence stir violently. His skin erupted in goose-flesh, and at his feet, fresh vines burst from the ground to coil around the body of the dead mercenary. Milo lurched back a few steps, horrified as the thick tendrils of plant matter smothered the lingering flames and dug deep in the open wounds like carrion worms searching for choice morsels.

He was so overcome he didn't realize he'd moved too far from his cover, and a shot ripped a bloody furrow across his calf.

Milo's leg buckled underneath him, and he pitched backward to the ground, shock robbing him of his voice.

"Ezekiel, you idiot!" Percy shouted from his hiding place behind the tree. "We need him alive."

"Cease fire!" Captain Saakadze shouted.

"Hold your horses, Percy. I just winged him." The cowboy chuckled. "Damned fine shot if I do say so."

His breath whistled between Milo's teeth as throbs of agony rolled up through his leg. In the back of his head, a voice was screaming for him to focus and grab the unguents from his coat, but by the time he'd gotten organized enough for the effort, hard hands were grabbing him and rolling him over. At one point, what must have been a foot brushed his wounded leg, and he let out a snarl of pain and thrashed. A knee was planted in his back, and he felt a barrel being pressed against the back of his head.

"Don't move," shouted a voice Milo was sure couldn't have come from a man any older than himself.

"Alive!" Percy called. "I need him alive."

"It's a witch!" Milo heard one of the mercenaries shout in Georgian.

"A *kudiani!*" another cried. "Iacob, don't touch it!"

"You let him go, and I'll drop you where you stand." Ezekiel's voice was much closer than before. "Keep him right there, and I'll hogtie the little witch."

Milo tried to twist his head around to see what was happening and caught a glimpse of the glade filling with the rest of the mercenaries and the advancing cowboy before his captor reacted.

"Face-down," a wide-eyed teen growled at him before ramming the barrel into Milo's face.

The unforgiving rim jammed hard enough into Milo's eyebrow to break the skin, and his blood dripped onto the soil. Between spasms of pain from his leg, he wondered if the gore-hungry vines would be drawn by his blood, it being so near, but a glance showed they hadn't moved an inch. All the same, he thought he should keep a weather eye on the earth as droplets of blood dripped from the corner of his eye. It turned out that he wouldn't have to keep his vigil long.

He heard Ezekiel's perpetual snuffling giggle nearly on top of him when Ambrose decided now was the time to open fire. The carbine roared from within the trees, and Milo felt something hot and wet spatter across the back of his neck. The weight on his back vanished. Careful of his leg, he rolled over as Ambrose hammered out a pair of shots. Milo saw Ezekiel pitch forward with a mad guffaw as another mercenary, one who must have been in the rear guard, slumped sideways with a shocked mewling sound. Captain Saakadze took a round through the shoulder and fell, but to his credit, he twisted as he dropped, attempting to bring his carbine to bear one-handed. Two more rounds punched through his chest as he hit the ground, and when the dust settled, he lay motionless and glassy-eyed.

Percy and the remaining two mercenaries ran for cover behind the standing stone opposite Milo's, chased by two more shots before a sharp *plink* sounded from Ambrose's sniper's roost.

The American and his goons seemed to understand the significance of the sound and swung clear of the cover they'd just entered to pour a torrent of leaden fire into the woods. Had Milo been paying attention, he might have laughed at the way their shots scattered like mad hail, none going anywhere near Ambrose except by accident, but he was otherwise occupied.

Ezekiel was on his hands and knees less than two meters from the magus, a strange sucking sound coming from his chest as he coughed out a garbled chuckle. Blood frothed from his lips began to well up from inside his buckskins in time with the sucking noise. Milo dared to hope that Ambrose had struck something vital in the fiendish scalp hunter, his pain-addled mind thinking of old stories of killing horrors with a wound through the heart.

Ezekiel gave an ecstatic heaving laugh and expelled a spray of blood upon the ground in front of him. Milo's stomach sank as he saw the clear glint of metal amidst the blood coating the ground, then the cowboy's Cheshire-cat smile over the bullet.

"My turn," he said, and his bloody smile gleamed black in the moonlight.

A corroded pistol slid free of the cowboy's belt as Milo scrambled back, hands groping around him for his cane.

Since the shooting had begun, none had noticed the growing sound of many large forms moving through the trees. Milo only became aware of the thunderous approach as imminent death sharpened his senses to a razor's edge and time seemed to slow. The rushing creak and groan of heavy limbs shouldered aside proved a counterpoint to the slow mechanical click of Ezekiel's pistol hammer being drawn back, while the dull thud of broad, heavy feet juxtaposed the sharp, incessant barks of gunfire.

Ezekiel grinned malevolently as he made a show of taking his aim, but his eyes widened comically as Milo felt something immense looming over him.

Milo had an impression of huge legs swathed in metallic scale greaves—or was it the creature's skin?—passing over him, then one elephantine foot descended upon Ezekiel. The cowboy's pistol fired up into the foot, but it didn't slow the step that smashed his body flat to the ground. Milo felt the impact reverberate up through the earth.

The other leg passed overhead. Milo flinched under its shadow, but it came to rest several meters away. Milo beheld the huge, vaguely humanoid shape before him, two huge legs leading to a massive abdomen that was girdled with patchwork leathers that could have served as sails before muscle-mounded shoulders emerged with several lumpy, hairy heads at the apex.

The gunfire in the glade ceased as every eye fell upon the many-headed giant whose enormous back was still to Milo as it stood upon the twitching body of Ezekiel.

"I AM BAKBAK-DEVI," the giant rumbled from several

throats at once, the sound like a chorus from the bowels of the earth. "I COME TO HONOR THE SACRIFICE. CEASE YOUR QUARRELS. THIS PLACE IS HALLOWED."

Without a word, all weapons were lowered, and an eerie calm descended over the glade.

Bakbak-Devi pivoted, foot still grinding the pitifully fidgeting body of the scalp hunter, then stooped to regard Milo with a host of yellow eyes, several of which did not occur in pairs.

"YOU ARE WELCOME, SUPPLICANT," the giant said, its faces breaking into tusk-snarled grins. "IT HAS BEEN SOME TIME SINCE ANY OFFERED A LIFE OF THEIR OWN KIND UPON THE STONES."

Milo's eyes strayed to the vine-smothered corpse, and his stomach knotted.

"I am looking for the marquis," Milo said, doing his best to push down the revulsion rising within him. "I need his help."

The Lernaean ogre drew back, and for a single trembling second, Milo wondered if he'd said something to offend it. Its yellow gaze narrowed, and it stooped even lower to draw in a heavy sniff with several snouts.

"YES, YOU HAVE BEEN AMONG THE FOLK," Babak-Devi declared, then with impressive gentleness, extended a hand to help Milo to his feet. "COME WITH ME, AND I WILL MAKE YOUR INTRODUCTIONS."

"I have a friend here with me," Milo called to the giant as he rose, balancing on his uninjured leg. "He will be coming with me."

With a rustle and snapping of twigs, Ambrose emerged from his spot and rushed over to Milo's side, snatching up the magus' cane and the Gewehr on his way over. Bakbak-Devi watched without comment, only straightening so Ambrose could slide a shoulder under Milo's arm.

"Thanks for not forgetting me," Ambrose muttered as he handed over the cane.

"Don't mention it," Milo said out the corner of his mouth as he continued to watch the giant. "Just next time, don't wait until I'm bleeding to start shooting. I'm tired of fixing this leg."

A wounded looked passed over Ambrose's face, but he hid it behind a cheery smile at the many watching faces.

"Ready when you are, big guy," he called up with forced verve.

Bakbak-Devi nodded and turned to go when two barks of a pistol pierced the stillness of the glade.

The giant spun back with frightening speed for a creature the size of a house, while Ambrose swung Milo around like a ragdoll to shield the magus with his body. The two remaining Georgians toppled over, bullet holes in their heads, as their blood and gray matter woke the standing stone they were standing next to. Percy Astor slowly lowered his pistol, his bandaged hand held up placatingly.

"My sacrifice made, I would also like to be introduced to the marquis," the American declared in a calm, clear voice before nodding at the smeared bottom of the giant's foot. "I will also be needing my companion to join me if you would be so kind."

15

——

THE AUDIENCE

With firm strokes of his punting pole, Bakbak-Devi propelled their raft up the languid river and into the deepening beauty of the Lost Vale. The moon crowned the sky, and its silver light danced across the dark pines. Each one seemed plated in the precious metal, argent needles susurrating softly on the wind. Down amongst the trunks, the mist wound and flowed with currents of its own, and upon those ephemeral streams could be seen miniscule shapes flashing and glinting like fireflies in shades of blue, yellow, and green to reveal tiny imitations of horses, serpents, and men, all borne on gossamer wings. Milo spotted stags and leopards moving amongst the mist, breaching the foggy tides like antlered leviathans or golden-eyed whales, barely sparing the humans a look as they went about their nightly business.

Drifting over everything was a sense of wonder as palpable as a haunting melody that was just beyond hearing, yet all this grandeur was wasted on the men on the raft. Seated upon pine stumps, they paid no heed to the enchanted wood unfolding around them, only having time to share suspicious glares.

"I still can't believe we ain't shootin' 'em both."

Percy gave a heavy sigh and pinched the bridge of his nose vigorously.

"And that is why you have your job and I have mine," he said sullenly under his breath before turning to Milo and Ambrose with an apologetic smile. "I'm terribly sorry. I could make excuses for him, but they'd never be sufficient. I'll have to beg your indulgence a while longer."

Milo, having been forced to repair his leg with healing unguents with both men looking over his shoulder, was not in the most diplomatic of moods.

"Don't worry," Milo replied coolly. "The feeling is mutual."

Ambrose gave a low grunt of assent.

"I'm sorry to hear that." Percy sighed, raising a hand to tip his hat. "Then I suppose we are better served by fixing our attention on the scenery."

Milo made a hard thrust with his chin and bared his teeth in a smile to challenge the one the scalp hunter wore.

"You first," he snarled through the unfriendly grin.

Shaking his head, the American turned his back to them. Ezekiel sat looking askance at Milo and Ambrose, his tongue lapping across his stained, smiling teeth. It was galling and terrifying in equal measure that even after being ground to paste under the ogre's foot, Ezekiel had recovered in minutes unmarked and unfazed. Milo felt a quiver of uncertainty as he stared into the dark, mirthless eyes.

For all his giggles and grinning, Ezekiel Boucher's eyes were as cold and soulless as anything Milo had seen in his short, terrible life, and that included the ghuls of Ifreedahm.

"Don't worry, I still owe you a barkin', partner," the cowboy cooed as he reached out to tickle the scalps hanging from his indestructible buckskins. "I haven't forgotten."

Milo was about to form a retort, but before he could say anything, a pine stump hurtled through the air and took Ezekiel in the chest. The slight man's chest buckled with a tremendous crack as the hefty disc of wood carried him over the edge of the boat. Percy gave a subdued "Oh, goodness" as he shifted away from the water thrown up by Ezekiel's exit from the raft, but soon returned to staring out across the Vale.

Milo looked to see Ambrose standing over him, limbs trembling with rage as he spat curses of remarkable poetry and potency in French.

"Thanks," Milo said, but the big man didn't seem to hear him.

Bakbak-Devi paused from his punting to dip his pole into the river, while half his faces turned to frown at Ambrose.

"DO NOT DO THAT AGAIN," the giant instructed, his tone as firm and long-suffering as someone speaking to a particularly willful child. "THE HEXED ONE IS A GUEST OF THE MARQUIS SAME AS YOU, GEHENNA-GET. DO NOT TEST MY MASTER'S HOSPITALITY OR MY PATIENCE FURTHER."

For a single moment, Ambrose looked as though he would challenge the many-headed ogre, but with a long trembling breath, he let the tension slide from his shoulders. His limbs ceased to quiver, and he gave a slow nod as he bowed his shoulders slightly.

"I understand," he said solemnly. "My apologies to you and to your master."

Bakbak-Devi returned the nod and turned all his faces to the river.

"Gehenna-get?" Milo asked softly, eliciting a shrug from Ambrose.

"A new one for me," the big man confessed, crossing his arms.

Milo frowned as he turned back and noticed Percy watching Ambrose intently, a curious gleam in his eye. It only lasted a second before he turned back to contemplating the river and the forest, but at that moment, a swelling sense of dread plucked warningly across his spine.

Just then, the punting pole emerged from the water with a sodden Ezekiel clinging to the timber. His hair and hat hung down, so he looked one step above a drowning victim, but his smile still stretched from ear to ear.

With his peculiar gentleness, Bakbak-Dovi deposited the cowboy on the raft and proceeded to send them gliding up the river.

"I notice you have no apology for my compatriot," Mr. Astor stated as he continued watching the vista beyond the boat.

"I most certainly do not," Ambrose rumbled.

"Oh, that's all right, Percy." Ezekiel chuckled as he rose to shake the water from his hat.

He turned to grin at Ambrose.

"Better luck next time, big fella,"

Ambrose grinned back but didn't budge otherwise.

"It was the smell, sweetie. Didn't want to spend any more time having to smell you."

The manse of the marquis sprawled past the water's edge, a vast estate whose whitewashed walls swept in a wide arc that formed a harbor in the midst of the river. Between these lantern-hung arms stood a dock whose planks were richly engraved with glowing patterns of knots and whorls, all of which seemed to move when Milo wasn't looking directly at them. The illuminated boards stretched from the dock up to form stairs to a hedgerow gate that led to the manse's gardens.

"Impressive," Percy commented, looking up at the giant. "It bears a striking resemblance to Château de Kerjean."

The many heads nodded.

"THE MARQUIS WOULD BE PLEASED TO HEAR YOU SAY SO," Bakbak-Devi replied. "HE RENOVATED THE MANOR AFTER VISITING HIS COUSIN IN THE FOREST OF BROCÉLIANDE AND TOURING THE DUCHY."

"Fey go on holiday?" Ambrose asked.

"I guess so," Milo muttered distractedly, his attention divided between watching the Americans and surveying the manor. The architecture and subsequent historical implications were lost on him, but Milo felt the power vibrating off the construction. The closer they drew to it, the more potent that was until Milo felt it as a low tingle across his skin. Like the hex upon the knife, it was different from essence or shades—less focused, yet more fluid and lively, and it saturated the structure. As the raft slid up to the dock, Milo wondered how much of what he saw was physical objects, stone, wood, mortar, and how much was some magical simulation of the material.

Bakbak-Devi lashed the raft to the dock and then led them across the boards to land.

"THE SECOND SUPPLICANTS SHALL BE INTRODUCED FIRST," the giant explained as he ushered them off the raft as gently as a mother hen. "AGAIN, I WILL REMIND YOU TO BE RESPECTFUL TO EACH OTHER FOR THE SAKE OF YOUR HOST. BREACHES IN COURTESY CAN HAVE SERIOUS CONSEQUENCES."

So warned, the Americans and then Milo and Ambrose followed him up the dock and to the hedge gate. Milo expected the Bakbak-Devi to produce an immense key or parlay with an eldritch gatekeeper, but instead, the ogrish servant waved a hand, and the gate swung open silently. Again, Milo felt a tickle of magic, but it was almost imperceptible amongst the background hum of so much magic around him.

Past the gate, they walked through a topiary garden where the plants had been worked into masterful statues of men and women at rest or at play. Their craftsmanship was so incredibly lifelike it took Milo a second to realize something was wrong when one of them raised its head from contemplating a small pool and gave a slight nod of greeting. Milo stared and then waved back.

Milo could animate a corpse through binding a shade or make

a wooden statue amble about, powered by a specter, but this was different. This was a living being, reshaped and elevated beyond its simplistic foundations, possibly even given a kind of sentience. Wonder and a jealous hunger to know more raced through Milo.

He was so distracted that he almost trod on Percy's heels, but Ambrose caught him by the shoulder. They stood in front of a vast round hedge that grew to eye-level with Bakbak-Devi, and inside could be heard the soft strum of harps and the murmur of comfortable conversation. Set into the hedge was a portal of Corinthian columns with a velvet curtain draped across the opening. Bakbak-Devi put a hand to the curtain and slid partially through before pausing to turn half his heads toward them.

"WAIT HERE."

Then, quicker and smoother than any creature so large had a right to, he disappeared through the portal. The music beyond the curtain stilled as the giant spoke to someone within, but the words were muffled and indistinct.

The Americans held a brief whispered conference while Milo and Ambrose moved shoulder to shoulder.

Ambrose muttered under his breath, "You did want to bring the cowboy along to show the marquis. Looks like you got your wish."

Milo eyed the whispering duo like he would a pair of vipers.

"I wanted to bring him in as a prisoner, not a guest," he spat. "I'm not sure I like the idea of them getting the first crack at the marquis. Ezekiel may be a bloody-minded idiot, but the snake in silk isn't. Whatever happened to first come, first served?"

"Old school etiquette, I think," Ambrose offered. "The last one into the room is the boss, last to sit is head of the table, the last one introduced is the one most honored."

"Let's hope," Milo said. "We need to get the marquis' help, and then we need to get back to the Rollsy. Can you get it working?"

Ambrose frowned and shrugged.

"Maybe," he said. "I won't know until we get back and I have a chance to look things over, but worse comes to worst, I know where we can get a truck."

He gave a slight nod toward the Americans, whose conversation had become more animated, Mr. Astor pointing a finger in Ezekiel's face repeatedly.

"I'd be worried a mad dog like Boucher would bite my finger off if I did that," Milo said at a volume that made it clear he didn't care if he was overheard. "That's the problem with those kinds of pets, isn't it, Ambrose?"

Ambrose crossed his arms over his chest and nodded grimly.

"True enough. They'll turn on you eventually, mark my words."

Ezekiel's smile stretched with each word until it was nearly a grimace when he turned to look at them. Percy whispered something sharply to the cowboy, but his words went unheeded, so he turned back to the curtain, his face in his palm.

"Funny thing you talkin' about turnin', seein' as you both turned your backs on your own kind." The scalp hunter tittered. "I may be a bad *hombre*, but at least I don't sign my soul away to work for 'em."

"I always heard Americans were ignorant," Ambrose shot back. "I see you're an exceptional example of your kind."

Percy sniffed at the remark but refused to turn around, while Ezekiel's wormy tongue played across his stained smile.

"I am what I am, damnation and all," the scalp hunter said at last, absently raising a hand to stroke the forelocks dangling from his arms. "But you yellow-bellied, back-shootin', pixie-lovin' sons o—"

The curtain suddenly drew back, and the many faces of Bakbak-Devi loomed over them.

"IT IS TIME, COME."

"Thank goodness," Percy groaned, and he and Ezekiel made to follow.

Milo and Ambrose caught a brief glimpse of a wide green space where plumes of smoke rose from braziers to cast everything in a soporific haze. Wavering like heat mirages, they saw strange and elegant creatures reclined upon couches and divans before a small but ornate pavilion.

Then the curtain fell.

"Maybe the marquis could help us with transportation," Milo said as they stood straining and failing to hear what was happening within. "Riding the wind like Rihyani does could put us back there quicker than driving, though I'd hate to leave the car."

"One favor at a time," Ambrose replied, casting a look over one shoulder then the other. "We're not even sure this marquis will help us."

Milo turned from staring at the curtain to meet Ambrose's gaze.

"I don't think Rihyani would send us here if we couldn't expect help."

He hadn't meant to sound so hot and scolding, but the words came out sizzling, and Ambrose raised one eyebrow and gave a significant pause before responding.

"I think Rihyani was desperate, like we all were," the big man said slowly. "She pointed us at our best shot, but that doesn't mean things are going to go smooth. I mean, she did say it would take some convincing. I think it would be better to go in assuming we're going to have to earn our miracle, rather than expecting it."

Milo bit back the irritated retort he felt surging up from his gut, taking time to nod. Even if Ambrose was wrong, it wouldn't hurt them to proceed with caution. Rushing things had more potential to foul them up than help.

"You're right, good point," Milo said and turned back to the curtain to stare until a thought struck him. "Doesn't it seem strange that once again, we are stuck waiting to be introduced to some magical despot?"

"Let's hope this one goes smoother." Ambrose huffed as he looked forlornly at the Gewehr on his shoulder. "I haven't got any ammunition for her yet."

"You've still got that," Milo said, nodding at the carbine strapped to his back. "And from what happened in the grove, I'd say it works fine."

"Machine-operated action, self-ejecting," Ambrose said, and Milo wasn't sure if it was disgust or awe in his voice. "Even a child could put eight rounds downwind without pause."

Milo studied his bodyguard's face, but the usually expressive features had formed into a sort of mask. Ambrose was locked away with thoughts he wasn't interested in expressing, but Milo thought he saw some of that same fear and despair that he had seen on the balcony.

"Sounds like it will come in handy if things go like they did last time," Milo said, hoping to coax him out of his malaise. "If we ever get to step past this damned curtain."

Beyond the curtain, there was a sound like raised voices. Both men paused, waiting for the many-headed ogre to emerge, but the shouting quieted, and their wait continued.

"I knew an American, different sort than those two, who served in the French Foreign Legion with me." Ambrose chuckled, his eyes sliding out of the middle distance. "He used to say that a soldier's business was largely a matter of hurry up and wait."

Milo sighed. "I suppose a magus' life is much the same."

"We're all prisoners in a world of petty tyrants." Ambrose grunted. "At least until we carve out our own little fiefdom. Then we get our turn, assuming we make it that far."

"You read that line in a book." Milo snorted with a sidelong glance.

"Nope, just a little nugget I've been polishing," Ambrose

replied loftily. "Thought I'd share it with someone who could use it."

"Thanks, but maybe you should keep your nuggets to yourself."

Ambrose pointedly refused to meet the long look Milo gave him.

"You still aren't as funny as you seem to think you are."

The curtain parted and the giant beckoned them.

The Marquis of the Lost Vale sat quietly in the shadow of his pavilion. Two braziers wafted fragrant smoke that filled the tent, so throughout his retelling, Milo could only see the vaguest impression of a seated tall figure. The marquis' sandaled feet and long hands were the only things that emerged from the shadow of the tent, pearlescent and sharp-clawed. In one elegant hand was a goblet that seemed to be fashioned from polished granite, which the fey would occasionally draw into the shadows to drink from. Milo imagined he saw two glinting eyes within the deep shade.

The marquis had listened without comment as Milo had told the story of Rihyani's injuries at the hands of Ezekiel Boucher and the discovery that her recovery was prevented because of the curse the murderous cowboy bore.

"So Contessa Rihyani sent us to Tsminda Sameba and we met the priest, who instructed us to come here," Milo said, sweat pouring across his whole body despite the coolness of the evening. "We were pursued by the other two supplicants and their mercenaries while following Father Zoidze's instructions."

Ambrose softly cleared his throat, and Milo nodded.

"If their presence has burdened you, we sincerely apologize," Milo added quickly. "We didn't intend for them to follow us."

He forced his eyes to remain fixed on the shadowed figure

inside the cloud of smoke, but he'd noted when they'd first been brought through the curtain that the Americans were nowhere to be seen. Milo couldn't begin to guess whether that was a good or bad thing, but he didn't imagine gawking across the tables would look very dignified.

His story done and his explanations given, Milo stood, arms stiff at his sides, waiting. After talking about his experiences in the court of Ifreedahm, he'd hoped he would be more comfortable with this sort of thing, but he'd found an audience with the Bashlek of Ifreedahm was no proof against the nervous energy that made his legs tremble and his mouth run dry. He felt the eyes of the creatures reclining around him pressing dully, slowly turning screws. More than once, a flash of magic sparked across his supernatural awareness, heightening his discomfort. He wanted to demand an answer or at least a response, but he knew that wasn't likely to produce the results he wanted.

He stood waiting and tried to silence the hammering of his heart in his ears as he forced himself to draw one breath after another.

Milo became aware of that ancient, ponderous presence whose slumber he'd interrupted, and again he felt himself in danger of collapsing under its scrutiny. He wanted to run away mentally as well as physically, but he knew to do that would be to forfeit any hope of saving Rihyani, and that was something he could not, would not accept. He'd come this far; he would not turn aside now.

Thus, he stood and bore the oppressive observation, upright and square-shouldered in both mind and body.

The haze of perfumed smoke stirred, and Milo heard Ambrose shuffle forward a little. Whatever the bodyguard thought was about to happen or what he could do about it, Milo appreciated the reminder that he wasn't alone, whatever was about to happen.

"What is it that you wish of me then?" came a deep, rippling voice from the pavilion.

Milo gaped for a second, not understanding how it could be unclear what he wanted, but certain that pointing such a thing out could only be construed as an insult.

"I want your help in breaking the hex so that the contessa may be healed," Milo said, his tongue sticking a bit at first.

Again, Ambrose gave the gentlest of coughs.

"Please," Milo said. "I want your help, please."

There was another long silence, then the marquis' fingers flexed around his goblet, producing a soft but distinct sound of bone grating against stone.

"If you wish for me to break the curse upon Ezekiel Boucher, I will not, despite how much I should like to," the marquis declared in a tone that brooked no contest or question. "But I can teach you how to loosen the bonds of the hex that has gripped the contessa so she may be healed."

Milo, whose heart had stopped beating when the marquis said he wouldn't break the curse, nearly collapsed with relief.

"Thank you, good Marquis," Milo said with a deep bow. "Thank you."

A single long finger rose, the hooked point of the nail aimed at Milo's heart.

"Yet, though the contessa is distant kin to us, we cannot grant this boon free of cost," the fey said. Milo wondered if the tingle he felt was the slip of the noose around his neck.

"I will do what I can," Milo said carefully, uncertain of what such a powerful being as the marquis could want from him.

"You are the first of your kind who has ever been taught the Art, and even in these dire times, I'd be a fool if I did not extract a geas from you."

Milo frowned but kept his eyes upon the marquis.

"I am not refusing, but I have to admit I do not know what a geas is," he confessed. "I do not want to swear to something I'm not capable of doing. That would dishonor you and put the life of the contessa at risk, both of which I don't want to do."

"Well spoken," the marquis said, and to Milo's surprise, there was genuine warmth in his tone. "I will instruct you on what a geas requires, and then you may give me your answer, though if your intentions are as noble as you claim, I'm certain there will be no contest to the matter. For now, though, I'd have you take your ease and dine with me, as I have other questions to ask you of a less immediate but no less serious nature."

Milo felt his muscles tighten across his whole body, and it was all he could do to keep from shouting "NO!" at the mention of dinner and conversation. It seemed to Milo that the marquis, like so many other petty tyrants, could not imagine a world where their timetable was not the single deciding factor.

"Thank you, and I mean no disrespect, but I'm afraid time is an issue," Milo said, trying to keep the anxiety in his voice in check even as the sincerity of it spilled out. "It took us almost two days to reach your domain, and it will take just as long to return. I'm afraid if things go on much longer, we may lose her."

For the first time since coming before the marquis, the assemblage of fey responded to Milo's words. At first, it was a soft giggle behind Milo, then some heartier chuckles, and then laughter swelled around him, echoing from every direction. He felt his cheeks burn, and a potent if juvenile anger swelled up in him at each wave of laughter that rolled over him.

"I don't understand," Milo said, struggling to keep his tone even. "What is so amusing?"

The marquis, whose voice had not joined the chorus, silenced them all with a wave of this hand.

"Fear not, Magus," the marquis began, his tone warm and sympathetic. "Some forget that the ways and realities of humans are not the ways and realities of our kind. All these things I will explain soon, but first, we must dine. To the manor, my guests."

A cheer went up from the assembled fey, and the murmur of

conversation and the sound of music returned as they rose and began to move toward the manor in cliques and coveys.

Milo turned to Ambrose, anger and despair wrestling for control of his tongue.

"What do we do?"

Ambrose looked around, eyes narrowed.

"Go to dinner, I guess," Ambrose said after a moment's consideration. "He said he wanted to talk to you. Maybe you can convince him that you'll be a lot more fun and festive once Rihyani isn't bleeding to death."

Looking into the inscrutable pavilion where the marquis sat unmoving even as his guests filed past, staring into the swirling smoke, Milo wasn't certain of anything.

THE INTRIGUE

"To the marquis!"

The cry went up for the fourth time and the entire dining hall answered in kind, then the fey downed their various horns, flutes, chalices, and goblets. It seemed that the marquis' guests were eager to celebrate their host, even if he wasn't present. Milo and Ambrose had been ushered in by a corvid butler in the wake of the other guests, but even as they were shooed in by the black-feathered servant, the marquis did not emerge from his tent. Now nearly an hour into the drinking and toasts, the lord of the manor had yet to make an appearance.

Milo ground his teeth as he glared at the drink in his hand, a crystal flute filled with dark wine. The shade of the vintage reminded him of Rihyani's eyes, and that only made the waiting worse.

"Why do you think they laughed?" Ambrose asked in a low voice as he stood with Milo toward the back of the dining hall. While the magus brooded, the bodyguard had watched the grace-ful, glowing fey moving amongst each other, suspicious of every elegant gesture. It seemed he'd decided they were in no imme-diate danger.

Milo shrugged, telling himself to control his temper but feeling as though he could hear the dripping of Rihyani's blood from cursed wounds.

"Maybe they think it's cute how much you care for her?" Ambrose offered as he watched an amazonian fey stride by, muscles rippling beneath her slit corset and skirt of studded leather. At her heels scampered red hounds the size of ponies with black spines running down their backs. Milo couldn't shake the thought that their jowled faces looked a little too human.

"What do you mean?" he asked distractedly as a small man scuttled by, suspended three meters in the air on a quartet of spider legs. The man's face was flushed and his suit coat was liberally stained with wine, or what Milo hoped was wine.

Ambrose stepped back to avoid being skewered by one of the chitinous limbs and cleared his throat.

"I mean, they might find it odd that a man, a human, that is, has such strong feelings for one of their kind?"

"Are you suggesting," Milo began, hearing the edge in his voice and not much caring, "that I want to save her for a reason besides the debt we both owe her and her usefulness to our mission?"

Ambrose frowned, his eyes scanning Milo's face before he went back to watching the crowd.

"No, I don't suppose I am."

"Good." Milo grunted and then spotted the butler from earlier across the hall. "Huh, did he just try to get our attention?"

"Who?" Ambrose asked, but then the raven-like servant locked eyes with them across the hall and motioned them over with a black-pinioned arm.

"Seems the old crow wants to have a chat," Ambrose said, adjusting his rifle over his shoulder. "Shall we?"

Milo nodded, and as quickly as the crowd allowed, they made their way to the butler, who stood watching them with large, dark eyes set into his sharp, pale face.

"My master asks you to attend him in his library," the butler cawed softly. His head twisted at the end of the question as he thrust his beaky nose forward.

"Lead on," Milo said, handing his undrunk wine to a passing server.

The butler bobbed once and led them on a winding path through the corridors of the manor. Uncomfortable memories of the tunnels in Afghanistan began to surface as they followed the raven-like fey down dim passage after dim passage that all looked very much the same, devoid of decoration. They passed simple dark wood doors and intersecting passages, but the former were always closed, and the latter looked identical to what they'd already walked down.

It was a shock when the butler came to a door that looked very much like all the others and paused to wave his hand much in the same way Bakbak-Devi had at the iron gate. The door swung inward and the birdlike footman hopped aside, bowing his head as he gestured them in.

The simplicity of the door did not prepare Milo for what lay within. He had been expecting a room, even a large room with several shelves of books and maybe a desk and some sitting chairs.

What he stepped into was nothing less than a temple to the written word. Shelves twice Milo's height swept around the vast circular space, and above them, walkways circled the room and gave access to even more shelves. Above those was a third layer of shelves. Rolling ladders hung from each shelf, and emblazoned on brass plaques were the categorical divisions and subdivisions of the books enshrined upon the ornate shelves of mahogany chased in burnished brass. Scattered across the polished marble floors were overstuffed chairs and plush couches, with small tables complete with what looked like table lamps, except instead of flaming wicks creating tiny islands of light, they had what looked like captured stars sat inside the glass bulbs.

Seated next to one of these tables was the marquis, who stood upon their entrance.

He was as tall as Beli at three meters but far more svelte. His appearance was stretched further by a pair of backward-swept horns that grew from his brow. The thick horns shone a steely shade of gray that was quite striking above his long countenance of milky skin. He wore a suit that might have been in fashion a hundred years ago, a Regency tailcoat ensemble of rich cream. Most everything seemed sized for a smaller creature, the collar not quite rising high enough to cover his long neck, while the coat and the trousers came to just past his elbows and knees respectively. In many ways, his whole form seemed stretched, yet he moved with easy fluidity Milo had come to associate with fey.

"Welcome," he said in that same subterranean voice. "I appreciate your patience. I'm sure it hasn't been easy, but as you will soon see, the situation is now not as dire as you first thought."

"I would be very thankful if you'd enlighten us, Marquis," Milo said as he and Ambrose closed the distance. Their footsteps didn't ring on the floor as they should have, and Milo guessed there was a chance that some sort of magic was at work to keep the library a place of quiet reflection.

"All in good time," the marquis said, smiling and reaching down with a long-fingered hand to gather up the books on the table he'd been sitting at. This close, Milo could see the fey's eyes possessed the horizontal pupils of a goat.

"I mean no disrespect, but I'm afraid that isn't good enough," Milo said, feeling Ambrose tense next to him as the words were spoken. "Contessa Rihyani is depending on me, and every second counts. I will do whatever it is you ask, but please, no more delays."

For his part, the marquis paused for a moment, and Milo felt the strange eyes sweeping over him. Milo couldn't quite remember if the huge presence he'd recognized before felt the same as the pressing awareness, but he imagined it was close. As the stare continued, he could almost hear Ambrose coiling like a spring next to him. Milo began to wonder if he'd made a mistake. He contemplated making an apology for the abruptness, but another smile, warm and admiring, stretched across the fey aristocrat's long features.

"There it is," he said softly, stepping closer, books in the crook of one long arm. "That fire, that immediacy. It is invigorating."

The towering fey leaned down, bending almost double with no sign of difficulty or discomfort to stare at Milo.

"That's what this is all about."

Milo met the goat eyes uneasily at first, the stare striking him as alien and sinister despite the gentle expressions of their owner.

"I still don't understand," Milo said, then squared his shoulders and planted his feet. "But I would learn. Please, explain."

The marquis waited for a second longer, studying Milo, then straightened and moved toward the shelves.

"Since you are assisting the contessa, I can only assume you are involved with the conflict between the factions commonly referred to as the Shepherds and the Guardians?"

"I am," Milo called after him, the volume of his voice seeming almost sacrilegious in the library. To avoid having to do so again, he moved to follow the marquis, Ambrose at his shoulder.

"Were you aware that I've been approached by both parties?" the marquis asked over his shoulder as he began to shelve the books.

"No," Milo admitted, feeling a prickle of anxiety race across his skin. "I wasn't aware of that."

The marquis nodded as he tapped a clawed digit down a row of books playfully before finding the cavity where the last book went.

"I haven't declared for either side yet, obviously," the fey said as he slid the final volume home. "This particular situation offers me a unique predicament and opportunity."

The prickling flared, and Milo fought the urge to sweep the room as the skin between his shoulder blades tingled. He knew Ambrose was doing that for him and would probably do a far better job, so he decided to keep his gaze fixed on the marquis.

"You're considering turning us over to the Guardians then?" Milo said, the words coming out hoarse and harsh.

"Oh, no, nothing so duplicitous," the marquis declared, his tone hinting at offense at the suggestion. "You are my guests and under the protection of my hospitality. No, I could win favor among the Guardians simply by refusing to help you. Contessa Rihyani is known to both factions, and while I could justify my actions to the Shepherds as not wanting to get involved, the Guardians would appreciate an enemy agent killed, even if simply by inaction."

Milo's fingers tightened around the raptor cane, but he reminded himself that the marquis hadn't said this was what he was going to do, only stated it as a possibility.

"Is that what Ezekiel and Percy asked you to do?" Milo asked. "Just let Rihyani die?"

The marquis frowned, an odd expression on his long, pale face.

"The Americans? No, they had other interests. In fact, if you are operating under the assumption that they are allied with the Guardians, I'm afraid they seem quite ignorant of the conflict."

Milo pulled back and narrowed his eyes as he studied the marquis. Seeing no sign of deception, Milo supposed the marquis, who so far had been quite forthright, had no reason to lie. He made a mental note to consider the new information later as he reminded himself that Rihyani's life still very much hung in the balance.

"So, you could let her die," Milo said, keeping his tone even. "Or you could help us and save her life."

The marquis nodded, his strange horizontal pupils fixed on Milo.

"I could, and I think I will, at least in part," he said slowly, gauging Milo's reaction. "I will give you something, and what you do with it will decide whether you can go and save the contessa. Also, your success or failure in this endeavor will be the deciding factor of which faction I put my support behind immediately."

Milo stared for a second, and during the pause, Ambrose cleared his throat to speak up.

"And by immediately, you mean…"

"If you succeed, I will not only ensure you have the means to save the contessa but also that you will reach her in time," the marquis declared solemnly. "If you fail, you will be given a day to leave my vale, and then I will call the hunt to pursue you both to the edge of the mountain's shadow."

Milo didn't need to study the fey's expression to know he was serious.

"No pressure, huh?" Milo swallowed.

"Do you accept my terms and agree to abide by them?"

Milo turned and met Ambrose's eye. He knew the answer, but he was glad to see Ambrose give him a determined nod and then a subtle wink. A hearty cheer or slap on the back couldn't have been more encouraging.

Magus and bodyguard looked into the marquis' face, jaws set and shoulders squared.

"We accept," Milo said.

The marquis nodded and then raised his long arms straight out to either side.

"Very good." He smiled, raising his face toward the moonlight beaming through the windows high above the looming shelves. "Now, for this next part, I ask that you please remain very still. It can be confusing, but please don't move."

Milo's expression changed from bemusement to shock as the room began to spin around them. Faster and faster the room revolved around them, all the more frightening for their silence as images of ladders, walkways, and shelves flashed by. Soon the room was an eye-watering blur of colors and light, so Milo fixed his attention on the fey standing in a cruciform posture at the eye of the soundless storm.

"You are both doing very well," the marquis said as the lights around them began to change color. "Almost there now. Just remember to not move. I'd hate for you to hurt yourselves."

Moments later, the spinning room came to an abrupt stop, and Ambrose gave a muffled heave and managed to stagger a dozen paces away to be sick in a convenient decorative vase.

Milo felt a flutter of nausea, but it was not so severe that he didn't realize they were no longer standing in the library.

They stood in a tall, narrow corridor where one wall was set with a series of portals that looked out over the marquis' dining hall. The noble's guests danced, and drank, and sang, and drank some more in what was fast becoming a bacchanalian revel below. The fact that the creatures engaged were alien combinations of beatific creatures and Boschian nightmares only made the scene more surreal.

Milo stood staring down for a moment, doing his best to block out the sounds of Ambrose hawking, spitting, and cursing. They were clearly in a gallery overlooking the hall, but Milo had stood on the floor below and couldn't remember seeing any such gallery.

"This wasn't part of the manor when we were down there earlier," Milo said, turning back to the marquis. "Is it invisible from below?"

The fey shook his head, a smile teasing the corners of his mouth upward.

"No, but that isn't a bad idea."

Milo stared at the marquis, then gaped at the structure that stretched the width of the hall and was decorated to match the rest of the manor.

"You don't mean to tell me you fabricated all of this out of thin air on a whim?" Milo asked, unable to keep the heady mix of incredulity and awe from his voice. He'd known fey magic was different from that the ghuls practiced, but he struggled to believe it was so much more powerful as to create such vast, complex structures with what seemed like very little effort. Milo's head spun with the possibilities.

"Not as you might imagine," the marquis began. "The first thing you must understand about the Art, which is what we fey call our magic, is that it is tied to our will, which is itself tied to our very natures as creatures of will."

Milo blinked like an owl at noontime, struggling to understand the fey's words.

"You just will things into physical existence?" he said, his tone approaching flabbergasted. "You think them, and they are real?"

The marquis laughed, and though it was a kindly sound, Milo could tell he was getting more wrong than right.

"We need to clarify two things," the marquis said, raising two clawed fingers demonstratively. "First, will and thought are not the same things, particularly among the fey. Will in the sense I talk about is an interwoven matrix of identity, intent, and desire. A thought is fleeting, a series of reactions to stimuli either internal or external. Will is fundamental and enduring, a consistent declaration.

"Second, something does not have to be physical to be real. The greatest disservice done to your kind was when many of you came to believe that only things that are real can be weighed on a scale or measured with little notched sticks. Just as lamentable was when you forgot that belief can be as tangible as water and stone."

Milo clamped his hand over his forehead and massaged his brow.

"So, this gallery is real but not physical," Milo said slowly. "And you made it with your will, not just because you thought about it."

The marquis smiled.

"Yes, in its simplest form, that is true," he said. "But I think we'll need to back up a step."

Milo nodded, bewildered but striving to remain hopeful.

The marquis stepped back and gestured to himself with a wide sweep of his elongated arms.

"Every fey is whatever they will themselves to be," he explained. "What you see of me is what I wish you to see of me and the truth of what I am that I reveal to the world. You may have noticed that amongst the fey, there seems to be little homogeneity in form, and you'd be excused for thinking the likes of my servant Bakbak-Devi and the butler who brought you to the library were different species or breeds of fey, but that simply isn't the case. Each of us is what we will, the pixie-formed sprite dancing on lily pads or the jotun king as huge as a mountain."

Ambrose, a little paler than before, had rejoined them and was alternating between staring at the marquis and the fey on the dance floor below.

"So those are all fey, just fey, and they can be whatever they want?"

"Yes, they are all fey, but no, not whatever they want," the horned aristocrat said patiently. "Wants tend to be transitory, symptoms rather than causes. The will of a fey like Bakbak-Devi is bent toward being a powerful, watchful guardian. He will not become the pixie or the swan-bride because that is not who he is."

Milo nodded and swept a hand toward all the fey below them.

"The characteristics of the fey may be mutable, but what he or she wants to be, what they will, isn't going to change, right?"

"Almost," the marquis said, his alien eyes twinkling with a flash of puckish mirth. "Will is fundamental, but even fundamentals can be bent or broken. And that is where the Art comes into play."

The fey passed a hand over his face, and the long, pensive features were replaced by a baphometian horror. A shaggy, goatish snout filled with slavering fangs snapped with bone-crunching force, while the huge head with a crown of barbed horns tossed left and right, sending ribbons of burning brimstone through the air. Each man felt the heat of the hellish breath against his face, and each nearly retched at the pungent aroma of sulfur and sweaty beast.

Milo and Ambrose fell back startled, their backs to the open gallery window. Hands fell to weapons, while their muscles bunched in equal preparation to leap into the fray or to an uncertain escape to the hall below. Milo's coat could bear him down safely, but he wasn't sure it could bear the additional weight of the stout bodyguard.

Before things erupted into violence, the transformed marquis drew back, and with another pass of his hand returned to his previous appearance. He was polite enough not to grin in their faces, but the mischief still shone in his eyes.

"Was that some sort of illusion?" Milo asked, ignoring the hammering in his chest. "A momentary bending of the fundament?"

"Yes," the marquis said but raised a warning finger. "But do not confuse an illusion of the Art with a mere trick of the senses. With the Art, my will acted upon you, and your unprepared wills accepted it. If I'd bent to bite, my fangs would have opened your flesh as surely as any beast's."

Milo looked at Ambrose, who only gave a bewildered shake of his head.

"Your will acting on ours makes it real, even if you physically didn't grow finger-long teeth?" Milo asked.

"Precisely," the marquis confirmed.

"This whole gallery formed because the Art pressed your will on ours to make it," Milo said, nodding, then his head drew up quickly with an idea. "Is this whole manor part of your will? The whole Lost Vale?"

The marquis beamed down at Milo and bowed his horned head slowly.

"Very good, Magus."

Ambrose gave a grunt, and Milo and the marquis both turned to see him scratching his whiskered chin, his brows knit in concentration.

"So, if we know this, all of it," he began, waving his hand to the gallery and the hall, "is just an illusion, why doesn't it stop being real? If our will has to accept it as true, but now we know it isn't, why doesn't it disappear? Or at least, why can't we see through it?"

"A fair question," the marquis said gently. "But knowing is not believing. Again, the difference between thoughts and will is the difference between the child blowing dandelion seeds and the wind that propels the man o' war. A life among mortal men has raised your will to believe what your hands touch and your eyes see is real, and you've spent some time under my influence *knowing* it's real. It takes more than a thought to convince your will to throw off what it believes—especially, if I may be so bold, when it is being affected by a practitioner of the Art as potent as I am. You are shackled to your experience, though with time and concentration, you could break free."

Ambrose frowned as he nodded in acknowledgment, clearly uncomfortable with the whole business.

"All right, I think I understand the principle," Milo said, drawing the marquis' attention back to him. "But as a human, how am I supposed to learn the Art since I'm not a creature of will like fey are?"

"At first blush, I would say you couldn't," the fey said, the mischief replaced by scholarly gravitas. "Few humans can muster the certainty and focus to push back against all but the weakest of our kind, and even then, it is only to resist, not to push their own will out. Yet your unique ability to do ghulish magic gives me hope that there is a possibility that with some assistance, you could intuit how to begin mastering the Art."

"How can I intuit something that is unnatural to me?" Milo asked, despair creeping into the corners of his tone.

The mischievous gleam returned.

"That," said the marquis, "is precisely where things become very interesting."

THE ART

The marquis had offered to transport them to a different portion of the estate, but Ambrose had politely but firmly declined, so they'd spent some time moving through the manor before exiting and heading for the conical dovecote in the expansive courtyard where they'd first met the fey master of the Lost Vale.

"The reason I did not join you at the feast was that I needed time to riddle out this conundrum," the marquis explained as they strode across the lawn under a huge yellow moon. "As you so keenly observed, Magus, the Art is intuitive and grows with the exercising of that intuition, but how to bridge that gap when the instinct isn't present?"

Milo felt a growing sense of foreboding the closer they drew to the structure, and not because he expected the marquis' challenge lay within. There was a vague but familiar sourness to the sight of the building. With each step, he found it more difficult to pay attention to what the marquis was saying.

"As is often the case, the answer was staring me in the face," the fey said, shaking his head slowly. "After all, the Art is pressing my will upon the world and minds of others, so there was little reason I couldn't impress some experience, especially upon a willing participant."

Only a few strides away from the door to the dovecote, Ambrose nudged Milo with an elbow and nodded at the ground. The grass was matted down as though something had been roughly dragged across it. Some of the blades glistened black in the moonlight.

"What was it?" Milo mouthed to Ambrose as they followed the marquis.

The big man shrugged, but Milo noticed he'd surreptitiously adjusted his grip on his rifle. He nodded forward, and Milo realized that their host was still talking.

"Once I'd reviewed those, it seemed clear what I'd have to do. I know it might seem silly, but sometimes the ritual and metaphor of these things are an essential part of the magic. I'm sure you understand?"

The marquis turned as he came to the door, looking at Milo, who realized after missing a beat that the last statement had been a question.

"Oh, um, certainly," Milo said lamely. "Whatever it takes."

"I'm glad you understand," the marquis said, and with a quick flourish of his hand, a bright red apple appeared between his claws. It shone with a throbbing light of its own, more fecund and vibrant than the pale gleam from the moon above. For a moment, all the three of them stood in silence, staring at the glowing fruit, one caught up in the drama of the moment while the other two were just confused.

"I have to eat?" Milo asked, pulling his gaze from the apple.

The marquis looked down at him, a little deflated.

"Well, yes. A bite, at least. I thought I'd made that clear."

"Just checking," Milo muttered as he reached out to take the apple from the fey's hand.

The marquis let it roll from claws to Milo's palm, who nearly dropped it in shock and surprise. The fruit was soft and warm and trembled like a living thing. Milo felt his skin crawl as though trying to retreat from the unnatural thing in his hand. He raised it to his lips, reminded himself it was for Rihyani and sank his teeth into the apple. The skin parted easily, and the flesh within was juicy and sweet in no way that any apple had ever been in his life, but there was a strangeness to the texture that Milo refused to focus upon. His jaw worked mechanically as he doggedly kept from making comparisons with all the things chewing it was like, of which any plant-based edible was not one. A few eternal seconds later, he swallowed the bite and looked at the marquis.

"I don't understand," he said, drawing a hand across his wet mouth. "What is supposed to—"

The marquis smiled as something like an experiential bomb detonated inside Milo's head and heart. It was a firehose of sensation, not only information, but memories and emotions racing through him, chasing and devouring and regurgitating each other in a mad carousel. Milo felt his legs buckle and he heard Ambrose's voice, but everything was surrendering to a swelling white overload. The expanding overstimulation flooded every aspect of Milo's mind, and for a moment, he was certain he was about to lose himself, drowned by experiences and will he couldn't even begin to process from a being who was alien to him. In a fitting way, it was like when he'd had to hold the transformation of his blood in check, only now it was his soul and not his circulatory system that was in danger of being snuffed out.

Then, like the dawn of the fortieth day, the tide stopped, and Milo's consciousness stood upon the last spit of his identity, on higher ground, looking over an ocean of experience that wasn't his. He hung there, and for a moment, he realized there was something clinging to that higher ground with him.

Before he could ascertain what it was, the floodwaters began to recede, some evaporating into the psychic ether, some soaking into his mind's aquifers of instinct. He felt them there, pockets of conviction that told him that if he willed it, the world would bend to him. It was not the same metaphysical muscle as that which shaped essence from necromist formulae, but it was similar to the sensation. When he controlled essence, he was drawing in, focusing it down to a point of combustion and transformation. This was pushing out, pressing against the walls of minds and realities until a crack was found to let his will fill that space.

The white-out of sensation began to shrink, and Milo came to with a jolt to find he was still kneeling on the bloodied grass. Ambrose was squatted in front of him, massive paws holding his head.

"I think he's coming around," Ambrose said, his eyes searching Milo's face fervently.

"Your hands are sweaty," Milo said slowly. "Are you nervous?"

A rush of relief followed quickly by irritation swept over the bodyguard's face, and he gave Milo a little shake.

"You are not funny," he growled before releasing him and rising. "Stop embarrassing yourself."

The marquis' chuckle rippled out, dark and rich in the night air.

"Oh, I can feel it, Magus," he declared triumphantly. "Your will has bloomed. You are ready to put this to use."

Milo wasn't sure he was ready for anything except a full belly and a long nap, but it was clear neither of those was in his immediate future. With a grunt, he climbed to his feet.

"Are you sure he shouldn't take some time?" Ambrose said, eyeing Milo skeptically. "You know, rest, and maybe get some practice?"

The door to the stone and mortar tower was sized to human proportions, so the marquis was forced to bend nearly double to take the ring in hand. He looked back at Ambrose, bemused, and gave him a wink.

"Time is of the essence, isn't it?" he said, then tugged the door open. "And this *is* practice. He will learn by doing."

Still bent over, the marquis ducked inside. With little choice, Milo and Ambrose followed.

The stone walls of the dovecote had an upward-spiraling series of alcoves that reached three-quarters of the way up the structure, while the last quarter was domino tiles that formed alternating bands of black and white around a central hole. Directly over this hole hung the immense golden moon, and in its light, Milo and Ambrose saw the source of the blood and drag marks outside.

Ezekiel Bouche knelt in the center of the floor, wrapped in graven chains that had been anchored to rings in the floor.

"Howdy, boys," he cooed as Milo and Ambrose followed the marquis in. "I was wonderin' where you two had run off to. Should've known you'd get busy makin' friends with king o' the old castle here."

Ambrose rounded on the marquis, his words coming out hot and hard like shell casings.

"What the hell is he doing here?"

The marquis drew himself up to his full imperious height in response, an unhappy frown on his features.

"I told you there would be a test that, if passed, would give you the answers." He sniffed. "This is it. The magus shall use the Art to discover how to save Contessa Rihyani. I will give him until dawn to extract the information from the cursed one."

Before Ambrose could protest, Ezekiel burst into a fit of hysterical laughter. It rang off the walls until Milo's ears ached.

"You think this milk-drinkin' greenhorn's got what it takes to break me?" he wheezed between snorts of laughter before turning his manic grin on Milo. "Boy, you better kiss your fey lover goodbye because even if he gave you a month of sunrises, you still wouldn't have the gumption to make me sweat."

Ambrose's fist balled up and he made to go for the leering cowboy, but Milo put a hand on his shoulder. Ambrose looked at him, green eyes afire, but when he saw the hardened intent in Milo's expression, he nodded and stepped back.

"Can I only use the Art, or are any other means open to me?" Milo asked, locking his eyes on the scalp-hunter's wild stare.

"You are free to do as you will," the marquis said before adding, "but I will tell you that the Art and the knowledge I've given you are your most certain path to success. Perhaps there are other ways, but I doubt it."

"Oh, now we're talking," Ezekiel said with a dark chuckle.

Ambrose unlimbered and put down his rifle in one smooth movement before he began rolling up his sleeves.

"If it's a matter of interrogation, I've got ideas that might make him a bit more talkative."

"Oh, don't tease me, fat boy." Ezekiel giggled. "Come on over here and let me have it. Come on now, give me your best shot. Don't hold nothin' back!"

Ambrose was standing over the cowboy, hands curled into claws, when Milo stopped him with a word.

"No."

Ambrose paused, glaring down at the tittering cowboy.

"The marquis gave *me* this test," Milo said evenly, taking a step forward into the pool of moonlight. "This is for me to do."

Ambrose tore his gaze from Ezekiel to meet Milo's stare.

"And if you can't?"

The question hurt.

Milo knew it shouldn't. He knew it came from a place of deep concern, of love even, for Rihyani and him, yet it still stung. Pride, defiance, and anger rushed to inflame the wound and swell it in a vain attempt to protect himself, but he clamped down on the instinct, thinking that way wouldn't help anyone. Instead, he reached out and squeezed the big man's brawny shoulder, looking deep into his troubled gaze.

"Then I die trying," he said.

Ambrose's eyes swam with his own maelstrom, but staring into Milo's, he found what he needed. He nodded and stepped back.

Ezekiel's jeering snigger drew Milo's gaze.

"Had a pair like you in a scalpin' posse I used to run with," he said. "One of 'em used to ride the other so much we wondered why he didn't get his boy fitted for a saddle and bridle."

Not deigning to reply to the taunt, Milo turned to the marquis and Ambrose.

"I'm ready," Milo said, appreciating that he sounded confident even as his stomach began to squirm. "Dawn?"

The marquis nodded, his expression inscrutable as he led Ambrose out, leaving Ezekiel and Milo alone.

For some time, the two men brooded in relative silence. Milo drew slow, even breaths, while Ezekiel muttered and giggled to himself in a low, broken voice that Milo couldn't understand.

Then the air rippled with spectral winds.

"Here we go." Ezekiel tittered in anticipation.

Milo's will ranged outward, groping toward the septic wound that was Ezekiel's psyche. Pushing through his disgust at the contact, Milo pressed in, drawing upon the dark corners of his recent memories.

The ghostly winds congealed into the mewling, many-limbed visages of shades, grasping and crawling up from the floor. Twisted, unnatural simulacrums of humanoid shapes wrapped in oily, ectoplasmic flesh, they excreted themselves out of the stones like huge, hellish maggots. Splintered, bony fingers scored the stones of the floor, and the temperature in the room plummeted so both men's breath was visible. The shades groaned and wailed with the heart-stopping voices of the damned as they turned too-bright eyes upon the bound cowboy. As they manifested around him, Milo had to remind himself that they were his own conjurations.

In a way he never could have apart from this experience, he began to appreciate what the marquis had said. Just because it wasn't physical did not mean it wasn't real.

"Spooky." Ezekiel chuckled as he watched the lurching advance of the illusory shades. "But it's goin' to take a lot more than this, kid."

The shades were now gathered around the cowboy, leaning forward and eagerly snuffling. As one, their gleaming eyes turned to regard Milo, their puppet master. Milo's gaze hardened, and he felt rime spread across his heart. He knew he was not a cruel man, but life had been cruel to him, and for Rihyani's sake, he was willing to do many terrible things. That knowledge encased his soul like frozen armor, even as Ezekiel laughed louder and louder.

"I'm sure knowing you can't die seems like a comfort," he said, meeting Ezekiel's gaze with a chilling stare as the cowboy guffawed. "But that only means I don't have to worry about you surviving anything I do to you."

Every shade's malformed mouth twisted into an obscene smile as sharp, jagged fingers stretched toward tender flesh.

Ezekiel's laughter rose to a shrill cadence that was indistinguishable from a scream.

"You are going to tell me what I want to know, Ezekiel," Milo said softly. "One way or another."

***

Ezekiel knelt, head hanging, mangy strands of his stringy hair dangling over his face. He might have collapsed forward, but the chains that bound him would not allow him to do more than hang his head, shoulders taut. His breath sawed in and out between brown teeth as a string of crimson drool trickled from his mouth.

The last illusion had been a living strand of barbed wire that slithered down the cowboy's raw, cackling throat to twist and gyrate as it worked its way through him and back. The curse had mended the worst of the experience as Milo's will flagged, but there were enough lacerations in Ezekiel's throat that blood welled up with every breath for some time. Milo, sweating and trembling with exhaustion and frustration, stared in disbelief as the trickle of blood lessened with each wheezing gasp.

With a fitful cough that spattered a fresh layer of crimson across the stone floor, the scalp hunter began to laugh.

Milo's head lolled back, and he stared through the open portal in the ceiling. The moon of the Lost Vale had shrunk back to a reasonable size, and Milo could see the sky. Were the first traces of a sunrise beginning to filter through depths of night? Was it his imagination, or did he see some strands of blue and gray?

"You can feel it, can't you, boy?" Ezekiel chuckled thickly through crimson-streaked lips. "Dawn's comin', and you've got nothin'. Plumbed the depths of that nasty mind o' yours, and you still haven't shaken ol' Zeke."

The cowboy threw back his head and let out a hacking, raucous laugh along with a spume of red.

"HAHA! Guess your fey bitch bet on the wrong horse, huh? HAHAHA!"

For the first time that night, Milo's temper snapped, and he descended on the scalp hunter in a terrible fury. The raptor cane, wreathed in snapping emerald flames, rose and fell over and over. Supernaturally powered blows tore through flesh and snapped bone as witchfire scorched and scoured flesh. Within moments, Ezekiel was a seared, broken thing, barely recognizable as human.

Milo stood over him, chest heaving, burning with despair and frustration, and watched as the curse worked its terrible will.

He'd witnessed Ambrose's regeneration, with bones snapping back into place and flesh regrowing, but this was different. Watching it was like watching wounds reverse themselves, split and blackened flesh slithering back into place as it shrank and the scorching faded.

In less time than it had taken to inflict the incredible damage, it had been undone, and Milo was eye to eye with the same maddening grin.

"When are you going to understand?" He laughed, shaking his head with enraging slowness. "You can't win."

Animal instinct released the cane in Milo's hand so he could form a scarred fist to drive into Ezekiel's face. The blow split the cowboy's lip, but the grin only widened.

"Hit me again if you like." He giggled, and Milo did, knocking his nose of kilter by a few degrees as blood gushed from the nostrils.

"Oh, come on, you can do better."

Milo slammed two hard hooks into one side of Ezekiel's face. The eye started to swell shut.

"That's more like it."

Another strike across the engorging hematoma, then the other hand knocked a tooth free.

"Don't stop now."

Three more hammering fists split the unswollen eyebrow and knocked the nose even farther the other way before Milo grabbed two handfuls of lank, sweat-slimed hair.

"Come on, you said you were gonna die tryin'!"

His repetitively rising knee mashed the nose, collapsed the cheekbones, and snapped his jaw. Finally Milo staggered backward and collapsed when his throbbing leg gave out. Breath came in despairing rasps as he watched things slide back into place and out of mangled flesh. Ezekiel's voice rose like the inevitable verses of a prophecy.

"Nothin'. There's nothin' you can do. Not with your pixie

tricks, not with your bone stick, not with your little fists. You've got nothin', boy."

Milo stared back, trying to regain that icy calm he'd felt at the outset, but it had vanished. What he found instead was the flagging energy to kick up and clack the broken brown teeth together in Ezekiel's jaw.

"Nothin' you have can hurt me," the scalp hunter murmured. "Keep tryin'. Keep tryin' to get lower, meaner, nastier, whatever. It doesn't matter because you've got nothin'. Nothin' you can do, nothin' you've ever known, nothin' you can imagine."

Scooting backward on his hands, Milo admitted to himself that was why he was so angry. Yes, he was terrified of failing Rihyani, but sitting there with a man's crusted blood on his hands and smeared across his pant leg, he knew that fear wasn't the root of his anger.

He was mad because of how quickly and how low he'd been willing to stoop with his new gift of the Art. Killing a man in the heat of battle was one thing, but here he'd let the ugliest parts of his will, his very identity, have free rein to work horrors upon Ezekiel, and nothing had come of it. It wasn't that the monstrous man didn't deserve it, but rather that Milo letting himself generate in the fabricated horrors had sullied himself as surely as blood now clogged his nails and clung to his knuckles. There was a stain upon him, and there was nothing to show for it.

"Nothin'," Milo repeated quietly to himself, then Ezekiel's words returned to him.

Nothin' you can do, nothin' you've ever known, nothin' you can imagine.

What made the declaration so awful and enervating was that it was not a statement of bravado or challenge. No, seeing past the grin and the perverse laughter, it was a certainty rooted in something.

Nothin' you can do, nothin' you've ever known, nothin' you can imagine. Nothin' can ever be as bad as that.

It was a declaration rooted in despair.

"You finally givin' up the ghost, boy?" Ezekiel asked with a smirk, and Milo stared deep into his eyes. Past the practiced leer, Milo looked hard, and to his dwindling shock, saw disappointment and sadness. How could anyone, even an immortal, be sad to be free of torment?

Milo kept staring, and a thought bubbled to the surface of his mind.

He wants to keep hurting because he hates his life, yet even as he gets what he wants, he knows it will never be enough. Why? Because it will never hurt as much as something else did.

Milo suddenly knew what he had to do.

"I've got one more spirit to conjure," the magus murmured as he shifted into a cross-legged position on the stone floor. There was a decent chance this wouldn't work, but Milo knew without looking up that sky was lightening. Time was slipping through his fingers, and this was all he had left.

He scooted closer until he and Ezekiel were eye to eye.

"You gonna braid my hair and tell me I'm pretty?" the scalp hunter asked with a sneer.

Milo shook his head and straightened his back as he kept staring into the man's eyes.

"Not quite," he said as his will remembered the night the wind was on fire.

Milo couldn't have said why he chose to conjure that night using the Art, but as he drew Ezekiel into those moments seared into his soul and thus his will, Milo felt a familiar tremble inside. He pushed it aside as he and the captive scalp hunter moved together down the kindling streets and then turned to see the many-legged things with stars in their hands.

Milo let the fear he'd felt flow around Ezekiel, an experience shared, given as a gift, not an intrusion perpetrated.

At first there was nothing, the cowboy's will like a stone in the midst of the stream. Then, little by little, as the pure, unguarded, unsullied fear of an innocent child saturated that stone, cracks began to form. Out of those cracks wept a truth that not even Ezekiel's despairing mania could contain for long.

"Run," Ezekiel whispered, the words spilling from his lips. "Run, girl. Run, baby."

Girl? Baby?

Feeling a ripple of Ezekiel's will, Milo shaped the Art around it, forming it around the part of the scalp hunter that had been shaken loose.

The illusory scene bled into itself, and they stood in a field with a bloody sky glowering over red wildflowers. A little girl in a white cotton dress raced between the flowers, her hair whipping behind her like a banner of cornsilk, familiar dark eyes huge with terror. There was the sound of thunder, and Milo saw painted horses and painted men bearing down upon the child, bows drawn, lances leveled, pistols aimed.

From within Ezekiel's skin, Milo felt his heart pounding in a heavy, sickened beat as more words tumbled from numb lips.

Thump-thump—the first pistol barks, and the little girl screams as the bullet hisses past her.

"Thought I got them all."

Thump-thump—an arrow cuts her shoulder and the little dress sports a red bloom.

"Didn't think they'd track me down."

Thump-thump—the lance lunges forward, not slowing in its passage through the child until its point snaps on the dirt under her feet.

"Couldn't imagine they'd find me with her."

Thump-thump—her feet tangle and she falls, but the haft of the lance props her up, a broken doll with cornsilk hair amongst a field of red flowers.

The stone of Ezekiel's will weeps once more, and Milo again gathers his Art around the wounded tears.

The blue sky is stained black with greasy smoke as wails and screams create a strange chorus amidst the thrumming crackle of flames.

Through Ezekiel's eyes, Milo looks down from a saddled horse at a pile of blackening bodies. The pyre has been going for some time, but the features of the corpses are still discernible even as the flames lick higher, polluting the sky with more smoke. Tiny faces and little hands are among the mounded flesh, burning, splitting, and bursting like the rest.

Thump-thump—amongst the cacophony of despair and violation could be heard the laughing of men.

"It didn't take much to rile 'em up."

Thump-thump—in one bloody, sooty hand, a torn and bloody white dress was held.

"The dress was a banner and an excuse for most."

Thump-thump—with a single flick of the wrist, the dress rippled through the air to settle on the pyre.

"It wasn't even the same tribe of savages."

There was a howl of wind, keening and pained, and it slashed through the smoke and snaked down next to the pyre. Standing now before the fire, eye to eye with Ezekiel, was a gaunt and beautiful creature, her dark hair heavy with blades of flint hanging between the locks. Her golden eyes sparkled with tears as her lips spat words that stung and gnawed. A pistol was drawn, but not before a feather-thin dart of flint sailed through the air.

Milo's perspective through Ezekiel's eyes changed. He was staring up at the desecrated sky, feeling the stony blade scrape between his ribs as it sought a heart to nestle in. The beautiful creature's golden eyes loomed overhead, hair and dangling flints prepared to descend.

Ezekiel's horse had lost its nerve and bolted, hooves trampling and toppling one section of the bonfire. Bodies, fat running and bones cracking, tumbled free. Ezekiel's gaze saw them flop awkwardly upon the ground a few feet from where he lay dying, and their marionette's collapse struck upon a final ugly chord inside him. A laugh, long and broken and bitter, tore from his lips.

The beautiful creature narrowed her eyes, then with obvious disgust, reached down and pulled the flint blade from between the ribs. A few whispered words later, Milo knew the wound had closed as the curse was sealed.

Thump-thump—the beautiful creature laughed with him as he rose to his feet.

"She made me like her."

Thump-thump—Ezekiel's hand closed around the fingers that held the gory blade of flint.

"She said I could live as I willed now."

Thump-thump—He drove the blade into her chest, laughing into her teary face as the flint bit into her heart.

"Or I could end it like her."

The beautiful creature fell back into the pyre, and as the flames kindled her hair and caressed her body, the vision melted away.

Milo and Ezekiel were in the dovecote once more, and for the first time, the silence was absolute. No laughter or muttering emerged from the scalp hunter as he knelt upon the floor, arms stretched wide.

The first rays of dawn, golden-pink and cleansing, danced through the aperture in the ceiling.

Milo slowly wiped away the tears that rested on his cheeks before stiffly sinking down to one knee. His eyes sought to make contact with Ezekiel's, but the manic grin and defiant stare were nowhere to be seen.

"You could be done," Milo said softly, still searching for the broken man's eyes. "You could end the pain and hurt, couldn't you?"

Ezekiel shook his head.

"Can't," he murmured.

"Why not?"

The cowboy's eyes rose, and Milo saw what had been buried under the wild smiles and incessant laughter: hatred. Except this weaponized emotion was pointed utterly and entirely inward.

"Because I don't deserve an end," he hissed as his teeth clenched.

Milo was amazed to find that he understood, though there was a bewildering ache in his heart all the same.

"But the longer you go on, the more you hurt others," he pointed out in a slow, sad voice. "You said it yourself; you are what you are. That means the longer you live, the more you—"

"The more I don't deserve an end," Ezekiel growled. "Not the first time I thought of it. I even thought going to Hell might balance things out, but I can't take the chance that there is no Hell. So, I'm stuck."

Milo nodded.

"And forgiveness?"

"I ain't no quitter." Ezekiel laughed, and the sound chilled Milo to the bone. "I'm goin' to Hell, come what may."

The silence lengthened between them in the echo of that laugh, and Milo stayed there thinking until his knees ached and his back began to cramp. It might have been a few minutes before either of them spoke.

"So, forgiveness undoes the curse," Milo whispered, then looked at Ezekiel, who watched him with hollow eyes. "That's it, isn't it? If you can forgive yourself, the curse is broken, and your life could—should—end. So, if Rihyani forgives you, the hex on her is lifted?"

To Milo's incredible relief, Ezekiel nodded.

A distant thought came to him that the cowboy might be

lying, but at some level that was deeper than intellect, deeper even than magic, Milo didn't believe he was. The magus believed he'd found the answer.

That only left one loose end, and looking down on him, something like a grim pity settled across Milo.

"What if," he began as he rose to his feet and stretched, "I told you there is some sort of Hell? That I know someone who's seen it, seen what lives there because he's been there. Would that be enough?"

It seemed Ezekiel might laugh again, but as Milo braced himself, the cowboy's face contorted with thought.

"Who?"

Milo smiled.

"You've met him."

Ezekiel's eyes narrowed.

"Fat boy?"

Milo nodded.

"Really?"

Milo nodded again.

Silence reigned once more, though in the stillness, Milo felt the presence of the marquis and Ambrose outside the door. Milo mentally whispered something like a prayer for a few seconds more.

"I want to look into his eyes," Ezekiel said slowly. "I want to see Hell there, and then maybe I'll believe you."

As though they'd waited for their cue, the door opened behind Milo. Nephilim and fey entered quietly, both eyeing the bloody gouges on the floor.

Milo turned back to Ambrose and motioned him forward.

The big man approached slowly.

Ambrose obviously sensed a difference in the cowboy. His eyes narrowed suspiciously at the subdued creature kneeling where the defiant Ezekiel Boucher had once been.

"We've reached a sort of understanding," Milo said, turning to

Ezekiel, who nodded stiffly. "He's going to ask you some questions."

"What am I supposed to do?" Ambrose asked, giving the scalp hunter a sidelong glare.

"Be honest," Milo said simply. When Ambrose looked at him with deep concern, he nodded. "Yes, all of it."

Ambrose sucked his teeth and his mustache twitched.

Milo feared for a second that Ezekiel would capitalize on the hesitation and mock his bodyguard, but the cowboy was silent.

"This will save Rihyani?"

Milo looked at Ezekiel, who hung there with his eyes downcast.

"I've already got what I need," Milo said quietly. "This is about something else."

Ambrose looked at the two and shook his head wearily.

"All right." He grunted, crossing his arms. "What do you want to know?"

THE RETURN

"This has been a most enlightening experience," the marquis said with a spritely grin.

Milo and Ambrose didn't respond. Both of them were weary but eager to return to Shatili. Ambrose had his head under the Rollsy's hood while Milo busied himself loading and securing the food and drink the marquis had insisted they take. The magus had asked if they had any fuel or the equivalent since he'd had detonated their reserves, but as expected, the fey did not have any stores of petrol lying around.

Milo wondered how far they'd go before the Rollsy died, assuming Ambrose said she was capable of making the journey.

"I understand that for the two of you, this was a desperate and serious situation," the fey said, his tone gentle only long enough to say the word before rising again with amusement. "But I think this is the first time I've cared about anything outside of my vale since going to visit my cousin in Brittany."

Ambrose, who'd been silent since his conversation with Ezekiel, looked up with a scowl. His jaw worked to grind up the rebuke he decided to swallow.

For his part, Milo knew he shouldn't argue with the potent

ally he'd won, but he almost snapped. Then exhaustion quenched the defiant fire. Though the gears of his mind were gummed with fatigue, they slowly wound, and he remembered Percy's conversation with Bakbak-Devi about the manor and the mention of Brittany. They'd left Ezekiel bound in the dovecote, but there had been no sign of the other American.

He saw the marquis studying him, his expression almost hopeful.

"What happened to Ezekiel's partner?" Milo asked with a surrendering sigh. He didn't believe for a second that the comment concerning Brittany had been offered by coincidence.

"Oh, Percival Astor is at my home waiting for you to depart," the marquis said with a shrug as though just thinking of the answer. "He negotiated his own bargain with me, but he agreed that his errand was less time-sensitive than yours and so agreed, quite graciously, to allow you both to depart first."

Ambrose's head whipped around with neck-popping velocity.

"Bargain?" he snarled. "I thought you said that if the magus passed your test, you would be on our side?"

The marquis' ungulate eyes glittered as he showed his teeth in an uncomfortably predatory smile.

"I did, and I am," the fey said slowly, as though explaining something to a child. "But as I said already, the Americans seem quite separate from the entire struggle between the Shepherds and the Guardians. Their goals are far more nationalist and thus far less consequential."

Milo studied the fey, feeling an uneasy twist in his stomach.

"What did you give them, and what was the price?" he asked hoarsely, his mouth suddenly dry.

The marquis shrugged, then flapped his hand as though the question was a pestering insect.

"A map and a little bit of information," he muttered. "And in exchange, I requested the use of Mr. Boucher for my own purposes. You saw how that went."

Milo slumped against the door of the Rollsy.

"What?" He groaned, a hand running over his face. "So, it was all an act? A setup?"

An angry growl rumbled out of Ambrose's throat, and the hood of the Rollsy was slammed down.

"Hardly." The marquis scoffed, refusing to show even a trace of concern at both men's reactions. "Nothing happens in these mountains and for miles beyond that I don't know about, so it was not hard to understand why you'd come. Once the Americans bumbled their way into an audience, it was clear what I needed to do. Neither of them knew what I planned, but Ezekiel's confidence in his invulnerability combined with Percival's disdain for his partner made it an easy thing to broker. I'm quite sure neither of them expected things to work out the way they did."

Milo and Ambrose took a moment to process the revelation, and when done, they shared a defeated stare. What could they do now?

"You're a dangerous creature, Ochopintre," Milo said, the priest's name for the fey odd on his tongue as he turned to regard him.

"Not the words I'd use," Ambrose added sulkily as he shuffled his way to the cab.

"Then isn't it a good thing I'm on your side now?" the marquis asked, eyes and teeth gleaming.

"Could be worse." Milo sighed as he moved aside to allow Ambrose to clamber into the cab and shuffle over to the driver's seat.

"Oh, most certainly." The marquis chuckled, and there was something in the sound that reminded Milo of the baphometian horror he'd seen in the gallery.

"Since you're so well-informed, I suppose you're aware of what's coming to Georgia," Milo said, unable to keep the petulant irritation from his tone.

The marquis' expression sobered, and he nodded slowly.

"A son returned to the land where his iron was mined," the fey said, his eyes growing distant. "But he's bringing something or maybe someone he didn't have before. His metal is brittle, but driven by the machine of his ambition, he could grind his home to kindling to light another fire."

Milo started, knowing much was soaring past him but not having any idea where to start.

"Prophecies and riddles aren't nearly as useful as intelligence," Milo remarked dryly. "As our ally, wouldn't it be useful to be a little clearer?"

The marquis sighed and shook his head as he gave Milo a pitying look.

"That depends very much on what you are looking for," he said. "In truth, I know little more than you do, I imagine. A name maybe, but I can give you more than that, though its value is far more to you personally than to struggles between factions."

Milo's hands knotted into fists as he ground his teeth at the perpetual teasing tone of the fey's revelations. Arms locked stiffly at his side and heels grinding into the earth, he looked at the marquis with jaw set and eyes fixed.

"I'll have them both, please."

"His born name is Ioseb Besarionis dze Jugashvili, though he goes by Joseph now," the marquis said. "And though he has never met you, his effect upon your life has been profound even since you were a child and you watched as the wind was on fire."

Milo's heart kicked hard in his chest, but he refused to give the insufferable fey the pleasure of seeing his reaction.

"Is that all?" he asked, locking each syllable into the vault of his memory.

The marquis nodded.

"Thank God," Ambrose groaned from the driver's seat before turning the key.

The Rollsy's engine turned over, and Milo turned with

unseemly haste to climb into the cab. He raised a foot to mount the running board, except the running boards weren't where he'd left them. He barked his shin on the metal rail, emitting a burst of profanity at the same time that Ambrose uttered his own curse.

The Rollsy's heavy metal frame floated above the earth as though it were making a go at imitating a zeppelin.

"What the devil?" Milo spat as he bent to rub his abused shin.

"Nothing so dramatic," the marquis replied with a sniff.

"What did you do to my car?" Ambrose shouted as he gripped the seat and door of the Rollsy with bloodless fingers.

The marquis stepped forward and ran his claws tenderly across the vehicle's battered hood. The tempo of the engine's rumble slowed to an appreciative purr. Milo felt a soul-deep buzz of static that, after a moment of reflection, he imagined was evidence of the marquis' will working upon his own.

"I did promise to make certain you'd return to the contessa in time," the marquis said archly. "I provided you with a glamour to make certain you reach her quickly as long as you don't dawdle."

Milo stared at the Rollsy and then looked at the fey.

"I don't understand," he said. "Illusions convincing bodies and souls that things are or aren't happening is one thing, but making us believe we're flying can't make us fly, can it?"

The marquis bent double and laid a long hand on Milo's shoulder.

"Oh, you'd be amazed what believing something can do," he said, his words a whisper that brushed Milo's mind. "And no one said that men and the Folk were the only wills you could bend. Once upon a time, men knew mountains slept and rivers raged, so would it not serve me to seduce gravity?"

With that, he raised up and looked over Milo at Ambrose.

"Gear determines altitude," he explained. "Everything else should be fairly familiar, but remember to not dawdle."

Mind racing but not needing to be told a third time, Milo climbed aboard the Rollsy, with the marquis' voice behind him.

"I expect we'll be seeing you very soon, Magus. Take care, and keep an open mind."

Milo sank into his seat and saw the fey had vanished.

"Should I be concerned about all this fey business being mostly illusions?" Ambrose asked, eyeing the gear shift nervously.

"Try not to think about it too hard," Milo said and quickly added, "Especially when we're in the air."

The mountains rolled beneath them like rocky waves breaking in shades of white and slate as they rose from a green sea. The majestic vistas passed beneath them, and had speed not been so vital, Milo would have liked to savor the beauty.

When first leaving the Lost Vale, Ambrose had refused to put the glamoured Rollsy in anything but first gear, which put them twenty or so feet off the ground. Eventually, Milo was able to cajole and taunt Ambrose to rise higher with needling jabs at the big man's pride. In third gear, they'd risen to several hundred feet off the ground, and it was just as well because they soon spotted a burnt-out farmstead on the horizon, a smear of soot and cinders on a hillside.

Milo's stomach slithered into a tight coil behind his ribs, and he shouted to Ambrose over the whistling wind.

"Higher," he called, jabbing a thumb upward. "We need to get higher."

Ambrose's face was pale tinged with green, but he nodded and shifted into fourth gear. The previous ascensions had been gradual, but this final gear was too ambitious for such gentleness. Both men were flattened against the seats as they rocketed up, stopping only once they were what must have been thousands of feet up. It took a minute or two before either of them did anything but breathe before they unclenched.

His heart hammering, Milo hung his head out over the cab door and surveyed the land below, stretching out in a perspective he'd not experienced since the zeppelin in Afghanistan. God's-eye-view he'd heard it called, and if that was so, Milo decided that explained a good deal about the deity. The world was beautiful but detached, and cold was all around.

Milo pushed the morose thoughts aside as he saw that the burnt farmstead was not an isolated incident. Winding like a ribbon of destruction unfurling south, Milo saw other homes and hamlets that had received similar treatment. The once-picturesque dwellings and settlements were now smoldering black blots on the landscape, throwing up choking plumes of smoke.

"Dear God," Milo muttered, oblivious to the irony of the exclamation as he sank back.

"Looks like Joseph already found his way home." Ambrose grunted next to him, his face purged of color. "Wonder where he's going?"

Milo willed himself to look again at the devastation's path.

"South," he said stiffly. "Towards Tiflis, maybe."

Ambrose nodded and gingerly applied his foot to the accelerator.

"Good," he wheezed, looking for all the world like he might pass out, vomit, or both at the same time. His knuckles stood out like great white knobs on the wheel. "Means he's not headed for Shatili. The contessa should still be safe."

"And Lokkemand will be furious." Milo groaned, feeling dark despair well inside him. "I was away when the enemy arrived. I'll be lucky if he doesn't shoot me on sight."

The Rollsy growled a little louder as its driver applied his foot. From this altitude, the earth stretched out in imitation of the maps Ambrose had copied, making navigation a trivial concern.

"One bridge at a time," Ambrose said slowly. "Let's save the contessa, and then we can worry about what Lokkemand will do."

Milo shook his head, feeling the black waves lapping at him again. His situation seemed impossible, and even though he'd known this was a possibility, he'd desperately hoped that it wouldn't come to pass. What had started out seeming to be the *only* right answer had devolved into another trade-off, a measure forestalling eventual collapse.

What good was saving Rihyani if it resulted in the usurpation of an entire country and the dissolution of Nicht-KAT? Didn't that put him in the same spot as before? No, it was worse, he realized, much worse. The selfishness implicit in the thought sickened him, but he couldn't shake it. He couldn't think of any other thing he could have or would have done, but that only made things worse.

He was playing a rigged game, and knowing that only deepened his disgust at his circumstances, and more intensely, his inability to escape them.

There was nothing he could do to escape the fact that he wasn't enough, that he—

"Stop it!"

The words tore themselves from Milo's throat with such force that Ambrose jumped, and his foot came off the accelerator.

"What the hell was that?" Ambrose shouted, but Milo was too busy to notice.

He was gripping his head and compelling his magical awareness inward.

The tide of despairing, suffocating thoughts had been in his own mental voice, but they were not his. They'd sprung from some cavity inside of him where something nested, subtle and clinging, but they were not his thoughts. Unbidden, he remembered that moment when the marquis' "gift" of experiencing the Art had nearly overwhelmed him and he'd been aware, for an instant, of something sharing the space of his consciousness.

Who are you? Milo asked the darkness within him and felt a shiver race through as he felt the toothy smile behind the answering voice.

You already know, my wayward pupil.

"Magus?" Ambrose called, inching his way across the seat to give Milo a shake. "You're making me nervous."

Milo felt the darkling awareness recede inside him at Ambrose's touch and words, but he knew it was biding time, not retreating. Gooseflesh rippled across Milo's body, and it was all he could do not to reach down and rip his flesh with wild, clawing hands.

"Milo?" Ambrose's voice was almost pleading. "What is it?"

The magus ran a hand across his brow where icy sweat had sprung, then stared at the dampened hand as though fearing it would twist into a ghul's claw or worse, the unnatural spidery talon of a shade.

"Imrah," Milo murmured, fighting to get the words out as he kept his gorge in. "Her shade. It's inside me."

Ambrose swore long and bitterly, then collapsed in the driver's seat.

"One bridge at a time," Milo offered hollowly, but he couldn't bring himself to grin at the joke.

Ambrose rolled his gaze back to Milo, and there was nothing but heartache in his green eyes. Milo, allergic as he was to pity, was uncomfortable under the weight of the stare, but neither of them had the strength to break free of the shared stare's gravity for several heartbeats.

Ambrose finally turned away, head shaking, as he straightened and drove his foot down on the accelerator.

"Let's go save the girl before we plummet to our deaths," he growled.

"One bridge," Milo murmured as the wind pulled across his face and hair, the two words a feeble candle against the dark inside of him.

It was better than nothing.

Their descent to the courtyard of Shatili was as disruptive as the sight that Milo and Ambrose witnessed once they sank out of the sky. The soldiers dropped their burdens on the cobbles of the courtyard, at least one crate splitting and spilling its contents, while they stared at the settling Rollsy.

"What are they doing?" Milo asked as he rose in his seat.

Ambrose carefully peeled his hands from the wheel, and with a steadying breath, he reached down and turned the key off, and the tires settled with a turgid thump. The engine was still clunking to a stop as Ambrose looked around, the first trickle of color rising into his cheeks. His face curdled as though he were smelling something foul.

"Looks like they're packing up to go," he said before throwing his shoulder against the cab door. "Where are you boys going?"

The soldiers blinked and gaped, then they exchanged sheepish looks and set about gathering up what they'd dropped in their shock.

"Was everyone struck deaf after we left?" Ambrose shouted as he slid out of the cab. "Don't tell me you are all so busy that you can't hear me."

Milo joined the big man on the cobbles, then took a quick look around and noticed more than one sour glare from soldiers attempting to appear busy. Whatever had happened since they'd left, it was certain that any allies they might have had before seemed to have had a change of heart.

"We need to find Rihyani," Milo said softly, but his words were lost on Ambrose, who stepped forward with an angry stomp.

"Where do you think you are going?" he demanded, hooking a thumb toward the ravaged countryside they'd passed over moments before. "The enemy's at the gates, and you're going to slink off with your tails between your legs?"

One of the soldiers struggling with the burst crate rose and shook a jagged spar of wood at Ambrose.

"We're escorts, not a bunch of commandos," he snarled before throwing the broken plank down in front of the big man.

"You're soldiers, aren't you?" Ambrose shot back, kicking the plank away disdainfully. "Or did your manhood freeze off during the winter?"

"Ambrose," Milo began, but a premonition of something coming at him had him twisting around in time to see Lokkemand's fist coming for his face. He dodged back and away from the crushing blow, so it took him in the chest instead of the jaw. The strike was like a mule's kick, and Milo was thrown backward. His back struck the hood with a sound like a gong.

"You've ruined everything!" Captain Lokkemand bellowed over the echoing note of Milo's impact.

Ambrose, moving with shocking speed, spun and leveled his rifle at the raging captain.

"Touch him again, and I'll empty your skull all over this courtyard."

Lokkemand's gray eyes were molten silver with ecstatic rage, but he checked his advance as he looked down the long barrel of the Gewehr.

"One word and you'll both be dead in a traitor's shallow grave," the captain snarled, sweeping an arm at the soldiers across the courtyard. With that single phrase, the muted embarrassment of the soldiers was transmuted into the crackling tension of promised violence.

"That's going to make little difference to you since you'll be dead," Ambrose said in a chillingly calm tone before raising his voice so everyone could hear him. "I've got five rounds in this clip. Any of you so much as calls the magus a name, I drop him and then four more. After that, you'll probably have me, but know five will die with me."

No one moved, and for a moment, no one even breathed. Simon Ambrose did not need to lie, and every man there knew it.

Trying to steady his thready breathing, Milo climbed back to his feet as he looked around the courtyard. His chest ached abominably, and his heart still felt like it was trying to catch up with the beats it had missed after the impact. Despite this distraction, he could plainly see the dueling instincts of fear and wrath in every soldier's eyes around them. None of them wanted to be responsible for Lokkemand's death, much less their own, but Ambrose had a gun in their commander's face. Every instinct honed in the mud and blood of the War told them unequivocally what the only answer could be.

It would take only a moment before one of them overcame his fear, or at least succumbed to the conditioning beaten into him, and men died needlessly.

"No one needs to die today," Milo croaked, one hand massaging his chest. "I know the enemy is here, but that isn't a reason to pack up and leave. We need to reconnoiter, to assess the best way to go after their commander and his connection to the Guardians."

Lokkemand stopped glaring at Ambrose to look down his nose at Milo and sniff contemptuously.

"Oh, now the Americans are not the primary concern, are they? My *laziness* is no longer responsible for your incomplete victory?"

Milo straightened painfully and nearly rebuked the captain for his taunt, but with a weary wheeze, he folded and bowed his head instead.

"You were right and I was wrong," he said softly but with enough volume to be heard across the courtyard. "The Americans were a third party, and they don't seem to be connected with the Guardians."

Lokkemand's smile at Milo's words was cold and sharp, without a hint of humor.

"I'm so glad you've come to this understanding, but it's too little, too late." He sneered. "All of this is too little too late. You weren't here when the enemy rolled to Tiflis, and without you, we had no hope of slowing his advance. Now the Georgian Bolsheviks are in power, the country is enemy territory, and the Transcaucasian Federation is on the brink of civil war."

Milo stared, mouth hanging open at the revelation of so much changed in so short a time. The captain leveled his accusation in condemning terms.

"Your *errand* has expanded the War into once-peaceful nations and resulted in the end of Nicht-KAT. Is this the kind of magic you perform, *Magus*, because I'm not sure this is what Colonel Jorge was hoping for?"

"Still don't see any reason for you to run scared," Ambrose said flatly, his cheek pressed against the stock of his rifle. "The situation has changed, but initiative and leadership are what an officer uses to overcome these situations. New challenges mean new tactics."

Lokkemand turned his withering gaze back on Ambrose, and for a moment, it was as though he wasn't under the scrutiny of a gun barrel.

"I don't need a lesson in leadership, deserter," he hissed. "And there is only one tactic. When a superior enemy force knows your position and makes clear their intent to wipe you out, you retreat. It's not heroic and it's not glorious, but it is sound and wise."

"How do you know they know we are here?" Milo asked.

Lokkemand laughed, and it set Milo's teeth on edge. He'd had quite enough of men laughing at matters devoid of humor.

"The Georgian command knew, and more than that, a message was delivered by local Bolshevik sympathizers this morning. I think some of them were the same men I paid off because of your nightly excursions. Any foreign forces still within Georgia within the week will be considered invaders and killed to a man."

Milo felt a pang of guilt accompanying the ache in his chest, but it was a distraction from the gnawing in his mind at the mention of the Bolsheviks. The marquis' enigmatic words of the enemy commander's connection with Milo, combined with nightmarish memories of the night he'd met Roland, would not be ignored.

"Did you expect this was going to be easy?" Ambrose taunted as he squinted down the Gewehr. "An officer leads his men to accomplish their mission. He doesn't run when things get complicated."

Lokkemand's nostrils flared, and the look he gave Ambrose might have set any other man ablaze with its intensity.

"An officer doesn't throw his men's lives away needlessly," Lokkemand snapped back. "Blood is the currency of war, but I never spend it freely. You were gone when we needed you, and now the mission has failed; it is simple as that. Maybe you couldn't have stopped what happened, but we'll never know because you. Weren't. HERE."

Lokkemand's eyes were back on Milo, and he felt the weight of the whole courtyard's gaze settling on him.

"Do we know who the enemy commander is?" Milo asked, hating how weak and small his voice sounded in his own ears.

"I'm surprised you haven't heard the Bolsheviks howling it drunkenly across the countryside," the captain spat sourly. "The name of Joseph Stalin has been toasted by every Marxist within a hundred miles."

Milo stared, and Ambrose raised his head from his rifle.

"Yes," Lokkemand intoned grimly. "*That* Joseph Stalin."

"The Butcher of Petrograd?" Ambrose muttered as he lowered his rifle, and the entire courtyard seemed to take a breath.

"The same," Lokkemand said, unable to hide that his body

relaxed. "Seems he's recovered much of the strength he lost fighting the Whites in Omsk but couldn't make peace with the Reds like Rokossovsky and Zhukov. He's come back home to start over."

"And the Georgians just let him?" Milo asked.

"What choice did they have?" Lokkemand said, his tone sympathetic. "Nearly a third of the people agree with the madman's socialist principles, and the rest realize he only got here by marching through German-held territory, showing he's either strong enough to defy us or that we are secretly in allegiance with him. It doesn't matter which. He's here, and we need to leave before we're rounded up for execution."

Milo took a moment to look around and stare into the face of every man in that courtyard. There was anger and fear and despair in each face, in their eyes and the set of their jaws. Some of them were brave men, some were not, but all of them were broken. To expect them to carry on wouldn't only be wrong, it would be pointless, and he knew it. The thought of facing what lay ahead without even a token allotment of soldiers filled his belly with ice, but there was nothing for it. They were done.

"Go," Milo said, and every eye swung toward him.

"What?" Ambrose and Lokkemand hissed together.

"Go," Milo repeated, straightening and meeting every man's gaze in turn. "You've done your duty and then some. This War will keep taking more and more until there's nothing but ashes and bones, but those bones don't have to be yours today. Go."

"This isn't a rout, damn it," Lokkemand began, his voice struggling to stoke the anger implicit in the words. "This is a reasonable retreat."

Milo nodded, hoping the sincere sympathy he felt was conveyed by his voice and face.

"I believe it," he said, turning to look the captain in the eye while addressing the courtyard. "I may not like him very much, but I do believe at bottom that Captain Lokkemand is a good man and a responsible officer. If he says it is time to leave, then it is your duty to do so."

A heavy quiet fell across the courtyard as men weighed their motivations and wrestled with their souls. Milo could read in their faces that some of them came up wanting, but he met their stares with the same unjudging expression.

"Go," Milo said one last time and turned to enter the fortress.

"What will you do?" Lokkemand called after him.

"What I intended to do all along," Milo said without turning back. "My duty."

THE BROKEN

Using the Art on a fey seemed to be both easier and more diffi-cult than Milo had expected. Rihyani's will was more accessible to his efforts than Ezekiel's had been but also more reactive. His probing attempts at her slumbering will were met with a powerful resistance that he imagined was habitual.

She was unconscious and so pale she seemed ethereal stretched out on the cot, her whole body sinking in on itself. For a creature who was nearly eternal, it was a chilling thing for Milo to see and think she looked old. It seemed wrong.

Upon seeing her this way, Milo had made a hasty play at her will and been rebuffed so quickly her nurse barely had time to climb out of his seat beside her.

"Are you going to wake her up?" Brodden asked, seeming to have aged ten years since they'd left him a few days ago.

"No," Milo said, looking away from Rihyani for a second. "I'm not sure she can be woken up, and I don't think she needs to be."

"If you say so." The medic sighed, settling back into a chair. "I don't understand how she's still alive, to be honest. It seems like will alone is keeping her here."

"You might not be wrong about that," Ambrose said softly as Milo turned back to Rihyani.

"I'll need you to not interrupt me now," Milo explained between steadying breaths. "You may see or feel strange things, but whatever you do, don't distract me."

Brodden shook his head and fell silent.

Milo pressed his will outward again.

The second brush of his will against hers was met with as much resistance as before, but rather than simply withdrawing, he pushed harder. He felt her will manifesting as suggestions of terrifying fates and lonely ends clawing and yowling to keep him at bay, but he turned the tables by instituting his own visions of bringing joy and resolution to those dire guardian visions. It was imperfect, and more than one magical insinuation pierced through, making him break out in a cold sweat and clutch his hammering chest, but he held fast all the same.

She could batter his mind with terrors all she wanted. He needed to reach her.

Her initial defenses diverted, Milo pressed out more and felt the response of her will against his own, a kind of static spark of psychic energy as contact was made.

Rihyani, can you hear me? he called to her, shaping words only she could decipher through the Art. They weren't just words but sentiments, fragments of thoughts and feelings, the likes of which he could never have explained. As the marquis had explained, it came intuitively to him.

Milo? came the soft, almost brittle answer. *You have learned the Art.*

Milo felt a weight slide off his chest. She was still there, or at least enough of her to hear and respond to him.

The marquis taught you? she asked.

In a way, Milo thought to her, uncertainty quavering in the communication. *I'll explain later, but first, we need to release you from the hex.*

Milo could sense the psychic sigh sliding from the fey's mind.

Yes, I do think I'm coming to the end of my resolve to resist, she replied, a response disturbingly nonchalant for what it portended. *You found the release for it?*

Yes, Milo answered eagerly, stretching out to take her hand in his, trying not to recoil at how cold her flesh felt. *It may seem crazy, but you must forgive Ezekiel. His curse is rooted in his inability to forgive himself and let himself die, so you must forgive him to break the hex's hold over you.*

There was a long silence, and only the trembling throb of Rihyani's will in his supernatural awareness kept Milo from assuming she'd died.

Rihyani?

That will be difficult.

Feelings and images flooded through Milo's mind, visions of Ezekiel's sneering, cackling face with a bloodied knife flickering in his hands. Fear, pain, and hatred accompanied the images, and through Rihyani's senses, Milo relived their duel between the trees in a single heartbeat and felt her soul-wrenching anguish not only at the death of her centuries-old companions but their desecration at his hands.

"Rihyani, please!" Milo cried, breaking the connection the Art provided for a moment to keep himself from becoming lost in the onrush of her will.

His eyes had slid out of focus, but in that breathless moment when he pulled away from her, Milo saw blood dribbling down his arm. Sympathetic wounds had opened along the same line as what Rihyani had experienced.

"Milo?" Ambrose rumbled at Milo's shoulder, not quite daring to rest a hand on his shoulder.

"I'm fine," Milo said with a gulping swallow as he watched his blood slide down his outstretched hand to Rihyani's gray grip. "It's going to be okay."

Ambrose didn't say anything, but Milo could feel his frown at his back.

"Please," Milo said as gently as he could. "I need to focus."

When Ambrose made no protest, Milo clamped his eyes shut and pressed outward.

I'm sorry, I was overwhelmed, Milo broadcasted to her as their wills connected. *I am here now.*

No, Milo, I'm sorry.

He felt waves of the fey's regret, not overpowering but steady and sincere.

I am struggling to keep myself together. The hex and the wounds are taking their toll.

Milo felt a thrill of fear, which made his next thoughts sharper than he intended, but off they flew like arrows.

Which is why you need to forgive him. The longer you hold onto this, the harder it will be. Please, before it is too late!

A caustic film covered her next thoughts, and Milo had to harden himself to blunt the worst of their fury.

You talk as though it is easy! I watched that monster butcher two of my oldest friends, who I met when Latin was still a trade language! You speak of forgiveness like it is a flower to be plucked in a field!

Milo fought a rush of matching anger. He wanted to demand she stop being so proud, so stupid, but he beat the feelings down mercilessly. Pushing back wouldn't help because he couldn't drive her to forgiveness. He could only invite her, and with a start, he realized that the invitation could only come one way that would be understood.

You want revenge, he thought, pressing toward her with an understanding that mirrored his own experiences with the desire. *But what if I showed you that revenge against Ezekiel is exactly what he wants, too?*

What?

He felt her will rebel against the seeming contradiction, pulling away from him, but he remained open to her even as she came to the cusp of severing the connection. Milo wondered if that happened, would she have the strength to continue interacting? Her will was potent, but he sensed a brittleness that threw up more cracks after each outburst.

I don't understand.

Milo squeezed her icy hand with his bloodied fingers.

Let me show you, he begged. *Let me show you what I learned. Then make the decision for yourself.*

Another aching pause followed, but finally, Rihyani called out to him from what seemed like a greater distance than before.

All right.

Milo felt invisible barriers falling and intangible wards coming undone, and he touched the fey's raw, undiluted will with his own. It was beautiful, precious, and frightening both in power and fragility. Tears sprang unbidden to his eyes.

He is a monster, Milo said as he drew upon the jagged shards of memory still embedded from his encounter with Ezekiel. *But even monsters can love in their own fashion, and that means they can hurt and regret and be given our pity.*

With as much agonizing immediacy as before, Milo relived the sad tale of Ezekiel Boucher's living damnation with Rihyani.

She saw and felt everything: the piercing of Ezekiel's child by the vengeful warriors, Ezekiel's grief fueling the slaughtering of innocents, the coming of the curse, and him murdering the fey who cursed him.

Milo thought having seen it before would harden him against the experience, but he felt tears welling up, the blows to his heart penetrating even harder. Knowing what came did not make it better but only heightened his dread at each coming blow and his disgust at each predestined atrocity. Bound in will, he and Rihyani bore witness and felt what Ezekiel felt, and even amid the blood and hysterical laughter, it was an awful, gnawing agony.

The vigil completed and the smells of burning bodies and

Ezekiel's laughter fading, there was a stillness of body and mind so profound that Milo didn't dare to disturb it. Eyes sealed, his will present but passive within the fey's, there was a quiet closeness the likes of which he'd never known. In the fearful presence of that undiluted intimacy, he both basked and cringed.

When she finally reached out to him, a surprised, shuddering breath wracked his body.

He is like so many humans, worthy of hate and pity in his brokenness. I suppose I can tighten my grip and let his jagged edges cut me to the quick, but perhaps I'd rather let him go.

Like a skein unraveling, the hex became null.

"Thank you," Rihyani breathed, and leaned in with a gentle kiss.

Brodden's face was a comical explosion of wonder and anxiety, eyes bulging even as his lips met the fey's. The kiss lasted barely more than a second, but the bedraggled medic emerged as though he were coming up from pearl diving.

"Nothing much," he sputtered sheepishly as he stumbled back. "Just my duty."

Rihyani was still sunken and gray from her ordeal, but her smile was a radiant thing.

"We both know that isn't true," she said softly, holding out one waifish hand that Brodden took between thick, shaking fingers. "You performed above and beyond, and for that, I will grant you a boon."

Brodden looked nervously from Rihyani to Milo and Ambrose, who stood beside her chair by the fireplace.

"A boon from a fey," Ambrose muttered out the side of his mouth in an overloud whisper. "Careful what you wish for, eh?"

Milo didn't say anything, only nodded grimly, fighting to keep his dour expression as he watched the color drain from the medic's blotchy face.

"W-what boon would that be, *f-fräulein?*" Brodden gasped, absentmindedly tucking his uniform back into place and doing a generally poor job of the business.

Rihyani's smile slid away as her eyelids drooped to half-mast, and she gripped the medic's meaty fingers in both of her delicate hands. She drew a deep breath and let it slide out in a misty, monotone voice that was quite unlike her usual lively tones.

"You will write to your sweetheart in the next week and ask for her hand in marriage," she said, her hooded eyes looking through Brodden. "She will write back with haste to tell you her answer is yes."

Brodden made to say something, but his mouth seemed ill-equipped. He only managed a hoarse splutter.

"Don't speak," the contessa warned in her medium's drone. "A single word could unhinge the magic and release an awful curse on both of you."

Brodden freed his fingers to clap both his hands over his mouth as he shuffled backward, his face seeming ready to split in half from terror and excitement. He rocked on the balls of his feet to the point that Milo thought the man might lose his balance and a new medical emergency would arise.

"Go now with this boon," Rihyani decreed, fingers still stretched out toward him. "And speak of it to no one lest the curse be visited upon both of you until your dying days."

Brodden staggered back and fumbled for his medical bags.

"Hurry, man!" Ambrose barked, making Brodden jump like a startled cat. "Before it's too late and goblins dog you all the way back to Germany."

Brodden was still juggling his pack as he tore out of the room, and the sound of his pounding boots could be heard through the entire wing of the complex as he fled. Only as the last of his hammering steps faded did the three left in the room allow themselves a hearty laugh.

"Did you see his face?" Milo gasped between hoots of laughter, "But goblins, really?"

"A bit much?" Ambrose asked as he chuckled from the depths of his vast belly.

"A bit." Rihyani giggled and threw him a wink.

It was a few more minutes before they were composed enough for Milo to ask the question that had formed as he'd taken part in the spectacle.

"That wasn't any kind of actual magic though, right?" Milo asked, glancing to where Brodden had stood moments ago. "I mean, I could feel your will at work, and I don't know how you could work on a will that isn't here."

"Oh, you'd be amazed what the Art can accomplish with a little ingenuity," Rihyani said, smiling up at him before fluttering her fingers. A glowing cigarillo appeared between her fingers. "Our magic may be temperamental, but it is remarkable what we can achieve."

Milo stared at her, chin lowered and eyebrows raised.

"Oh, fine. No, it wasn't magic," she said before taking a toke and releasing a fragrant plume of smoke. "Just a little bit of observation. To pass the time, he'd usually read his letters from home, including those from a lovely young woman named Johanna. I'm not sure if he knows this, but the man mutters every other word as he reads."

Milo and Ambrose stared at the contessa.

"You could hear even when you were out?" Ambrose asked.

Rihyani nodded and took a heavy drag.

"One of the wonders of being fey is that we are never absent or insensate," she said with a sigh as she looked into the fire. "We can disconnect ourselves from aspects of our physical bodies to free our minds to wander, and that is the closest we get to sleeping or dreaming. Or in my case, giving me a little buffer from my injuries."

She shuddered at that, and they lapsed into silence.

As Milo considered this fact in light of the extremely long, possibly immortal lifespans of the fey, he suddenly understood why they all seemed eccentric in one way or another. Centuries and no true sleep; no wonder they all seemed a little—or a lot,—odd.

"So, the nightwatch," Milo began, an uncomfortable thought worming its way through his mind. "What did it do?"

Rihyani looked at him squarely in his face, and he felt a pang as he remembered her pained cry as she came to.

"It made sure I knew you needed my attention," she said softly.

Milo felt his cheeks burning and struggled to hold her gaze.

"I'm sorry."

"You already said that," she replied.

Ambrose looked at the two of them, sensing more at play than a misunderstanding of fey physiology.

"Well, that sounds downright hellish," he said finally with a slow shake of his head. "If I couldn't enjoy a good snooze, I think I'd have eaten a bullet or four by now."

Not that it would've done you any good, Milo thought, and he felt a sudden thrill of fear as he glanced at the fey. He'd worried for an instant that she might have heard the sentiment, but then he remembered the disentangling after the hex was released, and he breathed a sigh of relief. That level of connection was something he still viewed like a blazing fire: powerful but more than a little dangerous. Yet, like dancing flames, he wasn't going to forget the warmth of it anytime soon.

Rihyani felt his gaze upon her again and she looked up at him, turning her head coyly with a teasing smile on her dark lips.

"Yes?" she asked coaxingly.

"Um-uh," he stammered as his mind scrambled. "I was just wondering if you know, uh, with no magic at play, if Brodden was in for a rather disappointing letter from Johanna?"

Rihyani shook her head, and Milo noticed that already her

hair didn't seem quite so lank or her cheeks so sunken.

"Oh, Brodden has nothing to worry about," she said brightly. "Even with missing every other word, I could tell the sweet Johanna's been practically burning with longing for him to ask her."

"And the poor fool needed a fey to bully him into it?" Ambrose chuckled.

"Some men need a little extra help," Rihyani said, and Milo couldn't help noticing the sidelong glance she gave him through a cloud of tobacco smoke.

By dusk, they all stood upon the battlements of the fortress to watch Lokkemand and his entourage depart. Ambrose muttered curses, most concerning Lokkemand and his parentage, while Rihyani, who was more herself by the second, watched with an enigmatic expression. Milo remained silent, wrestling with an odd combination of guilt and relief.

What might happen to Nicht-KAT, Jorge, and yes, even Lokkemand, troubled him, but the fact was, he was free to do as he saw fit. A nagging thought told him he'd behaved that way up to this point, but with Lokkemand now gone and everything declared a loss, anything he could salvage from the situation would be an unexpected success. He hadn't wanted things to turn out this way, but now that they had, he felt there was nothing holding him back.

And that meant preparing for what came next.

"The messenger said within a week," Milo related after the last lights of the last vehicle winked behind a concealing hill. "That means that we have four days to prepare for Stalin and his forces."

"I doubt very much if forces will be sent just for us." Ambrose grunted. "A decent number of Germans to drag out for a big show execution is one thing, but we aren't worth the time. He'll send a squad of conscripts if he sends anything."

Rihyani nodded but said nothing as she drew her heavy traveling cloak around her shoulders. She'd begun to show the traces of silver light in her complexion and hair, but she was still a long way from her usual brilliance. Milo had offered her one of his restoratives, but she had declined, saying that she was healing quicker than her appearance suggested. Milo found that incredible considering the ordeal she'd gone through, but he was counting on her rapid recovery.

"That's only because they think the Germans all left," Milo said, a smile hitching up one corner of his mouth. "But if they think the opposite occurred, like maybe an entire regiment marched in, they would have to make a show of force. There is more than a good chance that Stalin might send the bulk of his forces to make a clear statement."

Both fey and bodyguard turned to look at Milo with furrowed brows.

"And why would they think that?" Rihyani asked.

Milo kept staring into the coming night and smiling.

"Because we're going to use the Art to make it look like that."

"Milo," Rihyani began, her eyes narrowing as she studied his face in profile, "the Art can make others believe things and even be affected by those beliefs, but fighting a battle with an illusory army is beyond any fey's skill."

Milo turned away from the dark and looked at Rihyani, still smiling.

"We aren't going to fight them," he explained. "We're going to lure them out here, and with most of his men chasing phantoms, we're going to find and capture Stalin. With the head of the coup gone and the forces dispersed, the Georgian government will have a chance to recover. We can't fix it for them, but we can give them a chance while we take Stalin back to Nicht-KAT for interrogation."

Ambrose and Rihyani both looked doubtful but nodded slowly.

"It's halfway to suicide," the big man muttered. "But if you can convince the Reds that's what's going on, it might work."

"Not to sound bloodthirsty, but wouldn't it be easier to kill this Stalin?" the contessa asked.

"We need to know his connection to the Guardians," Milo explained. "We need to get a better understanding of what connections they have to German forces and outside, and questioning Stalin seems like the best bet to get some answers as to how his benefactor operates."

Rihyani considered the answer for a moment, looking out into the darkness deepening across the vista.

"And if the benefactor is there with Stalin?" she asked.

"Then we kill or capture him," Milo said evenly. "Probably the former rather than the latter. A human prisoner is one thing, but the Guardian is probably going to be too difficult for us to transport easily."

"And we still don't know exactly what kind of supernatural help this Guardian is giving Stalin?" Ambrose asked as he probed around his coat before drawing out his pipe and tobacco.

"Only that he has incredible control over his followers," Milo replied.

Rihyani sighed. "That could be anything."

"Does the name Joseph mean anything?" Ambrose asked, giving Milo a sideways glance. "Or Ioseb Besa…a…"

"Ioseb Besarionis dze Jugashvili," Milo said as they both turned to look at the fey.

Rihyani shook her head.

"Wouldn't want it to be too easy, now, would we?" Ambrose said around the stem of the pipe between his teeth. "Besides, doesn't change what we have to do, does it?"

"No," Milo said, forcing himself to keep the confident smile on his face. "No, it doesn't."

THE MESSAGE

Milo was surprised to see a familiar face among the men Ambrose brought to the fortress the next day before late afternoon.

To give the Red warlord time to gather his forces for a proper response, Milo thought it imperative that word of the arrival of a strong German contingent needed to be issued as soon as possible. As such, Milo had sent Ambrose to the village of Shatili to ask for local Bolsheviks and gather a few of them in the bed of the Rollsy for an introduction to the "German answer." The men had not come willingly, of course, but few knocks on the head and a few lengths of rope, and Ambrose had come into the courtyard frog-marching three bound and rather terrified men.

One of those men happened to be the farmer who'd sicced his dogs on Milo the night he'd been gathering hearth ash. The man didn't seem to recognize the magus, which was not at all surprising, not only because of the nature of their encounter but also because of the figure standing next to him.

"Are you ready for this?" Milo whispered out the side of his mouth.

"Absolutely," boomed a strong kettle-drum voice in thick German.

The man who made the declaration could have been the impossible offspring of Lokkemand and Ambrose. He was huge, as tall or taller than the towering captain but with a bulky physique like that of his other "parent," and upon his florid face sat a well-waxed mustache that would have left a walrus envious. He was dressed in an officer's black coat festooned with medals and sporting the red-banded knotwork of an *Oberstleutnant*, or lieutenant colonel, upon his shoulders.

"You're very convincing," Milo said with an appreciative dip of his chin.

"Naturally," rumbled the massive officer. Not for the first time, Milo had to keep his mind from reflecting on the considerably smaller fey inside the illusion. It was perhaps the least dramatic thing they'd be showing the erstwhile messengers, but it was the one Milo was most impressed by. She'd even woven a few shaving nicks onto the thick neck of her disguise.

"Eyes front, Volkohne," the *Oberstleutnant* puffed through his mustache, and Milo dutifully complied.

The trio of men staggered before them, their faces set and angry while frightened eyes roved the stones around them.

"What do you want with us?" the farmer Milo recognized asked, his voice convincingly steady.

The man had some steel to him, there was no denying that.

Milo made a show of looking at his superior, who nodded.

"You've been brought here because we were notified that you were Bolshevik sympathizers and traitors to your own country," Milo said, and he held back a smile as the protests and declarations sprang up like geysers.

Milo held up a warning hand, and the men quieted—except the farmer who spat on the ground and thrust his chin toward Milo and the disguised Rihyani.

"Execution, then?" he snarled, taking an angry step forward.

"You invade our country and think you have the right to execute us?"

"We were guests until a short time ago," Rihyani declared in the booming German officer voice.

All three men looked at the illusory officer with open trepidation, even the farmer, but Milo could tell they didn't understand the words that had been said.

"*Oberstleutnant* Hindenreich makes the point that we were only called invaders since the rise of the Bolshevik terrorist Stalin," Milo explained in Georgian. "And it is for this reason he and his forces have now come to restore the rule of law."

All three looked around the seemingly barren fortress, but only the brave farmer had the courage to respond.

"What forces?" he sneered. "Last we knew, you Germans were running north with your ears pinned back."

"That is why you are here now," the *Oberstleutnant* declared and raised a hand to issue a ringing finger-snap.

Every door in the fortress flew open and out marched streams of federated German soldiers, rifles at their shoulders or machine guns carried in teams. Milo's and Rihyani's wills working together ensured that the tromp of their boots, the smell of their sweat, and even the heat of their bodies brushed the senses of the three men. Milo had feared mounting pressure as the men sought to disbelieve what they saw, but even the farmer took the illusory information at face value. The marquis hadn't been wrong about how much men trusted their senses in the face of what they might have otherwise disbelieved.

The fabricated soldiers came to parade rest behind Rihyani and Milo, faces grim and eyes set forward. Perhaps soldiers might have noticed the fact that they were too perfect, but for the present company, the illusion worked fine.

"You are going to bear witness," Milo declared as he strode forward to put himself nearly nose to nose with the brave farmer. "You will return to your treacherous masters and tell them that the German Empire does not bow to threats and does not forsake its allies. You will be spared your miserable lives to deliver this message."

The farmer attempted to meet Milo's pale eyes, but his gaze kept wandering to the arrayed soldiers, and the defiance leached from his face.

Cowed, the farmer led the other two up the stairs and out onto the battlements. Ambrose, Milo, and Rihyani followed. They all looked out over the valley, the arms of the mountains sweeping to either side. For a moment nothing happened, and the three informants cast nervous looks around, glancing back behind at the courtyard where the soldiers stood and then at their captors. Ambrose grunted and pointed forward with a scowl that had all three turning back toward the valley.

There was a deep rumble as though the earth itself was awakening to bear witness, then across the valley, engines of war made their appearance. Tanks, armored tracks, and artillery pieces growled and chugged and snarled as they mounted the slope and stood glittering darkly in the late afternoon sun. Meaningfully, their weapons were leveled downslope, where the village stood quiet and unsuspecting. It took a moment, but soon all three men were whimpering, praying, and begging.

"My God," one groaned. "No."

"My family," another moaned.

"Please," the farmer cried, turning to Milo and falling to his knees. "Please, don't do this."

Overheard was the throbbing whir of zeppelins plying the skies. Milo hadn't expected those but pushed the thought from his mind as he looked into the informants' terrified faces. Rihyani must have been adding last-minute flourishes.

"Do you now understand the cost of treachery?" Milo asked,

feeling a little queasy as he watched the men squirm and grovel. "Do you now know what you must do?"

The farmer nodded vigorously, and the other two men followed suit as tears and snot ran freely down their faces.

"Go and tell the Bolsheviks we are here and they are welcome to try and drive us out," Milo commanded, nodding at Ambrose, who stepped forward to cut the men's bonds. "And that if they don't have the spine to defend their stolen prize, we will come and fetch them out like thieves from their den."

The men stared at their rope-worn wrists and stood trembling before Milo.

"Now go!" Milo roared, driving a spike of raw fear through his will and into the heart of each man.

Shivering and swearing on anything and everything they could think of, the men stumbled down from the battlements under the unflinching glare of the assembled soldiers. They found their feet as they passed through the gate and out onto the road, all three of them running wildly as their heads swiveled left and right.

The sight of their fleeing backs sparked something in his chest in a place next to his heart. There was a tightness, a contraction that was as much psychic as muscular, and Milo found he couldn't move, couldn't breathe. He wanted to scream, to gasp, but all control was gone. For an eternal second, Milo was locked inside himself, powerless to perform even the most basic and automatic functions, even as he felt his body cry out for air.

Then a mind not his own slid up from that cavity inside him and took control. It expelled the stale air from his lungs and drew in a fresh breath before looking skyward at the zeppelins. Like clouds of steel and thunder, they'd flown low over the fortress, and Milo's kidnapped eyes noted the way the barrels jutting from the gun turrets were now trained upon the fleeing informants.

"Perhaps," the-thing-that-was-not-Milo called out in a magically enhanced voice, "you need further encouragement."

Ambrose and Rihyani both looked at Milo, confusion written plainly on their features. Their questions were answered a second later when the zeppelins above opened fire. Everything, the flare of their muzzles to the hiss of the bullets cutting the air, even the spurts of dirt and dust they kicked up, were all illusory, but each of these elements heightened the terrified certainty of the fleeing men that they were being fired upon. Screaming, they put on speed and wove away from the intersecting sweeps of the chattering salvos.

"Milo," Rihyani called, traces of her real voice slipping between the booming officer's, "What are you doing?"

The men below were beyond frantic in their flight now, each pumping his arms and legs with a speed and determination born of mortal fear. Milo watched them through eyes he no longer controlled, his co-opted mouth twisting into a smile.

"Magus!" Ambrose barked, stepping toward Milo and grabbing him by the shoulder. "That's enough!"

The-thing-that-was-not-Milo turned and twisted the stolen face into a cruel sneer.

"Let go of me, or by Iblis, I'll burn you to cinders."

The raptor skull flared to crackling life, and Ambrose stepped back in surprise.

"Iblis," Ambrose muttered, his face knotting in confusion, but the usurper was already dragging his eyes back to the fleeing men. The zeppelins harried them, stitching lines of false fire, inching closer and closer to a strafing run that would prove fatal to the thoroughly convinced men.

"What is going on?" Rihyani demanded, shedding her disguise like shrugging out of an overlarge coat. "Milo, stop this!"

The farmer had stumbled, his leg turning under him as his foot struck a stone. The line of fire would sweep over him, leaving a terror-perforated corpse. It was only a matter of time, and the usurper was intent on watching it.

"It's not Milo," Ambrose growled. "IMRAH!"

The-thing-that-was-not-Milo swung kidnapped eyes toward Ambrose as the big man's fist exploded across his face. Milo and his captor fell together in the prison of his flesh. The shared head struck the stone of the walkway, and darkness rushed up to claim them both.

He was back in the alley, Roland pulling on his hand. He was staring at the bricks but didn't know why.

"We need to go," Roland urged.

But he didn't, he realized with a start. He didn't need to go because he wasn't a child anymore. Looking down at his hand, he realized that Roland's was now the small one as he towered over him.

Roland looked back up at him, his voice plaintive in a way it had never been, perhaps never could be.

"I want to go, please."

He shook his head to protest, but as he did, he watched scrawling lines of ink sprout across Roland's skin. Tattoos years too early unfurled as child Roland began to swell in front of him.

"Come on, little brother," Roland said, his voice cracking and then deepening as he spoke. "We need to go."

He tried to pull away and felt a familiar, insistent grip trying to keep him there.

"You need to come with me," Roland insisted, pressing forward so the nearly formed face was inches from him. After a second of hesitation, it became the cruelly beautiful face of the angry and ambitious young man he'd followed through Hell and the underbelly of Dresden more than once.

"I need you," Roland murmured into his face, breath sharp with vodka. "You need me."

He pulled his hand away and made to push the face away, but

it was as insubstantial as smoke, a misplaced memory vying for attention it didn't deserve.

He looked back at the brick wall and remembered the spaces between the spaces. His breath gathered in a single sharp inhalation, he drove his fingers between the memories.

It was cold on the other side, but not so cold he couldn't feel the slippery, squirming thing. His finger clamped down even as it tried to wriggle away, digging into rubbery flesh with a strength he hardly recognized in himself. Something tried to bite him, but its teeth blunted and cracked on his skin. There would be no escape from him now that he knew it was there.

With a heave like a fisherman hauling a prize catch onto land, he dragged it through the bricks and onto the floor of the alley. Its dark form glistened red under the burning sky as it curled at his feet in the fetal position, his hand still fastened around its neck. Despite the ectoplasmic slime, he recognized the quivering thing.

"Imrah!" he snarled but then paused, thoughts flickering in his eyes before they narrowed once more. "No, not her. Just her shade."

The creature writhed and snapped its teeth, but it was like a viper or some other venomous reptile gripped behind its jaws, gnashing at open air. He felt the phantasm's fear throbbing against his palm, and both quickly understood that whatever vulnerability of Milo's it had grasped was gone.

"You're a parasite," he snarled, stilling it with one hard shake. "And I think I'm going to do some exterminating."

His fingers began to tighten about the thing's neck, and he savored his strength. His might was born of focus, control, and will, constructed in the dreamscape, and he knew with a burst of certainty he could destroy the shade inside him. The text on shades had been ambivalent about this, but here in the kingdom of his mind and spirit, he knew he could.

The shade squealed, and its shrill cry gave him pause.

"Wait! Not yet! Please!"

He didn't tighten his grip further, but he didn't loosen it either.

"Why?" he demanded.

The shade began to snivel and gibber, but he shook it again and its plaintive whining congealed into words once more.

"We are not the shade of she who was Imrah, only splinter, a fragment, sent to make an offer."

Milo squeezed his fingers a little tighter as his eyes narrowed.

"What offer?"

"She offers to share all knowledge, all information with you if you make her whole."

Here in the dreamscape, rational thought was more difficult as his emotions and subconscious swam freely, but the cold, rational, and ruthless part of him stirred like a shark scenting blood. Suspicions and fears woke as well, but the predator's instinct was not so easily distracted.

"Make her whole?" he asked in a soft, deadly voice as he bent closer. "How would I do that?"

The fearful splinter-shade winced away, but his hand held it fast.

"She will explain!" it sobbed. "We don't know, we were only sent with a message!"

"And with enough power to almost murder a man," he growled, his fingers squeezing again. Tiny motes of spiritual debris floated away from the edges of his grip. Much tighter and the splinter-shade would come apart in a rush of psychic dust.

"Part of the message!" it squealed with further feeble thrashing. "To show, to demonstrate! Could have killed you, could have thrown your body from the wall or stopped its breathing! We didn't, not the message!"

Milo felt a tremor in his grip as he remembered the utter separation from his body, a helplessness he'd never known. He wondered if the reason he had absolute dominance over the splinter-shade was that it had spent its strength controlling him for those moments. Wrath and defiance at the memory made his hold fast in an instant.

He decided it didn't matter how it took control before. It wasn't going to get a chance to scurry away to some dark corner inside him. He had it now, and it would end.

His fingers flexed, and the feeble imitation of a ghul twisted helplessly in his grip.

"You are unharmed, message delivered!" it babbled. "Please! Message delivered! Please!"

"Message delivered, and I may even take the shade up on its offer," he whispered as his crushing grip sent up more of the fracturing shade. "Either way, I see no reason to let you cause more mischief."

The splinter-shade made to scream, but he snuffed it out like a candle wick.

"I am going to repeat for the hundredth time that I do not like this," Ambrose growled as he thumped down the stairs to the shade-warded dungeon. Milo supposed that the estimation of the number of times the big man had protested was fairly accurate, but as before, Milo pressed on.

When he had finally woken with a sizable lump on his skull and a few teeth that felt uncomfortably looser than they ought to, he'd quickly relayed his dream escapade after confirming that the farmer had not met an unfortunate end from illusory bullets. Once reassured of that fact and having finished his tale, his companions had been decidedly unhelpful by taking opposing opinions on the matter. Ambrose was determined that this proved that "messing with" Imrah's shade was foolish, and they should make sure her remains were never found by another living soul.

Rihyani, on the other hand, seemed convinced that the best option would be to at least hear the shade out because "if it wanted you or any of us dead, we would be."

In the end, much to the bodyguard's irritation, Milo had decided that one final interview with the specter of his old teacher would be worthwhile.

So now all three of them had come to the dungeon, willing or otherwise. The ritual to call for Imrah's shade was observed, only this time, the wraith's entrance was nothing like the horrid production he'd witnessed before. The horrifying, mewling thing with too many limbs and brightly gleaming eyes didn't emerge, nor did Imrah's form in some twisted parody of woman and ghul. The temperature dropped and a column of fog emerged, in whose center floated Imrah's ghulish face.

"I see you got my message," she said, a pure observation without irritation or humor.

"I did." Milo nodded, his arms crossed over his chest. "I don't suppose I should be surprised that your message involved almost killing someone."

The ridged brows of the ghulish face twisted into what passed for a concerned scowl.

"Not one of those two, I hope?" it said.

"Does it matter?" Milo spat in disgust.

The ghul specter gave him a wry look.

"Are you going to keep pretending it wouldn't?" it asked.

Milo shook his head but didn't say anything. It wasn't wrong. If Ambrose or Rihyani had been threatened, the remains of Imrah would have been reduced to cinders and the shade thoroughly dispersed by now.

"Whatever the case, are we done with games now?" Milo asked.

"It is not a matter of games, but of effort," the floating face explained in what sounded like Imrah's voice emerging from the bottom of a well. "Since my death, coherence is largely a matter of extreme effort, and until you were ready to listen, there was little reason to try."

For one jarring second, Milo felt as though he were talking to Imrah, so different was the shade from its previous appearance and behavior.

"Your death," he said, fresh suspicion narrowing his eyes and sharpening his words. "You want me to trust you, but you keep acting as though you are Imrah when we both know that is not true."

A ghulish smile spread across the levitating visage, and Milo felt nauseous.

"Very good grasp of the ephemeral principles, but unfortunately incorrect. One of the secrets I'd learned among the Guardians was a heretical version of the necromists' formulae. Very tricky, but it connected my spirit to my shade."

"That's not possible." Milo frowned. "Nothing I've ever read says anything about that."

The floating face just stared at him.

"That would be why they call it a secret," it remarked dryly. "But I have to confess, my attempt at the process seems to have been imperfect. As a result, mastering the shade and its entropic nature makes coherence and cohesion difficult."

Milo stared back, making no effort to conceal his incredulity. When he didn't respond, Imrah, if that was what it was, gave a short, irritable sigh, which Milo as her former pupil was quite familiar with.

"It might be difficult to believe, but I hope the messenger displayed my intentions, and what I'm going to ask should seal the deal, as you might say."

"I'm listening," Milo said, chin raised. Behind him, Ambrose uneasily shuffled his feet but voiced no objection, for which Milo was thankful. He didn't need anything dividing his attention right now.

"I want you to bind me to the cane I gave you," the cloud-swaddled ghul stated. "Without the structure inherent in a well-made fetish, I am losing the battle to keep the shade bound to me. If you do this for me, I will promise indefinite service and advice, until such time as you pass me on to another or deplete me unto destruction."

Ambrose muttered a disbelieving assemblage of profanity while Rihyani gave a small, silver-noted laugh.

"She certainly doesn't lack for determination, I'll give her that," the fey said, and Milo could feel her smile at his back.

"That's putting it mildly," Ambrose growled. "Magus, please tell me you're not taking this seriously?"

But Milo most certainly was, and as Imrah watched him, she could plainly see that.

"Unlike the rest of you, our young magus understands the position I am placing myself in to ensure my survival."

"She's not wrong," Milo admitted as he slowly nodded. "If I bind her shade to the cane, she becomes its power source."

"And a potent one at that," Imrah added with more than a hint of pride.

"And treacherous," Rihyani said flatly. "What happens in the heat of battle when you call on her and she isn't there? She's already proven that she's patient enough to wait for the opportunity to turn on you."

Imrah's eyes narrowed at the fey, thin lips curling with disgust above the nest of fangs. Apparently, the enmity between the two was enough to last beyond the grave.

"Or even worse," Ambrose chimed in quickly, "she decides to blast you or someone else with flames when you don't want her to? Waits until you're in a petrol refinery or something and then BOOM!"

Imrah drew her gaze from glaring at Rihyani and looked at Milo.

"Should I explain it, or do you wish to?" she asked archly.

Milo looked over his shoulder at the two behind him, hoping he didn't sound as haughty as his former teacher as he explained.

"Yeah, it doesn't really work like that," he began, eyes darting from Rihyani to Ambrose and back again. "A shade bound to a fetish like what she is talking about, as a sort of essence battery and not as an actual animator, means she wouldn't be able to do much of anything without me directing it. A necromist has to give her power direction and focus. Otherwise, it is all potential. She'd be bound inside forever unless I depleted her past the point of cohesion, and then she'd be gone forever. It's a possible eternity bound in a small, unmoving length of stone."

Silence followed his explanation, and out of the corner of his eye, Milo saw Imrah give a nod of approval.

"Why would you choose that?" Rihyani asked at last, staring uncomprehendingly at the ghul's face. "How could such a life seem worth living?"

"I knew eternal life would have a cost, and more than that, it affords me time," Imrah replied coolly. "The plan was to provide myself with a more suitable, enduring vessel, but best-laid plans and all. This keeps me from slipping into madness and the void and gives me time to plan for the future."

"Future of what?" Ambrose asked with a derisive snort. "Supporting old knees and being stood up in the corners of entryways?"

"Eternity is a long time," Imrah replied. "Perhaps in time, the magus will find new uses for me, and if not, maybe the person he passes me to will."

The room once more lapsed into silence, and in the quiet, Milo could feel the unease of those behind him. Yet for all of that, the potential gain couldn't be ignored. If she were bound inside the fetish, he wouldn't just gain absolute control over the potent repository of essence for necromistry, but also her knowledge. No more cryptic answers or dueling bluffs; he would ask her a question, and she would answer it as truthfully and completely.

Despite all the misgivings, could he let this opportunity pass him by?

"Tell me about the Guardian working with Stalin," Milo said, staring hard into Imrah's face. "Do that, and we could have a deal."

"Milo," Ambrose began sharply, but a shushing sound from Rihyani stilled him.

"I don't know for certain about Stalin, as the name is not known to me," Imrah began, but reading Milo's face was quick to add, "But if it is the Guardian I think it is, I have much to share."

"Go on," Milo said.

"His name is Zlydzen of Domov, a dwarrow, and one of the founding Guardians," she explained. "As you might've guessed from your readings, ghuls and dwarrow do not typically interact except violently. Zlydzen was different; seeing past rivalries and petty squabbles. He understood what was at hand."

"Which was?" Milo asked.

"Extermination," Imrah stated flatly. "Never numerous, our kinds were losing more and more ground to humans, and it was only a matter of time before we were discovered and slaughtered. Zlydzen was the first of the gathering revolutionaries who understood that if we did not gather weapons and allies, both old and new, we'd have no chance to stem the tide."

"How simplistically extremist of him." Milo chuckled dryly. "So what weapons, old and new, could he have given to his new ally?"

For the first time, Imrah looked uncomfortable.

"The possibilities are nearly endless," she replied woodenly. "Even before founding the Guardians, he'd been interested in designs and theories that had incredible, devastating potential. Nearly all of them were incomplete or untested, but if he's deigned to work with this warlord, then he most likely has several at his disposal. He was the sort who liked to keep his options open."

"What sort of designs?"

"Vessels of demonic contagion, machines to drive armies mad, and engines to level cities," Imrah said, a hint of impatience heating her words. "I wasn't exaggerating about the potential. If he's decided to make a definitive move, he more than likely has the means to do incredible damage even if the scheme fails."

The color draining from Milo's face as he remembered the horror and destruction of Kimaris. Imrah had mentioned that her mentor had shown her how to draw him into service, as ill-fated as that had been, and now Milo could be facing one who possessed innumerable such doomsday creations.

"And would you have any idea how to stop these sorts of weapons?" Milo asked, trying to force down the panic that threatened to bubble up into his voice.

"Perhaps," she said, her face growing pensive. "I was his acolyte, but as I said, the designs were incomplete, though with a working knowledge of the concepts, I could give you a better chance than you'd have alone."

Milo turned to Ambrose and Rihyani and issued a weary shrug.

"I don't see that we have much of a choice."

"There's always a choice," Ambrose growled, but Rihyani stilled him with a gentle hand upon his shoulder.

"True," she said gently before looking at Milo with golden pupils held steady upon his gaze. "Whatever you decide, I'll stand by you."

Milo gave her a thankful nod and turned to look at Ambrose, who was glaring past him at Imrah's impassive face.

"And you?" Milo asked quietly.

Ambrose's gaze settled on the floor, and he heaved a mighty sigh before looking up to meet Milo's stare.

"To the end."

Milo nodded once more and turned back to Imrah.

"All right," he said, drawing a centering breath. "Let's do this."

THE FIRES

"I'm never going to get used to this!" Ambrose groaned as he tightened his grip on Milo's and Rihyani's outstretched forearms despite the straps which suspended him between them. Despite his most desperate hopes, Rihyani had stated she didn't possess the potency of the marquis to carry the Rollsy, and they'd had to make do with a cobbled-together harness.

Ambrose's complaints had been renewed every few minutes since they'd left Shatili.

Milo wanted to join in but feared if he was distracted for a moment, his first real experience wind riding would end very badly. Instead, his watering eyes remained fixed on the horizon, and his will pressed outward like a vast sail.

The binding of Imrah to his cane and preparing a little surprise for the inevitable communist occupation had taken days, so when they made ready to leave Shatili fortress, things were rushed. He'd received a crash course from Rihyani on the basics of wind riding, which seemed to be about willing the very air around him to believe he was light enough to be borne on a cushion of it. As with most things having to do with the Art, it was a simple, intuitive thing to accomplish the basics, even though it seemed impossible from a rational perspective that he had to diligently remind himself to not think about lest everything come undone and he plummeted to his death.

Despite his basic proficiency, Milo recognized quickly that he was far from the sort of easy mastery Rihyani displayed. Even now sailing along beside her, he could tell most of their forward movement was due to her dragging both humans along. Milo may have been carried by the currents of directed air, but they were not in a hurry to get him where he needed to go, and he guessed on his own skill, he would be lucky to do more than float along like a rather turgid balloon. He also found he struggled to maintain a steady altitude, and more than once, he found himself incredibly thankful that he was connected through Ambrose to her since he might have sailed heavenward and lost his nerve.

A meander upward followed by a sudden and final descent seemed a rather poor way to end his first attempt at flight.

They'd set off in the evening in hopes of avoiding being spotted by Stalin's forces, and also not trusting that the full week of amnesty would last, given the message they'd sent. Thankfully, the darkness didn't seem to bother Ambrose or Rihyani, and Milo had taken a dose of nightsight before they'd left, so navigation over the night-blackened countryside wasn't too much trouble.

The mountainous land rolled by beneath them, scattered homesteads and farms with cheery, fire-brightened windows housing those blissfully ignorant of their passing. War and bloodshed were once more about to descend on a country that had known much in its long history, but the small homes built on hillsides or in valleys still housed families gathering to break bread. They seemed like tiny bastions to Milo, each declaring a silent, enduring defiance to the darkness. Milo wasn't certain the defiance was warranted, especially now in a world filled with monsters and demons, but if he could will himself to fly, he supposed he could will himself to believe that maybe some of those little holdouts of honest people enjoying simple pleasures could outlast what was to come.

They sailed over Roshka, a village in a river-gouged valley, and righted their direction for a straight run south. There were no major roads through this part of the country, the closest being rough tracks made by horses or shepherded flocks wandering familiar paths, but that mattered little to them, riding the nightly currents. The closest major road that could have borne vehicles lay to the south and west near Pasanauri, which might be considered a full-scale town and was nearly fifty kilometers away.

Milo expected that was where the Soviets would come from, and as he swung his gaze toward that area, his stomach clenched.

There, winding across the rough ground like a vast glowing worm, were the lights of the advancing Soviet column. Crawling but still advancing, he could see them: over a hundred armored vehicles and trucks chugging along, headlamps glaring into the night. Rippling like an escort of ants besides the undulating column of light were the ranks of marching men. There was no way to accurately assess their numbers in the dark, but Milo knew there couldn't have been less than three hundred and possibly twice or three times that number, depending on if any groups ranged too far ahead or behind to be easily spotted near the line of vehicles.

Seeing such a force arrayed against them, Milo understood Lokkemand's anger and decision to retreat. Before a force like this, his paltry escort was an afterthought, and with no magus to try to balance the scales, what choice did they have but to run?

"They'll get a surprise when they get to the fortress," Ambrose shouted, obviously having noticed the spectacle to the southwest.

"Won't hardly make a dent," Milo called back over the wind.

"But it will make them wary, and that will buy us time," Rihyani said, her smile flashing at him in the moonlight. "Our success depends much more on their delay and less on how many we kill."

Milo knew she was right, but it still galled him to think that he was supposed to be the tipping point in this war, but he still felt so small before the realities of industrialized battle.

They continued in silence as more of the countryside rolled beneath them, and they lost sight of the Soviets. The harness connecting Milo to Ambrose and Rihyani, fashioned from what must have been carriage leathers, was beginning to cut fiercely into Milo's shoulders and back when Rihyani pointed to the east.

Milo forgot about the harness as he watched an entire village being put to the torch.

Thatched roofs crackled brightly, a stomach-turning exaggeration of the welcome glow that should have shown from their windows. A line of trucks, ten or so, stretched through and out of the plaza of the village, where figures moved in and out of the firelight. No one seemed to be attempting to put out the flames. A venerable mosque with an aged minaret stood in solemn witness to the destruction, its darkened windows looking for all the world like downcast eyes in the firelight.

"What is going on?" Milo shouted, unable to tear his eyes away.

"Recruiting," Ambrose shouted back, nodding at the sight of figures being torn from small knots of people and dragged toward the trucks. "Conscripting the next round of meat for the Butcher."

Milo looked on mutely, staring as the flames leaped higher. He wondered if soon the flames would climb high enough that the wind would catch fire, and at that thought, something kindled inside of him.

"We're going down there," he declared, canting clumsily toward the burning village.

Rihyani didn't fight him, but their speed decreased markedly.

"What about Stalin?" she called. "If we stop him, doesn't that put an end to all of it?"

"We can't save everyone, Magus," Ambrose shouted, casting a forlorn glance at the destruction below.

Before Milo could reply, a tussle broke out amongst those extracting conscripts from the crowd. Rifles barked, and two figures crumpled as a third was dragged toward the trucks. The fire in Milo's chest melted any hesitation.

"Maybe," Milo hissed through clenched teeth. "But I can certainly save some of them."

He threw a fierce look at Ambrose and Rihyani.

The fey nodded, and Ambrose returned it with a grim smile.

"That or die trying!" the big man roared.

Their angle of descent and their speed increased.

Milo's fingers tightened on the cane, whose raptor skull was freshly graven with runes inlaid with silver.

Now we get to see what you can really do, he thought and a chill ran through him as he felt Imrah's spirit stir within.

I aim to please, master.

The conscriptors could be excused for not looking skyward as the trio descended upon them.

They were busy after all, dragging men, boys, and the sturdier women from their families. Their attentions were on selecting those who looked useful while threatening everyone else with further violence. They hadn't come with the intention of burning down the hovels and shooting the old woman and her enfeebled husband, but the backward peasants refused to see reason.

Though the Glorious Revolution had been forestalled by the pressing needs of the War, the cause still required bodies, and like it or not, these ingrates would have to do. After all, even such simpletons should have known that all worthy causes require sacrifice.

Being so distracted, they didn't see the trio touch down

behind the mosque, where they hastened to undo the jury-rigged harness. Even as they unbound straps and buckles, their eyes swept the deep shadows between the firelight as they endured the screams and wails of the beleaguered villagers.

From where he stood, Milo saw a knotted clump of shadows cast by families huddling away from the soldiers. The fury still burned in his chest, but he checked himself as he felt his muscles tensing to pounce. Though they hadn't planned on this fight, they couldn't play fast and loose with so many innocents at hand.

"Rihyani," Milo hissed as he crept toward the edge of the mosque's shadow. "I need you to find a way to get those people moving out of the village. I don't want them standing around and catching a stray bullet."

Looking around, he saw Rihyani frown in thought. Then she gave him a confident nod.

"I have an idea," she said. "But it's only going to work if you engage the soldiers."

Milo nodded and looked at Ambrose. "I think we should avoid gunfire as long as possible," the magus whispered. "We need to make sure one of those bastards doesn't hear shots and starts gunning down the civilians."

"Good idea," Ambrose murmured, his eyes sweeping across the burning village. "You have something particular in mind?"

Milo's face broke into a wolfish smile, his teeth catching the firelight.

"I read once that a commander burned the boats of his army to keep them from retreating," Milo said, his fingers tightening on his cane. "Imagine how quickly that army would have come apart if they thought only half the boats were burned."

Ambrose drew his bayonet blade from his belt and returned Milo's grin.

"I'm with you, Magus," he growled eagerly.

The soldiers out on conscription duty hadn't made any other stops up to this point, and so only two of the trucks were packed with poor souls. This village was the first of what was planned to be a long night of dragging honest folk from their beds, which left the trucks at the rear empty save for two soldiers left as sentries in each vehicle.

The first two to die never had a chance.

Ambrose was on them like a lion among sheep, his knife flashing left and right. Crouching, he was already moving toward the next truck as Milo stepped forward, and the raptor skull vomited flame over the vehicle. Green flames so pale they seemed woven with molten silver splashed across bed and cab, clinging and warping with terrible fury.

The soldiers watching from the next two trucks sprang from their cabs, rifles in hand, shouting and cursing in confusion. Milo stalked toward them, his will pressing outward to warp their vision of him with the Art. He became a host of wavering splintered silhouettes before the burning vehicle. Blinking in the sudden eye-watering brightness, they raised rifles whose barrels swept toward one phantom that vanished before chasing another. They were so distracted that when Ambrose's blade punched through their hearts, only the last man noticed that the other three were cooling in the dirt before his gaze emptied.

Two more trucks were set ablaze as cries and shouts sounded from the village, and they watched packs of soldiers racing between the burning buildings to see their handiwork. In one sweep, Milo saw no less than three dozen men emerging sporadically from the few unburnt hovels, what meager pilferings they could find in greedy hands.

Even sorely outnumbered, Milo felt his wrath increase as though it were fuel to the fire inside him.

His nightsighted eyes protesting at looking past the glaring flames, Milo spotted a flicker of movement behind the oncoming soldiers. For one second, he wondered if he'd vastly underestimated the enemy numbers, but then he saw a shadowy mob rushing away from the village. They seemed less like a mass of people than a low, scudding cloud of oily smoke.

"Rihyani," he said and turned back to the soldiers, who were already ranging out from the village. Their rifles and electric torches were in their hands, but Milo's befuddling illusion held, and they were unable to focus. Even from this distance, Milo could see fear glistening in eyes that reflected the flaming trucks.

The first few shots whistled into the dark harmlessly, but the sound and impotent fury stoked the rest of the men. Salvos, haphazard and aimed at nothing, tore through the night, while sergeants barked for good order to no effect. One squad of soldiers had even started firing at one of the trucks near the village, riddling the vehicle and the sentries with equal zeal.

Even with the illusion holding, the sheer amount of fire saw shots hissing past Milo and he needed to dart for cover. Spitting curses, he slid behind a low wall that had once marked the edge of the village proper as torch beams swept overhead and few more wild shots zipped by.

"I saw something!" a voice hollered in hoarse Russian over the sounds of men shooting and lever actions working frantically.

"Kill it!" another voice screamed, and the wall a stride or two from Milo sprayed mortar and chipped stone in all directions as the squad opened fire.

In a matter of seconds, the furious onslaught died off as soldiers fumbled for fresh magazines to ram home. Milo smiled wolfishly as he heard their sergeant cursing them for their poor order, and he was still wearing that toothy smile when he sprang up from behind the wall.

"My turn!" he snarled.

Lashes of flame tore across the firing line like huge infernal cats o' nine tails.

The luckiest caught the brunt of the sorcerous onslaught and were dead before their bodies hit the ground in a shower of cinders and ash. The less fortunate were not immediately slain but had time to scream as the unnatural flames lapped across their bodies. They managed to flail and floundered in the remains of the fortunate dead, but it was a short-lived struggle. In less than ten seconds, every man had succumbed, and Milo was left staring wide-eyed at the devastation he'd wrought.

One furious stroke and ten men lay dead.

"I didn't even know I could do that," Milo muttered, and he felt Imrah's chuckle grate against his mind.

I aim to please, master.

Milo realized he was gawking while more soldiers swept their torches toward the fresh fires. Milo dove behind the wall and scampered away as chunks of stone were punched out around him. Unlike the last batch, these soldiers seemed to be maintaining some semblance of order, their shots coming in overlapping volleys as they advanced in teams of three from cover to cover.

May I recommend using something less eye-catching than witchfire?

Milo swore as he scuttled through a breach in the wall and sprinted through a torrent of shots to leap through a house's open window. One shot plucked at the tail of his black coat and he felt the heat of another across the back of an outstretched hand, but somehow he landed on the wood floor unpunctured.

"I'm open to suggestions," Milo gasped as he crawled, winded and cringing, deeper into the house as the squad opened fire. Rounds snapped off plaster walls and whined off hanging pots and pans as Milo sought to move clear of the windows and looked for a back door.

The formula excites particles to make them ignite and burn, Imrah began with frustrating calm given the situation. *It stands to reason the opposite could be achieved by simply reversing the process.*

Milo heard orders being shouted and knew that in minutes, they'd be sweeping in to surround the house.

"Are you saying I can make things cold?" Milo asked. "What good is ice going to do right now?"

A boot thudded against the bullet-pocked house's door, and there was a splintering crash. Milo spotted a window big enough to climb out at the back of the house as he heard several pairs of feet thumping across the wood floor.

I thought humans loved their science? Ice is crystallized water, and what floods your fleshy bodies?

Milo was halfway through the window to the backlot when two soldiers rounded the corner of the house. Without time to think, Milo leveled the cane and launched a spike focus.

FREEZE

Faster than the eye could follow, something darted from the skull's sockets into the chest of the leading soldier. He had enough time to stare bewildered at twin shards of black ice in his chest before his body erupted in all directions in red shards. Two of these gory icicles pierced the shoulder of the man beside him, and he managed to scream in horror before he burst into a frigid imitation of a porcupine.

Both men collapsed to the dirt, accompanied by the musical tinkling of shattering icicles.

Ice has a greater volume than water, Imrah informed him smugly. *All that excess has to go somewhere.*

"Dear God!" Milo gaped as he stumbled the rest of the way out of the window.

I recommend relocating.

There was a shout inside the house, and a rifle roared as the window frame splintered behind him.

With nothing but an open stretch for several strides, Milo's options were bleak until he spied the roof and had an idea. Gathering himself physically and mentally, he leaped into the air.

Borrowing both the Art to make himself lighter and his necromist's work on his coat to form wings, he soared through the air. Black wings flapping, he rose level with the house, his feet stretching out to go skipping across the rustling thatch.

He spun back as three more soldiers clambered out into the back lot, casting glances upward in obvious confusion. Milo downed each of them with frigid darts before they could draw a bead on him, then he scrambled up the roof as he heard shouting from the rest of the squad in front of the house.

Two three-man teams were watching the house for targets, one batch hunkered behind a wagon and the other huddling inside a dry, dilapidated fountain. Their sergeant was bellowing for the other teams to sound off but was only greeted by the sounds of burning buildings and fighting somewhere in the distance

"Not quite the night you planned for, was it, boys?" Milo chuckled to himself darkly as he gathered for another leap.

With a huge beat of ensorcelled black wings, Milo flew into the air, and with an inverted incantation of the flaming lash, he sent out a wave of icy black javelins to scythe down on the cowering soldiers. Preternaturally hardened ice bit through flesh and fabric with ease, and whatever flesh it touched knew the ruin of utter cold in a single labored heartbeat.

Only the sergeant, his head raised to look for his missing men, had spied Milo and managed to flatten himself behind the lip of the fountain in time. The shard shattered on the stone above him and he sprang up, service pistol sweeping skyward. He chased Milo with a flurry of hasty shots, but the pistol clicked empty before the magus touched at the back of the fountain basin, faceless stone statuary rising between the two.

Drawing on the cane's physical enhancements, Milo spun with inhuman speed and shoved a lance of focus hastily through the end of the cane. The beak yawned, and a blade of ice three meters long and as thin as a sheet of glass flew under the statues' outstretched arms and pierced the sergeant through the shoulder.

The man screamed as the rifle he'd scooped up tumbled from his limp fingers.

Milo met the man's eyes, and behind the pain and hatred, he saw something move. For a single instant, something besides the dying man dangling from an icy lance stared at Milo, and Milo stared back at it.

Zlydzen has seen us, Imrah whispered, and Milo thought he heard a tremor of fear.

The presence vanished as the ice claimed him and life slipped from the man's eyes.

Milo stood for a moment, wrestling with looking in the eyes of a dying man and seeing his enemy watching him. Part of him, still warmed by the heat of his fury, gloried in the observation, confident in his display of prowess. A quieter, deeper voice was not so certain it was a good thing.

Milo shook off the thoughts, then realized the sounds of battle had passed, and only the crackle of flames broke the silence of the night.

From somewhere among the burning trucks, Milo heard Ambrose shouting and Rihyani's musical call.

"Milo! Milo, where are you!"

"Magus! Magus! You better have not gone and died on me!"

Despite the clinging sense of foreboding, Milo's mouth hitched up in a smile.

"Not as lucky as that," he shouted back.

THE BURDEN

"Mercy, please!" came the desperate plea, tears and snot smearing the commissar's face. "Please, just let me go!"

"You're not helping your cause with that bleating, comrade," Ambrose growled at the kneeling man. "If it weren't for the magus here, I'd have shot you on principle."

To punctuate, Ambrose tapped the man's forehead sharply with one blunt finger.

Milo wasn't certain if Ambrose was saying that to frighten the man into silence or not, but either way, the wretch recoiled and quieted some, his wailed pleas becoming sniffled mutterings.

"What do we plan to do with him?" Ambrose asked as he stepped back to stand beside Milo.

"Information would seem the most important thing right now," Rihyani offered, but an edge crept into her voice. "Though I would like nothing better than to feed him his own heart, slowly."

Milo looked at the fey and saw the vaguest ghost of the feral creature he'd witnessed fighting Ezekiel among the trees.

"Everyone wants this one to die," Milo said, not much caring that the sniveling prisoner could hear him. "Is there a particular reason?"

Rihyani and Ambrose shared a look.

While Milo had been fighting for his life, Rihyani had used the Art to conceal the villagers and compel them to flee before returning. She came back and helped Ambrose finish off the rest of the soldiers, who'd unnervingly fought to the last man without any thought of retreat. All except this blubbering man in a *voenkom's*, or war commissar's, uniform. He cut quite the pitiful figure, his uniform disheveled, glasses cracked, and his cap missing, leaving his sweaty dome of a head to gleam in the rising sun.

"This one's pants were still around his ankles when he came stumbling through the smoke," Rihyani explained. "The girl staggered out of the house he'd used. I could smell him all over her, despite the blood."

Ambrose growled, and there was something wet in his eyes.

"Tried to get the girl to run toward where the rest of the villagers were," he said hoarsely. "But at the sight of me coming toward her, she screamed and ran the other way. She ran right... right into...ri..."

Ambrose's voice faltered, and his hands tightened into shaking fists.

"Right into the line of fire," Rihyani said as she rested a hand gently on his broad shoulder. "There was a fireteam holding out in a stable, and they were shooting anything that moved. She was dead before she hit the ground."

Ambrose nodded and, with a searing glare at the commissar, turned and strode a dozen paces away, where he began pacing in tight circles. His voice, a low and snarled stream of French profanity, became ambient noise to join the fading snap and pop of the smoldering village.

Milo was tired, but not so much so that he didn't feel the flames of righteous rage spring up at this fresh atrocity. He banked them, forcing his mind to process questions that might be relevant.

"You said girl, but how old was she?"

Rihyani's face was a mask of restrained disgust.

"Human ages are difficult for me to tell," she began stiffly, her eyes remaining fixed in the middle distance, "but she had barely entered womanhood. She most certainly wasn't old enough to be a mother."

"So, you're saying she was a child?" Milo asked, his voice a snarl as he turned toward the cowering thing not three strides from him. "A child!"

Rihyani might have said something, but a rush of disjointed memories played through Milo's mind, pushing out everything except the sight of the commissar. Memories and feelings locked away long ago howled and rattled their chains, and before he knew what was happening, Milo had the man by the throat. His gloved fingers bit into the sweaty skin around the man's neck, eliciting a choked gasp as Milo dragged him up so they were nearly nose to nose.

"I think a bullet in the head is too gentle," he hissed into the man's face. "As a magus, I can think of a dozen much more painful ways to end you."

"P-please," the commissar croaked. "I could be useful. Pl...ack!"

Milo's grip continued to tighten, and the rapist began to paw at the hands around his throat. He managed to worm his fingers in enough to manage a desperate gasp.

"I'm Chief Commissar Beria!" he wheezed. "I can get you anything, please!"

Milo's hands bore down on the man's throat, and Beria's knees buckled.

"I want to see you die!" Milo snarled, spit flying from his lips. "I want you to feel helpless, abandoned, powerless, and then I want you to die!"

Beria's face was changing colors, his eyes losing focus behind his splintered spectacles, but in a last desperate twist, he pulled back enough to form another strangled plea.

"Please!" he cried, his voice barely above a whisper. "Stalin! I can give you Stalin!"

Milo recovered his grip, and for a single heartbeat, he didn't care about what he'd just heard. The cries from the vaults of his mind were too insistent, too indignant, too real to ignore. He was going to kill Beria, knowing it was the right thing to do, Stalin and Nicht-KAT and the whole War be damned.

But then he smelled the acrid smoke of the burnt village and heard a lively patch of embers give a crackling pop.

Milo's hands released the commissar, who collapsed to the earth, heaving huge sob after huge sob. He pressed his face into the sooty dirt as his hands covered his head.

Beria deserved death and worse, and if there was any justice in this life or the next, something horrible waited for him on the other side of the dirt, but there was more at stake than justice for one girl or even one village. Milo knew that the likes of Commissar Beria were a symptom, not the disease. They deserved eradication, yes, but there were always more to take their place.

"Listen to me very closely," Milo began, grinding each word between his teeth. "The only thing keeping you alive is your absolute cooperation, do you understand?"

Beria's bruised throat couldn't manage a reply, but his head nodded exaggeratedly even as he stared at the ground. Milo reached behind him and picked up his cane.

"One argument, one lie, one hesitation, and I will make your end into folklore," Milo snarled and drew a baleful light into the cane's eye sockets. He shoved the raptor's beak under the commissar's chin, dragging the ash-streaked face upward. Beria's eyes bulged as Milo held the glowing skull in front of the man's face.

"Your name won't be remembered, but they'll tell stories how no man has ever before or ever will again suffer such a terrible end."

Beria tried to turn away in a fit of gibbering tears, but the eagle's beak hooked his cheek and dragged his eyes back to the magus' face.

"Look into my eyes and tell me you understand," Milo said in a whisper-soft voice. "I want you to show me you understand what is at stake."

The commissar's whole body shook as though it took all his strength to meet Milo's eyes, but self-preservation lent him uncommon fortitude. With jerky movements and a wet gulping noise in his throat, Beria nodded vigorously.

"I understand. Yes, I understand."

Milo searched the terrified expression for several heartbeats before drawing the cane back and straightening. He realized then that both Ambrose and Rihyani were at his shoulders once again, their faces grim and their eyes locked on Beria.

"All right, *voenkom,*" Milo said with deadly softness. "Tell me everything."

Ambrose came back from tying Beria to the fountain like an untrustworthy pet, shaking his head as he hooked a thumb over his shoulder.

"I don't know that I believe a damn word that weasel said." He grunted as he settled on the steps of the mosque where Milo and Rihyani were sitting.

"With enough time, we could make sure he's not lying to us," Rihyani offered, but Milo shook his head.

"We don't have time," he said, frowning at the blue sky overhead. "We've been here long enough. If we stay much longer, there's a good chance that we'll be caught by another patrol."

"Or the villagers will return, and who knows how they'll react?" Rihyani said, her expression inscrutable.

"I'll give you three guesses what I think they'll do with him," Ambrose muttered as he did a quick spot clean of his Gewehr. "And doesn't matter what it is because it'll be better than what he deserves."

Milo bobbed his head, listening but unable to bring himself to say anything. Suspicions notwithstanding, Beria had been a fount of information, providing Milo with an abundance of information regarding Stalin's operation. He knew almost nothing about the supernatural influence, thinking it was only the force of Stalin's charisma, but even with this disappointment, the intelligence he provided was invaluable. One item in particular was rolling around his mind like a grain of sand on its way to becoming a pearl of a scheme. All this would, of course, be cold comfort to the elderly couple and the teenage girl they'd buried less than half an hour before.

Milo felt a heavy weight settle across his shoulders, and he dreaded what he knew came next.

"We can't bring him with us, though." Ambrose huffed as he let the rifle settle into the crook of his arm. "We can't fly with an extra man, and we can't drag him along by foot without risking him bolting at the first opportunity."

Rihyani looked at the commissar sitting in the fountain, head hung miserably. Her lips worked in a humorless smile, peeling upward to reveal lethal fangs.

"Are you intending to let him live?" she snarled in a low, throaty voice. "After everything he's done?"

"And what he will do if we let him go," Ambrose added.

Milo sighed and pressed a thumb to the hardening ache between his eyes, realizing that his jewel of a scheme might come apart if the commissar managed to warn Stalin.

"I know all the reasons why I should put a bullet in his head," Milo said heavily. "But I gave him my word that if he gave us information, we'd let him go. I don't see how I can go back on that when he kept his end of the bargain."

Ambrose snorted, and Rihyani suddenly found something interesting to look at in the sky above.

"What?" Milo demanded, eyes darting between the two of them. "You're saying you'd kill him even after he fulfilled his part of the deal?"

Ambrose nodded while Rihyani turned a flat, chilly stare on him.

"Yes," they said together.

Milo pinched the bridge of his nose and fought to keep his temper under control.

I agree with your companions, Imrah announced in Milo's head. The cane rested against one leg.

"Who asked you?" he growled, kicking the fetish away angrily.

"Even the ghul agrees with us." Ambrose chuckled.

"For all the wrong reasons, I'm sure," Milo spat, then raked his fingers through his hair. "Fine. Tell me, how does killing him now not make us just like him?"

Ambrose and Rihyani glanced at each other and back at Milo with an almost pitying look. Milo had no memory of his parents, but sometimes the wardens at the orphanage had shared similar looks when they thought their charges were being particularly stupid or naïve. Milo despised the look, and it took more self-control than he would have cared to admit not to throw something at them to dispel their condescension.

"Last I checked, I never raped a little girl," Ambrose said flatly. "Or forced civilians into service at gunpoint."

Milo ground his teeth together.

"I gave my word!" he roared as he sprang to his feet and began pacing. "That has to mean something. To me, if nothing else."

"Some creatures have chosen to be unworthy of such things," Rihyani said, her words tender and patient as she watched him, but it was no use. Milo felt the gravity of certainty grip him and he knew nothing could set him free.

Nothing except doing as he'd promised, as sick as it made him feel.

"Then I suppose I shouldn't have given my word," Milo snapped. "But since I did, I need to honor the terms. It is as simple as that. Maybe it'll ruin everything, but I'm doing it."

Ambrose opened his mouth to argue, then stopped, cocking his head to one side. Milo recognized the signs of Ambrose's inhumanly keen hearing at work.

"What is it?" he asked, eyes sweeping to the edge of town, but he saw nothing.

Ambrose shouldered his rifle and drew his bayonet blade.

"Time to go," he said quickly before heading toward the fountain where the commissar squatted.

"What are you doing?" Milo called after him, shuffling an uncertain step after him.

"You said you wanted him to go free," Ambrose answered over his shoulder. "Fine, let me go do it, so your precious word can be kept, and we can get out of here."

Milo felt a tremble of concern as he watched the blade glinting in Ambrose's hand, but something in the big man's voice told him to trust. After all, Simon Ambrose didn't lie.

Despite that, Milo stood fixed in place as he watched Ambrose trudge over and roughly cut Beria's bonds. The commissar rose and stood staring at Ambrose as the two exchanged words, then Ambrose turned and ambled back to Milo and Rihyani.

"Ready to go?" Ambrose asked.

Rihyani nodded as she rose, while Milo bent down and scooped up his cane.

Not a word, Milo warned Imrah before turning to Ambrose, frowning.

"What did you say to him?"

"Told him not to follow us, or I'd gut-shoot him and break both his legs." Ambrose shrugged. "Recommended that he stand there counting as high as he could before moving to make sure I didn't get the wrong idea if I heard him behind us."

Milo looked past Ambrose at Beria, who stood shivering in the dry fountain, staring at them with terror-stretched eyes.

"That's it?" Milo asked doubtfully.

Ambrose heaved a sigh and shook his head.

"Fine," he sputtered. "I also reminded him I was an excellent shot, and I'd love for him to give me an excuse."

Milo stared at Ambrose for a long moment and then nodded.

"Fine, let's get moving."

They gathered their things in short order, deciding to go by foot at least initially unless a patrol in the area spotted them and they came under fire. Carrying Ambrose, they couldn't fly high enough and would be moving too slowly to effectively avoid such an assault, so they trusted the rough terrain of Georgia to give them the concealment they needed.

They left Beria counting as they jogged past the outskirts of the village and the burned-out trucks.

Milo threw one last look over his shoulder and nearly stumbled as he saw movement at the opposite side of the town. His alarm dissipated when he recognized that the dark shapes all bore sooty faces and weary expressions. The villagers were coming back to what remained of their homes, sweeping around the village perimeter with wary eyes.

As he loped onward, Milo wondered if they'd scrape together what they could before leaving or stay and try to rebuild, but the thought flew from his mind when he heard an ear-piercing wail come from the center of the town where a dry fountain had sat in front of a venerable mosque.

"What was that?" Milo said reflexively as he looked at Ambrose, but something in the pit of his stomach told him.

"Proof that Beria could count higher than I expected." Ambrose shrugged and kept trudging as another terrified squeal was drowned out by angry, vengeful voices.

23

THE RUCKUS

Tiflis, a city of architectural heterodoxy, the capital of Georgia since the fifth century, curled and contoured around the green ribbon of the Kurgan River. Like many cities of the northern Near East, its buildings were as varied as the lords and tyrants who had held sway over it in its long existence. Marketplaces and cafes that would have been well-suited to Baghdad abutted against civic buildings fit for cities like Berlin or Paris, neo-classical and solemn. Bubbling up among the sloped streets, the voluptuous style of Orthodox churches and the picturesque Mediterranean structures seemed determined to root the city to its oldest origins, when the world still shook with Rome's crumbling.

Despite this variety and implied vibrance, everything seemed bleak and barren as the trio overlooked the city from the northern slopes. The sinking sun painted the city crimson, but the garish color could do little to lift it from the oppressive drabness that had settled over every building. From this distance, they could see it was a city occupied, its streets empty and its people huddled inside, awaiting what came next.

Only one place showed signs of life and activity, near the very center of the city. Here fires and red flags shone on a broad plaza as a line of trucks and other vehicles wound through. As they watched, flocks of people were disgorged from the automobiles, reduced to dark accumulations of squirming dots by the dying light and the distance. They milled about until other more determined specks converged on them and shuffled them toward one side of the city square or another.

"Looks like Beria was right," Ambrose spat as he squinted. "They were very aggressive with recruiting."

Rihyani shook her head, her eyebrows raised in dread wonder.

"They can't possibly think to bully all those people into service," she murmured. "Not with so much of their strength gone northward. It would be like equipping an army that could readily turn on you."

Ambrose heaved a weary sigh.

"You'd be surprised how much audacious men with guns can get away with."

"And let's not forget Stalin isn't just using intimidation," Milo said, pressing down on the welling anxiety inside of him. "Zlydzen is providing him with some way to influence their minds, make them fanatics."

That was exactly what gnawed at Milo as he thought of what they were going to try to accomplish. There were so many down there, almost enough for a brand-new army, and it could very well be that in moments, they'd transform from unwilling conscripts to fearless zealots. The thought made his stomach perform an acrobatic routine he could have done without.

"That makes me wonder," Ambrose said, his mustache fidgeting. "The soldiers were all more than willing to fight to the death. I mean, I didn't hear one man call for retreat, but why wasn't that filth Beria fanaticized?"

They all took a moment to consider the point before Milo finally shrugged.

"Maybe because he was a commissar, not a soldier, and a fairly high-ranking one. Levintry Beria was only out in the field to sate his needs. A fanatical soldier is one thing, but bureaucrats? They'd be getting in each other's way even more than usual."

Ambrose chuckled, but Rihyani, who also seemed to have taken the question in hand, stared intently at the scene in the square.

"It could also be a measure of insurance for the dwarrow," she said, her voice so soft she might have been talking to herself. "Long-term mental and emotional manipulation through magic can have side effects. Higher ranking members not being affected means that if Stalin dies or becomes unmanageable, his replacements won't be a bunch of damaged drones."

I concur, Imrah whispered in Milo's mind. Zlydzen understood that many of his tools for mental manipulation, potent as they were, couldn't control entire nations. Not yet, at least.

The final caveat did nothing to help Milo's stomach settle, but the knowledge that the upper echelons of the Red invaders could be as fractious and disorganized as any other band of power-hungry humans was a small comfort. Who knew, maybe they would get lucky and things would devolve into a massive power-play as they nabbed the Marxist warlord?

"We're not getting any closer to accomplishing this suicide mission standing here." Milo sighed. "We best get moving. We've only got a few more hours before Beria said the big show was going to start."

"I hate this part," Ambrose grumbled as he took the harness from his shoulder and began shuffling into it.

"It's just to get us in the city," Rihyani soothed as she stepped forward to offer a helping hand with a buckle.

"After which we'll need to secure transport quickly," Milo said, taking up a portion to belt around his waist. "The last thing I want is to have to start hauling our prisoner around like a sack of wheat."

"He says it as though there was any doubt who would do the actual hauling," Ambrose muttered to Rihyani, making certain Milo could hear him.

"He's looking out for you then," Rihyani said, throwing a wink over the big man's shoulder at Milo.

"Oh, *mon chéri*, you make a man's heart wander!" Ambrose whispered as he ran his eyes across the hardened contours of what could have been the Rollsy's prettier younger sister. It was not a Rolls-Royce fully armored and outfitted for battle, but a lighter command/reconnaissance model. With a longer hood to accommodate a large engine and an open extended cab, it seemed designed for greater speed and accessibility.

Just the sort of thing you'd need for a kidnapping.

The wind-riding trip over the city outskirts amidst the dying light had gone without incident, but they hit a snag when they touched down very near a checkpoint in the city's heart. Quick obfuscation by Rihyani had spared them from being spotted as their images melded with the building they'd landed on. They'd stood frozen for a moment, and the near-disaster had turned into good fortune as the fine specimen of a vehicle rolled up to the checkpoint.

Ambrose slowly drew his rifle to his shoulder, but before he could take aim, Milo settled a staying hand on his shoulder.

"Pretty sure we don't need a shootout just yet," Milo murmured, then smiled at Ambrose's stricken face.

"Won't be a shootout," he hissed, looking anxiously past Milo to where the driver seemed to be arguing with the guards at the checkpoint. "Four men and I've got five on a clip. I could practically do it with my eyes closed."

"It would still be too loud," Rihyani said. "I'm not sure I could cover the sound of that many shots coming so quickly."

The officer in the back of the cab was leaning forward and gesticulating irritably.

"We better do something," Ambrose muttered, nodding down at the unfolding scene at the checkpoint. "They're either about to shoot each other or at least make a call into a higher authority, and either way, we'll lose our best chance with that beauty."

The men below did seem to be on the verge of some sort of violent altercation since they were all shouting at the same time. One of the guards was now holding his rifle across his chest rather than slung over his shoulder.

Do you think you can take them all out with one volley of the frost shards? Milo asked Imrah as he raised his cane so the eye sockets could study the targets below.

Child's play, the disembodied ghul replied.

Milo drew his focus to a lethal point, and with a twist in the essential formula, bifurcated it twice. He felt Imrah's power seething inside the fetish, waiting to be released.

FREEZE

Four black shards of ice trailing a tail of rippling fog tore through the air with the barest of whines. The two checkpoint guards were struck in the chest, while the driver was pierced from the back. The officer had surged forward to swat at the nearest guard with an open hand, so the final shard missed. It slashed the shoulder of his jacket, leaving an ice-rimed epaulet.

"Child's play?" Milo remarked drily as he turned the cane to glare at the skull.

He moved, Imrah sulked.

Down below, the officer was shrinking down into his seat as he watched the profusion of bloodied ice spines erupting from his driver and the two guards. Mute with horror, he stared unmoving until they all collapsed in a chorus of crackling icicles.

"That'll take some getting used to." Ambrose grunted with a shudder as he moved to the lip of the building and leaped to the ground four stories below. There was a dull thump as his boots impacted, but otherwise, his impossibly absorbed jump was without effect.

"Show-off," Milo muttered before leaping after him and calling on his coat's wings to bear him down safely. He felt Rihyani's will reach out to the wind, which whispered back as it carried her in his wake.

They came down level with Ambrose, who was already moving toward the vehicle, Gewehr at his shoulder.

"How is it any worse than what you do with that old cannon?" Milo asked as he fell in step beside the big man.

"I dunno, just is." Ambrose shrugged before raising his voice to a commanding growl in Russian. "All right, time to come out of there."

No movement came from inside the cab except the driver, whose frozen body was slumped over the door. There was a series of sharp cracks, and the top half of the corpse fell out of the vehicle with a crash.

"That better not start to thaw on those seats," Ambrose snarled, throwing a scowl toward Milo as he advanced, rifle still at his shoulder. "You better get out of that car right now!"

The officer peeked his head over the edge of the armored door, spotted the rifle, and nearly ducked down, but Ambrose's venomous warning stopped him.

"Don't you even!"

So slowly it was almost comical, the officer climbed out of the vehicle with his hands raised, palms open.

"Where were you going?" Milo asked, planting the cane in front of him. "Isn't Comrade Stalin addressing the troops tonight?"

The officer, standing before them with both hands open, looked odd to Milo. His uniform did not fit him, apparently made for a man who was of a taller, more robust figure than the bookish, round-shouldered creature wearing it. With a broad forehead made even larger by a balding pate and small spectacles on his beady eyes, he seemed more suited to clerking than soldiering. His gray-speckled mustache made a bold play, but it left him as perhaps arch-secretary of the clerks at best.

For all this, when the man spoke, it was in a clear, unshaken voice.

"He sent you to retrieve me then," the officer said, casting a measuring glance over the trio, his eyes lingering longest on Rihyani. "*Koba*'s variety of agents is growing more eclectic by the day."

He paused long enough to eye the marred shoulder of his ill-fitting jacket.

"A little brazen, but your point is made."

Milo fought to keep the easy manner he'd adopted in the face of having no clue what the man was talking about. Striking a confident swagger, he strolled toward the Rolls-Royce, wearing the half-smile, half-snarl he'd perfected as a criminal youth.

"I think it would be an awful shame if you missed the excitement," he said, his voice softening to a menacing whisper as he drew up next to the cab. "Supposed to be quite the show."

The clerk in officer's clothing lowered his hands centimeter by centimeter even as he glowered at Milo, his mustachioed lips puckered in disapproval.

"First time you see that dwarf crank his damned organ, it's all very impressive, but after so many times, I've lost the stomach for it. I understand why *Koba* uses the little freak, but I don't see how it helps anything for me to stay here. In fact, judging from your methods, I imagine you probably understand how it works better than I do, and just so you know, this is him showing off."

Here he paused and looked at his driver's split corpse, failing to repress a shiver. Despite this, when he spoke again, his voice was steady as ever.

"But he can have his puppeteer parades because there is business in the north that needs addressing. Yezhov is a useful little animal, but he's neither an effective commander nor a proficient diplomat, which is why he hasn't reported since going north. I'm going up there to sort things out before he sets everything north of the Caucasus Mountains on fire."

Milo's mind was racing to process everything the man mentioned with the casual assurance of someone in the know. This clerk was someone to Stalin, and important enough that he expected that Stalin's agents wouldn't intentionally kill him. Also, the forces they sent to Shatili hadn't reported, and this fact made Milo smile.

His surprise for the Reds must have worked after all.

"Oh, I don't imagine you'll be hearing from Yezhov anytime soon," Milo said. He didn't bother to hide his wicked grin.

The man frowned down at Milo and heaved a sigh.

"I suppose it was only a matter of time." He nodded. "He only needs one poisonous dwarf, and his new one, while more disturbing, is certainly more useful."

Milo surreptitiously glanced at Rihyani and Ambrose, and their expressions matched his own feelings. This man was painting quite the chilling picture of what it was like to serve in the regime of the Butcher of Petrograd but also assuring that he was going to join Stalin, tied up in the bed of the Rolls Royce.

Milo nodded at Ambrose, who shouldered his rifle and fetched one of the straps of the newly repurposed harness.

"Is that necessary?" the man asked, sounding more irritated than distressed. "You made your point, and I'll go willingly."

Milo hopped up onto the running board so he was face to face with the man.

"Trust me, you'll be thankful for it before the night's over," Milo said as he reached inside and tugged the door open and then sprang back onto the street. "Now, if you please?"

In the central plaza of Tiflis, the conscripts had been forced into rough ranks by their captors and now stood shivering with a combination of fear and cold as the night time temperature began to plummet.

A stage had been erected in front of the Parliament building, with a series of amplifiers arranged to blast over the square. A tangle of cables ran to a single microphone at the center of the stage. Behind the stage, a glistening red curtain hung heavily, shielding whoever emerged from the Parliament building from the view of those in the square.

Thus, none but a handful of technicians scurrying about backstage saw the odd coterie that emerged and began the slow walk up the ramp that led from the Parliament building's steps to the stage. The conscripted men and women in the square hardly noticed the faint hum of the amplifiers coming on as they looked around, calculating. More than one of them had noticed that though they at first seemed surrounded by rifle-toting soldiers, there was only a thin line stretched between their serried ranks. Having had a few minutes in the growing cold to liven their senses, many of them began to cast about, and before long, some were even whispering.

They had their kidnappers ten to one, if not twenty to one. The soldiers who had dragged them from their beds, dazed and disoriented, were the only ones present in the city, it seemed. They weren't being conscripted to join a glorious army so much as to *become* the army, which now seemed absent. As this realization spread, a question formed in every brain worthy of the name amongst the conscripts:

Wouldn't it be an easy thing to rush the guards?

The whispers made their rounds as elbows nudged and chins jerked in surreptitious agreement. Another ten minutes, perhaps another five, and they would descend upon their abductors in an avalanche of vengeful bodies.

But then the curtain parted, the lights on the stage came on, and the hidden coterie emerged.

At their head was a squat, waddling figure pushing what might have been a madman's street organ in front of him. None of them were close enough to the stage to see the dwarf very well, but those who could acknowledged he did not look or move like anything they'd ever seen. Those closest noted his oddly drooping features and voluminous mossy beard and subsequently assumed the truncated man was in a costume to look so repellent. Eyes narrowed as he ambled to the right of the microphone, and those same eyes widened at what came behind the shuffling oddity.

Comrade Joseph Stalin, in a spartan uniform complete with long olive drab coat, strode forth, his movements sure but unhurried.

A pace behind him walked a pair of living effigies, a man and a woman, both statuesque and muscular, their bodies smeared in greasepaint so their skin glistened like polished ironwork and their hair seemed to be cast from bronze. The man was dressed in a worker's coveralls and held a hammer over his head. The woman wore a bare-shouldered blouse and a peasant skirt, and over her head, she held a sickle.

Comrade Stalin approached the microphone and stood for a moment, untroubled at the weight of so many eyes upon him. The pair marching behind him came to a stop a stride or two behind, where they promptly crossed the hammer and sickle in the air over their glorious leader's head. Neither showed the slightest discomfort or strain at maintaining the position.

Every eye, soldier or conscript, was upon the short mustachioed man before the microphone.

"Welcome, my countrymen," Stalin began, his voice soft, bordering on nasal, his Russian shot through with a strong Georgian accent. "Welcome, sons and daughters of my beloved homeland."

There was a subtle but distinct ripple across the conscripts, and Stalin acknowledged it with an easy nod.

"I know many of you are confused, or frightened, or even angry," he continued, nodding again with conciliatory grace. "Not so long ago, you'd almost forgotten me, I think—the wayward son gone north. Then suddenly I returned, at the head of an army none dared challenge."

More than a few of those in the square looked at the soldiers watching Stalin raptly, and their question was plain: what army?

"It seems I am to do what so many others have done in our embattled land: claim rule as a tyrant," he said, and this was not a ripple but a wave of men and women drawing back, their expressions souring. "You would not be unjust to curse me and shake your fists at me. Even strike me down if such were the case."

Here and there amongst the conscripts, men and women voiced their agreement, at first in whispers but then in growls and finally in shouts. Soon enraged knots formed in the ranks, as voices were raised with growing fury.

Stalin let it all wash over him, neither burdened nor smug. For all the world, he might have been a man waiting for his morning bus to work.

"Except I've not come as a conquering tyrant. I was elected to my current position in a special session proposed by former Prime Minister Zhordania."

For a moment there was silence, if for nothing but the sheer audacity of the claim. Why would the prime minister do anything of the sort? Did he expect them to believe this?

"Many of you may not remember this, but Zhordania and I are both cut from the same cloth. Both of us long for the fulfillment of the long-denied Glorious Revolution, and it is with his blessing that I now assume the mantle of leadership here."

The spell was broken, and the rows of unwilling conscripts began to collapse into mobs.

"I did not convince him with argument, but the reminder of a song," Stalin said, his amplified voice nearly lost to the cacophony of the crowd. "Now I offer the same to you."

Comrade Stalin turned ever so slightly and nodded at the dwarf, who laid a hand on the monstrous street organ's crank. The mobs forming in the city square had begun to surge toward the thin line of soldiers standing transfixed before their leader. From within the organ came clanging, grinding noises, and then like a record player finding its way to a friendly groove, a blast of sound emerged. Trumpets, drums, and less recognizable instruments thundered across the square, slowing the advancing horde.

Then a choir a hundred, a thousand, a million strong seemed to rise out of the machine. In Russian, yet striking every ear as the mother tongue, strong voices, male and female, were raised in thunderous outcry.

Stand up, ones who are branded by the curse,
All the world's starving and enslaved!
Our outraged minds are boiling,
Ready to lead us into a deadly fight

The riotous herd of conscripts slowed until many were only shuffling forward if they moved at all. Each one heard the words and felt them too. The words bore down on them, pressing through to their bones and then deeper still. In a way that even religious aesthetics could not relate to, the lyrics spoke to their souls in a ruthlessly potent and undeniably compelling voice.

The dwarf continued to turn the crank and so continued the anthem, a hand-turned tidal wave of sound.

We will destroy this world of violence
Down to the foundations, and then
We will build our new world.
He who was nothing will become everything!

Stalin's smile deepened into that of a man well content with his labors.

"You see, with a few words, I remind you of the truth you

knew all along." He beamed as the crash of symbols and rumble of drums heralded the refrain.

This is our final
And decisive battle;
Under the guardians
Man will serve in truth!

"Understand now that you are part of something grander and greater than you could have ever hoped for. Something much higher."

Stalin's words were not the rantings of a zealot or the bellows of a demagogue. Even as they rose over the anthem booming across the bewitched crowd, there was a quiet, reasonable conviction that infiltrated every ear and every mind before him.

"Listen to the song and remember—"

A piercing wail, wild and discordant, tore through the air, and Comrade Stalin faltered.

The organ crank turned, but for an instant, the anthem's choir stalled as though the legion of voices was momentarily distracted, even as the instrumental chords played on. Stalin turned to look at the dwarf with a scowl, but the creature was glaring at the northernmost entrance to the square. The voices returned strong as ever, but in their absence, some of the conscripts had begun to look around, clutching their heads or drawing hands across their faces.

No one will grant us deliverance,
Not god, nor tsar, nor hero.

Pressure began to build in the air like the herald of a storm. In the dragging current of the anthem, it hadn't been noticeable before the first cry, but now all felt it, though only one understood it.

We will win our liberation,
With our very own ha—

The ripping scream came again, and once again, the chorus lost time. The screech was quickly followed by its own feral choir, the sound of which seemed to unravel the chords of the anthem.

More conscripts began to shake awake, reaching out to glassy-eyed friends and neighbors beside them. Some they shook out of their stupor, some they didn't. Some responded violently to the intrusion. Shouts, blows, and confusion began to erupt across the plaza, and the thin line of soldiers could no longer ignore the growing pandemonium. They waded in with the butts of their rifles and curses. A few opened fire.

The anthem surged back, instruments and chorus launching ahead as though trying to make up for lost time.

—up the furnace and hammer boldly,
While the iron is still hot!

And then all hell broke loose in the heart of Tiflis as an armored Rolls-Royce roared into the square, trailing a storm of shimmering, shrieking horrors.

24

THE RED

"Was this what you had in mind?" Ambrose shouted as he cranked the newly christened "Rollsy" hard to the right to avoid a brawling knot of men.

"No," Milo shouted as his will was taxed by maintaining the horde of spectral horrors, sweat beading his forehead. "Not exactly."

Lapping around the Rollsy and forming in a wave behind them were ghostly apparitions. Some were skeletal horrors dangling etheric wisps of tattered garments and grave wrappings, their grinning face sending up wild, piercing cackles. Others were akin to the malformed shades of Milo's experience, sloughing features drooping around moaning, hungry mouths. Like a tide of terror, they plunged into the square.

The people in the square, already unsettled, erupted into utter pandemonium.

Conscripts, soldiers, and the phantoms Milo and Rihyani had summoned fought, chased, raved, and generally created chaos. Milo caught fleeting glimpses of violence and madness as Ambrose sawed his way through the churning bodies like a sailor tacking a sailboat through unfriendly waters. More than once, a body thumped against their flank as stray bullets sang off their hood, and a few times, there was a crunching *thump-thump* as the Rollsy gave a small two-stage jump.

The reality of what was going on might have provoked a greater reaction from Milo, except so much of him was pressed outward that sparing time for his physical senses was hardly worth the effort. He could feel the magical power of Zlydzen attempting to smother what he and Rihyani were doing, and dear God, was he strong. Milo recognized that his magic was different from anything he'd experienced thus far, a brutal, mechanical sort of magic. Necromist magic was uniquely chemical, exciting elements and letting them do as the formula dictated, while the Art was singularly psychological, bending and shaping impulse and determination into reality. This magic, perhaps all dwarrow magic, was intensely mechanical, a grinding and relentless force that would carry on like tides rolling in and out to batter at them as long as someone kept turning the crank on that machine. He and Rihyani could keep pressing their wills, like two travelers leaning into a headwind, but if they didn't find shelter soon, the wind would exhaust them.

That or I change the weather, Milo thought. Sparing what little he could of his awareness to squint through the windscreen of the Rollsy, he saw the shrunken figure at the street organ. Even given the erratic movements of the vehicle, Milo could tell the creature was glaring at him as it continued to turn the crank. Milo spared a further glance to see Comrade Stalin standing in front of the microphone, rigid and attentive, the man and woman behind him holding their positions flawlessly.

"We need to get to that stage," Milo shouted and gritted his teeth as they slewed to one side hard enough the Rollsy rose on two wheels for one heart-stopping second.

"What do you think I'm trying to do?" Ambrose shouted

before slamming his foot down on the accelerator again. "She's got some heft, but if I try and plow through, we'll just get clogged up."

Milo understood and even thought distantly that they couldn't just run over people. Not intentionally, anyway, since the majority in the square were prisoners, not enemies, even though some of them were doing a fair job acting like it under the dwarrow's influence.

"Rihyani!" he shouted, twisting to face the wind-riding fey behind them. "We need to get to the stage."

Rihyani looked down at him, her face partially twisted into that fearsome, bestial visage, and nodded as she surged forward. One hand reached down and took him by the wrist, her claws digging through the cuff of his sleeve into his flesh. With the miniscule will he had in reserve, Milo tried to wind ride. All he managed was to make himself lighter, but thankfully, it was enough.

"Meet us up there!" Milo shouted as he rose out of the cab and began flying in a low trajectory toward the stage.

He knew that if there had been even a few soldiers assembled near the stage, he'd have been riddled with incoming fire, but as it was, all he had to contend with were the astonished and sullen glares from Stalin and the dwarf respectively. His boots barely skimming the heads and raised fists of the battling souls beneath him, Milo was afraid he wouldn't clear the stage, but Rihyani, with a feral howl of effort, dragged him upward before her claws detached from his arm. He hurtled onto the stage as Rihyani arched upward gracefully in time to avoid colliding with the canopy.

Milo wasn't quite ready for his landing, but the lightening of his failed wind riding meant he came down without breaking both his legs. He did leave off the effort of pushing his will outward, and across the square, half of the monstrous specters dissipated. Milo knew he would need all his attention and energies here.

Milo staggered his first few steps but righted himself as he came to a stop, raptor-headed cane raising level with the dwarf. Ghostly green flames licked the sockets.

"That's quite enough music for one night," Milo said, straightening to his full height as he did his level best to not look like he'd almost fallen flat on his face.

Up close, the dwarrow was curious and grotesque. Milo had assumed dwarrow might look like those afflicted with dwarfism with some dash of inhumanity, but he struggled to see how anyone could mistake this creature for a human being. The proportions were all wrong, with a huge leathery face squatting on a barrel-like trunk amidst a profusion of wiry gray hair. The feet and hands were disproportionately outsized as well, nearly twice human proportions. Eyes like polished beetle shells watched him over a long, drooping nose that looked like it should have been planted in a garden, not hanging from a face.

"So, this is *De Zauber-Schwartz*," Zlydzen crowed in a rasping voice that grated on the nerves like a file. "You are younger than I pictured you."

With a rush of chill wind, Rihyani settled gracefully next to Milo, clawed fingers curled.

"He told you to stop the music, Zlydzen," Rihyani growled, a wet, leonine sound.

To Milo's surprise, the dwarrow ceased turning the crank, though he left a hand resting on the handle defiantly. His wide, parched-lipped mouth spread into a jagged saw-edged grin as he looked them both up and down appraisingly.

"I'd always supposed the Shepherds were working openly with the humans, but now I understand precisely how *intimate* this partnership is,"

Milo had to fight off the ridiculous impulse to justify himself to the Guardian even as Comrade Stalin stepped away from the microphone and moved toward the dwarrow. His movements were stiff, and he clutched his right hand to his abdomen as though it were wounded.

"Keep playing, you fool," he snarled. "What are you doing?"

Zlydzen didn't stop scrutinizing Milo and Rihyani as he answered with a cringe-inducing titter. Milo was certain that nails and slate going through a meat grinder would have sounded better.

"Oh, I'm preparing to give you up, *Ioseb*," the dwarrow declared. "You've served your usefulness to the cause—that is, my cause—and now I'm trading you for my escape. After all, you are here for him, aren't you?"

Stalin balked, but Milo shook his head slowly.

"No deal," he said as he let a little flame crackle around the outstretched cane. "We've got plenty of room for both of you, so I see no need to trade anything. Now, hands off the organ."

"You vile little—" Stalin snarled as he made to lunge at Zlydzen, dragging a pistol one-handed from his coat. Milo was quicker.

Snapping his cane down to strike the stage, a sheet of ice unfurled like a glassy runner. Stalin's rushing feet abandoned him in a rush that sent him reeling to land with a heavy grunt on the suddenly frozen floor. The pistol tumbled from his impact-numbed grip, skittering over to the feet of the pair still crossing hammer and sickle without acknowledging the world around them. Before Stalin could recover his breath, much less his weapon, ice began to creep up the back and arms of his coat, binding him to the stage.

Stalin swore and panted, but the ice held fast.

Zlydzen gave a hooting cheer and slapped his swollen hands together with ungainly exuberance, like a young child imitating what clapping looked like.

"Hehe, isn't that lovely? O-ho-ho, just marvelous."

This was the mastermind who won you over to the Guardians? Milo thought as he turned back to the dwarrow with narrowed eyes.

Do not underestimate him, the fetish-locked ghul warned. *He's the most dangerous being you've ever met.*

"Do you have any more?" Zlydzen cooed, looking at Milo with widening wet eyes. "Oh, come now, please show me a little more, at least."

Milo wasn't sure whether he was disgusted or amused and decided it was probably both.

"If you like that," he said, a smile touching the corner of his face, "you're going to love this."

Milo, don—

Milo's cane twitched toward the street organ, launching a burning lance of witchfire into the machine. He had braced himself for the shriek of metal, the splintering of wood, and even the rocking force of a small explosion. He was ill-prepared, however, for a sudden sonic assault that drove him to his knees. Hammering pulses of auditory stimulation, some heard, some felt, bludgeoned his mind and body. From his knees, he saw Zlydzen cringing as Stalin writhed, unable to raise his frozen arms to cover his ears. Pained gaze sweeping around him, Milo saw Rihyani's head gripped between her hands as she threw it back and screamed. Beyond her, the scene in the plaza seemed even more frenzied as some went into convulsions while others fought all the harder, eyes and ears bleeding freely.

A burst of amethyst light drew Milo's eyes back to the erupting organ, and he saw what for all the world looked like a tiny, dying star emerge from the crackling green flames devouring the machine. It pulsed rapidly, sometimes an orb of light, other times symbols, possibly a letter or sigil, and then with a wink, it was gone.

It took Milo a moment to realize that the brutalizing cacophony was over as blood-dampened hands came away from his ears. There was ringing amidst the static of his abused auditory function, but despite this, he still heard the dwarrow's nerve-shredding voice raised in command.

"Kill them both!" Zlydzen shrieked, stabbing a too-large finger toward Milo and Rihyani.

Almost too late, Milo turned to see the Soviet mascots bearing down on him with hammer and sickle raised.

They moved faster than Milo would have thought possible, their legs pumping like pistons across the stage, splintering wood underfoot as they came. Milo reflexively drew on the augmentative powers of his eagle-skull fetish, but even so enhanced, he had to throw himself to the edge of the stage to avoid being crushed flat and hacked in half.

Rihyani stood frozen in front of the oncoming assault, and Milo didn't have time to cry out before the hammer wielder brought his hammer smashing into her chest—only Rihyani wasn't there. The illusion dissipated, and the fey was suddenly behind her attackers; she raked her claws across their exposed backs. The rasping screech of a sharp edge on unyielding iron was all she got for her efforts as the hammer wielder spun. She vaulted into the air to avoid being flattened.

"They're golems!" Rihyani shouted. "Magical automatons!"

"Got it," Milo shouted, on his feet now, facing the sickle-wielding not-woman. He realized it sounded like he knew what he was doing, but the reality was that he had no idea. Battling magical machine-soldiers was not in his woefully limited repertoire.

Out of the corner of his eye, he saw Zlydzen moving toward the curtain before the sickle-wielder closed on him.

"Rihyani!" Milo shouted to the fey, nimbly dodging the hammer-wielding golem. "Stop the dwarrow!"

Milo didn't have a chance to see what if anything she did before his golem was nearly on top of him.

Out of habit more than anything else, he launched a blast of witchfire at the approaching murder-machine, but it quickly became apparent that the fire wasn't nearly hot enough. He only managed to set the costume ablaze, so he faced a flaming reaper who pounced on him with lethal speed.

That's not working, Imrah informed him redundantly as he wove away from a swing.

Snarling, Milo launched another bolt of fire point-blank into the golem's face. The machine staggered back a step but replied almost immediately with a stroke that nearly split Milo in two.

"I'm open to suggestions," Milo snarled as he barely managed to set aside a downward hack with the haft of his cane, and even then, only with magically enhanced strength and speed.

Metal grows brittle when cold, Imrah replied, and already Milo felt her essence seethe inside the fetish.

Milo desperately parried another sweeping cut and responded with a hard blow that would have shattered the spine of a living man but only managed to ring off the golem's arms as it staggered two steps to one side. The golem's heavy foot came down on Stalin's outstretched leg with a nauseous crunch, and there were a few shock-filled seconds before the man started screaming in agony. Milo ignored the warlord's plight as he scrambled backward, realizing this was about as much extra space as he could get between him and the lethal machine already turning back toward him.

FREEZE

Milo forced his mind into the formula, but rather than releasing it in a burst of frigid intent, he looped it into a heat-sapping stream. A ray of black that chilled the air around it into a sinking fog raced out and struck the golem in its sculpted iron bosom. For a single instant, the ray only seemed to put out the last of the fire clinging to the machine, and it closed half the distance in a stride. Its next step came at a languid pace, and its arms seemed to struggle to raise the weight of the heavy sickle even as it lurched forward. A low groaning and clicking sound issued from inside the golem as tiny spurs of frost began to emerge along hairline seams across its body. A second later, these spurs bloomed into a latticework of ice that encased the now-motionless golem.

Releasing the ray, and with the rest of the world coming back into focus, Milo looked up to see the sickle arched over his head, a single narrow icicle dangling from its tip.

"That was close," he said, stepping out from under the reaper's shadow as he hefted the beaked cane like a miner's pick.

One chop into the golem's chest created a widening spiderweb of fissures amidst a chorus of cracking noises. Milo drew back his foot and threw his weight into a supernaturally fortified front kick, and the golem exploded into jagged chunks. The sickle thunked on the stage and the frozen blade snapped in half, the hilt clattering to the floor.

Milo's moment was interrupted by the sounds of Stalin still screaming over his mashed leg and Rihyani's struggle at the back of the stage.

"Sorry, Joe," Milo muttered as he vaulted over the recumbent Red to help the embattled fey.

The scarlet curtains flapped and twitched as a lumpy form thrashed in their knotted embrace, while Rihyani and the hammer golem danced between the rippling waves of fabric. The golem bore dozens of jagged lines across its frame, the coveralls barely hiding anything anymore, but none of it seemed to be slowing the brute in the slightest. Rihyani pranced away from another swing, but from her lack of counterattack, Milo could tell she was struggling with what to do next. If Milo hadn't also given her the task of stopping the dwarrow, which must be what was thrashing in the tangled curtains, she could have brought her full power to bear against the golem. As it was, she was fighting the thing with her attention, and thus her will was divided.

To punctuate the point, the golem pulled its next stroke, and when Rihyani made to dodge the feinted swing, it reached out and grabbed her by her cloak. She snarled and lashed out with her claws, but they only spread more superficial gashes across metal limbs.

Unperturbed by the scratches, the golem slammed her down on the stage with bone-snapping force. For an instant, as Rihyani sprawled at the machine's feet, the curtains ceased their mad dance, and Zlydzen's nightmarish caricature of a face emerged from the folds, black eyes burning with hate at the fey.

"Kill her now!"

FREEZE

The frigid black ray snapped from Milo's outstretched hand and struck the golem even as it reared back for the executing stroke.

"Rihyani! Get out of there!" Milo shouted before pressing more of his mind and Imrah's essence into the enervating ribbon of unlight.

"Stop him!" Zlydzen hissed.

Milo only realized Rihyani had been thrown bodily by the golem as she came hurtling toward him, but he had time to break off the formula before she was caught in the crossfire. This did not, however, give him time to avoid being bowled over as he and the fey went down in a tangle of limbs.

Zlydzen cackled and Milo saw the golem stomping toward them, shedding flakes of frost with each step. He tried to draw on his mind for another burst of cold, but he was too dazed. Rihyani stirred on top of him groggily, and he felt her will clumsily pushing outward and only managing to swaddle the dwarrow in another layer of the curtain.

Get up.

As the murder-machine loomed over him, Milo fought to think, to will something to happen, but all he could do was watch the hammer rise overhead.

Get up, Milo!

The hammer descended, and a tremendous impact rocked the

stage. The whole world seemed to tilt perilously; the golem's strike had cratered the stage a few spare centimeters from Milo's head. He heard the full-throated roar of a large engine hard at work, and another shudder shook the stage, forcing everything to tilt even further.

MILO! Get up!

The golem yanked the hammer out of the stage, and in the process, toppled backward. Milo realized that he and Rihyani would be joining it as they began to slide. The world came into sharper focus and he saw that one entire section of the stage had collapsed, and he and Rihyani were sliding as gravity relentlessly pulled them down the newly created slope.

His grip tightening on the cane, Milo drew on the strength and energy within. Snarling with the effort, he began to scrabble upward, one arm wrapped around the still-dazed Rihyani. Slivers of wood bit into his hand and scraped his knees, but with a growl and a heave, he dragged himself and Rihyani onto a level portion of the platform.

Looking down at the fey, her eyes half-lidded, Milo feared that her injuries were more severe than he'd first thought, but then a drowsy smile, free of her ferocious fangs, spread across her face.

"Thank you," she murmured softly. "You saved me again."

"I think that makes us even, right?" Milo quipped, not sure why now of all times, all he could do was look at her lips.

"Not even." She laughed, but then her eyes flashed, and her hand shot out and gripped him by the back of the neck. "Look out!"

With more force than seemed possible for her graceful limbs, she pulled hard to one side, and together they rolled hard to the left. The golem landed heavily and nearly on the hem of their clothes from its herculean leap out of the wrecked half of the stage. Milo and Rihyani didn't have time to disentangle themselves but kept rolling as the automaton came after them, hammer raised.

Milo was nearing the point of nauseous disorientation when the beautiful sound of a Gewehr cracking off shots rang through the air. The rolling stopped, Rihyani on top this time, and both looked up to see the golem lurching drunkenly as shot after shot slammed into its iron body. Three of the shots left heavy dents in the iron chest and face, but two of them bit deep, punching holes in the shoulder joint of the hammer-wielding arm.

The golem turned its malformed face toward Ambrose, who was advancing from the edge of the stage, already ramming another magazine home.

"Get Stalin!" the big man shouted, and Milo realized his prisoner's icy prison had come apart with the stage's destruction.

Milo found his lips meeting Rihyani's as she bent toward him. The contact was so quick that had it not set his every nerve alight with a spark of desire, he might have thought he imagined it.

"We'll talk about that later," the fey said as she sprang off him, her predatory mien in place. "Right now, I've got a dwarrow to catch."

Milo fumbled to his feet, his lips tingling oddly even as he searched for where Stalin had gone. Thankfully, it wasn't far.

Dragging his wounded leg behind him, the Bolshevik warlord had managed to hop and crawl toward the back of the stage. As Milo watched the pathetic display, Stalin's hands groped across the knotted curtains for support.

"And where do you think you're going, *Joe*?" Milo hissed as he advanced on his quarry.

Stalin twisted at the taunting call and lost his balance, the thick curtains slipping through his sweaty, trembling hands. He tried to twist as he fell to spare his injured leg but only managed to have it be underneath him when he landed. An animalistic bleat of pain slipped past his lips, so unlike his calm, sure voice only moments earlier.

"Oh, how the mighty have fallen," Milo quipped as he came to stand over him.

"No," Stalin snarled as he fought to roll over and climb to his feet. "It can't end like this."

Milo stomped, knocking him back down onto the stage.

"End?" Milo said teasingly as he glared down into watering dark eyes. 'You're far too useful alive for this to be over so soon."

A struggle between indignation and relief writhed in the wounded warlord's eyes, then they narrowed as they roved across Milo's face.

"No," he gasped again, face straining toward Milo's with eyes beginning to bulge. "Are you a ghost?"

Wary of a deception, Milo straightened, reached inside his coat, and fished out a fetish, a simple-seeming coil of leather he'd prepared in Shatili just for this moment.

BIND

The leather sprang to life, and in seconds, it had wound its way around Stalin, forcing his legs and arms together with sharp tugs of its coils. Though he winced at the constricting movements, hissing as it pulled at his injured leg, Stalin never ceased staring at Milo, his eyes growing wider and wider.

"So, this is it, then," he murmured, sliding into his native Georgian as he sank back against the stage heavily. "Laid low by the sins of my past."

A cold, bitter smile slowly crept out from under his mustache.

"I should have known she was lying. Oh, clever little Petrovich."

Behind him, Milo heard a rending metallic crash, but that sound could never have struck him as hard as the name which passed Stalin's lips.

"What did you say?" Milo snarled as he reached down and grabbed Stalin by the leather web that ensnared him.

"Did you think I wouldn't recognize you?" Stalin asked, his

face still lit by his wintry smile. "That I wouldn't see her in your face, your mouth, your eyes?"

Milo's fingers twisted into the cords until his fingers ached, but the power of speech seemed to escape him.

"Magus!" Ambrose shouted. "Where's Rihyani? We need to go!"

Turning around from Stalin's leering grin, Milo saw the big man standing over the crumpled golem, the machine's hammer in one hand. If his heart hadn't been doing its best to pummel its way out of his chest, Milo might have laughed at the sight.

"She went after Zlydzen," he said, finding his voice at last and nodded toward the empty steps of the Parliament building where he'd last seen her. The gates into the courtyard were shattered and hanging off their hinges, and within, he heard the sounds of a violent struggle.

"Go get her," Ambrose said as he tossed the hammer to one side. "I'll get him in the Rollsy, and then we need to go. Things are getting wild out there."

Stealing a glance past the stage, Milo saw what he meant.

The square had become an abattoir.

Milo and Rihyani's specters were gone, and most of the Russian soldiers seemed to be among the piles of the dead, but that had not stopped the conscripts from tearing into each other with reckless abandon. Brother fought brother and neighbor fought neighbor as the dwarrow's broken manipulations turned men into mad beasts. In the flurry of blows and screams and blood, it was almost impossible to tell who had been driven mad by the street organ's broken enchantment and who was fighting for their lives to fend off the frenzied humans next to them.

At the far end of the street, he saw a fresh crowd entering the square, a rabble of scared and angry-looking citizens coming to see what new madness was gripping their city. Milo knew it was only a matter of time before the madness in the square turned its attention on them, or they waded in in some desperate attempt to restore order.

Either way, things were only about to get worse, and they needed to escape before they were inescapably caught up in the storm.

Spitting a curse, Milo spun and dragged Stalin up toward his snarling face.

"We're not done," the magus hissed, his pale eyes boring into the man's dark, defiant gaze. "Not even close to done."

Milo threw him back down and stalked toward the Parliament building.

Milo moved into the courtyard and was greeted by an odd sight.

Rihyani stood amongst the remains of a fountain, water gurgling up and around her feet from rent pipes as she faced Zlydzen. The dwarrow stood several strides away on dry paving stones. Neither fey nor dwarrow moved, each staring at the other.

Milo felt magical energies trembling in the air, Rihyani's will swirling about and probing at a hardened presence he could sense in the direction of the squat grotesque. The magical presence of the dwarrow was stolid and intractable but showed no signs of being willing or even able to lash out. The magic present was armor, not a weapon.

"It's over, Zlydzen," Milo called as he moved to Rihyani's side, kicking up little splashes. "Your golems are scrap metal, and your puppet is ready for transport. Give up now, and we can bring you in with some dignity."

The dwarrow's glittering black eyes turned toward Milo, and he felt his confidence wither inside of him.

"I think not, little magus," Zlydzen muttered. "You have Ioseb, who I will remind you I already offered, but as I expressed, I have work that is too vital to spend any more time dallying with you."

Milo gave a snort and began to prowl forward, not noticing that Rihyani's expression tightened as he moved past her.

Milo, he heard as her will brushed his. *Be careful.*

Milo almost lost his stride at the contact but was determined not to let it show.

"Seemed like you spent plenty of time dallying with that curtain." Milo chuckled as he came to stand a few paces from the dwarrow. "Which was amusing, but it's not your dancing that I'm particularly interested in."

A smile that could have curdled milk from a mile off drew Zlydzen's lips apart.

"What exactly are you interested in, little magus?" the dwarrow asked in a ragged whisper. "How far have you plunged into the dark? Far enough to start asking the right questions?"

Milo put on his best sharkish grin in reply and drew witchfire into the cane's sockets.

"Come with us, and you'll find out," Milo said with a voice that was sinister and silky. "Come quietly, and I might even ask my questions politely."

Milo, he's raised wards around himself, Rihyani warned. *No magic can touch him now.*

Milo's stomach twisted, and he wondered if that meant the ungainly little creature couldn't work any magic either.

"Tempting though your offer is," Zlydzen said, still smiling, "I'm afraid I'll have to pass. As I said, work and all that."

Milo took a menacing step forward, pointing with his cane.

"Just because you've warded yourself, it doesn't mean I can't beat you to a pulp and pour you into the trunk," he growled before drawing the pistol from his belt holster. "Or I could put a round or two in some nonvital parts and drag you back to the car and hope you don't bleed out. Your choice?"

Zlydzen's smile widened until his mouth seemed ready to split his huge head in half.

"Brave words." The dwarrow laughed from somewhere deep inside its chest. "For such a little fellow."

Zlydzen sprang forward, and Milo opened fire.

The first rushed shot sailed over the dwarrow's head, Milo's aim not adjusted for such a low-slung target. His second would not have the same problem as the dwarrow erupted upward and outward in a chorus of sickening pops and cartilaginous clicks. Milo's second shot struck meat, but not that of the squat, lumpy thing that had stood before him seconds ago

Zlydzen, like some monstrous jack in the box, had unfolded and was now a gaunt, looming monster four meters tall, coming for Milo with outstretched hands perfectly proportioned for his enormous stature.

Not seeming to mind the pinprick of a bullet hole or the second and third Milo opened, Zlydzen sprang at Milo, fists raised to flatten him. The magus, realizing this was certainly the reason why the fountain was the way it was, threw himself backward, calling on his coat to get him clear with a single black-winged beat.

Water and bits of shattered stone flew into the air, and Zlydzen gave a roar that combined the terrifying elements of an enraged bovine and ursine.

Milo came down from his soaring leap to land on his feet with a splash, but before he could snap off another shot, a chunk of broken masonry flew at him. He twisted away, but a corner of the missile clipped his shoulder and sent him spinning to the ground, his head striking stone with a wet *thunk*.

A shadow fell across him, and Milo realized the pistol had been knocked from his nerveless grip. He rolled over, trying to focus his impact-addled brain enough to draw on the cane's strength, but his brain felt like it was clogged, his thoughts thick and syrupy.

Zlydzen loomed over him, one huge foot raised to flatten him.

I tried to warn you, Imrah whispered to him.

There was a flash of silver through the air, and then like a hellcat, Rihyani was savaging the dwarrow's face. The crushing foot thudded down next to Milo's arm and he feebly swatted at it with his cane, but all that managed to do was knock the fetish from his weakened grip.

Meanwhile, Rihyani ripped and tore at Zlydzen, sending up ribbons of flesh and sprays of brassy blood with each rake of her claws or snap of her teeth. The dwarrow staggered backward, tripped on a piece of the fountain, and fell heavily onto his back.

Hands slapping about in the water, Milo tried to snatch up his pistol and cane as Zlydzen finally closed his huge hands around Rihyani.

The trollish brute squeezed hard, but the fey only dug deeper into his face. Both screamed, mouths filled with blood, as Zlydzen tore her from his face in a ripple of flexing sinew, losing the end of his tuberous nose. With a pain-maddened roar, he threw the fey and his nose at Milo.

For the second time that night, Milo was flattened by the impact of Rihyani's body striking him, and they both went down in a pile.

Zlydzen gave another bestial roar, but it was matched by the Rollsy's engine as Ambrose drove the vehicle through the broken gates into the courtyard.

The dwarrow's black eyes glared with utter venom at Milo as he lay soaking wet and panting with Rihyani, but then the huge mouth spread in another queasy smile made all the worse by the recent mutilation.

"Until we meet again," Zlydzen said in a well-deep voice, then turned to run at a dead sprint for the columned vestibule.

The Rollsy skidded to a stop in the fountain water as the dwarrow leaped and began to clamber with apelike agility up the pillars and onto the roof of the Parliament building.

"We need to go!" Ambrose shouted as he stood up in the cab. "We've got to go now."

Rihyani, on top of Milo once more, smiled down at him, her face smeared with the dwarrow's metallic gore.

"Don't tell me," she whispered with coppery breath. "You want another kiss, don't you?"

Milo stared at her, then his mouth hitched up in a smile.

"Would that make us even?"

25

THE ARENA

"Do you think you can raise one more toast to your victory?"

Milo turned from staring around the marquis' ballroom and saw Rihyani approaching with a pair of crystal flutes. An amber liquor rolled gently in the vessels as she stalked toward him, flecks of gold sparkling within to match her eyes.

"I'm not sure you can call it victory," Milo said, hating how sour he sounded. "But I don't think it'll hurt to have another drink."

He knew he wasn't being honest with himself about that.

Ever since they'd escaped Tiflis and headed north for shelter in the Lost Vale, it had been nothing but intoxicating celebrations. He thought the first time he'd had a drink shoved into his hand, he was still damp with fountain water, and everything since then melded into a blur of cheering, drinking, toasting, drinking, feasting, drinking, and even more drinking.

He'd crept off a few hours ago after realizing he was sobering up, and he had no idea how long it had been since he'd been in that state. Since then, he'd wandered the ever-shifting halls of the fey manse until he found his current perch. The overindulgence of elven wine and fair folk spirits hadn't left him with the physical maladies such excess should have entailed, but they made him merrily forgetful, and now he wasn't sure that was always a good thing. They'd need to be on their way soon, and he wanted his head clear and his memory intact.

Seeing Rihyani standing there with a glass in hand, her dark garments exchanged for a gown of blue velvet, he thought little harm could come from one last sip. After all, in his bleary recollections of the recent revels, her face featured not a little.

"Not a victory? Nonsense," the fey chided lightly, a smile on her dark lips. "You set out to capture a dangerous enemy from the midst of his followers, and you not only succeeded relatively unscathed, but you even captured one of his most useful subordinates."

Milo shook his head, torn between escaping the scrutiny of her gaze and longing to savor the sight of her.

"That last one just fell into our laps, so I don't think I can take any credit for it." Milo sighed and realized she was standing in front of him, arm extended with glass in hand. "Oh, sorry, I'll take that."

He took the flute, and they raised their drinks together. Rihyani's eyes locked onto his and he felt her will brush against his, as intimate as though she was whispering in his ear.

To your conquest of impossible odds, she thought, her will gliding across his like fingers across his cheek. *Both on the field of battle and in far more important arenas. May you always show such courage, determination, and cunning in whatever lies ahead.*

Hear, hear, Milo managed, not so practiced that he could casually commune in the Art as effortlessly as the fey.

The flutes chimed against each other and they both drank deep, each watching the other.

The amber liquor was cool on the tongue but warm in the throat and tasted of smoked honey and cloves. The warmth of it became a low fire in his belly, and with a sudden intensity he didn't quite trust, the hazy lethargy of the last few days of celebrating melted like fog in the summer sun.

Rihyani saw his eyes widen as everything came into sharp clarity and gave one of those laughs that made Milo's heart sore with longing. Up to this point, he'd never been sure what he longed for, but whether it was the liquor or a revelation, when he looked at her, he thought he might know now.

"S-so," he began and nearly cursed himself for the stammer, "now that you helped us, what is the plan? Will the Shepherds reassign you?"

Rihyani's eyes slid down to the dance floor, where the fey cavorted as the marquis sat at a vast table at the head of the chamber. The lord of the manor watched the proceedings with a venerable patriarch's assured ease.

"It doesn't quite work like that." The contessa sighed as she eyed the tall, goatlike fey. "But I do need to pass the word among our circles that the marquis has joined our side. I'm sure he's already made it known to some, but I'll need to verify the reports before he can be brought in on our operations."

Milo nodded, knowing he needed to say something. He also needed to stop bobbing his head up and down like an idiot, but standing there watching her, he didn't seem capable of anything else.

A smirk curled a corner of Rihyani's mouth, and for a second, he thought she was going to laugh at him. He wondered if he'd find that enchanting too, but then he saw her nod at the banquet table.

"They look like they're having fun." She giggled as Milo followed her gaze and then shared her smile.

To the marquis' immediate right and left were the seats reserved for Milo and Rihyani, while on opposite sides, Ambrose and Bakbak-Devi were engaged in yet another competition of consumption. That the half-human bodyguard had managed to win a few times against the many-headed giant was certain to be a matter of folklore among the fey for some time to come.

"I'm glad Ambrose is enjoying himself," Milo said and felt his grin buckling under a grim realization. "It's probably going to be a long time before we get a hero's welcome again. We're headed back north, and if we're both not thrown into the stockade on sight, it will be a mercy."

Rihyani turned back, studying his face, her smile giving way to pensive concern.

"You don't think your captives will be enough?"

Milo shrugged and shook his head.

"I don't know," he admitted. "They have vital intelligence about the Guardians and the Ewiges Reich, and they both seem practical enough to talk."

And that wasn't the only thing at least one of them knew. Milo felt a sudden urge to race out to the dovecote where Stalin was chained and ask him why he'd said a name scrawled on a tarot card in Milo's pocket.

"But?" Rihyani prompted, and Milo realized he'd trailed off.

"Um, but, uh…" He floundered for a second before seizing on the thread he'd left dangling. "But the military loves hierarchy, and I pretty much threw the book out not once, but twice. I'm not sure anything short of winning the war can guarantee I'll be spared."

Rihyani nodded and finished off the last of her flute before making it vanish with a flutter of her fingers.

"I still need you to teach me that one," Milo said. "If we ever get the time."

Rihyani turned back to the dance floor as she folded her arms in front of her. A smile tickled the corner of her lips as she gave him a sidelong glance.

"We could have the time," she said quietly, then he felt her will, faint and silken against him. *If you wanted it. If you wanted me.*

Milo stared at her, his mouth working for a second or two without making a sound.

"I mean, I didn't, not that I wasn't hoping," he babbled, then stopped himself and drew a steadying breath. "I mean, you're immortal, beautiful, wise, and pretty much everything I'm not."

Rihyani's laughed gently, and that familiar ache in his chest throbbed.

"Are you trying to talk me out of it?" she asked, giving him another quick glance out the corner of her eye.

"I guess I'm trying to say…" Milo began, then had to take an embarrassing few seconds to decide what exactly he *was* trying to say. "Well, I guess it, um, I mean, you just seem too amazing. It's like I'd be a fool to dare to hope for something so out of my reach."

With a smooth sideways step, Rihyani slid up next to him.

"Do I seem out of your reach now?" she asked, eyes fixed on the dancers below.

Almost without knowing what was happening, Milo's arms wrapped around her. Once the embrace began, it seemed to have a life, a gravity, a force all its own. She contoured to him and he to her. She raised her eyes from the hall beneath them, their foreheads resting gently against each other's.

It's not foolish to hope, Rihyani whispered to his soul. *Only the hopeful can know real triumph, and even when they fall, they do so daring greatly. I'll strive for you and you for me, and together we'll be valiant enough for whatever comes.*

Milo felt something new and potent burning inside him, and for once, it was not a matter of eldritch knowledge. It was a far simpler, far more potent power, and it shone inside him such that he thought he might begin to glow like the beautiful creature in his arms. For a single instant, he felt as though the long shadows and cold depths inside him were gone, banished before the light, and he couldn't decide if he wanted to laugh, sing, or cry.

He looked into Rihyani's eyes and decided he wanted something else altogether.

"Here's to hope," he said, then kissed her deeply.

EPILOGUE: ADVERSUS SOLUM

Petrograd was not what it once was, and it was whispered on some nights that the fires of the Red Revolution still burned in a city that was now little more than a ruin, inhabited by bandits, scavengers, and more of the same with grandiose ambitions.

"Yet those souls still need saving," Father Bunin would say. "And as long as the Lord grants me strength and the saints grant wisdom, I will be here."

The fact that those souls had sacked his little chapel on the road into Petrograd and had more than once cruelly mistreated the priest did little to discourage him.

"Everything is dark apart from the light of Christ," he would remind himself as he set about putting right what could be and clearing out what was broken beyond repair. "If our Lord could forgive the worst of these, how much more should I?"

From there, it was a matter of finding out what needed replacing, though the Orthodox church had abandoned the area nearly a decade ago. As such, the furnishings, decorations, and even the icons were of his own crude making. Unlike the teacher to whom he devoted his life, Bunin was no carpenter, but he did the best he could. The wood he hewed from the forest down the road, while nails and fastenings he collected from the crumbling outskirts of the city.

It was on one such scavenging expedition that Bunin discovered an odd sight.

A small, lumpy form huddled inside a burnt-out home.

This in and of itself did not seem strange since Bunin was regularly finding old, moldering corpses on such excursions. In fact, two-thirds of the bodies laid to rest beside his chapel were those he'd found in such a state. Father Bunin was no stranger to the sights and smells of death, living so near a cursed place like Petrograd.

What was strange were not only the proportions of the figure but also the fact that it seemed to still be alive despite what seemed to be a horribly disfiguring disease. Ragged breaths wheezed out through the ragged holes where a nose had been, and the whole body seemed swollen, most particularly the head. The poor wretch's beard was streaked with sour, crusted bile.

Despite its truly horrific state, Father Bunin squatted next to the creature and laid a gentle, callused hand on the clammy brow.

"Oh, my child," Bunin said in a tender whisper. "What afflicts you so?"

Bunin started when one eyelid peeled back from a glittering black eye.

"A witch," the wretch hissed between jagged teeth. "A fey witch."

Bunin nodded slowly, understanding that such superstitions existed among the folk of Russia. Father Bunin believed from the Scriptures that there were those who might consort with spirits and demons, like the woman from Endor or Simon the Sorcerer, but the simple folk found it easier to blame the harshness of their life on such creatures in place of simpler, harder answers. He didn't begrudge them this in their confessions, and he certainly would not begrudge a dying man such thoughts.

That he was dying was certain, the poor wretch. That he was

still alive even now was a miracle of either divine or infernal making. With a silent prayer, Bunin hoped for the former as he unlimbered the waterskin slung across his back.

"Are you thirsty?" the priest asked, holding up the skin.

The diseased man's other eye, as black and hard as its twin, opened, and he glared at the offering with open suspicion. Then a cough wracked his body, and his parched lips split in several places. The fluid that leaked from them must have been choked with disease because it looked and smelled quite unlike blood.

"Yes," he croaked, and without hesitation, the priest raised the waterskin to the befouled mouth.

"Slowly," he cooed, sliding his free hand behind the swollen head to prop the poor creature up a little. "There is plenty, and it's not going anywhere."

The wretch choked at one point, and a gush of water and coppery fluid sprayed out of his mouth. He had to be rolled on his side to keep from drowning in his own effluence. The fit passed, and Father Bunin rolled the creature gently back after placing his backpack as a support against the fellow's spine. Using a clean rag from the bag, he cleaned the wretch's mouth and gave him more water.

"What are you doing out here, my child?' the priest asked as he took the waterskin away to give the man a chance to catch his breath. "I've not seen you around here before, but being in such a state, I can't see how you could have come from very far."

"I came from Georgia," the wretch said with a gargle in his throat. "I had business there, and now I'm here, waiting for another business partner."

Father Bunin supposed it was nothing but fevered rambling, but he nodded and dabbed the creature's mouth with a clean corner of his rag.

"That is a long way to come, especially in your condition," the priest said before looking out through the scorched door of the flame-scoured building. "Will your friend be along shortly?"

"Should be any minute now." The poor man sighed, his blackened eyes sinking to half-mast as he leaned against the priest's bag. "I sent word by one of his cronies when I arrived yesterday."

Father Bunin, having endured so long in such an inhospitable place, had no illusions left about what kind of henchmen might be lurking around the outskirts of the ruined city. If the man hadn't killed this poor creature in such a vulnerable state, he only did so because he thought further profit or sport could be had by returning with friends.

"Perhaps," the priest said, resting a hand softly on the man's malformed shoulder, "you would like to come with me back to the chapel and wait there? We can leave a note for your business associates. There will be some food there for you while we wait for them."

The rattling rumble of a diesel engine put to death Father Bunin's hopes as it growled its way toward them.

"No need," the wretch observed in a small, unsettling voice. "He's already here."

A canvas-backed truck came to a stop before the husk of a house. Father Bunin could make out men's voices speaking over the engine, then a strapping figure appeared in the doorway.

A deep, velvety voice came from the silhouetted figure at the threshold. "Don't bother with that one, Father. Jesus didn't go to the cross for the likes of him, I think."

"What took you so long?" the wretch snarled with a forceful will Father Bunin wouldn't have thought possible given his condition.

"I came as soon as I could," the apparent business associate said as he stepped into the house. "But it took some time to find a vehicle that wasn't being used. That plan of yours is extensive."

Emerging from the shadows was a shockingly handsome man with dark, smoldering eyes and tattoos crawling up either side of his neck. One ink-scrawled hand raked through wavy locks of golden brown grown long in the front but shorn to the skin on the sides. Instead of the rugged, homespun attire common to most of those dwelling around Petrograd, this man wore a fine suit like a businessman from a bustling metropolis might wear.

It took Father Bunin a moment, but he recognized the man as a leader of one of the legions of bandit bands plaguing the area. The priest had only seen the man at a distance during one of his scavenging expeditions, but the forces the man commanded, as best as the priest could guess, were more like an army than roving thugs—hard-eyed killers, united by one that even such men could respect.

"What happened to you?" the bandit chief asked with an amused chuckle. "You weren't pretty before, but this new look is beyond the pale."

"Shepherd harridan," the wretch spat. "Her and that pet sorcerer. They didn't just do this, but they turned the marquis against us, too."

The chieftain, who'd begun to look at the burnt home with a mildly annoyed expression, perked up at that and turned an approving smile on the disfigured fellow.

"You limped all the way from Tiflis like that? I'm impressed."

The wretch didn't seem to appreciate the compliment.

"Just kill this fool and get me back to my workshop. I still have much work to do."

The bandit frowned as he spared a pitying look for the dumb-struck priest.

"He's a well-meaning fool. A simpleton with some hand-drawn icons at the edge of the city. Really, there's no need to kill him."

For one moment, Father Bunin thought about running, trying to escape. However, given what the man had said he must know about the chapel, Father Bunin's only chance of escape, assuming they didn't gun him down immediately, was to flee the area, and he knew he wouldn't.

Instead, he decided to draw out his simple wooden cross and begin to pray where he was, on his knees.

"*Our Father who art in Heaven, hallowed be thy name.*"

"He's seen too much," the wretch rasped as he shifted himself against the priest's pack.

"*Thy Kingdom come, thy will be done, on earth as it is in Heaven.*"

The bandit frowned, cutting an angry glance toward his mutilated partner before staring down at the kneeling priest

"*Give us this day our daily bread and forgive us our trespasses.*"

"Get it over with!" the wretch snarled, air whistling through his absent nose.

There was a metallic click, and Father Bunin looked up into the black eye of a pistol barrel. He forced himself to look past that abyss over the wrist sporting a skull and orthodox cross into the dark gaze of the young man holding the weapon.

"*As we forgive those who trespass against u—*"

The pistol barked, and the last priest in Petrograd fell to the scorched earth.

If you're looking for another double fisted tale of war, magic, and bloody conspiracies in the grim alternate history of the War to End All Wars, the story continues in *Wizard Born*, book 3 of the World's First Wizard series.

AUTHOR NOTES - AARON SCHNEIDER
OCTOBER 19, 2020

Dear Reader,

Wow, already book 2, and book 3 (Wizardborn) is coming in just a few weeks.

Let's hope you all can handle the short wait, and maybe even convince some other folks that Milo has something to offer. We may find it difficult to gather together, but we can certainly gather online to savor what, I hope, is a good book.

In the meantime, we've all got to keep living in this world that seems ready to tear itself apart at the drop of a hat or the scrape of a pen on a ballot. I pray by book 3 we'll see peace and rest for the coming Christmastide, but in the meantime, I'll ask us all to remember something, whatever our convictions.

Remember the words of G.K. Chesterton.

"Charity means pardoning the unpardonable, or it is no virtue at all. Hope means hoping when things are hopeless, or it is no virtue at all. And faith means believing the incredible, or it is no virtue at all."

Be seeing you soon dear readers.

Aaron D. Schneider

ACKNOWLEDGMENTS

For this book I wanted to take a second to acknowledge some of the amazing people who make these books possible.

First to my beta readers, the wonderful and enduring folks that you are, persevering past all my failings and inability to self-edit. You are honest and true, finding gems amongst all the muck. I value every suggestion and read every comment several times, so please know your efforts are greatly appreciated.

Second to Lynne and the Just in Time team, you are all saints the likes of which most people only hear about. You take this mess and with divine patience, sift and trim and cultivate and a thousand other metaphors for the marvelous job you do hacking a path through my unruly writing. God bless you.

Finally, to Kelly who keeps the wheels rolling on this crazy train. You right the ship and keep us steady, and I appreciate all of it immensely. Thank you.

All of the wonderful people I thanked in *Witchmarked* are just as worthy of my acknowledgment and thanks for this book as the last, but I hope they know they still have all my love and affection as before.

CONNECT WITH THE AUTHORS

Connect with Bradford Bates

Facebook:
https://www.facebook.com/authoraarondschneider/

Amazon:
https://www.amazon.com/Aaron-D-Schneider/e/B07H8WZ2HT/

Connect with Michael Anderle and sign up for his email list here:

Website: http://lmbpn.com

Email List: http://lmbpn.com/email/

Facebook:
https://www.facebook.com/LMBPNPublishing

Twitter:
https://twitter.com/MichaelAnderle

OTHER BOOKS BY AARON SCHNEIDER

The Warring Realm Series

War-Born

War-Torn

War-Sworn

Rings of the Inconquo

(with A.L. Knorr)

World's First Wizard

(with Michael Anderle)

Witchmarked (Book 1)

Sorcerybound (Book 2)

Wizardborn (Book 3)

OTHER LMBPN PUBLISHING BOOKS

To be notified of new releases and special promotions from LMBPN publishing, please join our email list:

http://lmbpn.com/email/

www.ingramcontent.com/pod-product-compliance
Lightning Source LLC
Chambersburg PA
CBHW031609100726
47898CB00006B/1714